What people are saying about …

ONLY BY DEATH

"Just when you think it's over, it's not … and the tension mounts. Young Jesse is brave, spunky, and lives out his faith. I want to be like Jesse when I grow up!"

Roxanne Henke, author of *After Anne*, book 1
in the Coming Home to Brewster series

"Kathy Herman's *Only by Death* hinges on a subtle principle from
God's Word [illegible] ppiness and
holiness—a [illegible] ue servants
of the Savi[illegible] y with the
protagonist [illegible] is not your
typical murd[illegible]

Eric Wiggin, MsEd, speaker, author
of *The Gift of Grandparenting* and *The
Hills of God*, rewritten as *The Recluse*

"*Only by Death*, book 2 of Kathy Herman's Ozark Mountain Trilogy, is filled with action, suspense, and surprises, as well as thought-provoking questions about what it really means to live the Christian life. Looking forward to book 3!"

Julianna Deering, author of the
Drew Farthering Mysteries

"What does it really mean to put God's will ahead of your own? Kathy Herman explores the question in a heart-stopping story that kept me on the edge of my seat from the very first line until the final page. *Only by Death* is a riveting book that will challenge your own concept of obedience and linger in your heart."

Carol Cox, author of the Arizona Territory Brides series

"*Only by Death* is not an easy read, just as the Christian life is not a sunny afternoon stroll. But the journey this book unfolds is worth the tension and danger. Both heartwarming and chilling."

Lyn Cote, *USA Today* bestselling author

"The tension in Kathy Herman's newest book builds slowly, then erupts and leaves you wondering—and worrying—clear to the end. One of her best so far, especially in the faith thread. It will challenge you at a deep level, making you question where you would stand if the same things happened to you. I highly recommend *Only by Death*—truly a must read."

Miralee Ferrell, award-winning author of *Runaway Romance*, also a TV movie

ONLY *by* DEATH

OZARK MOUNTAIN TRILOGY

KATHY HERMAN

BESTSELLING SUSPENSE NOVELIST

ONLY *by* DEATH

A NOVEL

ONLY BY DEATH
Published by David C Cook
4050 Lee Vance Drive
Colorado Springs, CO 80918 U.S.A.

David C Cook U.K., Kingsway Communications
Eastbourne, East Sussex BN23 6NT, England

The graphic circle C logo is a registered trademark of David C Cook.

LCCN 2017952633
ISBN 978-1-4347-0476-4
eISBN 978-0-8307-7271-1

Published in association with the literary agency of Alive Communications,
Inc, 7680 Goddard St., Suite 200, Colorado Springs, CO 80920.

The Team: Alice Crider, Jamie Chavez, Amy Konyndyk,
Nick Lee, James Hershberger, Jack Campbell, Susan Murdock

Cover Design: Kirk DouPonce, DogEared Design
Cover Photo: iStock

Printed in the United States of America
First Edition 2018

1 2 3 4 5 6 7 8 9 10

013018

To Him who is both the Giver and the Gift

ACKNOWLEDGMENTS

This is the first time in my writing career that my husband is not here with me to celebrate the release of a new book. My sweet Paul—best friend, business manager, sounding board, ardent supporter, and the other half of my heart—stepped into eternity before this book was finished. I have yet to find words adequate to describe how much I miss him. But though he's absent in body, his words of wisdom and encouragement still echo in my heart and mind, reminding me of why I do what I do. My success, to a large degree, is the result of Paul's partnership in my writing ministry, and his unselfish willingness to work our personal life around my deadlines and commitments. Without his support, understanding, and prayers, I would never have been able to write professionally. I am forever grateful.

I love Arkansas! After moving to the rolling hills of East Texas from the Front Range of Colorado, I discovered that anytime I missed the mountains, I could travel to nearby Arkansas to satisfy that longing. I chose the Ozark Mountains of northwest Arkansas to provide the backdrop for this series and many of the images I describe in the story. However, Sure Foot Mountain, Angel View

Lodge, Raleigh County, and the town of Foggy Ridge exist only in my imagination.

During the writing of this book, I drew from several resource people, each of whom shared generously from his or her storehouse of knowledge and experience. I did my best to integrate the facts, as I understood them. If accuracy was compromised in any way, it was unintentional and strictly of my own doing.

I owe a special word of thanks to Retired Commander Carl H. Deeley of the Los Angeles County Sheriff's Department for helping me to understand the finesse of obtaining a child's eyewitness statement; ways to legally obtain DNA evidence when a warrant is not justified; why and when an Amber Alert is issued; details about autopsies, postmortem bruising, and covert surveillance; and how a mobile command post is equipped and operated. Carl, you generously gave of your time and expertise. You're a joy to work with!

I want to thank my reader friend, Paul David Houston, former assistant district attorney, for advising me on trusts and power of attorney. Paul, we go back a long way. You've always been a trusted source of information. Thanks!

To my novelist friends in ChiLibris, who allow me to tap into your collective storehouse of knowledge and experience—what a compassionate, charitable, prayerful group you are! It's an honor to be counted among you.

To Nancy Godsey, Betty Mix, Martha Shelton, Sharon Mayville, and Gloria Langford, my friends at the Waterton Inn in Tyler, Texas, for falling in love with my books. Your newfound excitement lit a fire in me during a difficult year when grief had snuffed out my creativity. You will never know how God used you. He is faithful!

I'm immensely grateful to my faithful prayer warriors: my sister Pat Phillips; dear friends Mark and Donna Skorheim, Susan Mouser, and Susie Killough; my online prayer team—Pearl Anderson, Judith Depontes, Jackie Jeffries, Joanne Lambert, Diane Morin, Kim Prothro, Kelly Smith, Carolyn Walker, and Sondra Watson; and my friends at LifeWay Christian Store in Tyler, Texas, and LifeWay Christian Resources in Nashville, Tennessee. I cannot possibly express to you how much I value your prayers.

To my agent, Lisa Jackson, at Alive Communications, for being such an advocate for this series. I never have to wonder if you're looking out for my best interests.

To my editor, Jamie Chavez, for never being afraid to speak the truth—but with such grace. Thanks for affirming, instructing, and inspiring. Your suggested improvements to this story proved immeasurable. I'm looking forward to working with you again.

To Cris Doornbos, Dan Rich, Alice Crider, and the amazing staff at David C Cook publishers for believing in me and investing in the words I write; thanks for all you've done to support my writing ministry, and for giving me the opportunity to finish this series. I have loved being a part of the Cook "family" for an entire decade.

And most important, thank you, Heavenly Father, that I am Your handiwork, created in Christ Jesus to do good works, which You prepared for me before I was ever born. Open the hearts of my readers to see and understand that it is only by death that we live, only by death that we find our true selves. Let my words glorify Your Name.

PROLOGUE

"For if you live according to the flesh, you will die; but if by the Spirit you put to death the misdeeds of the body, you will live." Romans 8:13

Liam Berne was about to commit murder—at least according to Arkansas law. He blocked out the voice of his railing conscience as he clutched tightly to the wheel of his old Chevy Caprice, bumping and rocking over an unmarked road that led to a secluded bank on the Sure Foot River. Tall leafy trees and short-leaf pines lined both sides of the road and formed a tight verdant canopy, allowing only an occasional glint of sunlight to peek through.

He glanced over at his elderly mother, who had started rambling again.

"I do love ridin' the roller coaster," Dixie Berne declared, sounding as if she actually knew what she was saying. "But Roland'll have a conniption if he finds out I threw away hard-earned money on a carnival ride." She folded her hands in her lap and exhaled loudly. "How much farther's the church? We're fixin' to be late for the weddin'!"

"It's just over yonder," Liam said, trying to sound calm.

"Who're *you*?"

"I'm your son, Liam."

"You can't drive without a license, young man."

Liam smiled, then reached over and gently clasped her wrist. "It's okay, Mom. I passed my driver's test." *Nearly forty years ago.*

"Carry me to the bus stop!" she said, her voice suddenly frantic. "I need to get home and fry my chickens. Aunt Lena and Uncle Jack are comin' for supper."

Liam swallowed hard and rolled down the windows. He could do this. He had to do this. It might be his only chance. "Let's go to the beach. I know how you love the water," he said. "Smell that salt air? Feel the sea breeze?"

His mother giggled, her soft white curls tossed about in the crosswind of balmy September air passing through the open windows. "Okay, but don't tell Mama I haven't finished the ironin'."

His mother's delight soon turned to silence. Once again, she seemed distant, her eyes vacant and seeming to stare at nothing.

Liam glanced at his watch. If he could just keep his mother from getting out of hand in the next few minutes, her troubles—and his—would be over.

He had agonized, getting to this decision. Some would surely contend that what he was about to do was vile. Or, at the very least, immoral. It certainly wasn't legal. But it was kinder, more humane, than letting his mother's life drag on for years in this useless state while his parents' life savings went to pay the Alzheimer's hospital. Using that money to prolong her pitiful existence was unfair to everyone.

Colleen would never see it that way. His sister had been given power of attorney in their mother's affairs and was willing to use every cent available to her to ensure that their mother was well-cared for and comfortable. And why not? Colleen didn't need the money. She was single with a full-time teaching position, thirty-year tenure, and a good pension when she decided to quit. She had never been married or divorced. How could she understand what it was like to deal with a greedy ex-wife who never once held a job yet managed to get half of everything he'd worked for *and* eighteen months of alimony on top of that?

Liam sighed and glanced in his rearview mirror. Colleen had no clue how humiliating it was for him, at fifty-two years old, to be working full time at the poultry plant, and living under his sister's roof because he was too broke to pay rent. When Colleen asked him to move in and share the responsibility of caring for their mother at home, in lieu of paying rent, he was sincerely glad to help. But he was equally motivated to keep Colleen from spending their inheritance on their mother's long-term care.

That had worked for six months. But his mother's memory was getting worse, and she wandered away from the house more and more frequently. Colleen insisted they consult with the folks at Foggy Ridge Alzheimer's Center. The doctors there convinced Colleen that their mother should be admitted to that facility as soon as a bed opened up. Liam pretended to go along with it, but he had already decided what he would do if things played out that way.

"Stop!" His mother's agitated voice brought him back to the present. "Let me out this instant, or I'll call the police!"

"But we're almost to the beach."

She cocked her head and looked over at him. "Why, John Dillard. I haven't seen you in months. How's Monique?"

"She's just great." Liam exhaled audibly. *Just great.*

His mother's attention suddenly seemed focused on the buttons of her pink dress as she rambled on and on about getting together with girl friends to sew pearls on Cousin Margaret's wedding dress.

Between the trees, Liam spotted the glistening ripples of the river about fifty yards ahead of him. "Mom, look." He pointed his index finger toward the front window. "We're at the beach."

"Hush. Can't you see my baby's sleepin'?"

"Right. Sorry." Liam drove the car through some tall weeds and parked it in the shade of a cottonwood tree. He took a deep breath and let it out slowly, considering what he was about to do. This was the only choice that made sense. And this might be his only chance to end the madness. Did he have the courage to go through with it?

"Who're *you*?" his mother asked for the umpteenth time.

"Come on. Let's go to the beach." He doubted he would have much trouble convincing her they were in Galveston—at least long enough to do what he came to do.

Liam got out, his gut feeling as if someone had kicked it and left a shoeprint.

He spit out his gum and walked around to the passenger side and opened the door. He took his mother's fragile, bony hand and gently pulled her to her feet.

"Where am I? I want to go home!" His mother held tightly to his hand, wearing the expression of a lost child.

Liam took her face in his hands. "Mom. *Mom.* Look at me." Her expression softened and she seemed to recognize him. "We're in Galveston. Let's go swimming. We can stop at Winky's and get a snow cone," he said, his tone playful and coaxing.

Her dull blue eyes lit up like a child's at Christmas. "I want grape!"

"Now that's more like it. Let's go." *Before I talk myself out of this.*

Liam glanced in all directions and saw no one. But he'd never seen anyone here. He took his mother's arm and walked through the weeds and down a dirt path to the river's edge.

"Oh, Roland!" she exclaimed. "You brought me back! Thank you! What a surprise!"

"Come on. It's a beautiful day for a swim." Liam led her into the tepid water up to her shoulders.

His mother looked around, her thin white eyebrows scrunched. "Who's gettin' baptized?"

"*You* are, Dixie," he said.

His mother just stared blankly.

Liam, feeling as if his heart were being pummeled like a punching bag at the gym, kept his arms tightly around his mother. He had rehearsed this a dozen times. Keeping her head held firmly to his chest, he lowered himself into the water, up to his neck. His eyes stung as she wiggled and fought in vain for a gulp of air, and he fought the urge to change his mind.

"Mom, don't fight it," he said, his voice shaking. "Please, just let it happen. You'll be with Dad soon. I'm doing this for you." *Really?*

Liam silenced his conscience. This was the merciful thing to do, and the only way of ending her life that wouldn't produce incriminating evidence on an autopsy. He refused to accept that, by society's standard, it was murder.

Liam waited several minutes after his mother stopped fighting before he brought her limp body to the surface. He checked her pulse. Nothing.

He took his thumb, his hand trembling, and closed her eyes, tears clouding his vision as his mind flashed through a lifetime of memories of when his mother was vivacious, quick-witted, and nurturing. Dixie Regina Anderson Berne had lived a full life and had been a wonderful wife and mother—and a proper southern belle. But Alzheimer's changed all that, having stolen her beauty, her memory, her dignity, and any meaningful interaction with others. How could he sit by and let it take every last cent she had planned to leave her children? Maybe Colleen could, but he couldn't.

He unfastened the clasp on the platinum cross hanging around his mother's neck and dropped it into the river. The coroner would conclude she had wandered away and drowned. Or at worst, that she had fallen into the hands of a thief, who had stolen her jewelry and drowned her.

Her diamond anniversary band wouldn't budge. Finally, Liam forced it over her knuckle and into his palm, vividly remembering the glow on her face when she and Dad proudly showed it off the day after their twenty-fifth anniversary. He dropped it into the river and stared at the ripples for a moment. Then he moved his gaze to his mother's face, his mind flashing back to the time he accompanied her to the vet to have their beloved dog Amber put to sleep. As much as it hurt, it had been the right thing to do.

"I love you, Mom. So much. You're in a better place." He pressed his lips to her forehead, tears trickling down his cheeks. "Say hi to Dad for me."

Slowly, reluctantly, Liam turned loose of her earthly shell, surrendering it to the river's current. He watched her snow-white hair undulating as she slowly sank in the murky water, and deeply regretted that her body would have to be recovered, identified, and the cause of death pronounced by the coroner before they could give her the burial she deserved.

But what he had to focus on now was making sure every detail of the story he had concocted for Colleen and the sheriff was consistent so that he wouldn't come under suspicion.

A loud sneeze broke his concentration, and Liam jerked his head around and scanned the far bank. He froze, shocked to see a boy sitting on a rock, holding a fishing pole, its red-and-white bobber shimmering in the rippled water. How had he missed that?

Liam spun back around, his heart pounding. The kid was fifty yards away. If he'd seen what happened, would he have kept on fishing? Wouldn't he have shouted or run to get help? Then again, if he had a cell phone, he might have already called the authorities!

Liam trudged through the water, his back to the boy, adrenaline pumping through his veins. He walked up on the bank, his wet clothes clinging to his body. From where he stood, he couldn't see the car, which meant the kid couldn't either.

As he fought to catch his breath, Liam realized there was no turning back. He should just walk to the car nice and slow, like nothing was wrong—and stick to the plan.

CHAPTER 1

Kate Cummings heard the front door slam so loudly that the windows shook. Three seconds later, her twelve-year-old came charging into the kitchen, wearing a red-and-gray Razorbacks sweatshirt, a matching cap, and a toothy grin that told her his fishing outing had been better than just enjoyable.

"I'm back," Jesse Cummings announced as he made a beeline for the fridge.

"Yes, I heard. I think every guest at Angel View heard."

Jesse refilled his water bottle, then stood beside Kate at the stove, his fishy, wet-dog smell mingling with the aroma of the homemade pasta sauce she was stirring.

"Man, does that ever smell dee-lish!" Jesse put his face closer to the pot and took a big whiff. "Mmm … this is a *perfect* Saturday. The Razorbacks won. The Foggy Ridge Falcons won. Fishing was awesome. And now we're having the *best* spaghetti in the world for dinner."

Kate proudly stirred the sauce she'd made with plum and Roma tomatoes, Italian sausage, onions, peppers, mushrooms, and her own special blend of garlic, spices, and fresh herbs.

"So tell me about the fishing," she said.

"It was *awesome*—the most fish I ever caught. Sixty-two crappie and thirteen catfish. I forgot my stringer, so I let them all go. But I took a couple selfies with the biggest ones. Tons of them were legal keepers. I should take Hawk next time. Grandpa'd go nuts, but it's too far for him to walk."

"So where is this honey hole?" Kate said.

Jesse unscrewed the cap on the spring water, gulped down half the bottle, and wiped his mouth with his sleeve. "On the east bank of the Sure Foot, south of the bridge—on down toward Rocky Creek. There's this wide, flat rock that sticks out over the river. Such a cool spot. I caught one fish after another, and they were still biting when I finally ran out of bait. I practically had the place to myself, except for a man and a lady over yonder, wading in the water."

"That's dangerous," Kate said. "You do know that, right?"

Jesse rolled his eyes. "You've warned me a million times about the undercurrent. When I get hot, I take off my shirt, then fill my hat with water and pour it over my head. I just wish it felt like fall instead of summer."

"Why don't you go shower and clean up before dinner."

Jesse glanced in the dining room at the new navy stoneware, floral tablecloth, and the centerpiece his mom had made of fresh yellow mums and orange zinnias. He cocked his head and looked at her. "Cool, Elliot's coming for dinner. Why don't you just get married? He's here all the time anyway."

Kate felt her cheeks warm. "He's not here *all* the time. But we certainly enjoy each other's company."

Jesse ran his finger through a dollop of pasta sauce on the spoon rest and stuck it into his smiling mouth. "Well, it'd be fine with me if you got married. I like having Elliot around. You're over Daddy now, right?"

Her youngest son's candor pierced her. Had he been able to remember his father, perhaps he wouldn't have spoken matter of factly about the man she mourned so deeply—who had just vanished one day with Jesse's two-year-old sister, Riley.

Kate tilted Jesse's chin and looked into his eyes. "I doubt I will ever *get over* your daddy being murdered by some wayward mountain man who stole Riley from us for five years. But it's behind us, and I'm enjoying life again."

"Well, I think you and Elliot should get married."

"You do, huh?"

"Yep. I like it when you're happy." Jesse downed the last of the bottle of water. "I'm gonna go shower. Don't put the garlic bread in the oven till I get back. I love the way it makes the whole house smell good."

Jesse shot out of the kitchen, and she could hear his footsteps on the staircase.

Kate smiled. She *loved* being happy again and was glad Jesse noticed. For most of the years he could remember, she had been grieving the losses in her life. He couldn't possibly understand how afraid she was to open her heart again, despite the fact she was inexplicably drawn to Elliot and too much in love to run scared.

Elliot Stafford loved her more than she dared admit. He had been a supportive friend during the time Micah was missing, slowly falling in love with her, but never once telling her so or acting inappropriately. He was sincerely devoted to her and the kids, all of whom adored him. So why, every time he hinted about marriage, did she seek to change the subject?

❧

Liam Berne pulled his '95 Chevy Caprice into the driveway of his sister's red-brick ranch and then eased into his half of the garage. He paused to pull himself together, then got out and opened the trunk. He took out four plastic bags of groceries, spotted his sister standing in the doorway between the garage and the utility room, and walked toward her.

Act nonchalant. No matter what she says, don't react.

Colleen Berne blocked the door, her arms crossed, worry creases connecting her thick eyebrows. Her dull brown hair bore streaks of gray and hung down to her chin, straight as a two-by-four, same as her figure. Despite the fact that there wasn't an ounce of middle-aged fat on her, Colleen's most attractive feature was her designer tortoiseshell eyeglasses.

She glanced over Liam's shoulder. "I was hoping Mom was with you."

"Why would she be with me?" Liam said. "I told you I was going to run errands and stop at the grocery store."

"I know. When she wasn't in her room, I thought maybe I'd misunderstood and you'd taken her with you. I've been trying to reach you for almost two hours. Why didn't you answer your phone?"

"Sorry. My battery went dead and I didn't have my charger with me. So Mom's out wandering again?"

"Apparently." Colleen tucked her hair behind her ear. "I just got back from looking for her when you drove up."

"Did you call the sheriff?"

"Yes. No one had reported finding her. That's why I hoped she was with you."

"Surely someone will realize she's got Alzheimer's and wandered off," Liam said. "I'm glad we ordered that ID necklace with her name, address, and phone number on it."

"She's not wearing it." Colleen's lower lip quivered. "I told you she keeps taking it off. It reminds her of the dog tag Daddy wore in the army. She was wearing that platinum cross he gave her and won't even let me take it off when she showers."

"I'm sure Mom's fine." Liam forced a reassuring smile, finding it harder to lie to Colleen than he had anticipated. "The sheriff's department will probably call any minute, and we can go pick her up."

"They have my cell number. I can't just sit here and wait. I need to keep looking for her."

Liam squeezed past Colleen, the scent of Dial soap wafting under his nose, and walked through the utility room into the newly remodeled kitchen. Wood floor. Granite countertops. Stainless steel appliances. Wallpaper with an attractive flower-garden pattern. Colleen had better taste in decorating than she did in personal fashion.

Liam set the bags on the breakfast bar. "I'll go with you. It's pointless to split up if my cell phone's dead. Let's bring in the rest of the groceries and put away the perishables first."

Liam turned and walked back out to the garage, Colleen on his heels. He handed her a bag, then picked up the last three, slammed the trunk shut, and followed her into the house.

Colleen began emptying the bags. "Mom's living with us isn't safe for her anymore. I can hardly wait until there's a bed available at the Alzheimer's center."

"I know you're right. But it hurts me to think of leaving her there like some stray puppy we turned in to the humane society."

Colleen put down the yogurt carton, her eyes welled with tears. "Don't you think it breaks my heart, Liam? But we have to do whatever it takes to keep her safe. She's vulnerable when she's out wandering. I don't know what I'd do if something awful happened to her ..."

Liam was touched by his sister's raw emotion. What Colleen lacked in looks, she made up for in character. Her motives were pure and he knew it. His unspoken disagreement with her was concerning what was actually *necessary*. And in his opinion, watching his mother's life drag on in some sterile institution that would cost a fortune and not add one minute of quality to her life was *not* necessary.

Liam blinked away the image of his mother's limp body, weightless in his arms, and was hit with an unexpected swell of emotion. He coughed to cover it up—but not before his sister picked up on it.

Colleen came over and stood next to him, her arm around his waist. "I know it's hard. I hate it too. But it's really the best thing for her. She's been a wonderful mother." Colleen gently rubbed his back, her voice now compassionate and soft. "We can honor her by being strong and making sure she receives the necessary care, for however long she's still with us."

Liam nodded, glad to let her assume his upset was because of his reluctance to admit their mother to the Alzheimer's hospital.

Colleen pulled him closer. "Let's get this done and go find her."

The lump in Liam's throat seemed to have doubled in size. He was beginning to feel the finality of his actions. He would have to join in the search for their mother. And when they couldn't find her, Colleen would fall apart. The sheriff would be all over it. And Liam would have to give the performance of his life.

CHAPTER 2

Kate sat at the dining-room table between her dad and Elliot, and across from her four children. She smiled as Jesse dumped a mound of Parmesan cheese over his third helping of spaghetti.

"Mama, this tastes *so* good," Jesse said. "You should sell your sauce and make a fortune."

"A fortune, huh?" Kate chuckled. "I don't know about that, but it's always fun to serve it to this crowd."

"Seriously, Jesse has a point." Abby Cummings tucked her long auburn hair behind her ear. "Your sauce is perfect on all your pasta dishes: ravioli, manicotti, tortellini, lasagna—anything. We ought to put together a cookbook of your recipes and sell it together with a jar of your homemade sauce. I'll bet the guests would go for it. It's a great souvenir to take home for themselves or someone else. Especially if you autograph the cookbook."

Hawk Cummings nudged Abby with his elbow. "What a cool idea, Sis. And here I thought the entrepreneurial gene skipped you."

Abby looked up at him and grinned. "Thanks. I think there's a compliment in there somewhere."

"I appreciate your vote of confidence, everyone." Kate waved her hand dismissively. "But I'm happy to make it just for us."

"I wouldn't be so quick to blow it off, Kate," Elliot Stafford said. "People usually leave here with souvenirs, right? If we could find a clever way to package your cookbook and a jar of homemade pasta sauce, it'd be a great *personal* addition to the gift shop."

"We could sell it at Flutter's too," Abby quickly added. "We could use it in some menu items and make a display at the cash register. Great impulse item."

"Goodness"—Kate was sure her cheeks were pinker than Abby's sweater—"I didn't expect all this."

Riley dipped her garlic bread in pasta sauce and took a bite. "It's yummy. I never had nothin' like this before I came here to live."

Suddenly everything was quiet. All heads turned to Riley.

"I meant I never tasted *anything* like this before I came here to live." Riley giggled. "I keep working and working to say things right. But sometimes I just forget."

"You're doing great"—Hawk nudged her in the ribs—"for a pipsqueak."

Riley cocked her head, the corners of her mouth twitching. "I'm not a pipsqueak."

"Too bad," Hawk said. "Because if you were, I might let you pour the chocolate sauce on the spumoni ice cream I picked up at Sweet Stuff."

"Okay. Okay. I'm a pipsqueak. I want to pour the chocolate. But what's spanomi?"

"No," Jesse said. "Spoo-*moan*-ee. It's like this awesome cherry-chocolate-and-pistachio ice cream."

Abby tapped her spoon on her water glass. "I think Grandpa Buck has something he wants to say."

Kate's dad wiped the red off his white mustache with the flowered napkin that matched Kate's new tablecloth. "Before we set our sights on dessert," he said, "I think we should take a vote. All in favor of Kate printin' a cookbook to sell with her pasta sauce, raise your hand."

Jesse's arm shot in the air, as did everyone's except Kate's.

"Majority rules," Jesse said.

"Goodness, I'm overwhelmed." Kate moved her gaze from person to person. "I'd only be willing to go forward if it's a family effort."

"Let's get Jay involved too." Abby folded her napkin on the table. "He'd love doing the artwork—anything you want."

"Picking out the cover paper and binding shouldn't be hard," Kate said. "I've worked with the print shop on brochures and marketing pieces for the lodge."

Elliot reached over and covered Kate's hand with his. "Don't rule out self-publishing a *hardcover* cookbook. I could look into the cost difference. Hardcover would be classier. Your recipes are top notch, Kate. Way beyond just home cooking."

Hawk laughed. "My mama, a published author. I say, go for it."

"I'm a good salesman," Jesse said. "I could make sure shop owners in town know that Mama's cookbooks and sauce are in our gift shop and see if they would sell them too."

Riley didn't say anything. She sat with her arms folded, her lower lip protruding.

"Sweetie, what's wrong?" Kate said.

"I want to help too."

"How about you and me being in charge of distribution?" Hawk tugged one of her pigtails. "We'll make sure the businesses Jesse sells to stay supplied with Mama's cookbooks and sauce. We can make deliveries."

Riley looked adoringly at Hawk. "I'll be your number-one helper."

"Absolutely."

"I'm getting fired up about this," Elliot said. "If we get busy, we *might* get it in before Christmas. It's worth a try."

"Then it's settled." Hawk stood and pushed back his chair. "Okay, Pipsqueak, let's go dish up dessert."

Jesse slid his plate aside and cleared his throat loudly enough to get everyone's attention. "Isn't anyone going to ask me how the fishing was today?"

"Since you didn't say anything, I figured you got skunked again." Hawk laughed.

Jesse shook his head, a grin toying with the corners of his mouth. "For your information, I caught sixty-two crappie and thirteen catfish." He held up his hands and proudly displayed the gill nicks and rough fingers that were proof he'd taken a lot of fish off the hook. "I forgot my stringer, so I released them all. But I took selfies." Jesse handed his phone to Hawk. "I'm going back. The fish were still biting when I ran out of bait. Man, I hit the jackpot."

"I'll say." Hawk raised an eyebrow. "Where were you fishing?"

"It's my secret." Jesse pointed to himself with his thumb, seeming to enjoy having the family's undivided attention. "It's too far for Grandpa this time. But I'll take you there, if you want."

"I want," Hawk said.

"Can I go?" Riley's bright blue eyes were pleading. "Pleeease?"

"There's always room for a pipsqueak," Hawk said, "but I should go check it out first. I think your other big brother might be exaggerating. So, Jesse … who else knows about your fishing hole?"

"Just me. A man and white-haired lady were wading in the river, but I don't think they paid me much mind."

"How about you show me this place tomorrow after church?"

"It's gonna cost you." Jesse wore a playful grin. "Hey, I'm a businessman."

"So what's your price?"

"A ride down to Evans's Sporting Goods," Jesse said. "I want to spend some of my savings on a lighter rod and four-pound test line."

"Before or after we go find the fishing hole?"

"Before." Jesse folded his hands on the table. "It's nonnegotiable."

"Done." Hawk looked over at Kate and winked. "We've definitely got too many business heads in this family."

Liam heard the grandfather clock strike eight, and watched Colleen pick at the veggies on her plate. He had stifled his own emotions and managed a believable show of support as they searched for their mother. Colleen verbalized optimism that she would surface alive and unharmed, but he could see her resolve slipping. He just hoped their mother's body was discovered soon so they could get the autopsy over with, give her a proper burial, and proceed with dividing up the money. His worst fear was that her body wouldn't be found; and without a death certificate, the inheritance money would be on hold indefinitely.

He blinked the stinging from his eyes. He had done the only right thing. Nothing would ever make him believe otherwise. Ending their mother's life was more compassionate than letting her live out her days at the Alzheimer's hospital, babbling to strangers about the snippets of a life she could no longer remember.

"Liam?"

He was suddenly aware of Colleen's voice and realized she was standing next to him.

"Are you done?" she said.

He glanced at the half-eaten chicken breast and baked potato. "I guess so. Sorry I didn't finish. It's not that it wasn't good."

"That's okay. I'm not hungry either." She started to take his plate, but then lowered it back to the table and flopped down in the chair next to him. "What are we going to do?"

Was that a rhetorical question, or was she actually expecting him to answer?

"It's only been a few hours," Liam said. "I'll bet someone from the sheriff's department will call any minute, saying she's been found." Why was he giving her hope? He should be preparing her for the grim truth.

"I don't have a good feeling about this." Colleen sighed. "Let's split up this time and go look for her again. If we don't know something by bedtime, I think we have to file a missing person's report."

"Agreed." Liam gently gripped his sister's wrist. "But I'm going with you. I don't think you should be alone."

"Probably not. I can't just sit around here. I have to keep trying."

"Sis"—Liam paused until she looked at him—"I know it's hard to talk about this. But we need to prepare ourselves in case this doesn't have the ending we want."

Colleen shook her head. "I'm not ready to have this conversation. Let's just go look for Mom, okay?"

"Sure," Liam said softly, both dreading and hoping for the moment when they would get the call that their mother's body had been found. Would seeing Colleen heartbroken trigger the release of the pent-up emotion he fought to contain? Or would he be so focused on *not* raising suspicion that his emotions would be shut down and he'd have to fake a strong reaction?

Liam took in a slow, deep breath and let it out. Then did it again. Regardless of whether his performance was felt or contrived, it would have to be believable.

❧

Liam sat in the chair in his bedroom, staring out the window into the darkness. The stars no longer looked to him like diamonds on black velvet, but more like a million shards of broken glass crushed on the floor of heaven.

He and Colleen had come back from tonight's futile search and filed the missing person's report. The detectives had no trouble believing their mother had wandered off because she'd done it a number of times before.

Had he acted prematurely by taking his mother's life? It was a desperate move. But someone had to step up. It would have been unfair to sentence her to live out her days in emotional isolation, lost in some inner maze of mixed-up thoughts and incomplete sentences. No caregiver from the Alzheimer's center could give back her memory or her dignity. All they could do was make her hopeless existence *comfortable* in order to justify the high cost of keeping her there.

Liam blinked away the last image he'd had of his mother before he held her head under water.

"Who's gettin' baptized?"

"You are, Dixie."

He had used something sacred in order to deceive her in those last seconds. At least he got it over with quickly. He wondered if people in heaven knew how they had died. If so, his mother would surely thank him for ending her life before the disease rendered her subhuman.

Liam wiped a runaway tear from his cheek. Colleen always contended that every human life had value because God made it. But God hadn't made his mother without a memory. Disease stole it from her. She had been intelligent, clever, creative. Vivacious and bubbly, gracious and hospitable. She never knew a stranger until the Alzheimer's took hold. Half the time she didn't even recognize him or Colleen. Or remember her own name. How did that glorify the Creator?

Liam got up and stretched his lower back. Why was he arguing with himself when he needed to rest? The stress of sitting eye to eye with Deputies Duncan and Hobbs and filing a missing person's report while trying to look more worried than guilty had taken everything out of him.

Colleen still held fast to the hope that their mother was merely lost and would be found unharmed. She called the prayer chain at her church, and someone set up a conference call so that everyone on the prayer team could pray with her. That seemed to calm her, and she finally went to bed.

Liam had all the answers. So why was he wide eyed and staring into the darkness? He eased back into the chair and heaved a sigh. What was done was done. His mother was at peace. Half of the inheritance money would soon be his. What he had to do now was avoid raising suspicion. He needed to be a comfort to Colleen as they grieved their loss. Later on, when he finally got his share of the money, he would use it to get out of debt and buy back his independence. That was the best way to honor his mother.

CHAPTER 3

Kate sat with Elliot at an umbrella table on the back deck at Angel View Lodge, enjoying sweet mint tea and relishing the magnificent panoramic view.

The warm September breeze toyed with her hair as she looked out at the pristine expanse of earth, water, and sky. Beaver Lake, the color of blue lapis, sparkled beneath the lush Ozark hills, forming a maze of inlets and islands as far as the eye could see.

Sunday's azure sky was generously dotted with cloud puffs that cast shadows across the green hills. Soon all that rolling green would become a patchwork of crimson, orange, purple, and gold.

"A penny for your thoughts," Elliot said.

Kate moved her gaze to him. Elliot's thick salt-and-pepper hair was neatly in place despite the playful breeze, the twinkle in his steely-blue eyes an indicator that he was delighted to be in her company.

"I was just thinking that I've never taken this view for granted," Kate said.

Elliot nodded knowingly. "It was smart planning that you and Micah included so many huge windows and decks at Angel View."

"It was his idea," Kate said. "Micah had it figured out right down to which trees needed to be cleared to open up the view. He wanted to make sure every guest was privy to this incredible vista. In his mind, stewardship and ownership were synonymous."

Elliot squeezed lemon into his mint iced tea and stirred. "I'll say one thing, you've done a remarkable job of running this place by yourself. That's no small feat. I've seen what's involved."

"Dad's been a great help," Kate said. "The kids too. Carrying on the family business has helped them cope with losing Micah."

"He'd be proud of how y'all pulled together." Elliot seemed far away for a moment. "Have you ever thought about hiring someone to manage Angel View?"

"Not really."

"You want to work this hard forever?"

Kate smiled. "What else would I do?"

"Spend more time with me."

"Am I neglecting you?"

"Not at all. I just love spending time with you, and I wouldn't mind more of it."

Kate shifted her weight. "We've both got businesses to run, Elliot."

"Yes, but now that corporate's running Stafford Lumber, I don't need to be involved in the day-to-day operations."

"Well, I *do*. I don't have that luxury."

Elliot's gaze collided with hers. "My point exactly. Wouldn't you like to turn loose of some of the responsibility so you could just kick back and enjoy life?"

"I'm enjoying life just fine. But even if I wanted to slow down, I can't afford to hire someone to manage the lodge. I've got kids to support."

"What if"—Elliot ran his index finger through the condensation on his glass—"you didn't have that responsibility anymore?"

Kate was suddenly hot all over. She was not ready for this conversation.

"Darlin', when are you going to get serious about where we are in our relationship?"

"I *am* serious," Kate said. "You know that."

"I know we love each other." Elliot reached over and took her hand in his. "But anytime I try to talk to you about the future, you shut down. Maybe we should talk about why."

"I just like things the way they are—for now."

Elliot sighed. "Look, I get it. It took me years to get over Pam's death. I don't mean to push you. It's just that I love you so much. I'm ready to spend my life with you. Every time I bring it up, you seem to turn me off. I'd like to understand why."

Kate kept her eye on a great blue heron flying toward the lake. "I'm not still grieving Micah, if that's what you think."

"I would understand if you were. It's just coming up on two years since you learned that he was murdered."

"I did most of my grieving during the years he was missing. I had accepted that I would probably never see him again."

"Then why do you resist talking about our future together?"

Kate took her free hand and fiddled with the lemon wedge on the rim of her glass. "I'm not sure. Maybe I'm afraid of losing you."

"Of course you are. I feel the same way about you. But do you think if one of us died, the pain would be any less intense had we not gotten married?"

Married. Why did the word make her squirm? "Probably not," Kate said. "But, for now"—*until I can think about marriage with joy instead of panic*—"I'm comfortable with things the way they are."

Elliot kissed her hand, then let go.

Kate leaned forward on her elbows and waited until he looked at her. "Can you just be patient until my emotions catch up with yours?"

"Sure." He flashed a warm smile that belied the disappointment in his tone. "I'll wait for as long as it takes. I just don't want there to be any question in your mind what my intentions are. I love your kids too. I would never try to replace Micah, but I'd love a crack at being a stable male presence, especially for Jesse and Riley. Jesse's just a year away from being a teenager. And even though he and Hawk are close, Jesse really needs a father figure."

"I know. And he adores you," Kate said. "He told me yesterday that he thinks we should get married."

"Really?"

"Abby and Hawk have said basically the same thing, in more subtle ways."

"How about Buck?"

Kate felt the corners of her mouth twitch. "Dad's hinted a hundred ways to Sunday that you're perfect for this family."

"And what about you, Kate?" Elliot seemed to look right into her heart. "What do you think?"

Kate started to feel as if she were cooking from the inside out. Was she having another hot flash or just feeling overwhelmed?

She reached down and snatched today's church bulletin from the side pocket of her purse and started fanning herself. "I think the love we have is real and deep and is only going to get better. That doesn't mean it's God's timing for us to get married now."

"Apparently not, since we're not on the same page." There was an uncomfortable half minute of silence, and then Elliot said, "Well then, let's talk about your cookbook."

Kate laughed without meaning to. "Are you still on that kick?"

"I can't remember seeing the kids more excited," Elliot said. "This is the first real opportunity we've had to see how we can work together as a family."

Kate was suddenly aware that most tables on the umbrella deck had been vacated. She glanced at her watch. "We can talk more later. Sunday brunch is over. I should go check with Savannah and see what our customer count was."

"You want to take a paddle boat out later?" he said. "We're not going to get many more weekends like this one before it's too nippy on the lake. I promise to keep the conversation light and just enjoy being with you."

"Sure, I'd love it. I think Abby and Jay are going out too." Kate stroked Elliot's clean-shaven cheek. "I shouldn't be long here. Why don't you go change clothes and meet me back at the house in thirty minutes? How does that sound?"

Elliot winked. "Like a plan."

Kate stood, then walked down the wooden stairs and inside through the side door of Flutter's Café, feeling at the same time relieved and trapped. Why couldn't she talk to Elliot about a future together? They were just as suited to each other as she and Micah had been. Was she afraid Elliot could never measure up to Micah? That no one could? Sometimes she wondered if she had put Micah on such a pedestal that her memory of him was skewed.

Jesse sat with his legs dangling over the side of the large, flat rock that jutted out over the Sure Foot River, Hawk sitting next to him.

"I hope you weren't exaggerating about how great the fishing was." Hawk nudged Jesse with his elbow. "We've been here almost an hour and haven't had a bite."

"Just wait"—Jesse lifted the Razorbacks cap he wore and wiped his forehead with the back of his hand—"the fish are gonna turn on, and you'll see what I'm talking about."

"If it's as good as you say, I'll be surprised if that couple you saw yesterday doesn't show up over here with all their friends. Where'd you see them?"

"Over yonder." Jesse pointed to the other side of the river. "But they weren't fishing, just wading in the water. I think the man was teaching the lady to hold her breath."

"Pretty stupid to be wading in the Sure Foot," Hawk said. "The undercurrent's been known to drag a man down."

"I never do it 'cause Mama's warned me not to ever since I was a kid."

Hawk laughed. "I got news for you, Bubba. You're still a kid."

"You know what I mean."

Hawk pulled the bill of Jesse's cap down over his eyes. "I'm just razzing you. So where're the fish?"

"They're here. And when they get hungry, look out." Jesse put his hat on backward and looked out over the ripples. "Can I ask you something?"

"Sure."

"Do you think Mama should marry Elliot?"

"That's a loaded question." Hawk reeled in his lure and pitched it out again. "Doesn't matter what I think. It's her decision."

"Do you think she wants to?"

"All the signs are there," Hawk said. "I'd bet a dime to a doughnut that Elliot does. But I don't know if Mama's ready to remarry. Losing Daddy was traumatic. You were too young to remember."

"I remember Mama being sad and depressed all the time. Now she smiles a lot and is cheerful. It's easier for me to feel happy when she's happy."

Hawk nodded. "I hear that."

"So tell me straight … do *you* think they should get married?"

Hawk was quiet for a few moments, and then said, "If I knew it would make Mama happy, I'd be totally on board with it. Elliot's a great guy. Seems natural having him around."

"What's Mama waiting for?"

"You ask too many questions. Doesn't your mind ever stop working?"

"Nope." Jesse's bobber disappeared and he jumped to his feet.

"Got a bite?"

"Something's playing with my line. Come on, take it …" Jesse didn't move an inch, his heart pounding so hard he could feel it in his temples. A second later, his line went taut and without even thinking, he reeled down and yanked up on the line. "I got him! Oh man, feels like a big one!"

"Doubles!" Hawk's fishing rod was nearly bent in two, his grin wider than the Sure Foot. "Now *that's* what I'm talking about. You might've found us a new favorite spot. Let's hope those folks you saw across the way didn't realize what you found. We need to keep this a secret."

CHAPTER 4

Raleigh County Sheriff Virgil Granger, still dressed in his church clothes, walked up on the wraparound porch of his Victorian home, a plastic grocery bag in one hand. He smiled at the orange tabby cat that perched at the front door.

"What's the matter, Garfield—couldn't get a handout anywhere else?" Virgil chuckled. His wife, Jill Beth, couldn't say no to a garden slug, and this smart old tomcat knew she was the easiest mark on the block. "I'll tell my sweetheart you're waiting on the doorstep. She saved you some chicken."

Virgil opened the beveled glass door and was hit with the pervasive aroma of freshly baked bread—and the yelping of the handsome mutt they had adopted from Animal Rescue.

"Hey, Drake. I'm glad to see you too. Now mind your manners. Sit. No, *sit* ..." Virgil waited until the dog ran in circles a few times, his tail harmlessly swiping the glass-encased Victorian curio cabinet.

Finally, Drake sat on the shiny wood floor, whining, but holding his position.

"Good boy." Virgil bent down and slowly petted the dog, careful not to encourage his canine exuberance. Part German shepherd and part Australian sheepdog, Drake needed to run—every day. Until Virgil and Jill Beth had figured that out, Drake's boundless energy and wagging tail had demolished more antiques than their triplet boys had in all the years they were raising them.

"First let me read the Sunday paper," Virgil said. "Then I'll take you out and throw the Frisbee."

Virgil stood and walked down the hall to the kitchen.

Jill Beth turned from the sink and stepped over to him, wiping her hands on a towel and wearing a smile that would melt an iceberg.

"Hi, doll." He set the grocery bag on the table. "One gallon of two percent milk as instructed."

Jill Beth put her arms around his neck, her round puppy eyes playful. "You're a good man, Sheriff Granger. You won't be sorry. I'm fixin' to use some of that milk to make the low-fat chocolate pie recipe that LaDawn Mitchell gave me."

"Police Chief Mitchell's wife?"

"Uh-huh. I told you she volunteers with me at the food bank. She brought a slice in her lunch on Friday and let me try it. It's beyond incredible. And the fat and calorie count is low enough that you can have seconds, and I won't give you what-for."

"I'm loving it already. By the way, your buddy Garfield is waiting at the front door."

Jill Beth laughed. "I don't know why we don't just buy cat food and set it out. He's adopted us."

"Or the other way around. You can't turn away any animal, once you've made eye contact." Virgil picked up a lock of her dark, chin-length curls and studied her face. "If I haven't said so lately, I'm mighty proud of the way you keep yourself looking nice and keep things running slick as a whistle around here. After thirty years, it's still hard to believe I'm the lucky dog you chose to spend your life with."

Jill Beth giggled and removed her arms. "If you're after thirds on the chocolate pie, it's working."

Virgil smiled and picked up the milk and put it in the fridge. "Think I'll go change my clothes and read the Sunday paper before I take Drake out."

"I took the Home and Garden section," Jill Beth said. "Dinner at six, okay? Rob and Reece are coming. Rick's in New York on business."

Virgil's cell phone buzzed and he glanced at the screen. "It's Kevin."

"On a Sunday?"

"Can't be good news when my chief deputy interrupts my Sunday afternoon."

"No kidding." Jill Beth sighed.

Virgil put the phone to his ear. "What's up?"

"We've got a dead body," Kevin Mann said. "Elderly woman. Body washed up at the shallow end of Rocky Creek about an hour ago. Couple of trout fishermen found it. She fits the description of Dixie Berne, the lady Duncan and Hobbs did a missing person's report on. She's slight framed and white haired. Wearing a pink dress. Timing fits—she's been dead twenty-four hours, give or take."

"Any sign of foul play?"

"Not that I can see."

Virgil glanced up at Jill Beth. "All right, Kevin. Talk to Berne's family before they hear it on the news. See if they can ID her."

"Will do, Sheriff. I'll let you know."

Virgil disconnected the call and told his wife about the recovered body and the missing person's report on Dixie Berne.

"Ms. Berne has a history of wandering," Virgil said. "And she's the only woman currently on our missing person's list."

"Poor thing. Will there be an autopsy?"

Virgil scratched his chin. "Probably not necessary. Depends on what the coroner finds."

⁂

Liam sat with Colleen in the waiting room at the Raleigh County Morgue. His sister wrung her hands and sighed about every thirty seconds. What was taking so long? It was going to be crushing for Colleen to see their mother dead. He hoped he could fake his shock. At least his grief would be genuine.

"How're you doing?" Liam said.

Colleen exhaled. "What do *you* think?"

Liam put his arm around her. "I think you should wait here and let me do this."

Colleen shook her head. "It's sweet that you want to spare me the pain, but I need to see her for myself. That photograph Deputy Duncan showed us wasn't proof enough for me."

Of course it wasn't, Liam thought.

"There's no way Mom could've wandered that far. And why was all her jewelry missing? Someone must have stolen it and then drowned her."

"Whoa, Sis. The deputy didn't see any signs of foul play."

Colleen stood and walked over to an oil painting of black-eyed Susans, her back to him. "Deputy Duncan said the coroner found water in her lungs. She was alive when she went into the water. Someone did this to her."

"Hey …" Liam got up and put his hand on Colleen's shoulder. "Let's not get ahead of ourselves."

"Her ring was snug," Colleen said. "There's no way it came off in the water unless someone pulled it off her finger."

"You may be right. But as of now, we don't know much. Let's wait and see what the coroner has to say. I'm sure he'll order an autopsy if there's even a hint of foul play."

"There is. There has to be." Colleen folded her arms across her chest. "On her best day, Mom didn't have the stamina to wander two miles to the river."

"But if she was lost and scared, it's hard to say what she might do."

"Well, not that."

Colleen's cheeks flushed, the pink actually an improvement to her pasty complexion, and he could tell she was vehemently determined to push for an autopsy. Didn't matter. Liam had covered his tracks.

The door opened, and a bearded, middle-aged man in a white coat walked in. "Are you here to ID the drowning victim?"

"Yes," Liam said, shaking the man's hand. "I'm Liam Berne, and this my sister, Colleen Berne."

"I'm Dr. Levin. I work closely with the coroner."

"We're a little on edge," Liam said. "Could we just get this over with?"

"Yes, of course." Dr. Levin looked over the top of his glasses. "It's only necessary that one of you identify the body."

"I want to see her," Colleen said. "I saw the photos taken by the sheriff's deputies, but I need to see her myself."

Liam nodded. "Me too."

"Very well," Dr. Levin said. "Fortunately, the river was kind to this woman. I've seen drowning victims that were unrecognizable. There were no signs of a struggle. It appears to have been an accident."

"My mother had Alzheimer's," Colleen said. "There's no way she could've walked all the way to the river. If this is she, there had to be foul play involved. I'll want an autopsy done."

Dr. Levin stroked his beard. "The coroner would have to make that call, but I can tell you that there's nothing about this victim to warrant it. No indication of sexual assault. Or any trauma. All indications support a classic case of drowning."

"Well, she obviously couldn't have drowned at Rocky Creek," Colleen said. "The water's too shallow, and the deputies said she was found faceup."

Dr. Levin nodded. "We think she drowned in the Sure Foot. Let me explain. When a drowning occurs in a river, sinking takes place immediately, which results in the victim reaching the bottom close to the point she was last seen on the surface. Later, when the body begins to rise, it will appear on the surface not far from where it disappeared. Many people don't realize the current on the surface is different from the current on the bottom. While the speed on the surface may be ten knots, current speed will decrease with depth. There is virtually no current on the bottom. Consequently, the deeper a body sinks, the slower the current is acting upon it. The victim's body is almost always found downstream no more than one or two hundred yards from where it sank."

"So then, it's possible to determine where the victim entered the water?" Colleen asked.

Liam was suddenly hot all over.

Dr. Levin nodded. "Sometimes, yes. If the authorities suspect foul play and invest time and personnel to launch an investigation along the shoreline. But that kind of investment isn't routine with accidental drownings."

"It wasn't accidental!" Colleen snapped. "The deputies told us her jewelry's missing. Someone must've robbed her and then pushed her into the water."

Liam plucked a tissue from the box on the end table and handed it to Colleen. "Sis, there's no point in torturing yourself. Let's hold off speculating until we at least determine if the victim *is* Mom."

Colleen nodded and dabbed her eyes.

Dr. Levin motioned toward the door. "If you're ready, I'll take you to the viewing area."

Liam let Colleen go first, and they followed Dr. Levin down the hall to a windowless room with a large flat-screen TV monitor and a row of chairs.

"Please have a seat," Dr. Levin said. "The image on the screen is coming from the room where we keep bodies until they are identified.

I'm going to have a tech open one of those stainless steel lockers and pull out a drawer. Once the body is visible, the camera will move closer so you can see the woman's face. Ready?"

Liam nodded and grabbed Colleen's hand, not sure if she was shaking—or if he was. This was the moment of truth. Could he let out the genuine emotion he had been suppressing so that Colleen and Dr. Levin would believe it to be the response of a son racked with shock and grief?

Dr. Levin pressed a button on the wall and spoke into what appeared to be a speaker. "Bobby Lee, would you please pull out drawer number eleven?"

Liam gazed at the monitor, his heart pounding so hard he wondered if it might hammer him into the seat where he sat. He watched a young man walk over to a row of stainless steel lockers and slowly pull out a slab containing a body covered with a white sheet.

"Okay, would you do a close-up of the woman's face?"

Liam pretended to look, but couldn't bring himself to see his mother this way. He remembered how peaceful she looked when he gave her body to the river. He didn't want that image replaced by a cadaver on a metal slab.

Colleen gasped. "Oh, Mom! I'm sorry. I'm so sorry …" Colleen started sobbing and buried her face in his shoulder.

Liam allowed himself to glance for a second at the image on the screen, and then he turned his gaze to Dr. Levin. "It's her. It's our mom," he said, not sure if he had said the words out loud or merely thought them.

"You're certain?" Dr. Levin said. "Are there any physical characteristics that would confirm this?"

"She had … a birthmark … on the back of her left forearm. It was sort of heart shaped."

"Bobby Lee, would you hold up the left forearm so we can see the other side?"

A few seconds later, the camera zoomed in—there it was. Proof.

Liam felt as if some invisible force were pushing down on him, crushing his chest, forcing the air out of his lungs. And the tears out of his eyes.

"Thanks, Bobby Lee. That'll be all." Dr. Levin turned off the screen. "Try to relax. Take shallow breaths. This is *never* easy, even if you've already reviewed the photos."

"It's worse than I thought it would be," Liam said honestly.

"It's my fault she wandered off." Colleen sat up straight and blew her nose. "But someone killed her. I'm sure of it."

Dr. Levin pulled up a chair, then sat and faced them. "I can only imagine how shocking and earth shattering it is to see your mother this way, and wanting answers. Sometimes there just aren't any. She drowned. There's nothing to suggest anyone else was responsible."

"We're both in the state of shock." Liam shuddered without meaning to. "We need time to process all of this."

Dr. Levin nodded. "How about I leave you here until you feel ready to leave? My office is across the hall. When you want to leave, come get me, and I'll escort you back to the front."

Liam heard Dr. Levin exit the room and saw Colleen staring at nothing.

"You okay?" Liam said.

"No, I'm not okay." Colleen turned to him. "No one's going to pursue this because she was just an old woman with Alzheimer's.

Well, she was our *mother*, and I'm not buying that she drowned by accident. I want to talk to the sheriff."

Liam bit his lip. "The coroner didn't find any sign of trauma. He looked her over pretty well, Colleen. What we know *for sure* is that she's at peace now."

"Well, *I'm* not." Colleen stood. "I'm not letting law enforcement blow this off."

"That's what you think they're doing?" Liam said.

"I absolutely do." Colleen picked up her purse and draped the strap over her shoulder. "They have a limited budget, and an autopsy costs too much. The only way we're going to get justice for Mom is to fight for it. I'm going to the sheriff. Are you with me or not?"

Liam felt his neck muscles tighten. He knew better than to try to reason with Colleen when she was like this. Play along with her. Go to the sheriff. Let him convince her.

"Come on," Liam said. "I'll drive."

CHAPTER 5

Liam walked into Colleen's red-brick ranch, the garage door closing behind him.

He made his way through the utility room and kitchen and into the living room, just as Colleen tossed her purse on the couch and flopped down next to it.

"I can't believe the hoops we have to jump through," she said, "just to talk to the sheriff."

"Sis, it's Sunday. What'd you expect? We could've talked to the deputies on duty."

Colleen shook her head. "Why waste our time. We have to appeal to the sheriff to convince the coroner to order an autopsy."

Be sympathetic. You're not going to change her mind. "We'll try again," Liam assured her. "First thing in the morning."

Colleen put her hands to her temples. "What am I saying? I can't go in the morning. We're taking the seventh graders on a field trip to the battlefield at Pea Ridge."

"You can't really be thinking of your students right now," Liam said. "Both of us need to take some time off and get Mom's affairs in order."

"They're already in order. Almost everything is in the living trust. All I have to do is call her lawyer and he'll take care of everything." Colleen exhaled. "But you're right. I don't need to be worrying about my students. I'd better go call the principal and let her know what's happened. She'll need to get a sub."

"It'll keep for a few minutes," he said. "Relax. You've just been through one of the toughest days of your life. Neither of us is thinking clearly."

Colleen's eyes glistened, a tear rolling down her cheek. "I wasn't ready to lose her, Liam. I didn't resent the added responsibility. Or paying Mrs. Olsen to stay with her while we were at work."

"I know that."

"I was willing to go to the Alzheimer's center every day to see her."

"Look … I'm sorry Mom's life ended suddenly like this," Liam said. "But there's a blessing we shouldn't miss. Mom didn't have to live out her days lost in some crazy mental fog, confused and alone."

"She wouldn't have been alone. How can you say that?"

"Sis, people with Alzheimer's stop communicating. And nothing you say gets through. I'd say that's alone."

"Mom wasn't like that."

Liam raised his eyebrows. "Pretty close."

"No one really knows what people with Alzheimer's are feeling," Colleen said. "Mom didn't seem to be suffering."

"And that's your measure of a quality life? She also didn't know where she was half the time. Or who she was with."

Colleen folded her arms tightly across her chest. "It was what it was. None of us gets to choose what it'll be like when we're old. I loved her. I was willing to do whatever it took to make her comfortable. But the thought that someone took advantage of her … stole her jewelry and then drowned her like she meant nothing …" Colleen shook her head and bit her lip.

Liam wanted to tell her that's not how it happened. That he did treat their mother with respect. That he held her in his arms until she was gone. That he loved her enough to end her life before things got any worse. "You've got to stop speculating, Sis. The coroner said there was no sign of foul play."

"Then explain how she got to the river."

Liam shrugged. "I can't. But I've heard of wandering Alzheimer's patients doing some pretty remarkable things. Maybe she asked someone for a ride."

"Give me a break."

"Don't be so quick to pooh-pooh the idea," Liam said. "Yesterday morning, she rambled on and on about 'being late for the wedding.' Maybe she asked someone to take her to a church and wandered some more after that. We're just never going to know."

Colleen put what was left of a tissue to her nose and blew. "I'm sorry, but I can't accept that."

Liam sat on the love seat facing her, his heart stirred by his sister's angst. He felt his own pain and nagging guilt tighten his gut. An autopsy wasn't going to answer her questions. He had to find a way to talk her out of it.

"Do you know what's really involved in an autopsy?" Liam said.

Colleen raised her hand. "Don't. I know enough."

"Do you?"

"Liam, stop it. I wouldn't even consider it if I didn't think there was a real possibility that Mom was murdered."

"Even though there's no sign of struggle?"

Colleen pursed her lips. "You think I'm wrong to pursue this."

Liam got up and walked over to the couch and sat next to her. "I think you're a loving daughter who's grasping at straws to avoid the painful truth that Mom just got away from us."

The expression left Colleen's face. "Not us—*me*. It was my fault. I was home with her. How could I not know she had slipped out?"

"I don't hold you responsible for this," Liam said. "Mom was prone to wander. It was getting impossible to keep track of her every second. She could've gotten away from me just as easily."

"But she didn't."

"Don't go there," Liam said.

"I'm *already* there. She got lost on my watch."

"For crying out loud, Colleen, she was taking a nap, and you used that opportunity to get some stuff done. Even mothers leave sleeping kids and do chores around the house."

"I should've heard her leave."

"We never heard her leave any of the other times."

"Will you stop making excuses for me!" she said.

"No. This is ridiculous. You are *not* responsible." Why was Colleen doing this to herself? He never meant for her to bear the guilt.

"I appreciate what you're trying to do, Liam. But you don't have to sugarcoat it."

"Sugarcoat *what,* for Pete's sake—that Mom got up from her nap and slipped out of the house while you were hard at work in the utility room, doing everyone's laundry and ironing? It's not like you plopped down in front of the TV with a box of chocolates or a bottle of whiskey."

"I heard *you* go out the front door," Colleen said. "Why didn't I hear her?"

Liam's pulse quickened. *Don't react. There's no way she suspects I took Mom with me.* "Because she's quiet as a mouse and I tend to slam the door."

Colleen let out the same sigh she had been replicating all day. "I feel just awful that I was right there and she slipped out without me hearing her."

Liam put his hand on hers. "I wish it had been me instead. You're going to be a lot harder on yourself than I would be."

Liam mentally retraced the steps he'd taken the day before.

"Colleen, I'm leaving to go run errands," Liam had said as he approached the door to the utility room. His sister had placed several piles of dirty laundry on the floor, and set up her ironing board, blocking the door to the garage.

She set the iron down and lifted her gaze. "I suppose you need me to clear a path through this mess."

"Stay put," Liam said. "I'm way ahead of you. I moved my car out front when you were taking your shower."

"Thanks. I wish I had more room to work with so I wouldn't have to spread out like this."

Liam smiled. "I'm just grateful you're doing my laundry. Mom's sleeping like a baby. Maybe you'll have a chance to get some stuff done. I'll get everything on the grocery list on my way home."

"Thanks. That'd be a big help," she said. "See you later, alligator."

"In a while, crocodile—"

"Not too soon, baboon."

Liam turned to go, Colleen chuckling at the silly good-bye they had used since they were kids. He hurried to the living room, where his mother sat. He put his index finger to his lips, then took her by the hand, gently pulled her to her feet, and slipped out the front door …

Liam had known that Colleen would be in the utility room ironing, and that the sound of the washer and dryer would make it easy for him to sneak their mother out of the house without his sister knowing it. The driveway was hidden from neighbors, on one side by high shrubs and the other by a privacy fence. The other side of the street had not been developed and was mostly woods. Liam was sure no one had seen him leave with her.

But if Colleen were able to convince the sheriff to investigate for foul play, the sheriff's deputies would likely interview neighbors and press Liam and Colleen in an effort to expose any guilt. He knew from watching TV that they always put the family under a microscope. He'd covered his tracks. There was no reason for anyone to suspect him.

Jesse set the baggies of fresh crappie fillets in the refrigerator and high-fived his brother. "We did it! We got our limit—fifteen keepers each."

"You're the man," Hawk said. "You found the spot."

Their mother smiled. "Tonight's out, but what night this week should we have a fish fry?"

"Let's do it Tuesday night," Hawk said. "I'll bring Laura Lynn, and Abby can bring Jay. It's a good excuse to get everyone together."

"Coleslaw and fries?" Kate said.

"Mmm … and baked beans." Jesse rubbed his stomach in a circular motion. "You make the best. Don't forget to invite Elliot." He winked at his mother, then went over to the stove, took the lid off a big pot, and inhaled the delicious aroma. "Beef stew. Yum."

His mother was suddenly distracted by something on the TV. She turned it up.

"The elderly woman's body was discovered by two fishermen in the shallow end of Rocky Creek just after ten o'clock this morning. According to the coroner, the cause of death was drowning. He estimated Berne had been dead between twenty and twenty-four hours. The victim's two adult children filed a missing person's report last night after Ms. Berne had wandered away from the residence earlier in the day and didn't return.

"Authorities believe Ms. Berne, who suffered from Alzheimer's, may have fallen into the Sure Foot River and drowned, the river's current moving her body downstream to where the river branches off into Rocky Creek. Foul play has not been ruled out. Anyone who may have seen this woman is asked to call the sheriff's department.

"Dixie Berne, eighty-five, is the third person to drown in the Sure Foot this year. In other news tonight—"

"Hey, I think that was her," Jesse said. "The lady I saw when I was fishing yesterday."

"Are you positive?" Kate said.

Jesse shrugged. "Sure looks like the lady I saw. Her white hair stood out in the sunlight. She was with a man. They were wading in the river."

Jesse put the lid back on the pot of stew and walked over to the table and sat. "Should I tell Sheriff Granger? Just in case it's her?"

"If you think that was the woman you saw," his mother said, "we definitely need to call Virgil."

CHAPTER 6

Sunday night, just after seven, the chiming of the doorbell filled the Cummingses' log house.

"I'll get it!" Jesse slammed his math book shut, ran out of his room, slid down the banister, and landed on his bare feet. He hurried to the front door and opened it.

"Hey, Jesse," Sheriff Granger said.

"Evening, Sheriff. You're dressed like a regular person. I'm not used to seeing you without your uniform."

The sheriff smiled. He had kind eyes. "I'm not *officially* working tonight. But while your memory is still fresh, I wanted to hear about the man and woman you saw wading in the river."

Jesse opened the door wider. "Come in. Mama made peanut-butter chocolate-chip cookies."

His mother came out of the kitchen and hugged the sheriff. "So good to see you, Virgil. How's Jill Beth?"

"She's great. Still doing volunteer work and treating me like a king."

"How are the triplets—I guess I should say, your three young men?"

"They're great too," the sheriff said. "Still running their software company together. Still inseparable. I wonder sometimes if we'll have a triple wedding one of these days. Wouldn't surprise me."

Kate laughed. "Wouldn't that be something? You want to sit here in the living room or out in the kitchen?"

"Whatever suits you is fine with me."

"I'd rather sit in the kitchen," Jesse said, a smile tugging at the corners of his mouth.

"Closer to the cookies?" His mother sounded amused.

"Well, yeah. They're best when they're still warm."

"All right, come on."

His mother led the way to the kitchen, and Sheriff Granger followed her, Jesse on his heels.

Jesse took a seat across from the sheriff, a plate of cookies already set in the middle of the table between them.

Kate laughed. "Don't look so surprised, Son. I know how your mind works. Everyone want milk?"

"Me!" Jesse's hand shot up.

Virgil chuckled. "I'm sure not going to pass. I haven't had peanut-butter chocolate-chip cookies since I had the measles."

Jesse studied the sheriff for a moment. "That's just an expression, right?"

"Yep."

Jesse heard a knock and then saw Grandpa Buck standing in the doorway. "I wouldn't mind nibblin' on a cookie and listenin' to what Jesse has to say."

"Same here." Hawk's head appeared over Grandpa's shoulder.

"No problem," the sheriff said. "Come in and get situated. Let me set this up."

Hawk and Grandpa sat on either side of Jesse. His mother set four glasses and a half gallon of milk on the table, then sat next to the sheriff.

Sheriff Granger took something out of his pocket and laid it on the table. It resembled a small cell phone. "I'd like to record this for accuracy. Is that okay?"

"It's all right with me," Kate said, filling the glasses with milk. "Jesse, you okay with that?"

Jesse nodded, grinning without meaning to.

"Okay, here we go." Sheriff Granger reached down and pressed a button. "This is Raleigh County Sheriff Virgil Granger. It's seven fifteen on Sunday night, September fifteenth. I'm at the home of Jesse Cummings, 100 Angel View Road. Present are: his mother, Kate Cummings; his brother, Hawk Cummings; and his grandfather, Buck Winters. I'm here to follow up on the drowning death of Dixie Berne, case number 20170914. Jesse, would you state your full name and age?"

"Jesse *Buckley* Cummings." He smiled at Grandpa Buck. "I'm twelve years old."

"Jesse, state your whereabouts on Saturday, September fourteenth."

"Fishing on the Sure Foot River, just south of the bridge toward Rocky Creek."

"Can you estimate how far south of the bridge?"

"I'd say a couple hundred yards."

"Were you fishing from the bank?" the sheriff said.

"No, sir. I found a round, flat rock that sticks out over the water. I was fishing there."

"What time did you arrive, Jesse?"

"Around nine o'clock in the morning. I stayed in the same spot until I left about four. I paid attention to the time because my mother makes spaghetti on Saturday night, and I didn't want to miss dinner."

"Okay, great," Sheriff Granger said. "Which side of the river were you fishing on?"

"The east side."

"Do you recall what was on the other bank?"

"Mostly trees. But over yonder, and down a ways, there was a clearing on the bank."

"Where was that from where you fished?"

"Straight across and to the left a few yards. You can't miss it," Jesse said. "It's the only clearing in that area."

"Did you see anyone else out there?"

Jesse nodded. "I saw a man and woman, wading in the river—right off that clearing on the bank."

"Can you guess how far away that was from where you were fishing?"

Jesse mused and looked at his brother. "I'd say fifty yards, give or take."

Hawk nodded in agreement.

"What time did the man and woman arrive?" the sheriff said.

"I'm not sure. I didn't see them get in the water. I just looked up and noticed them there."

"What time was that?"

"Almost exactly eleven. Sometimes I look at my watch and don't really pay attention to it. Kind of a habit. But that time I did."

"What can you tell me about them?"

Jesse took a bite of cookie and washed it down with a gulp of milk. "They were both white. They'd waded maybe ten yards from the bank, but I could still see their arms above water. I noticed the woman had white hair. I was catching fish like crazy and didn't pay that much attention to them."

"When you did pay attention," the sheriff said, "what did you notice? No detail is too small."

Jesse bit into a cookie and thought as he chewed. "The man put his arms around the lady and went down into the water up to his neck. And she went under the water—like he was teaching her to hold her breath. Kind of like parents do with a little kid."

"Did you notice if there was any splashing?"

"I didn't see any." Jesse stuffed the last bite of cookie into his mouth and washed it down with milk.

"Did you see the woman's head come back up?"

"I wasn't really watching. The crappie were biting as fast as I could get my bait back in the water. I remember glancing over yonder and seeing the lady floating on top of the water. It looked like the man was holding her up, like he was teaching her to float."

"Was her face up or down?"

"Up. I was concentrating on the fish and only glanced over there a few times. I did think it was weird for them to be wading that far from the bank. The undercurrent is dangerous. Didn't seem like a safe place to teach someone to swim."

"Okay, good. Now, this is important, Jesse. Do you remember what the woman was wearing?"

"I'm sure it wasn't a bathing suit. And I'm pretty sure it was pink."

"You're doing great. Tell me about the man."

"He turned toward me when I sneezed, but I couldn't see him very well because the sun was so glary. I did see him from behind when he walked out of the river and up on the bank, then disappeared in the trees. His shirt was short sleeved—maroon or brown, I think. Hard to be sure because it was wet. He might've had on jeans. He didn't look real tall or real short—just in between."

"So he was fully clothed?"

"Yes, sir."

"Could you tell how old he was?"

Jesse shook his head. "Not really."

"Was he heavy or slender?"

"Just average."

"Was there anything about his face that stood out—despite the glare?"

"Not that I could see."

"What color was his hair?"

"Dark brown, I think. It wasn't wet. I know that."

"Anything that stood out about how he walked?"

"I didn't really notice that." Jesse pushed his glass out of the way and folded his hands on the table. "I was looking for the lady but didn't see her anywhere. I thought maybe she got out first, and I just didn't see her."

"When the man walked out of the water," the sheriff said, "did he turn around? Or turn and look downstream?"

"He didn't turn at all. He just kept walking. Then the trees hid him. Do you think he drowned that woman?"

"That's what we're trying to figure out," the sheriff said. "It's certainly suspicious, since we found a white-haired woman's body downstream about a hundred and thirty yards, where the Sure Foot branches off into Rocky Creek. So the location fits. We'll have to get out there and search the area for clues. This is very helpful information, Jesse. Thanks."

Jesse smiled when Grandpa winked at him. "You're welcome."

"Is there anything else you can remember that stood out?" the sheriff said. "I don't care how unimportant it might seem."

"I heard a phone ringing while the man was walking away," Jesse said. "I couldn't see where it was. But the ringing was coming from that direction."

"Any idea what time that was?"

"Twelve minutes after eleven," he said proudly. "I remember that because *I'm* twelve."

"Excellent, Jesse. This is all such good information. Depending on what our investigation uncovers, later on we might need you to work with a sketch artist and see if we can get a better idea of the man's face. You might have seen more than you realize."

Jesse smiled. "Sure."

"But now I have to ask you—and everyone in your family—not to tell anyone outside the family that you saw anything. It may turn out that you witnessed a murder without realizing it. If so, you do not want that kind of information getting back to the person who did it."

"Goodness," Kate said. "I don't like the sound of that."

The sheriff shook his head. "Don't worry. We protect the identity of witnesses by not releasing their names to anyone. But we have to rely on witnesses and their families to help keep it anonymous by not telling anyone they know. Can you do that, Jesse? Can you keep this important secret?"

Jesse nodded. "Yes, sir. I won't tell anyone."

"Kate, you'll need to sit Abby down and explain what's going on."

"I will, but she won't be able to keep this from Jay any more than I could keep it from Elliot. As far as I'm concerned, they're family. I trust them."

"All right," Virgil said. "I don't recommend telling Riley anything; just make sure she doesn't overhear you. You all need to commit to keeping silent on this. If it does turn out to be a murder, the last thing we need is for the media to get wind of it. They won't print Jesse's name because he's a minor, but there's nothing to stop them from hounding the rest of you. As you know, word of mouth travels fast in this town, which means the guilty party could find out."

"You really think someone would try to intimidate Jesse?" Kate said.

"To keep from being arrested for capital murder?" The sheriff's eyes grew wide. "What do you think?"

"Should I be scared?" Suddenly Jesse had a bad feeling about this.

The sheriff shook his head. "No one besides a trusted few in my department—not even the victim's children—will know that you saw anything. And keep in mind, we aren't even sure that what you witnessed was a murder. We have some investigating yet to do. For now, just keep the information right here among yourselves, and you'll be fine."

"I'll make sure Abby knows," Kate said. "I agree that Riley doesn't need to know any of this. She's finally quit having nightmares."

The sheriff looked stern, but his voice was calm and gentle. "Jesse, I've known you since you were five years old, when your father and Riley disappeared. You know me. You know I tell it like it is. There's no need to be afraid. Just keep this within your family. We need to do some more investigating before we'll be able to say whether or not we believe you witnessed a murder. We might come to an entirely different conclusion."

"Okay," Jesse said. "I'm good at keeping secrets." *I think. I've never really had one this cool before.*

Jesse lay across his bed, flat on his back, his knees bent. He heard a knock at the open door.

"Can I come in?" Hawk said.

"Sure. What's up?"

Hawk came in and sat on the side of the bed. "Just checking to see how you're doing."

"Sheriff Granger said not to be scared, so I'm not. Well, maybe a little. But not much. They don't even know for sure that lady was murdered."

"And they might never know. I just don't want you to worry about it. No one in this family's going to bring it up to anyone."

"Maybe you and Riley should lend me your guardian angel," Jesse said.

Hawk smiled. "I'm sure you have one of your own. If you need to talk, come find me, okay?"

Jesse turned over on his side, his elbow firmly planted on the mattress, his head resting in his hand. "It really creeps me out that the guy might've been drowning the woman while I was busy catching fish. I really never thought anything was wrong."

"Why would you," Hawk said, "since the woman didn't cry out for help?"

"If I knew what he was doing, I would've screamed bloody murder. Maybe he would've run away before he drowned her."

"First of all, we don't know yet that a murder took place. If it did, it's not your fault that you didn't realize what was happening. But if it turns out to be a murder and the cops arrest someone, what you saw could be really important. You're probably the only person on the planet who can pinpoint the time of the murder, who was there, and saw how it probably went down. It's your chance to man up."

"Wow." Jesse sighed. "Seems like a lot of responsibility."

"This could just as easily be a slam dunk," Hawk said. "The guy could plead guilty, and it'd be over before it even got started."

"Think that happens very often?"

"Often enough. If he knows there's a witness, he might plead out and bypass the courts."

"Or he won't, and I'd have to testify?"

"Let's just wait and see. Maybe it was just an accident."

Jesse looked up at the ceiling fan. Just when he was finally involved in something important, he couldn't even tell his best friend.

CHAPTER 7

Jesse hiked up the front sidewalk of Foggy Ridge Middle School. Giant Arkansas oaks, showing just a hint of autumn gold, stood on either side of the ivy-clad stone building that had been there since Grandpa Buck was his age. He pulled open one of the red doors and walked into the spacious foyer, alive with Monday-morning buzz and ample light streaming in from the skylights. He spotted his best friend, Dawson Foster, and waved.

Dawson said something to the kid he'd been talking to, then hurried across the foyer and met Jesse halfway.

"Hey, man. What's up?" Dawson stood six inches taller than Jesse, his smile a bright contrast to his polished dark skin.

"You're famous," Jesse said. "I saw on the school's website that we beat the Hornets twenty-one to fourteen and you scored the winning touchdown in the last ten seconds."

Dawson bumped fists with Jesse. "The Foggy Ridge Falcons remain undefeated."

"I wanted to see the game," Jesse said, "but Hawk had to work Saturday and I couldn't get a ride over to Hoover Springs."

"No sweat," Dawson said. "The next two are home games. So what'd you do this weekend?"

Besides witnessing a possible murder? "Well, I found this awesome fishing hole on Saturday. I took Hawk with me yesterday after church and we both got our limit."

"Cool."

"Mama's having a fish fry tomorrow night. Want to come?"

"Aw, you're killin' me, man. I've got football practice. And I have to study for a major math quiz on Wednesday. If I don't get a C minus or better, I'll get benched."

"You can't get benched. The whole school will freak out."

The warning bell rang, signaling five minutes until classes started. Students began scrambling in all directions.

Jesse slapped Dawson on the back. "See you second period."

Jesse turned and walked briskly down the opposite hallway toward his homeroom class, pleased that Dawson wasn't ashamed to be seen with him since becoming a big football star. The two had been best friends since kindergarten, but the really popular kids wanted Dawson to be part of their group. Jesse didn't fit in with that crowd—not that he wanted to. Some of those kids were stuck up and picked on the students who weren't so popular. He could never be like that and couldn't imagine that Dawson could either. His friend was sensitive to other people's feelings, maybe because he didn't have a dad either. Or because he had such an awesome mom. Or because all those sermons at church had rubbed off.

Jesse hated that he couldn't tell Dawson about being a witness to a murder. That was almost as cool as scoring two touchdowns.

Jesse glanced at the black-and-white clock on the classroom wall. Where was his English teacher? The bell signaling the start of second period had rung four minutes ago.

Jesse heard footsteps, and a few seconds later, the principal, Mrs. Arnold, breezed through the doorway with a blonde lady who didn't look that much older than his sister Abby. The two stood in the front of the classroom, saying nothing until the murmuring stopped.

"Students," the principal said, "I have an unfortunate announcement to make. Miss Berne will be out on leave for a week or two. Her mother passed away over the weekend. Drowned. Maybe some of you heard about it on the news."

Heard about it? Jesse thought. *I was there!*

"Meanwhile," the principal added, "Miss Northup here will be filling in. Nothing else will change. You're still going on the field trip to Pea Ridge this morning. The buses have arrived, and you'll be boarding them shortly. First, let's observe a moment of silence for Miss Berne and her family for this terrible tragedy."

Jesse glanced over at Dawson and then stared at his desk, his heart nearly pounding out of his chest. The woman who drowned was his English teacher's mother! How weird was that? If it turned out to be a murder, it was going to be hard coming to class every day and never letting on that he had seen something.

Jesse felt awful for Miss Berne. He would never forget the crippling sadness that had plagued his family the five years his father was missing, and then after they'd discovered he'd been murdered.

"All right, class," Mrs. Arnold said. "I want you to introduce yourselves to Miss Northup and I'll announce over the intercom when we're ready to start boarding the buses."

Liam lifted his gaze as two uniformed male officers walked into the interview room at the sheriff's department, where he and Colleen were seated on one side of an oblong table. He recognized the tall, fiftysomething man as Raleigh County's sheriff, Virgil Granger.

"Sorry to keep you waiting." The sheriff introduced himself and Chief Deputy Kevin Mann, and then the two sat across from Liam and Colleen.

"I'm very sorry about your mother," the sheriff said. "I understand that you're insisting an autopsy be done."

"Our mother's drowning couldn't have been an accident," Colleen blurted. "She was incapable of getting to the river by herself. And her jewelry is missing—a diamond ring and a platinum cross necklace. Just because she had Alzheimer's doesn't mean she didn't matter ..." Colleen paused to compose herself. "I think the mystery surrounding her death justifies an autopsy."

Sheriff Granger folded his hands on the table. "Do both of you understand what's involved in performing an autopsy?"

"To be perfectly honest," Liam said, "the thought of subjecting our mother's body to an autopsy seems premature to me. If she was robbed and murdered, I certainly want justice. But could an autopsy even tell you who did it? I mean, without that, what's the point of violating her that way?"

"You never know what the coroner might find." The sheriff leaned forward on his elbows. "If we determine she was murdered, other evidence could come into play."

"Would you elaborate?" Colleen said.

The sheriff nodded. "I'm sure the coroner's office explained what happens when a person drowns. Our best guess, based on where your mother's body was recovered, is that she went into the Sure Foot within two hundred yards of where it branches off into Rocky Creek. I'm getting teams in place to comb the bank for clues, just as soon as it's light enough."

"What kinds of clues would you search for?" Liam asked, not liking the optimism in the sheriff's voice.

"Trash, aluminum cans, gum, Kleenex, anything that might have DNA. Also foot impressions, shoe impressions, tire impressions—anything that could help us determine where she entered the water and who was with her."

Liam took a sip of Coke, trying to remember how he'd disposed of his gum. "But is that enough to find a killer? Without an eyewitness, wouldn't all that be speculation?"

"By itself, yes. But put it all together, and it might tell a story. And if we found fingerprints that matched someone in the criminal system, it could be a huge break." The sheriff moved his gaze from Liam to Colleen. "I spent considerable time reviewing the case, and I tend to agree there's cause for suspicion."

"So you'll order an autopsy?" Colleen said.

The sheriff seemed lost in thought for a moment. "Miss Berne, the cause of death is not what's in question here. It's whether or not her drowning was an accident. It's unlikely an autopsy would tell us that. But a blood panel would tell us what drugs were in her system, and I definitely think that's in order. I'd like the coroner to reexamine your mother, with the idea that she may have been forced into or held under the water."

"But he already did that," Colleen insisted.

"True. But now that we know more about the victim, I want him to look with new eyes. Why don't we let him make the recommendation whether or not to proceed with a full autopsy? Does that sound reasonable to you?"

Colleen looked at Liam. "I'm okay with that. Are you?"

Liam nodded, confident there was no way they could link his mother's death to him. "I want to do the right thing. But if we can avoid subjecting Mom to an autopsy …" Liam put his fist to his mouth and pretended to choke back his emotion. "I just don't want to do it unless we absolutely have to."

Colleen reached over and took his hand. "Neither do I. I'm willing to go by the coroner's recommendation, especially since the sheriff's deputies are going to search the banks for something that could show where she entered the water. I just didn't want Mom's death to be handled like an open-and-shut case. If someone killed her, I want him found and locked up."

Liam nodded, avoiding eye contact with the sheriff.

"Okay. I'll talk to the coroner," Sheriff Granger said. "While I've got you both here, would you mind going over the events leading up to your mother's disappearance? It's in the report my deputies made, but I'd prefer to hear it from you."

"I noticed Mom missing about one thirty Saturday afternoon," Colleen said. "I was home alone with her and she was taking a nap. It's not unusual for her to sleep for long periods. I was out in the utility room, doing laundry and ironing. But I have a keen sense of hearing. I'm just shocked that I didn't hear her slip out the front door."

"I keep telling Colleen it's not her fault," Liam said. "Mom had gotten out several times before, and we never heard her any of those times."

"Mr. Berne, where did *you* go after you left the house on Saturday?" the sheriff asked.

"I left around ten to run errands. I went by Foggy Ridge Bank and got cash at the ATM. I washed and gassed the car. I stopped by Walmart to get supplies for deer hunting. Let's see ... I went by the shoe repair shop and picked up Colleen's heels. I ate lunch at Sammie's Subs and read a bass-fishing magazine. Went to Salisbury's Supermarket and got groceries. Then I came home."

"Do you remember what time you arrived home?"

"About three thirty, I think." Liam looked over at Colleen.

She nodded. "Yes, three thirty. I was frantic. I hoped Liam had taken Mom with him. I thought that maybe I had misunderstood what he told me just before he left to run errands. I couldn't reach him. I tried for almost two hours."

"My cell phone was dead as a doornail," Liam said. "I had forgotten to recharge it."

The sheriff's gaze was intense, and Liam tried not to squirm or react in any way.

Chief Deputy Mann cleared his throat. "Sounds like your mother was becoming quite a handful to care for at home."

Colleen sighed. "She really wasn't that much trouble, except for her wandering. We couldn't keep her safe anymore and were waiting for a bed to open up at the Alzheimer's center. We hired a woman from my church, Doris Olsen, to come sit with Mom during the day when we were working. But Liam and I shared the responsibility of caring for Mom after work and on the weekends. We were so close to getting her into a protective environment. This is just tragic."

"Devastating," Liam added.

"I understand how hard this must be for you," Mann said. "I just have a few questions. Mr. Berne, did you keep the receipts for all the purchases you made on Saturday?"

"I'm sure I did. I always save receipts."

"Good. We'll need to get copies of those receipts to keep on file," Mann said. "And we'll want to talk with Doris Olsen. She might be able to provide important details none of us thought to ask. By the way, did your mother have a will?"

Colleen nodded. "All her assets are in a living trust."

"I imagine the two of you will inherit everything?" Mann raised an eyebrow.

"Yes," Colleen said. "Mom named Liam and me as equal beneficiaries. She wasn't a wealthy woman, but her assets are worth about three hundred and fifty thousand dollars. Is that relevant?"

"Just information for the file. Would anyone else have access to her money? Or stand to inherit anything?"

"No," Colleen said emphatically. "I'm the oldest, and she gave me sole power of attorney over her bank account and all medical decisions, including her DNR."

Mann tented his fingers. "And have you had occasion to use your power of attorney?"

"I used it quite often when it came to her medical care. Mom also gave me power of attorney over a ten-thousand-dollar bank account to be used for her incidentals: shoes, clothing, co-pays on drugs and doctors, and other miscellaneous items. I've dipped into that account as needed. But I've always made sure Liam and Mom's estate lawyer knew about every cent I used and the balance in the account."

"My sister's done an incredible job," Liam said. "Always with Mom's best interest in mind. Why are you asking these questions?"

Mann leaned forward on his elbows. "Standard protocol. We need to eliminate any suspicion that the family was involved."

Colleen put her hand on her heart and sat back in her chair, her face flushed. "I assure you Liam and I loved our mother with every fiber of our being. There's no way either of us could ever hurt her. I'm appalled that you could even suggest such a thing."

"Please don't take offense to my questions," Mann said. "We have to cover all bases. So, Miss Berne, you were alone when you discovered your mother missing, 'round one thirty Saturday afternoon?"

"That's correct."

"Can anyone else confirm that?"

Colleen eyes filled with tears. "I guess not, other than I left several messages on Liam's phone. You can check the phone records."

"And what time did you call the sheriff's department?"

"I think it was around two fifteen." Colleen glanced over at Liam. "When I couldn't reach my brother, I wasn't comfortable just assuming Mom was with him, so I checked with the sheriff's department to see if anyone had found her. And then I went out looking for her myself. I hadn't been home long when Liam came back from running errands, and we went out together looking for her. When that failed, we called and made a formal missing person's report."

"Clearly, the two of you were devoted to your mother," Sheriff Granger said.

"She meant everything to us." Liam put his arm around Colleen.

"I'll speak with the coroner and have him reexamine your mother's body," Sheriff Granger said. "I'll let you know as soon as I know something. In the meantime, let's see if the search produces any clues." He stood and shook hands with Liam and Colleen. Mann did the same.

"I'd appreciate it if you would make copies of your receipts from Saturday," Mann said to Liam. "I'll have one of my deputies come by and get them—just to help document your whereabouts for the file."

"Not a problem." Liam downed the last of his Coke and rose to his feet.

As Sheriff Granger and Chief Deputy Mann left the room, Liam thought back on what he'd told them about running errands the day his mother died. He had deliberately left out details, such as after stopping at the ATM, he took his mother to the river and drowned her. And afterward, when he gassed and washed the car, he disposed of his wet clothes in the dumpster behind the service station. And then when he went to Walmart, he was there only fifteen minutes. He did pick up hunting supplies, but just so he would have a receipt that showed the date and time of purchase. The receipt showed the time he had left Walmart, not the time he had entered. But if the authorities did the math, they would know it took six minutes to get from the ATM to Walmart, and then an additional hour and three minutes until he checked out. The hour and three minutes that no one could dispute made a very believable alibi.

"What are you thinking about?" Colleen said.

The sound of her voice brought Liam back to the present. "Mom. I miss her so much. But I guess in some ways, I've missed her for a long time."

"I feel empty …" Colleen's voice cracked. "I wasn't ready to let her go. And certainly not this way."

Liam pulled his sister into his arms, and she sobbed quietly. Part of him wanted to sob with her. It hurt knowing he was responsible for her pain. He just wanted to move past the deception and get the authorities looking in another direction. Being under the sheriff's microscope was not unanticipated. But it was nerve racking. For now, he would have to cooperate with the authorities. It would all be over soon. Their mother would be buried with the dignity she deserved. And the inheritance money his mom and dad had hoped to pass on would give him his life back. He had done the right thing.

You don't really believe that.

Liam slammed the door on his conscience. He wasn't going to feel guilty about having done what was necessary. He had been gentle with his mother, and ended her life quickly. How could her going to heaven not be better than adding to the number of walking dead at the Alzheimer's center?

CHAPTER 8

Later Monday morning, Sheriff Virgil Granger sat at the conference table in his office with Chief Deputy Kevin Mann and Deputies Billy Gene Duncan and Jason Hobbs. He glanced out the tall, narrow window at the huge maples on the courthouse lawn, a few leaves showing a tinge of red and the promise of more to come.

On the sidewalk, people lined up in front of Miguel Perez's familiar blue-and-yellow rolling cart to buy breakfast tacos.

"Okay," Virgil said. "Kevin and I read the report you made on the Dixie Berne drowning. We called this meeting because some new information has come to my attention."

Virgil put his recorder on the table and pushed the button, replaying the interview he'd had the night before with Jesse Cummings regarding the man and elderly woman Jesse had seen in the river. When the recording finished, Virgil turned off the device and moved his gaze from man to man. "Gentlemen, it's possible that Jesse witnessed the drowning murder of Dixie Berne. The timing fits. The location fits. The activity he saw in the water suggests it."

"We're a long way from deciding it was murder," Kevin said, his arched eyebrows matching his wavy carrot-red hair. "But the Cummings kid's statement certainly raises more questions."

Jason folded his muscular arms on the table, his smooth dark skin looking almost bronze under the fluorescent lights. "I'm shocked that the Cummings family's in the middle of this. Those poor folks have been through the mill."

"Tell me about it." Virgil sighed. "After Kevin and I met with the victim's son and daughter this morning, I spoke with the coroner about doing some further investigating. We know Dixie Berne drowned. That's not in dispute. The only question is whether it was an accident or murder. I want the coroner to take a second look. A confused elderly woman wandering the streets would've made an easy target. Her missing jewelry and the fact that it was impossible for her to get to the river by herself certainly suggests the likelihood of foul play."

Jason and Billy Gene nodded.

"As you noted in your report," Virgil said, "the son and daughter are both single working folks, living at the same address with their mother, and seemed to be genuinely devoted to her. They shared the responsibility of caring for her. After her wandering became more frequent, they feared for her safety and put her on a waiting list for admission to the Alzheimer's hospital. They also shared with Kevin and me that their mother had a trust fund with ample financial means to ensure she got the care she needed. I think we can eliminate them as suspects."

"Except that, upon their mother's death, they stood to inherit a nice chunk o' change," Kevin added, "about a hundred and seventy-five grand each. Not exactly the lottery, but nothing to sneeze at—especially for a couple working stiffs."

Virgil pursed his lips. "True. But they came to us, insisting we consider an autopsy. If they were involved in her drowning, I'd think they'd want to avoid an autopsy, if for no other reason than to get this case closed as soon as possible."

"I agree. But there *is* one thing gnawing at me." Kevin laced his fingers together on the table. "It seemed just a little rehearsed that Liam could tell us each place he went on Saturday, from A to Z, without even stopping a second to think about it. I couldn't tell you every move I made *this morning*, without thinking about it."

"He just seemed prepared," Virgil said. "He had to know we would ask that question. The receipts he provided correspond to the stops he crossed off his to-do list. Nothing about his demeanor or speech made me suspicious."

"Me either." Kevin folded his arms across his chest and sat back in his chair. "It just struck me as a little too perfect, that's all."

"Billy Gene, you're awfully quiet," Virgil said. "Thoughts?"

Billy Gene stroked his dark mustache and seemed lost in thought, the lines in his forehead disappearing when he looked up. "I'm fixin' to take another gander at the case file. I'd like to listen to the kid's statement again. Did you tell the victim's son and daughter that we might have us a witness?"

Virgil shook his head. "No. And I'm not going to put Jesse Cummings's statement in the file either. If the coroner thinks Dixie Berne was murdered, then Jesse becomes a potential eyewitness, and for his safety, we'll need to protect his identity. I want this information to remain off the record—just between the four of us and the boy's family for now. Understood?"

"Yes, sir," both detectives said at the same time.

Virgil put the recorder back in his pocket. "I've already contacted Police Chief Mitchell. He's providing some officers to help us search the west bank of the Sure Foot for a couple hundred yards upstream from where it branches off into Rocky Creek. Kevin will oversee the search and divide everyone into teams."

"Which is another reason for this meeting," Kevin said. "I'm assigning just the two of you to search the area where Jesse saw our male person of interest get out of the water. Look for footprints, tire marks, discarded trash, bottles, cans—anything that could help us determine who was out there. You're the best we've got. I'm counting on you."

"If there's evidence out there, we'll find it," Jason said.

Billy Gene flashed a toothy grin. "Guaranteed."

"All right, then." Virgil laid his palms flat on the table and stood. "Let's get to work."

⚘

Kate stood at the kitchen stove, aware that the front door had opened and closed.

"Dad?"

She smiled when she felt a silent presence behind her. A second later, a pair of arms slid around her waist, a smooth cheek next to hers, the scent of Calvin Klein Obsession filling her senses.

"No fair," Kate said. "You wore that cologne to distract me."

Elliot tightened his embrace and whispered in her ear. "Is it working?"

"Almost—if I wasn't in the middle of frying apples to go with tonight's pork chops."

He kissed her cheek. "Then I'll extend an invitation for later."

"What invitation?"

"I thought we could walk down to the gazebo after dinner and smooch."

Kate laughed. "Do you realize how corny that sounds?"

"I wasn't planning to let anyone else in on it." Elliot's tone was playful.

"I always feel a bit like a teenager sneaking out to be alone with her boyfriend."

"We're fifty years old, Kate. We don't have to ask permission to steal a few moments for ourselves." Elliot turned her around and looked into her eyes. "Nothing wrong with two people in love kissing and holding each other. And it's not like we have much privacy *here*."

"I know." Kate met his waiting lips and let the tenderness of her response register her agreement. "Well, the answer's *yes* if you're okay with us not staying long. I'll need to get back and listen to Riley read a chapter. I'm amazed that her reading and comprehension are a grade level ahead. It never occurred to me that her voracious book reading would also teach her grammar. I'm surprised at how seldom I have to correct her now."

"I've noticed."

Kate stroked Elliot's cheek, then turned back around and continued stirring the simmering apples. "I've been distracted all morning, thinking about Virgil's investigation. I dread the idea that Jesse may have witnessed a murder. He's had enough exposure to death and heartache. It's time for him to just be a kid."

"Maybe it will turn out to be an open-and-shut case," Elliot said, "and Virgil won't even need Jesse's testimony."

Kate nodded. "That's what I'm hoping. He was smiling when he left for school and seems to be handling it well—even thinks it's cool to be a witness. Can't say that I share his perspective. It scares me."

"I know." Elliot's warm hands massaged her shoulders.

He was the only man besides Micah whose touch had ever made her skin tingle and her heart flutter. It was exhilarating being cherished again, the sole recipient of a good man's love and commitment—and his passion. So why did she seem to shut down anytime he wanted to talk about the future?

Elliot gave her shoulders a squeeze and then walked around the kitchen island where he could see her face. "One of the reasons I came by was to tell you I'll be in a board meeting all afternoon but will be here in plenty of time to help Riley set the table and go over her spelling words."

"Thanks. She has a test tomorrow."

"I honestly don't know how you do it, Kate. You've got two full-time jobs, and you're pretty incredible at both."

"That means a lot coming from you." She wasn't letting him lure her into another discussion about hiring someone to manage Angel View. "Hope your meeting goes well. I'll see you when I see you."

"Okay. Need me to pick up anything while I'm out?"

"No, I think we're set. But thanks."

"I look forward to our short-but-sweet gazebo date this evening."

Kate laughed without intending to. "Me too."

Kate sat on the living-room couch, nestled next to Riley. Riley munched on an oatmeal-raisin cookie while Kate reviewed the math papers her daughter had brought home from school.

"I got all my problems right," Riley said, "so Mrs. Lyons stamped 'Superb' on my chart again today. I've gotten all Superbs so far, except for one Good Effort because I got mixed up and missed two. I knew how. I just went too fast."

"You probably won't make that mistake again," Kate said. "But there's nothing wrong with Good Effort."

"Well, I want all Superbs." Riley looked up, her smile almost perfect, replacing the endearing jack-o'-lantern grin that had marked those first precious months after her return.

"Sweetie, I'm proud of how hard you've worked." Kate brushed cookie crumbs off the front of Riley's shirt. "You don't have to get Superb on every paper to make me happy."

"I know." Riley shrugged. "I just want to."

The front door opened and Jesse charged through it, dumped his backpack in the chair, then looked at Kate. "Can I talk to you about something—in private?"

"Sure," Kate said. "Riley, why don't you go find Halo and give her two of the hairball treats the vet gave us, and then brush her."

"Okay." Riley jumped to her feet. "Here, kitty, kitty! Halo …"

Riley hurried into the kitchen, and Jesse sat in a living-room chair, facing his mother.

"You'll never guess who the lady was who drowned," Jesse said. "Miss Berne's mother!"

Kate stared at her son and let her mind catch up with his words. "Goodness. When I heard the victim's name on the news, I never connected it to Colleen Berne. Was she in class today?"

Jesse shook his head. "No. The principal told us and introduced us to our sub, Miss Northup. Mama, it was so weird not telling anyone I saw the whole thing."

"If I remember correctly," Kate said, "you were busy catching fish and saw a man and a white-haired woman in the water."

Jesse grinned sheepishly. "Well, maybe I didn't exactly *see* the whole thing, but I'm the only witness."

Unfortunately. "I trust you kept your promise not to tell anyone?"

"I didn't say a word. But it's going to get really nuts when Miss Berne comes back to school and I have to pretend I don't know anything. Creeps me out to think that her mother might've been killed while I was having fun catching crappie. If I'd realized what was happening, I could've yelled at the guy. Maybe he would've left and Miss Berne's mother would still be alive."

Kate shook her head. "None of this is your fault, Jesse. But we can't know for sure whether her mother was murdered until Virgil gets the coroner's findings."

"It's still hard not telling my friends."

"You can't. Virgil made that clear. And why."

"I know. Don't worry, Mama. I didn't even tell Dawson."

"I appreciated that you didn't say anything in front of Riley either, since we agreed not to tell her."

"I won't slip." Jesse stared at Kate, a twinkle in his eye. "So … is Elliot coming for dinner?"

"What do you think?"

Jesse flashed a wide grin that reminded her she needed to make an appointment with the orthodontist. "Just checking. I'm starved. Are there any cookies left?"

"I made a fresh batch of oatmeal raisin."

Jesse popped up out of the chair. "I'll be in the kitchen."

"Don't spoil your appetite," Kate said out of habit, unable to recall a single instance when she had to prod her number-two son to eat.

She glanced up at the fireplace where she'd hung the family oil portrait that Abby's boyfriend, Jay Rogers, had painted after Riley was found and came home again. Micah was conspicuously missing. Even after seven years, it still seemed strange to see her family pictured without him. Her gaze moved from child to child and stopped on Jesse, who had shot up six inches since the portrait was done. It was hard to believe he was already twelve and growing into a responsible, caring human being, despite the obstacles he'd faced—or perhaps because of them. He had finally begun to smile and laugh again after being saddled with the family's grief and depression during those years after Micah and Riley disappeared. She did *not* want what was left of Jesse's childhood tainted by months or years of being the sole witness in a murder case. He did not need to be burdened with so dark a responsibility.

A chill crawled up Kate's spine. *If* Dixie Berne was murdered, the killer was still out there, and Jesse was the only person who saw him. She immediately dismissed the thought that had haunted her all day. Before she started to worry, she should at least wait to hear Virgil's findings.

CHAPTER 9

Liam waved as Colleen drove away from Praise Chapel, where they had arranged for his mother's memorial service to be held as soon as the coroner released her body. He opened the arched wood door and walked softly across the glossy marble foyer, then entered the sanctuary with its rows of polished oak pews—all empty. Like his heart.

He slipped into the back row and sat, studying the familiar stained-glass windows that adorned the old stone structure that had belonged to First Methodist Church when he was growing up. Most of his Sundays had started here. Though his dad had shown zero interest in spiritual things, his mom had insisted that Liam and Colleen go to Sunday school and church, and did so herself.

Sometime between his wedding day and his divorce, though, Liam had lost interest in church. Trapped in a bad marriage, he fell victim to depression and anger. God seemed irrelevant and the list of thou-shalt-nots impossible to live by. But he hadn't come here to defend his choices, past or present. There was just something immeasurably sad about the finality of his mother's death.

He refused to call what he had done murder, no matter how the law regarded it or how anyone else would judge it. He had released his mother from isolation and set her free. She was rejoicing with the angels instead of wandering the neighborhood, lost and confused, her memory locked away in some impenetrable mental fortress. And the money she intended to leave Liam and Colleen would go to them and not the Alzheimer's center. She would have wanted it that way.

Taking her life was a choice, harder than he'd imagined, and letting her go would be an agonizing process.

He studied the stained-glass window behind the pulpit, which depicted the resurrection of Jesus. *Where, O death, is now thy sting?*

He smiled despite his mood. His mother was okay.

Liam had never told her that he stopped going to the community church in Foggy Ridge a few years after he and Lynn Ann were married there. Vowing to spend his life with that woman had been a huge mistake. She turned out to be lazy, antisocial, and about as passionate as a barn door.

Trapped by his circumstances *and* his vows, his life had become at the same time cluttered and empty. He stopped going to church. Stopped socializing. Stopped caring. He filled up his evenings and weekends surfing the sports channels and fantasizing about what it would be like to have a different woman in his bed. He hadn't been much of a father either. Months and years passed and he and Lynn Ann basically lived separate lives. Though for his son's sake, he had waited to file for divorce until after Corey was settled at college. The judge ordered Liam to pay alimony, even though Lynn Ann had never made an effort to contribute one dime of income and spent a large part of her "workday" on the phone, social-media sites, or watching soap operas. The little they each got after the sale of the house and its contents went to pay for Corey's college.

Liam was glad to be rid of Lynn Ann, though he hadn't anticipated that divorcing her would strain his relationship with Corey. Or leave him broke enough to have to go live with Colleen.

He looked up at the stained-glass window behind the pulpit. The risen Jesus seemed to look right into his heart. He couldn't deny that his need for the inheritance money had influenced his decision to end his mother's life. But wasn't his love and concern for her genuine? And hadn't he put an end to her suffering as painlessly and quickly as he could? Surely Almighty God could see that.

Liam shuddered. He should have known better than to come in here, thinking that he wouldn't end up feeling guilty.

A hand on his shoulder caused him to jump.

"Son, are you all right?"

Liam looked up into the kind dark eyes of Pastor Austin Windsor. "I–I just need a moment."

"Did you hear back from the coroner already?"

"No. That's not it." Liam cracked his knuckles. "I have good memories of my mom here. Colleen told you we grew up in this church. I went here until my ex-wife and I were married, but that was a long time ago. A lot of water's gone under the bridge since then."

"And yet, you're here now." Pastor Windsor sat beside Liam and seemed to study the stained glass. "Is there anything I can do for you … I mean, besides doing the memorial service for your mother?"

Liam shook his head. "I just need a place to gather my thoughts of her."

"Your mother's at peace now."

"Well, if anyone deserves it, she does." Liam shifted his weight.

"Try not to imagine how she died, son. Picture her in heaven—whole and happy."

"I don't let myself dwell on the *how*," Liam said. "Colleen's the one who's obsessed with it. I'm just glad Mom's free."

The pastor sat erect in the pew, his arms folded across his chest. "I don't pretend to know how it feels to lose your mother this way. But if the coroner determines foul play was involved, as Colleen believes, I do hope forgiveness for the killer will be your goal, even if it takes time. Bitterness will eat you up, and it won't change anything."

"I get it," Liam said. "I'm not going to let that happen."

"Good." The pastor stood and put his hand on Liam's shoulder. "It'll truly be an honor to do the memorial service for Dixie. She was a lovely woman and a wonderful Christian example until the Alzheimer's got so bad. We can rejoice that she's with the Lord. If you ever want to talk, Liam, remember my door is always open."

"I appreciate that."

Pastor Windsor turned and walked up the side aisle and disappeared through a doorway.

Liam rubbed the back of his neck. He had a whopper of a secret to protect and shouldn't open up with anyone right now. With his mind so cluttered, he might say the wrong thing. Or get his story mixed up. The worst was over. He just needed to let things play out.

Sheriff Virgil Granger took off his Stetson and hung it on the wood coatrack in his office, then stood at the tall, narrow window and looked out at the grounds in front of the Raleigh County Courthouse. The red maples still had green leaves, but it wouldn't be long before autumn's spectacular fashion show beckoned countless fall tourists to the region. The traffic jams would be a small price to pay for the boost to the local economy.

The light turned green at Main Street and Commerce, and a young woman in hot-pink running shoes jogged across the intersection pushing a baby carriage. Old Melvin Mayfield lay sleeping on one of the wrought-iron benches, his knees bent, the bill of his blue fishing cap down over his eyes.

Virgil glanced at his watch. It was after three. He had expected Billy Gene and Jason to be back by now.

A knock at the open door caused him to turn.

Kevin walked in and handed him a manila envelope. "The coroner just sent this over."

Virgil hurriedly opened the envelope and pulled out the cover letter and scanned it from the top down. He stopped on one particular paragraph and read it aloud. "A number of antemortem bruises were noted on the victim's arms, wrists, hands, and ankles, consistent in individuals taking blood thinners. No injuries or defensive wounds were found. Significant bruising was discovered on the victim's back, but was clearly the result of hypostasis from the body being stored in a supine position."

Virgil moved his eye to the bottom of the letter. "After careful reanalysis, I stand by my original conclusion that the cause of death for Dixie Berne was drowning. Water in her lungs proves she was alive when she entered the water, but I found nothing to suggest she was forced, nor any physical signs that she had been assaulted, poisoned, or drugged. The toxicology findings will be needed to confirm this. However, proceeding with a full autopsy would not alter my finding that Dixie Berne drowned nor would it produce any physical evidence that a crime had occurred. Therefore, it is my professional opinion that a full autopsy is unwarranted."

Virgil exhaled and looked up at Kevin. "Well, there we have it. We can forget the autopsy."

"You're not satisfied?" Kevin arched his red eyebrows.

"Are you?"

Kevin smiled. "You know me, Sheriff. I don't let things go that easily. Just because the victim didn't have injuries or defensive wounds and wasn't drugged isn't conclusive proof that her drowning was an accident. The kid's statement holds a lot of weight and shouldn't be thrown out because the coroner can't find anything incriminating. But unless we find something that *is*, we may be spinning our wheels."

"Agreed," Virgil said. "I'm eager to hear what Billy Gene and Jason discovered on the riverbank where Jesse said he saw our person of interest get out of the water."

"Well, let's hope they found something. The victim's jewelry hasn't shown up at any of the pawnshops."

Virgil hung up the phone after talking with Jill Beth. He could almost smell the aroma of pot roast as he stood, prepared to call it a day. He heard a knock at the door and hoped it wasn't a problem.

"Come in."

The door opened and Billy Gene and Jason entered, their faces flushed, their hair damp with sweat.

"You finished your investigation?" Virgil sat, motioning for them to do the same.

"We swept the area." Billy Gene took a handkerchief and wiped the sweat off his forehead. "Bagged the usual stuff: bottles, bottle caps, aluminum cans, junk-food wrappers. Kleenex. Also chewing gum and cigarette butts. An empty snuff can. An old whisk broom. And some other stuff we couldn't make heads nor tails of."

"Any distinguishing footprints or tire tracks?" Virgil said.

Billy Gene and Jason both shook their heads.

"The dirt was dry packed on the riverbank," Billy Gene said. "Didn't find anything worth making a cast of."

"We did see where a vehicle'd been parked recently," Jason added, "in the tall weeds under a shade tree. No tire tread marks but some fresh oil and we got a sample."

Billy Gene nodded. "Also saw the flat rock that juts out over the water, where the Cummings kid said he'd been fishing. It was right where he told you, Sheriff, about fifty yards across the river. Bottom line: we didn't find anything out of the ordinary, at least not that we could tell right off. We'll have to wait for the lab to tell us whether any of it's got DNA."

"What about the victim's daytime caregiver?" Jason said. "Was Deputy Mann able to catch up with her this afternoon?"

Virgil nodded. "He's putting his report in the computer now. Said Doris Olsen was very cooperative, but she didn't offer us anything new. However, she did confirm our feeling that Liam and

Colleen Berne were extremely devoted to their mother, and also concurred that Dixie Berne didn't have the stamina or the presence of mind to walk to the river by herself.

"We all agree that since her jewelry was missing, the idea that she was robbed makes sense, even though the coroner didn't find a mark on her to substantiate that theory. And then this afternoon, we got back the coroner's final report after examining the body a second time. He stands by his initial findings and thinks an autopsy's unwarranted."

"Well, shoot," Billy Gene said. "If an autopsy wouldn't be worth a plug nickel, where do we go from here?"

Virgil placed his hat on his head. "Well, *I'm* going home and having dinner with Jill Beth. I suggest you two go home and get some rest. I'm not sure yet how to proceed. But I'm not convinced that this was an accidental drowning."

CHAPTER 10

Kate stood on the gazebo on the back grounds at Angel View Lodge, arm in arm with Elliot, the western sky ablaze with streaks of lava orange, hot pink, and golden purple. A great egret, its white wings catching a glint of the sunset's rays, moved effortlessly across nature's stage with the grace of a ballerina. Kate was vaguely aware that Elliot had said something and resisted for a moment leaving this state of total contentment.

"I'm sorry," she said. "I was lost in the sunset. What did you say?"

Elliot squeezed her hand. "Just that dinner was terrific, as always. Which reminds me, we need to get busy working on that pasta cookbook."

Kate counted the last Angel View rental boat pulling up to the pier. "I don't want to rain on everyone's parade, but I'm not eager to take on another job that *has* to be done. I need time to work up to it."

"Maybe not, if we use the sauce you just finished canning. Pick out the recipes you want in the cookbook. Buck and I and the kids will do the rest."

"I suppose I can do that much. Abby convinced me to write down all my pasta recipes last year, and we've tested them all. I'm just not sure I can handle anything else on my plate right now."

Elliot was quiet for a moment. "I'm sorry, Kate. You make it look so easy that I forget how much pressure there is running this place and being a single mom. Especially one as involved with her kids as you are."

"I don't know how to be anything but involved," Kate said. "Sometimes to a fault."

"A fault?"

Kate nodded. "Like this witness situation with Jesse. I'm probably overreacting to be so uptight, especially since the coroner didn't find anything to support that his teacher's mother was murdered. But when Virgil called this evening, I could tell by his tone of voice that he's not satisfied her drowning was an accident. I don't want Jesse caught up in a murder case. He's been through enough."

"Your feelings are perfectly understandable. I had never experienced that protective instinct until I fell in love with your kids. I'd do about anything to keep them out of harm's way."

"I'm sure they sense that. Abby and Hawk think you're the greatest. And Riley and Jesse think you hung the moon."

Elliot laughed. "You didn't tell them differently, did you?"

Kate turned and looked up at him. "Not a chance. Where do you think they got the idea?"

Elliot stroked her hair, then slowly, ever-so-gently kissed her mouth, his deep, longing passion sending a tingle through every fiber of Kate's being. She trusted the self-control he had shown during all those years Micah was missing. But the intensity was building in her, too, making it increasingly difficult to sidestep the question of where they wanted to take their relationship.

"I love you," he whispered.

"I love you too." Kate clasped her hands behind his neck and looked into his eyes. "Sometimes it scares me how much. I never thought I could love any man after Micah."

"I thought the same thing after Pam died. She'd been my first and only love. Some part of me died with her."

"Exactly. And yet ..." Kate laid her hand over Elliot's heart. "We both seem to have found the courage to love again. And I do mean courage."

"I doubt anyone who's experienced a deep loss jumps back into a relationship without some soul searching." Elliot brushed the hair out of her eyes. "For me, it happened slowly, over time. I didn't set out to love you. It just evolved. But now that I do, I can't imagine my life without you. And I believe you're as much a part of God's plan for me as Pam was."

"I wish I had your perspective," Kate said. "I still have trust issues with God. Oh, I love Him and want to serve Him. But He allowed some agonizing suffering in my life, and I struggle with fear that He might do it again."

Elliot pulled her into his arms. "Sweetheart, everything He allows He will give you ample grace to endure. How sad it would be if we didn't let ourselves love again out of fear of loss. Why mess up the joy of today by speculating about what might happen tomorrow? Most of what we worry about never happens."

Elliot was right. Kate knew that in her head and had even given similar counsel to Abby and Hawk. Maybe it was time to take her own advice.

She looked out at the last of the simmering glow on the horizon. "We told the kids we were coming here to watch the sunset. We probably should head back before they start to wonder what's taking us so long."

"They know exactly what's taking us so long." Elliot smiled and tilted her chin. "They think it's sweet. So are we going to smooch some more, or not?"

Kate giggled and yielded herself playfully and tenderly to this man to whom she had entrusted her heart, but not her future—a strange dichotomy she was more comfortable accepting than trying to understand.

❧

Virgil sat in the glider on his front porch, his navy uniform shirt unbuttoned, a cricket choir filling the darkness with the familiar chorus that used to put him to sleep as a kid. The night breeze carried the happy sounds of neighbor kids playing hide-and-seek and the intoxicating scent of gardenias that hung in baskets along the eaves. Garfield rubbed against Virgil's ankles, meowing at the top of his lungs.

Virgil took a sip of lemonade. "I don't know why you pester *me*. I told you I'm a dog person."

The fat orange tabby jumped up on the glider and nestled next to him and began to purr.

Virgil smiled. This stray tomcat was growing on him, probably because Jill Beth was so fond of it. The cat's purring was calming and made the day's pressures seem irrelevant in the momentary peace that settled over him. He closed his eyes and rested them in the quiet, thinking if he could bottle the feeling, he would be a rich man.

He heard the door open, and Jill Beth came outside and sat on the swing, Garfield content to stay put.

Jill Beth laughed. "Something's come between me and my man."

"You've created a monster," Virgil said. "Sir Feline here seems to think the world revolves around him."

Jill Beth picked up Garfield and set him on her right, then moved over next to Virgil and slipped her arm in his. "Better?"

"Much."

"I wanted to finish our dinner conversation," she said. "So have you actually closed the drowning case?"

Virgil shook his head. "It's premature. It's possible that something our investigative team put into evidence will yield useful information."

"But you said the coroner didn't find anything to suggest she was murdered."

"That's just one piece of the puzzle, darlin'. There's more to consider."

"Anything you can tell me about?"

"Not yet," Virgil said. "But I'm not convinced the drowning was an accident. I owe it to her kids to find out."

"You will. You always do." Jill Beth squeezed his hand. "I forgot to tell you, I ran into Elliot Stafford at the gas station this afternoon. He'd been to a board meeting at the lumber company and was going to Kate's for dinner. You should have seen the glow on his face. That man is smitten."

"I think you're right. I noticed it when I was at Kate's last night—" Virgil winced. So much for keeping Jesse's statement to himself.

"You were at Kate's? Why didn't you tell me?"

"I hadn't intended to say anything just yet. Only a handful of my deputies know."

"Know what?"

Virgil turned and slipped his arm around Jill Beth. "Jesse may have witnessed Dixie Berne's drowning. He saw a woman fitting her description wading in the river with a man. I'm not making this public knowledge."

"I've been keeping your secrets for almost three decades, lawman. I won't say anything."

Virgil knew she wouldn't. He told her every detail Jesse had given in his statement.

"As it turns out," Virgil said, "the time Jesse saw the man and woman in the water fits her time of death. And the location is about a hundred and thirty yards upstream from where Dixie Berne's body was recovered with all her jewelry missing. That, plus the fact that Jesse remembers seeing the man get out of the water but not the woman, supports the feasibility of her having drowned in the Sure Foot."

Jill Beth's eyes widened. "And no one else saw anything?"

"No one else has come forward. As far as we know, Jesse is the only witness to whatever occurred out there. I'm trying to keep it close to the vest. If Dixie Berne was murdered, I don't want the killer knowing we have an eyewitness, especially one as young and vulnerable as Jesse."

"How does Jesse feel about that?"

Virgil raised his eyebrows. "At the moment, he thinks it's cool to be the sole witness. Kate doesn't share that sentiment."

"I don't blame her. If you catch the guy and it goes to trial, poor Jesse would be right in the middle of it. And if you don't catch the killer, the Cummingses will have to deal with the knowledge that he's still out there."

"It's unfortunate that Jesse's involved in this," Virgil said. "But I can't ignore what he saw. I think I'll get our sketch artist to work with him. Even though he thinks he didn't get a good look at the guy's face, he might have seen more than he realizes."

Liam pushed away his dinner plate and watched Colleen pick at her broccoli with a fork.

"Your dinner's cold," he said. "You want me to warm it in the microwave?"

Colleen looked up at him blankly, as if his words hadn't quite registered yet. "Uh … no, thanks. It's sweet of you to offer, but I'm really not hungry."

"You need to eat anyway. It's going to be hard to stay strong if you don't."

"I need something that doesn't feel like a brick in my stomach. Maybe I'll have a yogurt later."

Liam nodded. "I'm glad we got Mom's arrangements made. The pastor at your church is warm. I'm glad he's doing Mom's memorial service."

"Pastor Windsor is a kind man. And he knew Mom personally, which means a lot to me."

"That's what matters. I doubt there will be more than a handful of people there."

"It might surprise you how many people from my church will come to support us. They won't be strangers. A lot of them knew Mom before the Alzheimer's."

"I doubt either of us will be thinking about other people. I just want to get it over with."

Colleen's red-rimmed eyes looked tired. "So do I. But I also want Mom to be remembered for the beautiful person she was most of her life. And I want to be with my church family to celebrate her going home to Jesus. That's important to me."

"Then it's important to me."

Colleen seemed to study him. "Did you ever hear back from Corey?"

Liam took a sip of water. "Just a text message saying he's sick about his grandmother's death. But that he just started a new job and can't get away right now, which is his way of saying he doesn't want to see me. He'll never forgive me for divorcing his mother."

"You didn't really expect him to come for the memorial service," Colleen said, "when you haven't seen him in three years?"

"I guess not. But a part of me was hoping this might be the time to break the ice."

Colleen reached over and put her hand on his. "I think laying Mom to rest is all the pressure either of us can handle right now. But you can bet I'm not done seeking justice for her death."

Liam looked into Colleen's sad eyes. "Sis, if the sheriff can't prove it was murder, what other recourse is there? Mom's gone. She's in heaven—whole again. Doesn't it make sense to let it go and move on?"

"I'm not sure I can do that."

"I understand. I really do." Liam tenderly squeezed her hand. "But I'm not sure we have another choice."

Colleen shot him one of her I-beg-to-differ looks. "Speak for yourself. I certainly do. I can use my half of the inheritance money to hire a private investigator. If it takes every cent, I'm going to find out what happened to Mom."

"You think a PI could find out what the sheriff can't? Or that Mom and Dad would want you to spend your inheritance that way? It's their gift to us."

"I could never enjoy spending that money," Colleen said, "knowing how we got it."

Liam bit his lip, careful not to react. It was just the grief talking. A month from now, she would change her mind.

CHAPTER 11

Two weeks later, Jesse missed the Monday-morning bus and hitched a ride to school with Elliot, who came to his rescue so Kate wouldn't miss her dental appointment. They were almost to school and Jesse had hardly said a word.

"What's wrong, sport?" Elliot glanced over at him. "You're awfully quiet."

Jesse stared at his hands. "Miss Berne is coming back today. I'm worried about what I should say to her."

"Well, when your mom and I saw her at the funeral home, I just told her I was very sorry about her mother. That's all you need to say."

"What if she can tell I know something?"

"She can't. How could she?" Elliot turned in behind a line of cars in the circle drive in front of the middle school. He reached over and put his hand on Jesse's knee. "The sheriff said he's not telling the victim's family that he has a potential witness unless he makes an arrest and it goes to trial. Your teacher doesn't know anything about you or what you saw. Just be yourself."

"Kind of hard to do when I might've seen her mother get murdered."

"Or not." Elliot inched the car forward. "There's no proof that's what happened."

"You don't think it's weird that the coroner said her mother's time of death fit the time when I saw a white-haired lady wading in the river with a man—and both of them were dressed in regular clothes?"

"Of course I think it's weird." Elliot pulled the car forward and stopped. "But the point is, unless the sheriff can find the man and question him, we will never know for sure. That's why he's talked to you several times and pressed you so hard to remember every detail you could."

"I remember lots of details. But I only saw the man's face for a couple seconds. I'm not sure that what I gave the sketch artist helped very much. But I'm ninety-nine percent sure the woman I saw was Dixie Berne."

Someone waiting behind them tooted the horn, and Elliot pulled forward.

"I guess I'd better get going," Jesse said.

"Just relax and have a good day. Tell Dawson I said he made an awesome catch on that last pass."

"I will. He's everyone's hero. Thanks for the ride. I'll make sure I don't miss the bus home."

"See you at dinner," Elliot said.

Elliot drove off, and Jesse walked up the front sidewalk of the ivy-clad stone building. He pulled open one of the red doors and walked into the spacious foyer, bright with golden sunlight and buzzing with the usual Monday-morning chatter.

He spotted Dawson standing near one of the tall windows, his polished dark skin enhancing his bright smile. He was surrounded by a group of cheerleaders and a few teammates. They were all laughing and seemed to be having a great time. Dawson didn't see him. Or pretended not to. Jesse decided not to interrupt him and headed down the hall to his homeroom class.

It was almost impossible to get Dawson's attention anymore. Between his new clique of friends, homework, football practice, and games, he didn't have time for much else, not even his best friend. Jesse suddenly felt really sad, but he pushed away the feeling. He wasn't a crybaby. If Dawson wanted to hang out with him, he'd find the time. Too bad he was so busy. He was missing some great fishing.

Jesse didn't get much studying done in homeroom. He couldn't stop thinking about what it would be like to walk into his second-period English class and pretend he didn't know anything about how his teacher's mother had died.

Finally, the bell rang, and he grabbed his backpack and headed down the hall, blending into the fast-moving stream of students.

"Jesse, wait up!"

In the next instant, Dawson walked beside him, keeping perfect pace. "Hey, man. I didn't see you before school and thought maybe you were sick today."

"I was running late and barely got in the front door when the bell rang," Jesse said, the lie pricking his conscience.

"Sorry I didn't text you over the weekend," Dawson said. "I played in the game on Saturday and went out with the team for burgers afterward. Then Mom took my phone away till I finished my homework—which took most of what was left of Sunday after church."

"No sweat," Jesse said. "I spent most of the weekend fishing. I wish you could see the crappie hole I found. Hawk and I can't pull them in fast enough. Even Riley's been catching one after another. It's been that way for a couple weeks. It's awesome."

Dawson winced. "Man, you're killin' me. I miss fishin' with you. I just wish I had more time. School's hard this year. And if I want to play football, I've gotta get the grades."

Jesse slowed to a stop and glanced up at the door to their English class. "Miss Berne is supposed to be back today."

"I'm glad. Aren't you?" Dawson waved at one of his football buddies, as the jock strutted into the classroom from across the hall. "I like her a lot better than the sub."

"Me too." Jesse followed Dawson into the classroom and saw Miss Berne writing something on the blackboard. Grateful not to have to face her, he turned down the second aisle and took his seat next to Dawson.

Other students poured into the classroom. Several walked up to Miss Berne's desk and left what appeared to be cards. One girl brought a small vase of zinnias. Jesse wondered why he hadn't thought to at least bring a sympathy card.

A minute passed and the bell rang, signaling the beginning of second period. The chatter and whispers died down quickly as Miss Berne turned around.

She wore a pretty blue dress and the same cool glasses, but she looked pale. Skinnier and older. Jesse didn't remember her having so many wrinkles on her forehead. Her lips were pressed tightly together and her hands clasped in front of her as she seemed to survey the cards and flowers.

Finally, she looked up and smiled. "Thank you, students, for this thoughtful display of sympathy and caring. I'm glad to be back with you. Miss Northup has kept me up on your progress. I'm proud of the work y'all did in my absence. It's been a difficult couple weeks, but I'm ready for us to pick up where we left off and get back to creative writing."

The students reacted with rumblings and sighs.

"Lest you think it's drudgery," Miss Berne said, "I want you to try a fun exercise. Each of you will need to get with your writing partner. The assignment is for the two of you to brainstorm and come up with a story. One of you is going to write the first half. The other, the second half. Y'all decide who goes first. All I want you to do today is figure out the story line. You'll have forty minutes to brainstorm. We'll start on the writing tomorrow. Because it's such a beautiful day outside, I'm going to let you sit in the courtyard and work on this assignment. So grab some paper and something to write with and let's quietly file through the cafeteria and out to the courtyard."

Jesse glanced over at Dawson, then joined a single file of students, crossing the hall to the cafeteria, his mind racing with an idea for a story. It could work. Unless Dawson could think of something better.

Jesse stepped out of the cafeteria and into the courtyard that made up the school's inner campus. He flopped down in the grass, and Dawson dropped down beside him.

"I hope you have some ideas," Dawson said. "I stink at writing. I have trouble writin' a thank-you note."

"Actually, I do." Jesse grinned. "Ready?"

Dawson nodded. "Go."

"Okay … one summer day, a kid about our age is fishing on the river and sees a murder."

"Cool!" Dawson said. "What kinda murder?"

"He sees a man and woman fishing off a dock but doesn't pay much attention because he's into a school of crappie. Later he notices the man by himself, throwing something into the water that makes a big splash. He can't tell what it is and doesn't think about it again until he hears on the news that a woman's body has washed up in the river—and realizes he might have witnessed her murder. His mom calls the sheriff, and he gives his statement. Come to find out, he's the only witness. He's not allowed to tell anyone about it—not even his best friend—because the killer is still out there and might want to silence the witness."

"*Way* cool," Dawson said.

"Even better, the kid finds out later that the dead woman was kin to his math teacher—and he has to see the teacher and all his friends every day and pretend he doesn't know anything. Pretty cool idea, huh?"

Dawson's eyebrows scrunched, and he seemed to study Jesse. "This is awesome, man. The kid would be dyin' to tell someone. But he couldn't. I like it. So how's it end? Does he finally spill the beans?"

"Uh, I don't know. I mean, I haven't gotten that far."

"Well, I say he does. Nobody could keep somethin' that big from his best friend. Besides, his friend'd be able to tell somethin' was wrong."

"Not necessarily." Jesse cracked his knuckles. "Maybe his friend was busy with school and sports and they hadn't hung out together for a while."

Dawson locked gazes with him. Jesse could feel his cheeks flush and looked away. This was a dumb idea.

"What's wrong?" Dawson said.

"Nothing."

Dawson gave Jesse's shoulder a slight shove. "Come on, man. Don't mess with me. We've been friends since we learned to talk. What aren't you tellin' me?"

"The ending of the story," Jesse said. "Come on. Help me think of a neat ending and maybe we'll get an A."

Dawson chewed his lip and looked intently at Jesse. "Why is your face red?"

"The sun's hot." Jesse smiled. "If you weren't black, your face'd be red too."

Dawson laughed. "So how'd you think this up?"

"I have a good imagination, remember? I've thought a lot about Miss Berne's mother drowning. It could've been murder. Nobody really knows. Now that I think about it," Jesse quickly added, "it'd be better if the kid in the story saw a murder somewhere besides the river so Miss Berne won't be reminded of her mother."

"How 'bout Beaver Lake?" Dawson said. "The story's great. I don't think anyone's gonna top it." Dawson seemed caught in a long pause, his gaze fixed on Jesse. Finally, he said, "You know somethin' you're not tellin'?"

"Ha! Now *you're* the one with a good imagination." Jesse was careful to show no reaction, but he felt hot all over.

Dawson continued to stare at him. "Did you see somethin', Jess? Is this about *you*?"

"I never said that." Jesse started to sweat. Why did he have to open his big mouth?

"But you'd never keep somethin' like that from *me*, right?"

Jesse's heart nearly beat out of his chest. He wanted to run somewhere—anywhere—to keep from breaking his promise to the sheriff. But he'd never lied to Dawson before—not even once.

Thirty minutes later, Miss Berne signaled the students to return to the classroom. Jesse trailed behind Dawson, then sat at the desk across from him.

Miss Berne waited for all the students to be seated. "I hope you found this exercise to be fun. Tomorrow, you're going to write your stories. I'll give you ten minutes first to review how you want to do it, and then you won't be able to discuss it with your partner again. One of you will write the first half. The other, the second half. On Wednesday, we'll read them aloud. I'm eager to hear what you've come up with. Any questions?"

One girl raised her hand and asked a question, but Jesse wasn't listening. What had he gotten himself into?

The bell rang and brought his focus back to the present. He grabbed his backpack and walked out into the hall and headed for his next class, Dawson keeping pace with him.

"Remember," Jesse said, "you can't tell anyone what I told you."

"You can trust these lips, dude. I don't know how you can keep this a secret, though. You're a celebrity. I'll bet you're the only kid in this school who's ever seen a murder and can identify the killer."

Jesse wiped the sweat off his forehead. It was bad enough that he'd gone back on his word, but why had he exaggerated the story? "Dawz, it *has* to stay our secret."

Dawson flashed a bright smile. "What a shame. People write books about stuff like this and make a ton of money. It's so cool."

"I know," Jesse said, grinning without meaning to. "But I'm not telling anyone else."

After dinner that evening, Jesse lay across his bed, trying to focus on how he intended to write the first half of his story in class tomorrow. He and Dawson had reworked the story so that the boy witnessed a body being dumped overboard on Beaver Lake. Jesse regretted telling Dawson his secret and felt even worse that he'd stretched the truth.

A knock at the door caused him to jump. "Come in."

His mother entered the room and closed the door, then walked over to Jesse and sat beside him on the bed. "What're you up to?"

"Just homework."

"You were awfully quiet at dinner. Is everything all right?"

"Just because I'm in a quiet mood doesn't mean something's wrong."

"I know." Kate smiled with her eyes. "But I'm used to you talking our ears off at dinner. I kind of like it."

Jesse laughed, despite his mood. "You should be glad I gave everyone a break. I know I talk too much."

"I'd say just about right."

"Well, Abby made up for it," Jesse said, "the way she gets all ooey-gooey when she talks about Jay. She's liable to get married before you and Elliot."

"The way I see it, there's no cause to rush either of us." His mother's eyes narrowed. "If there *was* something wrong, you know you could come to me, right?"

"Sure I do." *Just not this time.*

Kate paused for several seconds and seemed to be thinking. "Jesse, you've said very little about how it was to see Miss Berne for the first time since her mother died. Was it as awkward as you feared it would be?"

"Not really. Elliot reminded me that she doesn't know I saw what happened."

"What you *think* happened. Don't get ahead of Sheriff Granger."

Jesse cocked his head and looked at his mother. "Two grown-ups—in regular clothes, not bathing suits—go wading in the river, something every kid knows not to do, and the man gets out of the water by himself. Then a lady's body washes up in Rocky Creek. Come on."

"Be that as it may," his mother said, "without any suspects or concrete evidence, Virgil won't be able to pursue this. And that's fine by me. I'd just as soon you not be dragged into a court case, especially when you only saw a glimpse of the man's face from fifty yards away."

"But what if the guy saw *me*?" Jesse said. "He looked over at me when I sneezed. Maybe he thinks I can identify him. Maybe he's looking for me."

"I doubt that. But even if he did see your face, he couldn't possibly know who you are or how to find you as long as that information stays in the family. Virgil will probably close the case soon, and that'll be that."

Jesse nodded, hoping his mother couldn't tell his heart was practically beating out of his chest. He was ashamed of breaking his promise. But if he had to blow it, at least it was with Dawson—the one person he trusted not to say anything.

CHAPTER 12

The next morning, Jesse walked in the front door of Foggy Ridge Middle School, aware that Dawson and his circle of friends had turned their heads in his direction.

Dawson left the group and hurried over to him, smiling sheepishly. "Before I say anything, just remember I was only tryin' to help."

"Help what? Why is everyone staring at me?"

"Well, you're kind of … famous."

"Since when?"

"I guess they think you bein' the only witness in a murder case is super cool."

"You *told* them?" Jesse felt as if he might lose his breakfast.

Dawson lowered his voice. "No, just Bull Hanson. I hoped he'd want you to join the group. I knew everyone else'd follow his lead. Which they are. Trouble is, he told them everything after he said he wouldn't. I'm sorry, man."

Jesse blinked the stinging from his eyes. "How could you do that when I asked you not to? The sheriff isn't even sure it *was* murder.

And I exaggerated. I told you I could identify the guy. I only got a glimpse of his face. I couldn't even describe him to the sketch artist."

Dawson sighed. "Dude. Why didn't you just say that instead of lyin' about it?"

"You weren't supposed to tell anyone!"

"Neither were you," Dawson shot back. "Looks like we both messed up."

"Yeah, except *I'm* the one who's in big trouble. What if Miss Berne hears about this?" Jesse swallowed the ball of emotion in his throat. He couldn't cry here. Not in front of his peers. For the first time ever, he really wanted to punch his best friend in the nose.

Dawson put his hand on Jesse's shoulder. "Look at the positive side. Now you'll be popular too. And we can hang out with the same crowd."

"You don't get it, do you?" Jesse whispered. "I don't want to hang out with them."

"You will. Just stick with me. You'll see. They're really okay."

"No. They're not." Jesse pushed Dawson's hand away. "They put down everyone who isn't part of their group. They laugh at us. Think they're better than everyone else. That's wrong, and you know it."

"Most of 'em aren't like that," Dawson said. "They just don't wanna rock the boat."

"What about you?" Jesse said. "Are you okay with following the crowd even when they do things you know are wrong—just so you can hang on to friends that aren't really friends at all? Did you just blow off everything we talked about at youth group?"

Dawson folded his arms across his chest, his lips pursed, his eyebrows furrowed. "You don't know what you're talkin' about. You're judgin' us without even givin' it a chance. Bull did you a favor. If you walk away now, the guys'll never accept you again."

"That's not the kind of acceptance I'm looking for. I want a friend I can trust."

"I said I was sorry, Jess." Dawson threw his hands in the air. "I just wanted the group to accept you so we could hang out more."

Jesse saw the sincerity on Dawson's face and softened his tone. "I know. But what do I do now? Miss Berne's not supposed to know that I was out there when her mom drowned. If it gets back to my mom and Sheriff Granger, I'll be grounded for the rest of my life."

"Why'd you lie to *me*?" Dawson said.

Jesse glanced over at the group of kids looking in their direction. "I guess I wanted to impress you so I'd feel important."

"You *are* important. You're my best friend." Dawson made a fist and punched Jesse's shoulder. "But I have other friends too. Here's your chance to join us. At least give it a try. You can't just say 'Thanks, but no thanks' when they're offerin' to let you in. Most guys at school would die for that chance. I promise you, if you walk away, they're gonna take it as a slap in the face."

"That's their choice," Jesse said.

"Well, it's your choice too. If you disrespect them, they'll make things miserable for you. I won't be able to stop it."

Jesse looked over at Dawson's friends, who suddenly looked like a band of smiling Goliaths. Could he really afford to make enemies of them?

Virgil sat at his desk, clearing out his in-box and coming to grips with the fact that it was already the first of October. His life seemed to be moving at warp speed.

The intercom buzzed and he picked up the phone. "Sheriff Granger."

"It's Kevin. You free for a minute?"

"Just tackling my in-box. Door's open."

Thirty seconds later Kevin marched into his office, holding a brown envelope. "We've got a new development in the drowning case. The lab found Dixie Berne's DNA on a Kleenex that Billy Gene and Jason bagged at the river. It had a partial tire mark on it, but nothing definitive."

Virgil pulled out the lab report and perused it. "This sure adds credibility to Jesse's statement that Dixie Berne is the woman he saw in the water. I'll talk to the victim's son and daughter and make a statement to the media that this is now a murder investigation. But we need to keep the specifics of this DNA evidence close to the vest. And the fact that we even have an eyewitness. If Ms. Berne *was* murdered, I don't want her killer tipped off."

Kevin nodded. "Agreed. I'll talk to Billy Gene and Jason."

"I'll talk to Kate." Virgil looked out the window and mused. "It takes a real lowlife to drown a helpless old lady with Alzheimer's. He could've easily stolen her jewelry and let her go. It's not like she could identify him."

"Guess he wasn't taking any chances."

"Well, neither am I." Virgil handed the report back to Kevin. "We're going to nail this creep."

Jesse sat in the middle school courtyard with Dawson. The students had each been given ten minutes to get with their partners and review their plan for the story they were about to write for English class.

"Jesse, talk to me," Dawson said. "I can't afford to flunk this assignment."

Jesse glared at him. "You know what to do. Write your half of the story. And I'll write mine."

"Why are you so mad at me? Everyone in the group's jazzed that you're one of us now."

"You shouldn't have told Bull. Or anyone else."

"Will you just try lookin' on the bright side?"

"What *bright* side?" Jesse pulled up a handful of grass. "I have to suck up to a group I don't want to be in or they'll make me a total outcast. And I've got an even bigger problem if the sheriff finds out."

"He's not gonna find out."

"He will if Miss Berne hears about it."

"She won't. Quit bein' paranoid. Just leave it alone. What's the harm in lettin' the guys believe you got a good look at the man's face? They'll think you're cool. It's not like you lied to the sheriff."

"I broke my promise, Dawson. That's as bad as lying."

"Not if he never finds out."

Jesse sighed. "You really don't get it."

"Or maybe *you* don't. Why don't you man up and stop whinin'? You just got accepted into the coolest group at school." Dawson looked over at Miss Berne motioning for her students to return to the classroom. He stood and pulled Jesse to his feet. "Someday you'll thank me."

"I doubt that." Jesse yanked his hand free from Dawson's grasp. "Just write your half of the story the way we agreed. You need to get a good grade. We wouldn't want the *group* to freak out because their star receiver got benched."

Jesse got off at the bus stop and walked up Angel View Road toward the lodge. He had artfully avoided running into Dawson and his teammates, who met at the flagpole every day after school before they went to practice. If only he had the courage to tell them he didn't want to be part of the group. But there would be serious consequences. They would get even by intimidating anyone who tried to befriend him after that. If only he'd done what he had promised the sheriff, none of this would be happening.

Jesse spotted the roof of his family's log house and took off running. He bounded up the steps and stood on the porch for a moment, catching his breath. He was suddenly aware of someone sitting in the swing.

"You coulda set a track-and-field record with that sprint." Grandpa Buck looked over the top of his glasses, a smile appearing under his white mustache. "Mighty fancy legwork."

Jesse grinned. Grandpa always made him feel as if he were better than he really was—at most everything.

"School okay?"

Jesse shrugged. “I guess.”

“The sheriff was here earlier,” Grandpa said. “Your mama’s waitin’ to tell you about it. She just made a fresh batch o’ brownies.”

“Yay! I’ll be in the kitchen.”

Jesse pushed open the front door and was hit immediately with the delicious aroma of warm chocolate. After shedding his backpack on the couch, he hurried into the kitchen, where his mother sat at the table with Riley.

Riley popped a bite of something into her mouth, got up, and grabbed her American Girl doll. “Ella and I are going to go read my book. ’Bye, Mama. Hey, Jesse.”

“Hey yourself.”

Riley skipped past him, her pigtails swaying, looking as if she didn’t have a care in the world.

Jesse looked up at his mother. “Grandpa said you made brownies.”

“Right here waiting.” She pointed to the plate of brownies on the table.

Jesse grabbed a glass, filled it with ice-cold milk, and sat at the table, across from his mother. He took two big bites of a warm brownie and savored the flavor. “So what’d Sheriff Granger have to say? Grandpa said he came by.”

Kate folded her hands on the table. “They’ve uncovered new information and are moving forward with the drowning case as a murder investigation.”

“I knew it!” Jesse said. “So what’d they find?”

“Virgil couldn’t say while the investigation is still open. But he must think you witnessed Dixie Berne’s murder.”

“It was her,” Jesse said. “I’m almost positive.”

"Well, Virgil wants you to work with the sketch artist again and see if you can remember more about the man."

"Why? I wasn't much help before," Jesse said.

"I know, but the case just took an important turn. Virgil thinks it's worth a try."

"So am I still the only witness?"

"Unfortunately." His mother didn't look too pleased. "But unless and until Virgil makes an arrest, he's not going to tell the media or even the victim's family that he has a witness. You can't tell anyone either, no matter how tempting it is."

"I know." Jesse's heart pounded so hard that the front of his sweatshirt was moving.

"Are you sure you're okay?" Kate said. "I know this is a lot to handle."

"Don't worry. I can handle it." Dishonesty and shame burned his cheeks.

Jesse desperately wanted to tell his mother the truth but couldn't force the words out. He wasn't sure which he dreaded more—her disappointment or the consequences he knew would follow.

Liam parked his car in the garage and went into the house. Colleen stood at the stove, stirring something that smelled delicious.

He glanced over at the table set for only two. He still wasn't used to that. "Mmm ... what's for dinner?"

"Chicken and dumplings." Colleen put the lid back on the pot and turned around. "Speaking of chicken, how was your day?"

"Same old. My supervisor's cutting me some slack. I think she feels bad about what happened to Mom."

"Well, the sheriff called earlier. They—"

The doorbell rang.

"They what?" Liam said.

Colleen took off her apron and set it on the countertop. "I'll tell you over dinner. Let me see who's at the door."

Liam walked down the hall and stopped at the door to his room, waiting to see who had rung the bell.

"Ruth—hello." Colleen's principal stood on the doorstep. "What a surprise. Please … come in."

"Thanks," Ruth Arnold said. "I can only stay a minute."

"Would you like something to drink? Coke, sweet tea, water?"

"I'm fine, Colleen. I apologize for dropping by unannounced, especially at dinnertime. But I was at the grocery store a few minutes ago and got a call from Coach Patterson. He picked up on a rumor floating around school. Before I do anything about it, I wanted to run it by you."

"Why me?" Colleen said.

"It involves you. I hate having to ask you this, but do you know anything about Jesse Cummings being an eyewitness in your mother's drowning?"

Liam's pulse quickened. He stepped into his room and stood behind the door, listening intently.

"I certainly have not," Colleen said. "Where did Coach Patterson hear it?"

"Bull Hanson was talking to some teammates at practice. The coach overheard the conversation and got involved. Bull told him that he heard it from Dawson Foster, who heard it directly from Jesse."

"I–I'm speechless," Colleen said. "This is the first I'm hearing of it. The sheriff called shortly after I got home. He told me some evidence had surfaced in the case and said he was going forward with Mom's drowning as a murder investigation. He wanted me to tell my brother but said he couldn't discuss the details with us while the investigation was ongoing. But he didn't say *anything* about having a witness."

"You should call him back as soon as you can," Ruth said. "I don't know how much of this is true."

"Ruth, I need to hear everything the coach told you," Colleen said, "so I can be informed when I confront the sheriff."

"According to Bull, Jesse witnessed your mother's drowning and saw a man in the water with her. Jesse claims he can identify the man and is the sole witness. And that the sheriff told him not to say anything to anyone, for his own safety."

Liam closed his eyes and laid his forehead on the back of the door, his worst nightmare realized.

"Have you talked with Kate Cummings?" Colleen said.

"I haven't talked with anyone. I thought I should start with you. Regardless of whether it's fact or just gossip, we need to put a stop to it."

"Thank you for your sensitivity." Colleen's voice was shaking. "Don't call Kate Cummings. Let me check with the sheriff before we do anything further."

"You're sure? I don't mind calling Kate."

"No, don't. Please. Let me talk to the sheriff. I'll get back to you."

"All right. I'm really sorry to drop a bomb like this, but I didn't want you to hear it from a student or someone on staff."

Liam took a slow, deep breath, and then another, and another, shaken to his core by the cruel irony of this unwelcome development. The one kink in his plan, the one detail that he could not have anticipated, was an eyewitness. And of all the kids in Foggy Ridge, it just happened to be one of Colleen's students!

CHAPTER 13

Jesse stared at his computer screen. He was supposed to be researching the Battle of Vicksburg for his American history class, but all he could think about was how much trouble he was in.

He glanced over at the Bible on his bookshelf. It was wrong to hide the truth from his mother. How could facing her disappointment—and the sheriff's—be any more difficult than carrying around all this fear and guilt? It would be humiliating, though. And he would still be trapped. If he walked away from Dawson's big-shot friends, they would make it impossible for him to make *any* friends. Some choice.

He heard footsteps on the staircase and then a loud knock at his door. "I'm doing homework."

"It's me," his mother said. "I need to talk to you—*now*."

Jesse winced. The tone of her voice told him that this could not be good. "Come in."

Kate walked in and closed the door. "Jesse, I need you to turn around so I can see your face."

Jesse's heart beat so fast he was almost paralyzed for a moment. Finally, he spun around in his computer chair and looked at his mother.

"Is something wrong?" Jesse said.

"Oh, I think you know exactly what's wrong. I just got off the phone with Virgil. There's a rumor floating around school that you are the sole eyewitness to Dixie Berne's drowning. That you saw a man in the water with her—and can *identify* him." Kate sighed. "That information could only have come from you. Jesse, it's bad enough that you broke your promise, but saying you can identify the man is over the top. This entire family is trying to protect you by keeping this information under our roof—and you go right out there and put yourself in danger!"

"I didn't mean to, Mama. It was kind of an accident."

His mother arched her eyebrows, her face pinker than her apron. "How could you *accidentally* reveal an enhanced version of the very thing—the only thing—you were asked not to talk about?"

Jesse wanted to be anywhere but here, talking to anyone besides his mother. "We had this writing assignment," Jesse said. "Dawson was my partner and we had to come up with a story, then each of us would write half."

Jesse told his mother everything that had happened from the time they started the process of deciding on the story line until Jesse came back to school and discovered that not only had Dawson shared his secret with Bull Hanson but that Bull had then told everyone in the popular kids group.

"I know Dawson was just trying to help me fit in," Jesse said, "but I never wanted to be friends with his friends. They think they're hot stuff and that being in their group is what everyone dreams of. Not me. I hate the way they put people down and act all high and mighty. But I can't tell them or they'll feel disrespected and get even with me by intimidating anyone I try to be friends with. I messed up. I'm really sorry."

"If only you'd kept it to yourself, like Virgil asked you to," his mother said. "And by exaggerating what you told Dawson, you might have made yourself a target! Your life could be in danger! Do you realize how serious this is?"

Jesse nodded. "I don't know what to do."

"Why didn't you come to me right away, before it got this far?"

"I was ashamed that I broke my promise. I was hoping it would all go away and you and the sheriff and Miss Berne would never find out."

Kate's eyes welled with tears. "Let's hope the killer doesn't find out. Jesse, you've made it difficult, maybe impossible, for Virgil to protect you. This is what I desperately wanted to avoid."

"Maybe the rumor will stay at school, and I won't need protecting. Foggy Ridge is pretty big. There's a good chance the man I saw is never going to hear about it. He might not even live around here."

"We can hope and pray that's the case. But we're talking about your life, Son. This is no small matter."

"So what do I do?" Jesse said.

"The first thing we do is get the family together, tell them what's going on, and pray. Riley's asleep, so Elliot is getting the others right now."

"Is he mad at me too?"

"Both of us are extremely disappointed," Kate said. "But we're far more concerned for your safety. God is in control, but you have choices. This investigation could go on for some time. I wish you hadn't witnessed the drowning, but you did. So you have to get serious about doing what Virgil tells you. And maybe, just maybe, we can contain the damage you've done."

Liam paced in front of the window in his room, both angry and nervous that Sheriff Granger had been so vague during the earlier phone conversation when Liam and Colleen had called him back. He said they were going forward as a murder investigation, but that's all he could tell them right now. He wouldn't confirm or deny whether the sheriff's department had a suspect or a witness. All he would say about the rumor at the middle school was that he was looking into it.

Liam raked his hands through his hair. How much did the kid see? Was he just boasting when he told his buddies he was the sole witness and could identify the man he saw wading in the river with the victim? Could Liam afford to just sit back now and hope that the kid didn't see him as clearly as he saw the kid?

A knock at his door caused him to jump.

"Liam," Colleen said softly, "are you awake?"

"Yeah, come in."

Colleen opened the door and flopped down on the side of the bed. "I'm getting madder by the minute. I feel like an outsider in our own mother's murder investigation."

"I don't like it either, but that's the way law enforcement works. We can't take it personal."

"But it *is* personal! She was our mother. We deserve to know what Jesse told the sheriff and not just the version he told his friends. What if they have a suspect?"

"I didn't mean the *situation* wasn't personal." Liam sat next to Colleen on the bed. "I just meant that the sheriff follows the same protocol in all cases. While they're piecing the facts together, no one but members of law enforcement are privy to the information."

"I'd say that's pretty much blown in this case, wouldn't you?"

"Maybe not," Liam said. "It's possible this kid made up the whole thing to impress his buddies, and once that's confirmed, it'll be the end of it."

Colleen's eyes narrowed. "Then why didn't the sheriff just say that?"

"Because law enforcement never divulges information *or* opinions about an active investigation."

"Fine," Colleen said, "then I'll just ask Jesse myself if it's true."

"How well do you know this kid? Would he talk to you?"

Colleen shrugged. "I really think he would if I appeal to his sensitive side. His dad and sister were missing for five years, and he knows how uncertainty can haunt a family."

"Wait a minute ..." Liam's pulse quickened. "Jesse *Cummings*. The kid from Angel View Lodge, whose father was killed and sister kidnapped by that crazy mountain loon?"

"Yes. And I think because of that, he might talk to me, especially if I approach him as a daughter who desperately wants to know what happened to her mother."

"The sheriff isn't going to like that."

"The sheriff isn't the one whose poor, defenseless mother was drowned by some lowlife who could just as easily have robbed her and let her go. I have a right to know what Jesse saw. And I don't plan to ask the sheriff's permission."

Liam mused. This could be the perfect way for him to find out how much the kid knew. "Good for you. There's no law against a teacher asking a student if a school rumor is true or not."

❧

Kate said, "Amen," then opened her eyes, warmed to see the show of support on the faces of each family member in the circle, but chagrined that the tightness in her chest was still there.

Jesse looked relieved after having confessed to breaking his promise and exaggerating the truth.

"What were you thinking?" Hawk finally said. "Sheriff Granger couldn't have been clearer in what he told us."

Jesse shrugged and said nothing.

"I think Jesse's suffered enough," Kate said. "I'm sure he's learned his lesson. Virgil will tell us if we need to do anything, other than *not* discuss it with Riley or anyone outside the family. Of course, we don't consider Elliot and Jay outside the family."

Abby looked over at Jay and smiled, then turned to Kate. "Not even Dawson's mother?"

"That's right," Kate said. "Virgil doesn't want me calling Olivia Foster or any of the other boys' mothers. He wants us to let him do the damage control. He will talk to the principal and make sure that Jesse's teacher doesn't approach him about it. But if any of us are approached, we're to say we've been asked by the sheriff not to comment on an active investigation."

"Isn't that like admitting it?" Hawk said.

Kate sighed. "It's really all we can say, despite what anyone's heard."

"How am I supposed to go to school and not answer questions?" Jesse said. "And even if Miss Berne isn't allowed to talk to me, I'll know what she's thinking."

"I can't keep you home, Son," Kate said, "or everyone will assume the gossip is true. You're going to have to walk through this one for a while. But if you're too uncomfortable with Miss Berne being your teacher, the principal can transfer you to another English class."

Jesse's eyes welled. "I'm sorry. Y'all did what you were supposed to do, and I didn't. The last thing I wanted to do was worry Mama or any of you." A tear escaped down his cheek.

Grandpa Buck put his arm around Jesse and pulled him close. "We're in this together, boy. What does the Word say? If God is for us—"

"Who can be against us?" Jesse answered. "I guess that's a good one to think about right now. Just because I made a mistake doesn't mean God won't protect me."

"Of course it doesn't," Kate said, less sure than she sounded.

Jay Rogers cleared his throat. "I'd like to say something. Y'all know I was Jesse's age when I thought I'd accidentally shot a man dead and didn't have the courage to tell my mom. I know what it feels like to be twelve and trapped in a huge mistake with huge consequences. Jesse, be glad you got caught. At least now you can stop lying before things get even worse. Like your grandpa pointed out with that verse from Romans, if God is for us, nobody can be against us. Nobody. God protected Abby and me when we nearly got ourselves killed trying to find your dad and Riley. He's big enough to take care of you too. You've gotta trust Him."

Here we go again, Kate thought. Just when her life was finally happy and her worries few, she had to put another of her children totally in God's hands. Maybe she was overreacting. What were the odds that whoever killed Dixie Berne would find out Jesse was the eyewitness?

❧

Liam sat alone in the dark, his thoughts racing faster than his heart, the reality finally hitting him that one of his sister's students might actually be able to identify him. Surely any description this kid gave the sheriff would be general at best, fitting thousands of men. How good a look at him could the boy have gotten in just a couple seconds? How seriously would the authorities take that kind of testimony? Still … the implications were unsettling.

It had been gut wrenching taking his mother's life. He would never be able to shake the memory of it. And he hadn't come this far only to lose his inheritance because Jesse Cummings sneezed and Liam glanced over his shoulder for two seconds. By this time tomorrow, he should know whether the kid posed a threat.

And if he did? Liam looked up at the night sky, suddenly feeling one with the darkness and dreading the options. Nothing was going to stop him from getting his inheritance. He'd already paid too high a price.

CHAPTER 14

Virgil glanced up at the wispy swirls of golden pink and purple on Tuesday morning's sky, as he and Kevin walked in the teacher's entrance of Foggy Ridge Middle School. They were met by the maintenance supervisor, who led them to the principal's office.

Virgil removed his Stetson as he entered a pleasant pale-yellow room with walls of framed certificates and motivational posters.

The principal, an attractive fiftysomething brunette, rose from her desk to greet them and extended her hand. "Sheriff Granger. Good to meet you. Ruth Arnold."

Virgil shook her hand, the smell of freshly brewed coffee permeating the room. "This is Chief Deputy Kevin Mann."

"Pleased to meet you both," she said. "I've certainly seen you on the news a time or two. I appreciate your willingness to meet with me so early. I need some direction before classes begin. Please, sit down and make yourselves comfortable. I have a fresh pot of coffee. Any takers?"

"I'd love some," Virgil said. "Black is fine."

Kevin nodded. "Yes, ma'am. Same here."

Virgil and Kevin sat at a small table on one side of the room while Ruth walked over to a coffeemaker that was set on a counter in the corner. She brought two mugs of coffee and set one in front of each of them, then got one for herself and sat at the table.

"Sheriff," Ruth said, "I told you over the phone every detail I know of the rumor circulating that Jesse Cummings witnessed Dixie Berne's drowning and saw the man who was with her in the water."

"Who *allegedly* was with her," Kevin said. "That hasn't been established."

Virgil nodded, regretting that, for Jesse's sake, it would be imprudent to say more. "You know we can't comment on an ongoing investigation, but you can understand how that kind of information out there in the public arena, true or false, could make Jesse a walking target. So we need your help to contain the rumor."

"Sheriff, that's a tall order," Ruth said. "Once a rumor is out, there's no putting it back in the bag."

Virgil took a sip of coffee. "I know. What I want to do is protect Jesse as much as possible from having to comment on it, so that the rumor will die off by itself."

"How?"

"In my experience, kids this age get bored and stop asking questions if they don't get an answer."

"They're liable to turn on him," Ruth said. "Bull Hanson can be downright cruel, and he manipulates his teammates. I've already had to address their verbal bullying a few times, and the school year's barely started."

"That's a real possibility," Kevin said, "but one that can't be avoided. Jesse started the ball rolling on this. He's been told how making this kind of claim might have put him in danger."

"How can I help?" Ruth folded her hands on her desk.

"I've spoken to Colleen Berne," Virgil said, "who, I understand, is Jesse's English teacher. She knows that Jesse could be in danger because of the rumor, and that my department is currently investigating the story Jesse told his friends. It would be very helpful if you'd reinforce that she is not to have any—and I mean *any*—personal conversations with Jesse."

"I can do that," Ruth said. "I already planned to get with Colleen before classes start."

"Our recommendation is that you transfer Jesse to another English class. It will be almost intolerable for Colleen *and* Jesse otherwise."

Ruth had a faraway look and seemed to be thinking. "That can certainly be arranged easily enough. But I don't think Colleen's going to be a problem. She's a reasonable woman."

"With all due respect," Virgil said, glancing briefly at Kevin, "no one in a victim's family can be considered reasonable when their loved one has died, leaving unanswered questions, and a potential eyewitness so accessible. Though Colleen may be a wonderful teacher and a great human being, she is the grieving daughter of a woman who may have been murdered. The temptation for her to talk to Jesse could be overwhelming."

Ruth bit her lip. "Do you think it might be better if Jesse were transferred to another middle school?"

"Truthfully, no," Virgil said. "A transfer would likely raise more questions and perpetuate the rumor on *two* fronts, actually increasing the risk to Jesse's safety." Virgil scratched his newly shaven chin. "I'm sure you're aware of his family's tragic history. And I know you would want to spare them more heartache. I really think we can contain the damage already done if you will talk to Miss Berne and put Jesse in another English class. No one would question the wisdom of you doing that during an open investigation."

"All right," Ruth said. "I'll take care of it before second period. Jesse and Colleen won't have to cross paths. That should help. But what about Jesse's peers? They are going to barrage him with questions."

"Which he won't answer," Kevin said. "He's been coached on how to respond. We believe his peers will tire of the whole thing in short order. Unfortunately, they'll probably give him a hard time in the process."

"Sheriff," Ruth said while drawing a circle on the desk with her finger, "do *you* think Jesse saw a man with Colleen's mother when she drowned?"

"As Chief Deputy Mann already pointed out, that hasn't been established," Virgil replied. "The point is, Jesse has led his peers to think so. Right now, we have no reason to believe the media or anyone outside this school has picked up on it. We don't plan to talk with any of your students or their parents. We don't want to fan the flames even slightly. We caught this early and are in a good position, with your help, to contain the rumor and let it fizzle out on its own."

Ruth nodded. "Maybe by taking the steps you mentioned, we'll be able to do exactly that. But when *I'm* approached by students, parents, teachers—or, heaven forbid, the media—how should *I* respond?"

"Without using Jesse's name, just tell the truth: that the sheriff is working to establish whether the rumor is true, or whether it's a product of the student's imagination, or an attempt to impress his peers. Beyond that, you have no comment. Can you do that?"

"Yes. I'm sure I can."

"Good. Make it clear to your teachers that you're the *only* one authorized to speak to the media. If they're approached, they need to direct all inquiries to you." Virgil looked over at Kevin. "Anything else you can think of?"

Kevin pursed his lips. "Maybe you could choose a group of trusted staff people to keep an eye on Jesse without him realizing it. They'd be able to spot any student or teacher who seems to have him cornered and could interrupt the conversation with some made-up excuse."

"I'm sure I could arrange that," Ruth said. "At least we don't have to worry about strangers in the school. We screen people very carefully."

Kevin folded his hands on the table. "That's good to hear."

"Sheriff, is Jesse's situation putting my students in danger?" Ruth said. "I have a right to know that much."

"I really don't think so," Virgil said. "If anyone's in danger, it's Jesse. Just to be on the safe side, I'll be assigning two deputies to cruise the area around the school and keep an eye out for anything that doesn't look right. But let me emphasize," Virgil said, "that all of this is precautionary. I don't perceive your students to be in any danger whatsoever. This is about Jesse."

"Well, you have my full cooperation." Ruth glanced at her watch and stood. "I will talk to Colleen as soon as she gets here. And I'll make sure Jesse is transferred to a different second-period English class."

Virgil went out the side door of the school, the sun now visible just above the horizon. He placed his hat on his head and walked back to his squad car, Kevin keeping stride.

"I hated having to withhold what we know from Ruth Arnold," Virgil said.

"You did the right thing, Sheriff. And to be fair, we haven't found any *evidence* to corroborate Jesse's testimony, other than that Kleenex. Containing the rumor is our primary objective. I think we just might get it done."

"When I tell Kate what we're doing, her first impulse will be to transfer Jesse to a different school. I've got to convince her it won't help."

"Yeah, either way, the kid's in for a real kick in the pants," Kevin said. "Some of his peers will taunt him unmercifully when they question him about being an eyewitness and he tells them he's not allowed to comment on an open investigation. We've got to convince him to stay strong and be consistent."

"Let's hope they get bored with it quickly and leave him alone." Virgil pulled his keys out of his pocket. "But Jesse's bound to lose some friends who feel they've been lied to."

"Unfortunately, this thing could drag on for some time." Kevin's red hair caught a glint of sunlight. "We're not even close to finding a suspect."

"That's why I want our sketch artist to try again to jog Jesse's memory. And I want you to sit in on it. You're the best we've got at that. Jesse's a kid with twenty-twenty eyesight, who made eye contact with our man of interest from just fifty yards away. I'm not convinced we can't get him to remember what the guy looked like."

"Then again, he was sitting on a big school of crappie." Kevin flashed a crooked grin. "I wonder how tuned in I'd be to some guy across the river if I'd found a spot like that."

Liam was just about to clock in at the poultry plant when his cell phone rang. He glanced at the screen, then stepped out in the hall and put the phone to his ear.

"What's up, Sis?"

"The sheriff has already been here," Colleen said. "The principal moved Jesse to another English class. I've been *instructed*—which is just a polite word for forbidden—not to talk to Jesse. Can you believe it?"

"Sheriff Granger sure didn't waste any time."

"Liam, why would he go to all that trouble unless Jesse really saw what happened? Why are they so afraid I might find out what that is? What is the sheriff hiding from us?"

Liam felt as if his lungs were in a vise. Did the sheriff suspect him?

"Well, they can't keep me from talking to Jesse," she said. "I'm not going to just sit back and wonder what's going on. I want answers!"

"Colleen, don't," Liam said. "Don't jeopardize your career by talking to the kid. Give it time to play out. We have nothing to gain by defying the sheriff. He's the one person we need to stay connected to."

Colleen paused for several seconds, then exhaled into the receiver. "You're right. I want answers *five minutes ago*, but that's not the way the system works. We need to follow the sheriff's instructions. He knows what he's doing. I just wish I didn't have this unsettling feeling that he's hiding something."

"Like I told you before, he's just following department protocol." Liam kept his voice steady, careful to hide the panic he felt.

"And in all fairness to the sheriff," Colleen said, "he did listen to us. Even without an autopsy, he's agreed to investigate Mom's death as a murder."

Or is it because of something Jesse told him? The pounding of Liam's heartbeat seemed almost audible.

"Thanks for letting me vent," Colleen said. "I wish I could stay as calm as you do. You remind me of Dad."

"It's just a guy thing. Take a deep breath," Liam said, talking more to himself than to Colleen. "Do what the principal asked and don't question the kid. We'll talk more when I get home."

Colleen exhaled. "Okay. I think I'm okay now. I need to sit here and gather my thoughts before the bell rings. I'll see you tonight. Love you."

"I love you too." Liam disconnected the call, his hands shaking, and stuck his cell phone on his belt.

His mind raced in reverse through every detail of his mother's drowning and the cover-up. Things had gone flawlessly. There was no way the sheriff would find any tangible evidence to charge him with murder. The only thing standing between him and his inheritance was the word of that kid.

The same dark feeling came over him that had engulfed him the night before. Mom's attorney had nearly completed all the necessary steps for the dissolution of her trust, and Liam was just a couple weeks away from getting his one-hundred-and-seventy-five-thousand-dollar inheritance. How far was he willing to go in order to keep this Cummings kid from ruining everything he'd worked so hard to set in motion?

CHAPTER 15

Kate walked into Flutter's Café at Angel View Lodge, the delicious aromas of fried bacon and warm bread filling her senses. She spotted Abby pouring coffee for Grandpa Buck and his friend Titus Jackson. Abby looked up and smiled, then walked over to her.

"There you are," Abby said. "Elliot's sitting over there by the glass wall. He already ordered for you. Breakfast should be up in just a couple minutes. I'll get your coffee."

"Thanks, honey," Kate said.

"You look intense."

"Do I?"

Abby's smile faded and she seemed to study Kate's face. "I know you're freaked out about Jesse being a witness, but don't be. This case isn't high profile like when Daddy and Riley were missing. The media probably won't even give it much attention."

"Let's hope."

"Relax." Abby nodded toward Elliot. "Go enjoy a few minutes with your sweetheart before you open the office."

"I will." Kate turned and walked to the table where Elliot was seated. He seemed mesmerized by the sea of white fog blanketing Beaver Lake, which gave the illusion of being high above the clouds.

"Lost in the view?" Kate said.

Elliot flashed a perfect smile worthy of a toothpaste ad. "It has to be one of the most beautiful sights in the country. And it's right here at Angel View Lodge. You and Micah were so wise to buy this property when you did. It's sure prime."

Kate sat at the table opposite Elliot and looked out at the postcard view she had never grown tired of.

"How'd you sleep?" he said.

"Not well. I'm probably overreacting to the whole thing with Jesse. But I've been through tragedies and near misses with every one of my children, not to mention my murdered husband. I'm worn out with it."

"I know. That's why we have to trust God."

"I do. I think." Kate sighed. "I'm trying. Let's talk about something happy."

"Okay … marry me."

Kate looked into his gentle eyes and felt her heart sink. "I thought we agreed to put off this conversation until I feel ready to talk about it."

Elliot took a sip of coffee. "You said to talk about something happy. I can't think of anything that would make me happier." Elliot reached across the table and took her hand. "Kate, I didn't sleep well either, knowing you were all alone, wrestling with your fears. All I could think about was how much I wanted to lay beside you, hold you in my arms, and reassure you that everything's going to work out. We're better together than apart. You know it too."

"I never said we weren't. I just like things the way they are for now."

"So is that a firm no?"

Kate smiled without meaning to. "For now. There's plenty of time to have this conversation."

"I don't know, I just passed the half-century mark. I wouldn't push the envelope, if I were you."

Kate laughed. "Give me a break. You're fit as a fiddle. You make it sound as if you have a long white beard and walk with a shuffle."

Elliot's eyes twinkled with delight. "I love it when you laugh. I just want to make you happy."

Abby was suddenly standing beside the table pouring coffee. "Your breakfast is up next. What are you two lovebirds laughing about?"

"Lovebird things." Elliot winked.

Abby looked at her mother, the corners of her mouth twitching. "I'm probably out of line to say this, but if you don't marry this man, I'm going to take you in and have your head examined."

Kate felt her cheeks get hot and glanced around the room, relieved that no one was staring at them. "I don't remember asking for your opinion."

"But you're the one who said I was wise beyond my years." Abby giggled and took a step back. "I'm just sayin' …"

Abby turned and started pouring coffee refills for the folks at the next table.

"Honestly, she's just like her father," Kate said, more amused than she wanted to admit.

"Really?" Elliot said, tongue in cheek. "Because I was thinking she's just like you."

Jesse sat in the middle row of Mrs. Richie's second-period English class. When he had arrived at his first-period homeroom, he was told he needed to go see the principal. That's when he learned he was being transferred out of Miss Berne's class and was not to communicate with her.

He was aware of a number of students stealing glances at him. What were they thinking—that it was cool he was a witness to Dixie Berne's murder? Or that he made it up to get attention? Either way, he just wanted to disappear.

Mrs. Richie had introduced him without explanation and said he was joining their class. But the gossip had already spread, and he figured every kid in the seventh grade had heard the exaggerated version that he could identify the man who had drowned Miss Berne's mother.

The bell rang. Jesse breathed a sigh of relief, then grabbed his backpack, hurried out into the hallway, and almost ran into Bull Hanson, who grabbed his arm.

"Hey, slow down, man," Bull said. "Where've you been? You weren't at the flagpole yesterday after school."

Jesse felt his cheeks burning. "I had to take the bus. If I'd met y'all, I'd have missed it."

"How come I didn't see you this mornin'? You're always a few minutes early for school."

"Not today. I was running late." Jesse bit his lip as if that would conceal the lie. His bus had arrived fifteen minutes early, and he had walked behind the school, waiting until after the bell rang before going inside.

"How could you be runnin' late if you rode the bus?" Bull said.

"Well, no. I mean, my mom drove me this morning. But I *usually* take the bus." Jesse's gut tightened. Could he keep track of all the lies?

"Look, man. You're either in or you're out. I did Dawson a favor by convincin' the others to let you in the group. We're tight. We do things *together*."

Jesse looked up into Bull's face, suddenly feeling very short.

"Be at the game Friday night." Bull pushed his index finger into Jesse's chest. "The team's goin' out for pizza afterwards. Come with us. If you're gonna be part of us, we hafta get to know you."

Jesse pasted on a phony smile. "Okay. Sure."

Bull looked over at two guys standing outside the music room. "What're you stooges starin' at?"

"Nothing," said the taller of the two, his face crimson. "Just waiting for someone to unlock the door."

Bull went over to the kid who'd answered him and got up in his face. "You and your pal eavesdroppin' on me?"

"I–I swear we weren't, Bull. We just happened to be standing here. That's it."

"If one word of what I just said gets back to me, I'll know where to find you."

"We didn't hear anything."

"Keep it that way." Bull turned around, snickering, and walked back over to Jesse. "Did you see the look on their faces?"

"I really don't think they were eavesdropping," Jesse said.

"That wasn't the point. It's about respect. No one messes with us. You'll see." Bull glanced at his watch. "I've gotta get to class. Think of Friday night as initiation night. You're runnin' with the big boys now, baby."

Jesse met Bull's gaze and faked a smile, then rushed down the hall toward his next class. How many guys would give anything for an invitation like that? But all Jesse could think about was how to find a legitimate excuse to get out of it.

Liam knocked and then walked into his supervisor's office.

Marilyn Donovan looked up from her desk, the roots of her bleached hair matching the heavy mascara she wore. "What is it, Liam?"

"I should go home," he said. "I've been throwing up and feel really bad. Must be a virus."

Marilyn studied him. "You look a little green. Go on. You've got plenty of sick leave and I don't want you passing it around. If you're still puny in the morning, I need to know before seven thirty so I can get someone in here to take your shift."

"Thanks. I'll let you know."

"I haven't had a chance to talk to you much since your mother died," Marilyn said. "I heard on the news that the sheriff is now pursuing her death as a murder investigation. I'm sorry."

Liam nodded.

"I appreciate the fact that you've been able to do your job. Can't be easy right now."

"No. But Colleen and I take a lot of comfort in the fact that she's in a better place."

"Still … it has to weigh on you." Marilyn's gaze was intrusive. "Let me know if you need a little time off. Or want to cut back on your hours for a while."

"Thanks, but it helps to stay busy." Liam put his hand over his mouth. "Sorry, I'm feeling sick again."

"Go," Marilyn said. "Be good to yourself. Get some rest."

Liam nodded, his hand clasped over his mouth, and ran out into the hall and into the men's restroom. No one else was in there. He waited for about a minute and then headed down the hall and out of the plant. He had no intention of going home yet.

❦

Jesse rested his head against the bus window and was nearly lulled to sleep when he heard his cell phone beep and saw that he had a text message from his mother.

Sheriff Granger is sending a sketch artist to the house at 4:00. Come straight home.

Jesse sighed. He wished he hadn't gone fishing the morning of the drowning. It felt as if his entire life had been turned upside down ever since.

The bus stopped on Angel View Road where it intersected with Skyline Drive. Jesse put on his backpack and got off with the Moyer sisters, who walked in the opposite direction.

The scent of pine filled the crisp October afternoon and brought a smile to his face. He loved the outdoors, and Sure Foot Mountain was a giant playground of endless discovery. He couldn't imagine being stuck in the city limits of Foggy Ridge.

Jesse started up Angel View Road, the only sound the rapid drilling of a woodpecker on a nearby tree. The hardwoods had just barely begun to turn, but they would be magically transformed in the next couple of weeks as autumn's patchwork covered the hills.

Jesse heard a twig snap. He stopped and listened. Nothing. Probably a deer.

He started walking again and heard an unfamiliar whistling noise coming from the woods. What kind of bird was that? He slid out of his backpack and set it in the grass on the side of the road, then walked slowly toward the tree line, listening intently. He walked gingerly into the woods and looked around, but the only whistling he heard was the wind in the trees. He wanted to listen longer and try to determine what had made the interesting new sound, but remembered his mother had told him to come straight home.

He turned around and started walking back to the road when he heard another twig snap. Then something powerful bulldozed him from behind and slammed him into a tree trunk. He felt crushed by the weight of it. He couldn't move. Could hardly breathe.

"Make a sound and I'll gut you like one of your crappie," whispered a gruff male voice. "I'm only going to say this once, so listen up. You didn't see a drowning. You didn't see a man in the water. You made it up. Got that?"

Jesse tried to nod, but his head was pinned. "I … got … it."

"I know where you live, kid. I know you have a mother and two pretty sisters. You can't imagine what I'll do to them unless you tell the sheriff, your mother, and your classmates that you lied. That you made up everything you told them about the drowning. Is that clear?"

"Yes." Jesse's heart was pounding so hard he thought it might explode.

"I promise you," the man whispered, his breath warm in Jesse's ear, "if you tell anyone about this conversation, I'll carve up each person in your family, one by one, and leave you for last. Convince the sheriff you didn't see anything. And you'll never hear from me again. And believe me, you do not want to hear from me again."

"I … under … stand," Jesse said, a cold chill crawling up his spine.

"I'm going to turn loose of you now. Keep your eyes shut. Don't make a sound or move a muscle. Count slowly to two hundred. Then go home and tell your mother you lied, and get her to call the sheriff. Either convince the sheriff you made it up or be responsible for your family dying. Badly. I've got eyes and ears in the sheriff's department. I'll know if you double-cross me. It's up to you. I'm watching."

The pressure was suddenly released and Jesse gasped for air, hugging the tree trunk and slowly counting to two hundred. Even after he finished counting, he was paralyzed with fear. What if he couldn't convince his mother he'd lied? What if Sheriff Granger didn't buy it either?

Jesse felt sick to his stomach. He had already lost his dad. He couldn't lose his mother. Or be responsible for the deaths of anyone else in his family.

CHAPTER 16

Kate heard the front door open and close, listening for Jesse's robust declaration that he had arrived home from school. Instead, she heard footsteps charging up the staircase.

"Riley, why don't you go give Halo her treat, and we'll finish your spelling right after dinner."

"Okay, Mama." Riley picked up her American Girl doll and kissed Kate's cheek. "If I get one more Superb on my work, I'll be first in my class."

"You don't have to be first in the class for me to be proud of you."

"I want to be first so *I'll* be proud of me."

Kate smiled. Riley was self-motivated like the father she would never know.

Kate left the kitchen and went upstairs. She knocked on Jesse's door. "It's your mother. Since when do you ignore me when you get home? Don't you want a snack?"

"I'm not hungry."

"Are you sick?"

"Just tired."

"I'm coming in," Kate said.

She opened the door and went inside. Jesse lay in his bed, facing the wall. "How was your new English class?" she said.

"Fine."

"Virgil said that Miss Berne has been instructed not to talk to you."

"She didn't talk to me. I never even saw her."

"How were the kids? Did they ask you lots of questions?"

"Nobody said anything about it."

"Well, that's good. Right?"

Jesse didn't answer.

"I would sure appreciate it," Kate said, "if you'd look at me when I'm talking to you."

"But I just got comfortable."

Kate sat on the side of the bed, her arms folded across her chest. "I'm going to sit right here until you tell me what's bothering you."

"Nothing."

"Jesse Cummings, I can't remember the last time you came home from school and weren't starved." Kate put her hand on his back and rubbed. "I know middle school was challenging, even before Dawson exposed your secret. But if you'd done what Sheriff Granger asked, you wouldn't be in this pickle. I can't erase the consequences, but I'll help you deal with them. Come downstairs and have something to eat. The sketch artist will be here in twenty minutes."

"I already told him what I know."

"Deputy Mann is coming with him this time. He's good at helping people remember things they aren't even aware they saw."

"I didn't see anything."

"I'd say you saw quite a lot."

There was a long moment of silence.

Jesse sat up and turned around, his cheeks, nose, and forehead badly scraped and scratched.

"Good heavens! What happened to your face?" Kate tilted his chin and took a closer look at his wounds. "Please tell me you weren't fighting."

"I tripped and fell on the way home. It's nothing."

"I would hardly call that nothing."

"Mama, I need to tell you something, and you're not going to like it." Jesse's eyes welled with tears. "Everything I told the sheriff was a lie. I never saw Dixie Berne or a man in the water with her. I made it up. All of it."

Kate stared at her son, dumbfounded, trying to process what he had said.

"You made it up—just like that?" Kate said, trying to keep a level tone. "Jesse, you told me, right after you got home from fishing, that you saw a man and woman on the other side of the river, wading in the water."

"I did." Jesse glanced up at her. "But they were about Hawk's age. When I saw on the news that a woman's body had been found, I made up the whole story about seeing a white-haired lady with a man in the water."

"Why?"

"I don't know. Maybe I wanted to feel important, like Abby, Jay, and Hawk were when they rescued Riley." Jesse hung his head. "I'm sorry."

"Sorry?" Kate sighed, her mind racing with the repercussions. "Son, this might have been an accidental drowning, and you let the sheriff believe it was something more. You, of all people, should know how a family suffers when a loved one is murdered and the case is unsolved. Can you imagine how this has hurt Miss Berne and her brother?"

"I didn't think they would find out. Sheriff Granger said he wasn't going to tell the victim's family that he had a witness."

"He didn't," Kate said. "The rumor at school is responsible for that. But Virgil took your statement seriously. He had all his people and officers from the Foggy Ridge PD combing the riverbank, gathering evidence. And now you're saying it was all a lie?"

Jesse wiped his tears with his sleeve. "I never meant to hurt anyone."

"I know you didn't, but do you understand how serious this is? Virgil is pursuing this case as a murder, mostly because of what you claimed to have seen."

"That's why I have to tell the truth now—before it goes any further."

Kate felt at the same time relieved, and as if she'd been kicked in the gut. She was glad Jesse hadn't witnessed anything. But how upset would Virgil be that another of her kids had sent his deputies on a wild goose chase? "Jesse, I'm hurt and disappointed that you let this lie go on, even though you knew how worried I would be for your safety. After all this family has been through, after all *I've* been through, how could you be so insensitive?"

"It was wrong. I'm sorry. I just wanted to feel important."

"You *are* important." Kate held his gaze. "How could you not know that? We've got to call Virgil before Deputy Mann and the sketch artist get here."

❧

Liam lay on the couch watching TV. He heard a door open and close, and then footsteps walking through the kitchen. He pushed the off button on the remote and messed up his hair. A few seconds later, Colleen came into the living room.

"I was surprised to see your car in the garage," she said. "Why are you home already?"

"I left work early." Liam made sure his voice sounded weak. "Don't get too close. I've been throwing up."

"Don't worry about me," Colleen said. "Middle school is a petri dish. I'm exposed to something all the time. You want me to make you some chicken soup?"

"Thanks, but I'm not sure I could keep it down. Anything else happen with the Cummings boy?"

"I didn't see him today. Our principal made sure of that."

"Doesn't it frost you?" Liam said.

"You bet it does. But I can't afford to jeopardize my teaching career over it. Maybe it's all overblown. Twelve-year-old boys have been known to brag and make up a story as they go along."

"Is that what you think happened?"

"I don't know, Liam. Maybe. There must be a way to find out. My hands are tied. But nobody said *you* couldn't talk to Jesse."

"No way am I getting in the middle of this."

"The worst the sheriff could do is slap your wrist. And maybe Jesse would tell you what he saw. He didn't have any problem talking to his friends about it."

Liam shook his head. "No. We need to cooperate with the sheriff and with the principal. Antagonizing either is a dumb idea. Besides, there's no guarantee the boy would tell me the truth. And if he denied it, would you be satisfied?"

Colleen sighed. "Probably not."

Liam slapped his hand over his mouth and jumped to his feet. "Sorry, I'm going to be sick again." He hurried down the hall and into the bathroom and shut the door.

He would have to redirect Colleen's thinking. He could not allow himself to be pressured into a face-to-face encounter with Jesse—the one person who saw his face and could place him with his mother in the river at the time of her drowning.

His plan had worked so far. Jesse should be afraid enough to tell everyone he lied.

Hope you're proud of yourself.

Liam was plenty ashamed of having to put terror in the heart of a kid who already knew what it was to lose a parent. But it was either that or risk losing everything himself.

Kate opened the front door and instantly saw the concern on Virgil's face.

"Come in," she said. "I'm truly sorry. I would never have dreamed in a million years that Jesse would do something like this."

"Let me talk to him." Virgil took off his hat and brushed past her into the living room, where Jesse sat in a chair facing the couch.

Virgil walked over and sat on one end of the couch, and Kate sat on the other.

"Would you like something to drink?" Kate said.

"I'm fine, thanks." Virgil looked over at Jesse. "Your mother tells me you made up the story about having seen the white-haired woman wading in the river with a man."

"Yes, sir." Jesse stared down at his hands, folded in his lap. "I saw a young couple playing in the water. That's all."

"You went to an awful lot of trouble to give me your statement, Jesse. What made you decide to tell the truth now?"

"It's been bothering me that I lied."

"I see," Virgil said. "If it was bothering you that much, why did you tell your friend Dawson the same story? Especially when you'd promised your mother and me that you wouldn't let it go outside this family?"

Jesse shrugged. "I just did. I'm sorry."

"That's not good enough, son. I need a reason."

Jesse glanced over at his mother. "I was afraid of losing Dawson as my friend. He's a big hero, and I'm not. I wanted him to think I'm cool, even if I don't play sports."

Kate listened as Jesse told the sheriff the story of how and why he had shared his secret with Dawson.

"Dawson's betrayal has made a lot of trouble for you," Virgil said. "Just as your betrayal has now made some problems for me."

"I'm sorry. I didn't mean to."

"Nonetheless, I'm still going to be faced with questions about the rumor that you witnessed the drowning."

"You can say it's not true, right?"

"Jesse, I never acknowledged that you were a witness in the first place—or that I even had a witness. I never talk to the media about that kind of detail until we've made an arrest. The best way to reverse the rumor is for you to tell your friends the truth and hope it spreads as fast as the lie did."

Jesse's eyes welled with tears. "No one will ever speak to me again. I'll be a big joke."

"For a while," Virgil said. "But when the dust settles, your true friends will be there."

"I don't think so. Bull will scare off anyone who tries to be friends with me."

"You can't worry about that now," his mother said. "You just need to tell the truth."

"I am. I didn't see anything. I'm not a witness."

"Can you describe the young couple?" Virgil said. "Maybe they saw something."

"I wasn't paying attention to them."

"Can you tell me anything about them?"

"I think the lady was blonde," Jesse said, "but I'm not sure. I never saw their faces."

Virgil was quiet for longer than Kate was comfortable. What was going through his mind?

"Can I go now?" Jesse said.

"Not just yet. I still have a few questions. How did you skin up your face?"

"I slipped on some gravel and fell on the way home. It's no big deal."

Virgil was quiet for several seconds, then cleared his throat. "Jesse, has anyone come to you, wanting to discuss the case—other kids? Their parents? Teachers? Anyone?"

"I haven't said anything to anyone else."

"That's not what I asked you," Virgil said. "Have you been approached by anyone, perhaps someone who told you to back off?"

"No, sir. I just don't want to lie about it anymore. I'm really sorry I caused everyone so much trouble. I guess now that you don't have a witness, it's not a murder case."

Virgil tented his fingers. "I never said that. My decision to move this forward as a murder investigation went beyond just your statement."

"But I thought—"

"We're building a case, son. Whether you saw anything or not, we have good reason to believe Dixie Berne had been on that riverbank."

"What reason?"

"I can't discuss that with you either," Virgil said.

"How can it be a murder investigation if you don't have a witness?"

"You let me worry about that. You're absolutely sure you never saw anything?"

"I made it up, Sheriff."

"I suppose if I asked you under oath, you'd say the same thing?"

Jesse nodded. "I'm really sorry I lied. I didn't see anything."

Virgil scratched the stubble on his chin. "All right, then. You're officially excused as a witness."

Jesse blew the hair off his forehead. "Good. Now can I leave? I've got to go get up the nerve to tell Dawson I lied. There's going to be a lot of pressure on him to dump me as a friend."

Kate felt as if her stomach had done a flip-flop. She dreaded that Jesse would be ridiculed and rejected for lying. And that it might end his friendship with Dawson. Hopefully, there would be a deeper lesson in it that would strengthen his character.

"I don't have any more questions right now," Virgil said. "But let me caution you not to talk to Miss Berne about the case. I do *not* want her to know that you gave me a statement or that you were ever considered a witness in the case. Let her hear the rumor that you made it all up. Understood?"

"Yes, sir. I really am sorry."

"I know you are, Jesse. I'm sorry you're going to feel the thunder from the other kids. I can't protect you from that."

Jesse stood. "I need to go think."

Kate reached over, took his hand, and squeezed it but couldn't think of anything worthwhile to add.

Jesse left the kitchen, and she could hear him running up the staircase.

Virgil exhaled. "You believe him, Kate?"

"You don't?"

"I'm the sheriff. It's my job to weigh all sides. But he's your son and you know him better than anyone. Do you think he was telling the truth?"

"I think so, Virgil. But then, I never doubted him before. I'm as floored as you are that he recanted."

Virgil seemed to stare at nothing. "Keep a close eye on him. I want to know if you see any red flag that suggests he might not be telling us everything."

"What do you mean?"

"It's possible someone is leaning on Jesse to back off."

"You mean threatening him?"

"I admit it's unlikely that a middle school rumor has spread to the person who drowned Dixie Berne, if indeed she even died at the hand of someone else. But we can't rule it out. That could explain Jesse's recanting his story."

"Or he simply had a guilty conscience," Kate said, "and had to get it off his chest."

Virgil stood. "That too. It's going to be a tough go for him now. Kids that age show no mercy."

"Maybe I should put him in private school."

"You could, but I don't think it will solve anything. The rumor will follow him, and the fact that he changed schools will add fuel to the fire and make it look like he's hiding something. Perhaps you should let it run its course rather than try to rescue him from the consequences."

Kate bit her lip. "The mother side of me wants to protect him. But if Micah were here, he would tell me to let Jesse learn from his mistake."

"Having raised three boys myself, I would agree. I just want to make sure that Jesse's doing this of his own accord, and not because he's being muscled into backing off."

"I don't see how that's possible," Kate said.

"It probably isn't. But just as a precaution, pay attention. Let me know if you see any red flags."

"How would I even know what to look for, Virgil? I imagine Jesse's going to be withdrawn and a little depressed because he's disappointed in himself for letting us down and because of the rejection he's going to face at school."

"I know. Just do what you can to stay on top of it. If anything doesn't feel right, I need to know about it."

Kate walked Virgil to the front door and waited until he drove off, dismissing the heaviness that hadn't yet dissipated. Jesse was going to pay a high price for having lied. But at least now he wasn't in danger.

CHAPTER 17

Virgil stood at the window in his office and looked out beyond the courthouse lawn and row of shops across the street to the shadowy hills of the Ozark Mountains. The sky off to the west was blazing pink as Wednesday's sun bid farewell. How he loved Foggy Ridge. He was an Arkansas boy to the core. His love for this community and its residents went way beyond the job.

A knock on the door broke his concentration.

"Come in."

Kevin walked in his office, followed by Billy Gene and Jason.

"Sit down, gentlemen," Virgil said. "Looks like we just lost our witness."

The two deputies sat at the conference table, and Virgil took a seat across from them and next to Kevin, his fingers laced in front of him, and told them every detail of his conversation with Jesse and with Kate.

Kevin sat back in his chair, his arms folded across his chest. "That's just great. Without the kid's statement, Dixie Berne's DNA on the Kleenex won't be enough to suggest she was murdered. We can't even get a definitive make on the tires from the tread-mark impression."

"That pretty much blows our entire case," Jason said.

Billy Gene raised his eyebrows. "Yep."

"Not so fast," Virgil said. "It remains to be seen whether Jesse's telling the truth about having made up the story, but the odds are off the chart that the victim's DNA was found on the exact riverbank that Jesse named in his recorded statement."

"So we go forward with the murder investigation?" Kevin said.

Virgil nodded. "Sure we do. Even without Jesse's testimony, the fact remains that the victim's jewelry was missing, and it's near impossible for her to have gotten to the river by herself. We're on to something. We need to keep digging. And let's continue to keep Jesse's statement just between us."

Kate watched Jesse pick at his mashed potatoes for quite some time, seemingly oblivious to everyone else around the dinner table.

"Earth to Jesse," Hawk said. "Why are you moping around? No one here is giving you a hard time."

Kate flashed Hawk a scolding look. He knew better than to allude to Jesse's dilemma with Riley sitting at the table.

Elliot squeezed Kate's hand. "Riley, how about you and I going into the living room and review your spelling words?"

"Yay!" She jumped up from the table. "I'll go get my list."

Kate smiled at Elliot, ever amazed at his ability to read her.

As soon as Elliot followed Riley out of the dining room, Hawk spoke up. "I think we need to get this out in the open," he said.

Kate nodded. "All right. But remember, your brother has already punished himself ten times over."

"I don't want to punish him." Hawk turned to Jesse. "I'm just trying to understand how you could lie about something this important."

Jesse shrugged. "I just did, *okay*?"

"No, it's not okay." Hawk's voice went up an octave. "Do you realize how worried Mama was that you might end up having to testify in a murder case?"

"I said I was sorry."

"He can't go back and undo it," Abby said. "How about a little grace?"

Grandpa Buck nodded. "I'm for that."

"So am I," Kate said.

Hawk wiped his mouth with a napkin and stood. "Just don't pull something like this again, little brother. Your family may forgive you, but your friends won't. And just for the record, I think Dawson was a real jerk for blabbing it in the first place. He may be a football star, but he sure has a lot to learn about being a friend."

"Dawson thought he was helping me get accepted by his teammates," Jesse said. "He didn't mean for this to happen."

"Maybe playing football has given him pigskin for *brains*."

"Hawk, that's enough," Kate said. "What we need to do now is help Jesse deal with the consequences. I have a feeling it's going to be a rough couple weeks."

⚜

Jesse shut the door to his room and tossed his backpack on the bed. A piece of what appeared to be white computer paper fell on the floor. He picked it up and unfolded it. The words gave him chill bumps: *It's up to you. I'm watching.*

Jesse shuddered, remembering these as the words his attacker had said just before he left Jesse clinging to a tree trunk, gasping for air.

He reached in the small pocket of his backpack and pulled out his cell phone. He looked up Dawson's home phone and keyed in the numbers.

"Hello."

"Mrs. Foster; it's Jesse. May I speak to Dawson, please?"

Mrs. Foster was quiet for several seconds. "He's doin' his homework. You know he can't talk until he's done."

"Yes, ma'am, but I *really* need to speak with him now. It's important. I promise it'll only take a couple minutes."

Mrs. Foster exhaled into the receiver. "I heard about what happened at school, Jesse. Dawson told me everything. I'm really sorry."

"Thanks. Me too. So can I talk with him?"

"Five minutes?"

"Yes, ma'am."

"All right. I'm going to hold you to it. I'll get him."

Jesse's heart pounded. Could he sound convincing? He heard voices and then footsteps getting closer.

"Hey, man. S'up?" Dawson said. "Can't believe Mom's lettin' me talk. She stuck my cell phone in her dresser drawer till my homework's done."

"I figured. That's why I called the house," Jesse said. "I–I need to tell you something. You'll probably be mad."

"Tell me you're not backin' out of Friday night. 'Cause I gotta tell you, that's a really bad idea."

"It's worse than that." Jesse breathed in, then exhaled. This was it. Once he said it, his life would be forever changed. "Dawz, I made up the story about being a witness. None of it's true."

"You better be jokin'."

"I'm not. I met with the sheriff this afternoon and told him the truth. My family too. I need you to tell the team."

"What am I supposed to say? I vouched for you, man."

"Just tell them the truth."

"I can't. I made you out to be some kinda celebrity."

"Only I'm not."

"You know what's gonna happen if I tell them you lied: they'll make you pay. Why don't you just leave it alone?"

"I can't," Jesse said. "It'll be in the news, and I'll keep getting asked about it. I'm not lying anymore."

"It's social suicide. No one'll dare be friends with you."

"I know. Neither will you."

Several seconds of dead air passed, and then Dawson said, "Maybe I can fix things with the team."

"You can't."

Jesse heard Mrs. Foster's voice in the background.

"You better go. Good-bye, Dawz." Jesse pressed the disconnect button and dropped the cell phone on his bed. He lay on his back, his hands clasped behind his head, feeling the same kind of aching void he felt when Riley and his dad were missing. At least now his family would not be hurt. It was a sacrifice he was willing to make.

A tear trickled down one side of Jesse's face and then the other. He rolled over and buried his face in a pillow and let his pain turn to sobs, carefully muffled from the loved ones he was determined to protect.

God, I've made a mess of everything. Show me what to do. Keep my family safe.

❧

Liam gave up trying to sleep. He put on his jacket and went outside to the patio and sat in a lounger. He filled his lungs with the crisp autumn air.

His mother's attorney had called earlier and told Colleen that, maybe as early as next week, he would have the distribution checks ready. Liam could hardly wait to get a check for his share. He would finally be free of credit-card debt. Free of the chicken plant. Able to get his own place. And to start his handyman business. Everything was riding on the Cummings kid doing what he was told.

How disappointed and disheartened Liam's mother would be if she could see her son now. If she knew that, in his desperation to get her money, he'd been willing to resort to mafia-like tactics to silence a young boy who knew the truth about her drowning.

Liam pulled his jacket collar up around his neck.

How long before the kid figured out who he was? The thoughts that ran through his mind were disturbing. He needed to calm down.

Let the kid recant his story with his friends and family. And most of all, the sheriff.

Liam shuddered, then sprang to his feet and began pacing in front of the patio grill. Threatening the boy might have bought his silence, but it couldn't erase what he'd seen.

❦

Kate nestled with Elliot on the porch swing, a quilt wrapped around them, the night sky black velvet and diamonds, the only sound the hooting of a barred owl.

"It's late. I should go home and let you get some sleep," Elliot said. "But I hate to move when everything's so perfect."

"I don't want you to move." Kate nestled closer. "You have such a calming effect on me. Nothing seems to rattle you."

"Only because I let the Lord take care of things."

"I haven't mastered that yet," Kate said. "Maybe it will rub off."

Elliot smiled. "As easy as that sounds, we both know that not worrying is a choice. And it takes practice."

"Well, heaven knows, I have plenty to practice on. At least I can stop worrying that Jesse's going to end up in the middle of a murder trial."

"He didn't seem as relieved as I would have expected," Elliot said. "It must have been a huge burden lifted from him after he admitted he lied about witnessing the drowning."

"I think he's feeling as much remorse as he is relief. It's not like Jesse to be untruthful."

"Adolescence can be a crazy, mixed-up time," Elliot said. "But Jesse's a great kid with more character than most twelve-year-olds I know. He'll come out of this stronger."

"I doubt he'll confide in me," Kate said, "when the boys at school give him a hard time. He's much more likely to open up with you."

"I'll be there. That goes without saying."

"You've always been there for us. Even when you had nothing to gain. Honestly, Elliot, you're the most selfless person I've ever known." Kate smiled. She knew a compliment like that would leave him speechless.

A brisk breeze seemed to stir out of nowhere.

"How about warming me up before you leave?" she said playfully. "It's freezing out here."

"Let me see what I can do about that."

Elliot slipped his arm around her and tilted her chin, the warmth of his lips radiating through her. But even the thrill of his kiss didn't distract her entirely from the irrational heaviness that had settled over her since Jesse's confession earlier. Maybe it was just a combination of her disappointment in him and her uneasiness about the consequences he was facing that was still weighing her down.

Elliot put his hands on her cheeks, then slowly, reluctantly ended the kiss. "Okay, Cinderella. I guess I should leave before you turn into a pumpkin."

He stood and pulled her to her feet, then kissed her forehead. "Get some rest. Try not to worry about Jesse. Let's take it a day at a time. Things will work out. They always do."

Kate stood on the porch and waved as Elliot pulled out of the driveway. She then went inside, missing him and wishing he could have stayed. No matter how hard she fought it, it was becoming apparent to her that she no longer felt complete without him. Perhaps when things normalized again, she would put aside her irrational fear of commitment and start talking about marriage.

Kate walked across the living room and into her bedroom, all too aware that the heaviness still hadn't left her. Maybe after a good night's sleep she would be able to let go of what didn't come to pass and just help her son deal with the consequences of his lie.

CHAPTER 18

Jesse opened his eyes and saw only darkness, and realized he had cried himself to sleep. He rolled out of bed and turned on his lamp, the wind outside whistling eerily, probably ushering in the predicted cold front Grandpa Buck had mentioned at dinner.

Jesse glanced at the clock. Five thirty. His gut tightened, knowing that in thirty minutes his mother would knock on his door and he would have to get ready for school. He could deal with the ridicule that awaited him, knowing that pretending to have lied was the only way to protect his family. But now he had no close friend. No ally. No one to stand with him. He couldn't imagine life without Dawson. They had been friends since the first day of kindergarten.

All through grade school Jesse and Dawson were inseparable. Anytime Jesse was at Dawson's house, Mrs. Foster treated him as if he were part of their family. During the years Jesse's mother had been cloaked in sadness, yearning for Daddy and Riley Jo to come back, Dawson's home had been a haven from the sadness. Jesse wasn't just losing Dawson as a friend, but also losing an entire extended family that he had grown to love.

Jesse blinked to clear his eyes and to make his mind change the subject. It was going to be rough at school. It was important to remember why he had told Dawson that he'd lied about being a witness. This was all about protecting those he loved. The sacrifice was not too great.

Jesse got down on his knees on the side of the bed and bowed his head.

Lord, even though I feel alone, I know I'm really not. You're there all the time. I'm sorry I had to change my story and lie. I know lying is wrong, but I didn't see any other choice. Don't let that man hurt us. You helped Abby, Jay, and Riley through much worse trouble than this. Keep us safe, and help me through this day at school. In Jesus's Name. Amen.

Jesse stood and sat on the side of the bed. He opened the drawer in the nightstand and pulled out a snapshot of Dawson and him taken after the first football game of the season. He was proud of Dawson's athletic ability and was glad he had decided to go out for football, even though it was the first time either of them had gotten involved in a major school activity without the other. Jesse learned to do some things without Dawson, but he had counted on the routine going back to normal after Thanksgiving, when football season was over. But this was the new normal.

It wouldn't be much fun shooting baskets alone, or playing video games at Milner's Drug Store, or exploring the hills for arrowheads and fossils. And he could forget their annual tradition of flooding Dawson's backyard and turning it into an ice-skating rink over Christmas break.

He had better get used to doing things by himself. Bull Hanson would make sure no one hung out with him ever again. He might as well be a hermit!

Jesse hated that the killer knew who he was. And where he lived. And that he didn't have a clear picture in his mind of what the guy looked like. Was the man a thief as some people suggested? A real creep who saw a poor old lady with Alzheimer's wandering alone and took advantage of her? Perhaps a cold-blooded killer who wouldn't think twice about making good on his threat to kill everyone in Jesse's family?

Jesse combed his hands through his hair. None of this seemed real. Maybe once the sheriff decided to drop the murder investigation, the man would go away forever.

Regardless, life as he had known it was over. If only he'd kept his promise to the sheriff.

Kate sat with her dad at a table next to the glass wall at Flutter's Café, watching the morning mist that had settled over Beaver Lake.

"That granddaughter of mine is somethin'," Buck said. "The way she can juggle her classes at the junior college after putting in a hard morning here. Reminds me of you."

Kate looked over at her older daughter, who looked so grown up and confident it was hard to believe she was only eighteen. "Abby's doing an amazing job of orchestrating the morning shift while Savannah's on vacation. But we're nothing alike. Abby's more of a dreamer—like Mom was. And Micah."

"You're more alike than you are different, Kate. And watching Abby is like watching you at eighteen. Long auburn hair. Smile that'd stop a clock. You're still a fine-lookin' woman. I promise you Elliot thinks so."

Kate smiled, remembering how nice it was snuggling with Elliot on the porch swing.

"You ever gonna get serious about settlin' down again?" Her dad held her gaze.

Nothing like getting right to the point. "Well, not this morning." Kate took a sip of coffee and glanced at her watch. "I hope Jesse will be all right. I can only imagine what Dawson's friends will do when they find out he lied."

"Don't you go worrying about Jesse," Buck said. "The principal told you she's got a few teachers keeping an eye on him."

"They can't watch him every second."

Her father stroked his white mustache. "Well, Jesse's got angels lookin' out for him, and plenty of prayer to back that up."

"I'm disappointed that Jesse lied," Kate said. "But just between you and me, I'm almost grateful too. I know that sounds awful, but at least now I can stop worrying that he's going to get enmeshed in a murder trial."

The front door opened and closed, and Kate watched Titus Jackson come into Flutter's.

"There's your breakfast buddy." Kate got up and kissed her dad on the top of his head. "I need to get over to the office."

"Try not to worry about young Jesse," Buck said. "The Lord'll use this to build his character."

Kate smiled wryly. "I've about had it with character building for a while."

Virgil sat at his desk and looked out the window at employees arriving at the courthouse, all bundled up in their warm coats and hats.

Miguel Perez's blue-and-yellow food cart was conspicuously absent from the sidewalk at Main and Commerce, though it was too early in the season for him to close up shop. Mother Nature was merely toying with them. Once the cold front moved on, the mild weather would return, drawing thousands of tourists to the exquisite display of fall colors that would soon transform the landscape.

Virgil's intercom buzzed. "Sheriff Granger here ..."

"You about ready for us?" Kevin said.

"Yeah, come on."

Virgil heard heels clicking on the marble floor, and stood just as Kevin, Billy Gene, and Jason filed into his office and sat at the conference table.

Kevin held up a file. "Great news. The lab found DNA on a wad of Dubble Bubble chewing gum collected on the riverbank. Doesn't match anyone's in the system. But according to the lab, it'd been exposed to the elements about the same length of time as the Kleenex. Both had been out there less than forty-eight hours. Everything else put into evidence was far more degraded. Seems significant, since the area appeared somewhat secluded and relatively free of trash. The odds are much higher that these two pieces of evidence are related than they're not."

Virgil pulled out a chair, sat at the table, and perused the report. "Now all we need is a suspect whose DNA matches."

"Looks like we're back in the game," Jason said.

Virgil sat staring at his hands. "Gentlemen, I wish I had a better feeling about Jesse. I hardly slept last night. Every time I started to drift off, I saw Jesse's scratched-up face. Someone's threatening that boy. I feel it in my gut. He told me that he slipped on gravel and fell, but I'm not buying it. The knees of his jeans weren't scraped or torn, and the palms of his hands didn't have a scratch. I've known Jesse since he was five, back when I worked the case all the years his dad and sister went missing. I've been a friend to his family and have had many occasions to observe Jesse at various stages of development. I think he was telling the truth when I recorded his statement. I'm not sure yet why he recanted, but I'm not willing to gamble with his safety.

"Therefore, starting tomorrow morning, I want Billy Gene and Jason in plain clothes and an unmarked car. You need to have Jesse Cummings in your sight from the time he leaves home to catch the school bus until he's in for the evening. Obviously, you can't have eyes on him when he's inside the school, but the principal has several teachers watching him throughout the day. Don't hesitate to blow your cover, should the need arise to protect him. But otherwise, I want you to stay invisible." Virgil leaned forward on his elbows. "Kevin will assign other deputies to work the burglary cases. I want you two focused on this special assignment."

Billy Gene nodded. "How long do you reckon we'll need to keep tabs on the boy, Sheriff?"

"Until I'm convinced he's not in danger. And," Virgil added, "this will be a covert operation known only to the four of us—and Kate Cummings. I've arranged to have a meeting with her this afternoon. She needs to know what we're doing, but Jesse doesn't.

"Needless to say, there's no one in the department that I trust more than you three. I'm counting on you to get this done right and completely off the radar. Any questions? … Okay then." Virgil rose to his feet. "Let's get this done."

⁂

Liam stood in the assembly line at the poultry plant, deboning chicken wings as fast as they passed in front of him, his mind reliving yesterday's surreal encounter with the one person who had the power to wreck his life. Had his threat worked? Was Jesse Cummings scared enough to back off?

Liam regretted that it had come to this, but what else was he supposed to do? He had come too far to fail. His half of the inheritance was almost in his pocket. All he wanted the kid to do was forget what he had seen and get on with being a kid.

You're better than this. His dad's voice echoed in his head. That's what he had always said anytime Liam disappointed him. Just what he needed: a guilt trip from the grave. He was not a monster. Killing his mother was merciful. And no matter how cruel his actions might seem to some, he wasn't going to sit back and let some middle school kid point a finger at him so he could spend the rest of his life behind bars.

"I didn't expect to see *you* today." His supervisor's voice behind him startled him.

"I'm feeling better," Liam said. "Not a hundred percent, but well enough to do my job."

"Stay focused," Marilyn said. "I don't want you cutting off a finger."

Of course she didn't. Might mess up her precious safety record. For almost thirty years, he'd hated everything about this place, especially the smell of it. When he got his money, he'd finally be able to pay off his credit cards, give notice at the plant, and go into business for himself. He could fix almost anything, and handymen were high in demand. It would be so great to work for himself and not punch a time clock or be under the gun to work faster so his already well-paid supervisor could get a big bonus.

He was close to finally getting the financial millstone off his back. That's what his mom would have wanted. All he had to do now was to make sure Jesse Cummings kept his mouth shut.

CHAPTER 19

Jesse sat at one end of a table in the cafeteria, two empty spaces between him and some giggly sixth-grade girls who whispered among themselves and seemed oblivious to his fallen social standing.

Dawson sat on the other side of the room, stealing an occasional glance at Jesse. Though Dawson joined in the bursts of laughter coming from Bull Hanson and the others seated at his table, Jesse knew his heart wasn't in it. But that was little comfort. He and Dawson were done. Nothing could change that now.

Bull rose to his feet, a smug grin on his face. He said something that evoked another round of laughter, then turned and walked in Jesse's direction.

Jesse wanted to run, but he felt as if his behind were glued to the chair.

Bull stopped at Jesse's end of the table, his muscular arms folded, his shaved head tilted the way it always was anytime he was about to show off for his buddies. "So, Jesse"—Bull reached down and took the plastic bag of Oreos out of Jesse's lunch pack and put it in his own pocket—"how come you're eating with sixth-grade girls? Why aren't you having lunch with your friends? Oops. That's right, you don't *have* any friends."

Jesse didn't say anything. He just wanted Bull to go away.

"Bet you thought you were really clever," Bull said, "letting us believe you were a big-shot witness in a murder case. *Humongous* mistake. Now you're pond scum. Worse than pond scum. You're nothing. Zero. Zippo." Bull leaned over, his palms flat on the table. "You don't exist. Not to me"—Bull made a sweeping motion with his hand—"or any of *them*."

Jesse felt the heat scalding his cheeks in a moment of pin-drop stillness that eventually was interrupted by another round of laughter. He could almost feel the stares. He wanted to shout at the top of his lungs that he wasn't a liar, that he was protecting his family. And that he didn't care what Bull thought anyhow. Instead, he sat biting his lip and looking at his hands.

In the next second, Miss Berne was standing next to Bull.

"Mr. Hanson, I suggest you get back to your seat," she said, "before I send you to the principal's office."

Bull took a step back. "You, of all people, should realize what a loser he is."

"And you, mister, should know that intimidating a fellow student is grounds for suspension. I don't care if you are the star quarterback. Now go back to your seat."

"Yes, ma'am." Bull shot Jesse a this-isn't-over look and strutted back to his seat and the snickering faces of his peer group.

Miss Berne stood there, holding Jesse's gaze. She looked as if she wanted to say something, but didn't. She turned and walked over to

Mr. Jones, the other cafeteria monitor, who didn't seem happy with her. The two of them stepped outside into the hallway.

Jesse glanced over at Dawson, who wasn't laughing.

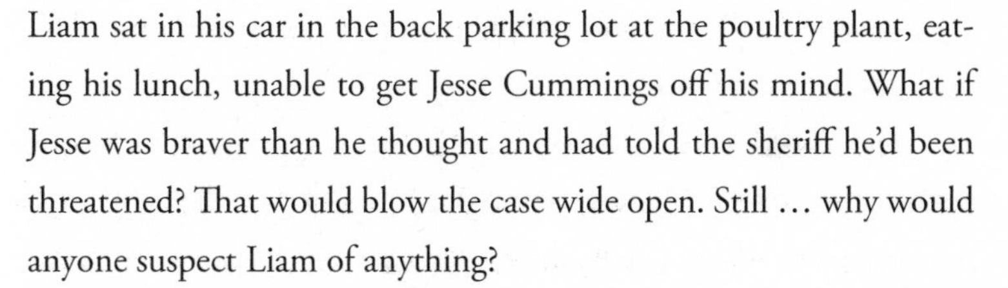

Liam sat in his car in the back parking lot at the poultry plant, eating his lunch, unable to get Jesse Cummings off his mind. What if Jesse was braver than he thought and had told the sheriff he'd been threatened? That would blow the case wide open. Still … why would anyone suspect Liam of anything?

His cell phone rang. He glanced at the screen, then put it to his ear. "Hey, Colleen."

"You'll never guess what just happened," Colleen said. "I got summoned to Ruth Arnold's office and chewed out royally—all because I did my job. I was a cafeteria monitor today and saw Bull Hanson, our football captain, giving Jesse Cummings a hard time. I intervened and sent Bull back to his table. I didn't say a word to Jesse. Not one word. But Gerald Jones, the other cafeteria monitor, was furious that I didn't let him handle it, so he reported me."

"Why *didn't* you let him handle it? You were told to stay away from Jesse."

"Whose side are you on?" Colleen snapped.

"It was just a question." Liam stuffed a potato chip into his mouth. "I'm sorry it happened, but Arnold did tell you to steer clear of Jesse."

"Well, what I called to tell you is that it's a moot point now because—"

"Jesse recanted?"

There was a long pause.

"How did you know that?" Colleen said.

Liam's heart skipped a beat. How could he have blurted that out without thinking? "Lucky guess. But I've said all along that he made it up to impress his peers."

"Well, you were right. According to Mrs. Arnold, it's all over the school now that Jesse called his friend Dawson last night and recanted the story, said every word of it was made up. He apologized to Dawson for lying and asked him to tell the team. Poor Jesse. Those boys let him in their inner circle, something that never happens. They won't let him live it down anytime soon. Bull Hanson can be mean, even without a reason."

Yes! Liam pumped his fist. "I imagine Bull felt foolish for believing him."

"Probably. I know I did."

"So why did the principal chew you out for helping Jesse, if she knew he'd recanted his story?"

"All she would say was that it didn't change the fact that I'm not to communicate with Jesse. I really should call the sheriff and see what he thinks about Jesse changing his story."

"He probably thinks that, without a witness, he doesn't have a murder case."

Colleen sighed into the receiver. "I don't believe that. Mom *was* murdered. I think Sheriff Granger believes it too."

Liam knew better than to argue with her. Colleen was like a pit bull. Once she made up her mind about something, she wasn't about to let go of it.

"Well, at least Jesse came clean. I wouldn't want the sheriff going forward with false expectations."

"I just can't figure out why Jesse would tell his peers that he lied," Colleen said. "He had to know the punishment he would take from Bull and his cocky friends."

"Maybe it was even worse living with a guilty conscience."

"Worse than being a social outcast?" Colleen said. "It makes more sense to me that someone pressured him into denying what he saw."

Liam's heart leapt. "That's completely baseless."

"Maybe. But Jesse's either exceptionally brave or exceptionally scared."

"Colleen, listen to me ... You've got to stop this nonsense. You're reading into things without a single fact. You're going to drive us both nuts."

"Our mother was murdered, Liam. Whether Jesse witnessed it or not. And even if the sheriff doesn't have any conclusive evidence, I will never be at peace until I know the truth."

"Never is a long time," Liam said.

"Well, I'm a long way from just letting it go. Jesse's hiding something. You should've seen the way he looked at me."

Liam only half listened to her rambling after that. He knew Colleen well enough to know that she would figure out a way to confront Jesse and find out for herself if she believed he had seen something. He had to make sure that Jesse stuck to his denial.

⁂

Virgil sat at his desk, reviewing everything they had on the Dixie Berne case. He listened again to the interview he'd had with Jesse Cummings. Nothing about Jesse's voice gave a hint of dishonesty. And what were the odds that Jesse had made up the story, when later, the victim's DNA was found on the riverbank next to where he indicated he'd seen a man and woman wading in the water?

His administrative assistant's voice came over the intercom. "Sheriff, Mrs. Cummings has arrived."

"Great. Bring her to my office."

"Yes, sir."

A minute later, Kate Cummings knocked on his open door.

"Come in." Virgil stood and went over to greet her. "I'm glad it worked out for you to come by. Saved me a ride up the mountain. Let's sit here at the conference table. Would you like something to drink?"

"No, I'm good." Kate sat and folded her hands on the table. "What's on your mind, Virgil?"

Virgil pulled out a chair and sat facing her. "I'm having a hard time believing that Jesse initially lied about having seen the man and woman wading in the river."

"Why?" Kate said. "Do you realize what it cost him to admit to me, to you, to his family and friends that he lied about being an eyewitness?"

Virgil studied Kate's face. "If I were twelve, I might admit to my parents and even the sheriff that I made up the story. But I just don't see myself telling my middle school peers."

"He didn't, exactly. Jesse called Dawson last night and told him the truth. He asked Dawson to tell the others. But the painful consequences will be the same."

Virgil picked up a pencil and twirled it in his fingers. "The thing is, I went back for a third time and listened to the recorded interview I had with Jesse, and nothing in my mind has changed. I studied him the entire time I did the interview and never picked up any indication that he was making it up. I have a lot of experience in spotting inconsistencies. His story totally fits with our investigation into Dixie Berne's death."

"Must be coincidence," Kate said. "I just don't believe Jesse would lie to me *again* and say he made it up if he didn't."

Virgil tented his fingers. "He might, if someone threatened him. Told him to keep his mouth shut."

Kate's face went blank. "You hinted at that once before. I know my own son. It took a lot of courage for him to tell me he made it all up. Jesse's usually a truthful kid, and this really bothered his conscience."

"I hope you're right," Virgil said. "But I'm not convinced. In order to get those nasty scratches on his face, Jesse would have to have fallen headlong on the ground. Neither the knees of his jeans nor the palms of his hands had a mark on them. But Jesse's quick recanting of his story is enough cause for suspicion."

"Meaning what?"

"Just that, until I'm convinced that Jesse isn't being coerced into silence, I want to keep a close eye on him." Virgil leaned forward on his elbows. "I want a couple of my deputies in plain clothes covertly watching him. That way we will see if someone approaches him."

"You're really that concerned?" Kate arched her eyebrows.

"I just want to be sure. And for now, that seems like the best approach. It's important that Jesse not be aware that he's being watched. I want him to act naturally."

Kate tapped the table with her fingers, her eyebrows furrowed. "I can't believe another of my children could be in danger. How much can happen to one family?"

"Maybe nothing's happening," Virgil said. "But we need to be sure. Remember, don't say anything about this to Jesse or anyone in the family. I'll have someone in place when the bus picks him up tomorrow morning. My deputies will keep tabs on him from the time he leaves for school until he is home for the evening. Mrs. Arnold has a number of teachers watching him when he's inside the school. And you need to make sure he doesn't leave the house by himself."

Kate sighed. "You want me to check the emails on his computer and text messages on his phone?"

"Sure, couldn't hurt," Virgil said, "though anyone threatening him would probably be smart enough not to leave a trail."

Liam knocked on his supervisor's door.

Marilyn looked up. "What is it, Liam? Come in."

"I was wondering if you'd allow me to leave an hour early to keep an appointment and let me work through my lunch hour tomorrow to make up the time. Joe Spalding says he's got my back, if I need to cut out early."

"All right. As long as you make up the time."

"Thanks. We're finally getting my mother's estate settled and I need to sign some papers."

Marilyn waved her hand as if to shoosh him. "See you tomorrow."

Liam clocked out and hurried to his car. He knew what he had to do.

CHAPTER 20

Jesse stepped off the school bus behind the Moyer twins. The girls walked down Angel View Road and looked over their shoulders at him, giggling the way girls often do when they're enjoying petty gossip. It didn't matter much what they thought of him. But getting the cold shoulder from all the seventh-grade boys had been hard to take.

He wondered what Miss Berne had been thinking after she had come to his rescue in the cafeteria and stood staring at him. Had he been able to hide his guilt? How he wished he could have told her the truth. Though it might be easier for her to get over her mother's death if she believed the drowning was an accident.

Jesse hooked his thumbs on the straps of his backpack and headed up Angel View Road. The pale-blue sky was dotted with interesting cloud puffs of all sizes. He relished the scent of pine, then filled his lungs with crisp mountain air, glad for the beginning of his favorite season, but unable to shake the heaviness in his gut that reminded him that Dawson would not be around to share his adventures. At least he'd done what the killer demanded. His family was safe now.

A calico cat stood at the tree line, meowing loudly. Jesse smiled and took off his backpack. He went over to the cat and knelt, holding out his arms until she came to him.

"Chestnut, what are you doing out here? Are you lost?" Jesse gently stroked the cat, which had had two litters of kittens, including his own cat, Halo. Should he leave her here or try carrying her to the Lamberts' house, which was on his way?

A second later, he felt an arm clamped around his neck, cutting off his air. Someone forced him into the woods.

"Don't fight me and I'll let you breathe," said an all-too-familiar voice. "I'm going to let go now. Don't turn around. And if you try to move or call for help, I'll strangle the life out of you. Got it?"

Jesse nodded.

The man loosened his grip, and Jesse gasped and coughed until he could finally breathe normally.

"Did you tell your mother you lied?" the man said.

Jesse blew out a breath that ended with a barely audible "Yes."

"What about the sheriff?"

"Him too," Jesse said.

"Then why is he still talking to the media like it was a murder?"

"I don't know," Jesse insisted. "I told all my friends too. No one believes I'm a witness anymore."

"What about Miss Berne? What have you said to her?"

"Nothing. I'm not allowed to talk to her."

"She's convinced you know something."

"I don't! I didn't see anything."

The man thumped Jesse on the back of his head. "Now *that's* the spirit."

"No, I mean it. I never saw your face. Honest. You have nothing to worry about."

"Nice try, kid. But if I saw you, you saw me. You're the only thing that stands between me and a bright future—and quitting my stinking job. Do you understand what I'm saying?"

He didn't. But he nodded in agreement, his heart banging against his chest.

"I'm watching your every move. If you even *think* about double-crossing me, I'll start picking off your family like a lion stalking wildebeests. They'll die one by one. It won't be pretty, and it'll be your fault. Their blood will be on *your* conscience. I don't have one. Now lay facedown and put your hands behind your head."

Jesse did as he was told, aware of pine needles sticking his cheeks, and the guy's boot pushing a meowing Chestnut out of the way.

"Slowly count to two hundred and then run home and don't look back. Tell *anyone* about this, and your family dies. You won't get another warning."

Jesse lay shaking on the forest floor, his hands clasped behind his head, Chestnut rubbing against his side.

The instant he finished counting, he jumped up, grabbed his backpack, and ran toward Angel View Lodge, his mind racing faster than his pulse.

Jesse wondered if he was doing the right thing by handling this by himself. Should he tell the sheriff he was being threatened? Could he trust Sheriff Granger to protect his family from a man he couldn't even describe? All he was sure of was the guy's voice. It could be anyone.

Virgil stood with Kevin outside the front entrance of the courthouse, holding a late-afternoon press conference for persistent reporters.

"As I stated earlier," Virgil said, "there is an ongoing investigation into Dixie Berne's death. At this time, we're treating it as a murder investigation."

"Do you have a witness?" said Sarah Halloran, a seasoned reporter for the local TV station.

"I'm not going to comment on that while we're still investigating," Virgil replied.

"Can you at least confirm that a student at Foggy Ridge Middle School claims that he witnessed the drowning?"

Virgil kept his voice sure and even. "Since you're on top of this rumor, Sarah, I'm sure you know the student recanted that claim and admitted to lying. So let's move on."

A bearded man raised his hand. "Do you have any suspects?"

"We haven't made an arrest," Virgil said, "but that's all I'm going to say right now."

"Have you determined the exact location of the drowning?" Sarah scribbled something on her notepad.

"It's guesswork at this stage," Virgil said. "We have thoroughly combed the banks of the Sure Foot for two hundred yards upstream from where we discovered the body."

"Did that uncover any evidence?" said a balding man in thick glasses.

Virgil pursed his lips. "I'm not going to comment on what we might or might not have in evidence."

"Sheriff, what *can* you tell us?" said an attractive redheaded woman in a navy dress. "You don't seem to have answers to any of our questions. Our citizens could be at risk if a killer is on the loose."

Virgil forced a smile. Why did the media play this game when they knew he couldn't give them what they wanted? "I agreed to meet with you because I want you to know my department is serious about getting to the bottom of this. There is only so much I can comment on at this stage, but let's be clear: every effort is being made to uncover details of what happened in this case. It continues to be an active murder investigation. I ask you to be patient with the process and remember it takes time for facts to unfold and additional time for us to put it all together. I'll be back when I can tell you more. Thank you."

Virgil turned and went inside the courthouse and made a right down the first corridor, Kevin keeping stride with him, their heels clicking on the shiny marble floor.

"That was short and sweet," Kevin said. "Think they believed the kid recanted?"

"I hope so."

"I don't know what to think," Kevin said.

Virgil lifted his Stetson and wiped his forehead. "Jesse knows the pain and grief a family goes through when a loved one goes missing and is found dead. I just don't see him making this up. I have to consider that he recanted because he was threatened."

"I'm not so sure," Kevin said. "I can see a middle school kid doing something like that to impress his peers, especially the star players on a winning football team."

"You don't know Jesse like I do."

"Well, his mother knows him better than anyone," Kevin said. "She believes him."

"That's because Kate doesn't want Jesse pulled into a murder case. She *wants* to believe he made it up. She can't be objective."

Kevin was quiet, which usually meant he had his own opinion. Finally, he said, "At least she's on board with our covert operation. I hope it's not a waste of time and manpower."

Virgil stopped and held his gaze on Kevin. "What aren't you saying?"

Kevin seemed trapped in a long pause. Finally he turned to Virgil. "May I speak freely?"

"You know you can."

"I'm going to go out on a limb here and ask you something, just friend to friend. You don't have to answer me, Virgil, but be honest with yourself. Would you be going to this extreme to protect Jesse if he wasn't Kate's son?"

Jesse stopped running when he reached the top of the hill. He leaned over and grabbed his knees, trying to catch his breath. He looked down Angel View Road and didn't see anyone. At least he was safe for now. The cawing of a crow echoed through the trees and seemed almost like an omen. Creepy.

He waited until his pulse slowed, then stood up straight and walked the last fifty yards to the two-story log house his dad had built. He bounded up the front steps to the long porch, where Grandpa Buck sat on the wooden swing, nibbling sunflower seeds.

"Hey, Grandpa."

"Hey yourself. Been prayin' for you off and on all day. How'd you do?"

Jesse shrugged. "Okay, I guess. As okay as a guy can when he doesn't have any friends. But I already knew Bull would make sure no one talked to me."

"That might change with time," his grandpa said. "Bull will probably lose interest after a while."

"No, he won't. Nobody makes Bull Hanson feel stupid and gets away with it. I guess that's part of the consequences. It's my own fault for lying."

"Give yourself some credit for tellin' the truth, boy. Wasn't easy admitting you lied. It cost you plenty."

If you only knew! Jesse studied his grandfather's kind face. "Thanks for saying that."

"Feel better?"

"Not yet. But I'll think about what you said."

"Good. And don't forget who it is you belong to when you walk into that school. Bull may be a football hero, but you're the son of a King."

"I'm not sure Bull'd be impressed," Jesse said.

"But are you? That's what counts. It's really somethin' to belong to *the* royal family." Buck winked.

Jesse smiled despite his mood. "I never thought of it like that."

"Your Father, the King, is just waitin' for you to ask Him for help."

"I'm pretty sure He's mad at me for getting myself into this mess."

"I doubt that," Buck said. "But He might be disappointed unless you trust Him to help you out of it."

"I'm not sure there *is* a way out of it." *Any of it!*

"He can still help you. Don't think you're all by yourself just because you made a mistake."

Jesse considered his grandfather's words. "How come you always know what to say?"

"I don't always," Buck said. "But this is a no-brainer."

"I guess I do need to remember who I am. Bull makes me feel like a nobody, and I get down on myself. But what hurts most of all is losing Dawson. It's like I've lost a brother."

His grandpa looked over the top of his glasses. "Oh, I wouldn't count Dawson out just yet."

Kate set a plate of cookies on the kitchen table and heard the front door open and close.

A few seconds later, Jesse stood in the doorway.

"I saw you talking to Grandpa." Kate got up and walked over to Jesse. "Want some oatmeal-raisin cookies?"

"Thanks, but I'm not hungry right now. I have homework to do."

"How was school?"

"Not great. None of the guys are speaking to me. I told you they wouldn't."

"It'll pass, honey. Give it time."

"I don't have much choice. I'm going to go do my history report. It's due Monday, and I don't want to have homework this weekend."

"Sure you don't want a cookie?" Kate said. "They're still warm."

"No, thanks."

Kate saw something in Jesse's hair and picked out a clump of pine needles. "How'd you get these?"

"I saw Chestnut at the edge of the woods. I went to get her and tripped over a tree root. At least Mother Nature doesn't laugh at me, even if I am a klutz." Jesse turned and went upstairs.

Kate went back in the kitchen and sat at the table, across from Elliot. "He's upset. Did you see the look on his face?"

"We knew school would be a challenge for a while," Elliot said. "I'll talk to him later, after he's had a chance to be alone with his thoughts."

Kate sighed. "Thanks. He really respects you. He's getting to the age where he needs to hear a male perspective."

"I'm your man," Elliot said, taking Kate's hands in his. "I love Jesse."

"I know. He's crazy about you. They all are. Jesse and Riley don't remember their father and thrive on your attention. They listen to everything you tell them."

Elliot smiled. "I look forward to the day when I officially become their stepdad."

"I'm not sure things would be different than they are now. You're already wonderful with them."

"Thanks, but they don't need a part-time dad." Elliot gently squeezed her hand. "They need to know I'm there for the long haul—no matter what."

Kate didn't say anything.

Elliot tilted her chin. "A few hours from now, I'll go home to an empty house and think of you alone in your bed, wrestling with the pressures of being a single parent."

"I don't handle it alone," Kate said. "You're a lot of support."

Elliot was quiet for a moment. "And I always will be. But, Kate … have you stopped to think about what it's like for me?"

"What do you mean?"

"I've been in love with you for the biggest part of seven years. It's become almost torture for me to go home alone, night after night, especially when I feel like such a part of this family. I *want* you, Kate. Body, mind, and spirit. And I want to share all that I am and all that I have with you."

"Elliot, I—"

He touched her lips with his fingers. "Just let me say it. I've built a relationship with each of your children. I'm there whenever you need me. I've shared Christmases and special events and holidays for years. I run errands, do dishes, babysit, help with homework, help with crises of all kinds. I love this family. I adore *you* and every moment we spend together. So why aren't we together?"

"Other than physical intimacy, what do you think is missing?" she said.

"I happen to think physical intimacy is pretty great, by the way. But that's just part of it. What's missing is the oneness. We're still two. You have your life. I have mine. It should be *our* life. We should grow together and learn to know each other on a deeper level than we do with anyone else. I had that with Pam, and you had it with Micah, so don't pretend you don't know what I mean."

She did know. "Why are you bringing this up now when I'm in the middle of a crisis with Jesse?"

"*We* are in a crisis with Jesse."

"Fair enough, but I can't think about where this relationship is going when I'm preoccupied with his well-being."

"You're hiding, Kate. It's always something. You seem afraid to accept that you could have a bright future with me. I have so much love I want to give you and these kids. Plus, I can offer you financial security. You can keep Angel View Lodge without owing a dime on it."

Kate let go of his hands. "I love you, Elliot. But I won't be pressured into making such a life-changing decision."

"I'm not trying to pressure you, honey. I just want you to know how I feel. I want to share all that I am and all that I have with you. It isn't as though we don't know what it's like to be a family. We've got that down pat. But this aching in my heart is not going to go away until you marry me."

Kate looked into his gentle eyes that were not quite blue and not quite gray, and felt as if he could see into her very soul. She looked away, sure that her face was flushed. "I–I know you're right. Something in me just wants to freeze this stage of my life. I'm afraid to move beyond it."

"Maybe if you'd talk about it, we could figure this out."

"What if marriage changes things?" Kate said, surprised at her own words. "I *know* what we have now is good. But after we're married, the kids might resent you suddenly being the head of the house. At the moment, they adore you. Will they feel that way when your role changes and you help to enforce the rules?"

"Why don't we ask them?" Elliot said. "Hawk and Abby are adults, for all practical purposes. I want to be there for them, but they don't need me the way Jesse and Riley do. We can just explain to the kids that I'm not trying to take their father's place, but that I love them and want to stand in as their dad. And that I'll be watching out for them, just like you do. Kate, they're going to resent me at times. It comes with the territory. The key is making sure they know how much I love them. It's not like I haven't had time to think this through."

Of course you have. Kate felt as if her mouth were stuffed with cotton and her head would explode. How was she supposed to answer him?

"I didn't start this conversation with the intention of putting you on the spot," Elliot said, kissing her hand. "But it's time we *both* got serious about how we want to spend the future. The kids are growing up fast. This family can only be stronger with two parents. And I'm miserable living apart from you. I'm not content with things the way they are."

Riley came into the kitchen and crawled up in Elliot's lap, her arms around his neck. "You said you would help me with my spelling words before dinner."

"So I did. Let me finish talking with your mother, and I'll be right there."

Kate jumped to her feet. "That's okay. You go ahead. I need to fold the laundry."

She forced a smile and gently tugged one of Riley's braids as she brushed past her on the way to the utility room, glad to have her conversation with Elliot interrupted. But there was no escaping the big decision that only she could make. Was she really going to let fear render her incapable of saying yes to the most wonderful man she could ever hope for?

CHAPTER 21

Liam stood in Colleen's garage and tapped the dried mud off his boots, then entered the utility room and strolled nonchalantly into the kitchen, where Colleen was making dinner.

"Something smells terrific," Liam said.

Colleen smiled. "Fried chicken and twice-baked potatoes. Hope you're hungry."

"You kidding? I'm starved."

"Where have you been?" Colleen said.

"What do you mean?"

"I called your cell and left a message and then called the poultry plant. Your supervisor said you had asked to leave an hour early."

"Oh, that." Liam suddenly felt hot, his mind grappling for a believable answer. "I told her we had some papers to sign. The truth is, I just needed to get out of there. I've had it with that place. In fact, after the distributions are made and I've got the money in hand, I'm going to give notice."

Colleen stopped stirring whatever was on the stove and looked up. "You're *quitting*? When did you decide that?"

"I've been thinking about it since Mom died. I think she'd be pleased if I used my inheritance money to go into business for myself."

"Doing what, Liam?"

"I want to start a handyman business. I know how to fix almost anything. I think once word gets out, I'll be busy all the time."

"What if it doesn't pan out?" Colleen said. "Are you really going to throw away a job you've held for nearly thirty years? It's risky to switch jobs at your age."

"That's why I didn't tell you. You're already expecting me to fail."

"I suppose I'm projecting my feelings onto you. I'm too big a coward to make a change like that. There's security in having tenure, and I've learned to focus on the positives and overlook the things I dislike about teaching."

Liam sat at the table. "But I dislike *everything* about working at the poultry plant. My job is monotonous. It doesn't pay enough, and there's no such thing as tenure. Any of us could get caught in a layoff. Standing all day makes my feet hurt. And the stink gives me a headache. I've stayed there because it's a steady job. Now I want to see what I can do on my own. Can't you just be happy for me?"

Colleen sighed. "Of course I can. But I'll never feel comfortable spending Mom's money unless it's to help find whoever killed her."

Liam studied his sister's face. It hurt him to see her so sad. "We've already talked about that. I think you're making a big mistake blowing your inheritance on what will probably be a dead end. I don't think Mom or Dad would want you doing that."

"I have to do what I think is right," Colleen said. "And would you please return my calls when I leave you a message? I needed you to stop and get bread and some of that deli corned beef for your lunch tomorrow. I hate going out after dinner."

"Sorry, I'll go right now, before dinner. Just so you know, I did check my messages when I left work. Then I turned off my phone while I drove around to think. This is a big step. I need to have a plan."

"You're really serious?" Colleen said.

"Very. I'm counting the days until I hold that inheritance check in my hands. If we had to lose Mom, at least I can honor her by bettering myself with the money she left."

"Why am *I* just now finding out about this?" Colleen arched her eyebrows.

"Because I'm just now realizing this is what I want. I haven't told anyone else."

"Well, I'm not spending a penny of that money on myself until I find out who killed our mother—even if I have to pay a private investigator."

"That's just crazy," Liam said, more forcefully than he intended. He softened his tone. "Do you really think Mom would want you to obsess over this? No matter what happened, you can't change it."

"Finding her killer is the only thing that will bring me closure." Colleen put the lid on the pan and turned off the stove. "I'm as determined in my endeavor as you are in yours. At least if I spend my share and fail, I'll still have a job."

Liam ignored her sarcasm and stood. "I'd better get going. Anything else you need from the store?"

"Couldn't hurt to get another gallon of milk."

"All right." Liam grabbed his keys. "I'll be right back."

He walked out to the garage, his head spinning. What could Colleen possibly uncover? Even if she put a PI on it, what was there to find out? The only threat to his getting his inheritance money was Jesse Cummings—and he would make sure the kid stayed too terrified to open his mouth.

❦

Jesse double-checked the lock on his bedroom window. It would be dark soon. The only thing scarier than living with a death threat was living with the fear that the killer could sneak up on him again. For some reason, the second threat was even more terrifying than the first. He was tempted to talk to the sheriff this time. But without knowing what the killer looked like, how could the sheriff protect his family? All Jesse could do now was stick to his denial and pray that the guy got caught.

A knock at the door caused Jesse to jump. "Who is it?" he said, his heart racing.

"Elliot. Can I come in?"

"Sure."

Elliot came in and shut the door, then sat on the side of the bed, his hands folded between his knees. "I know it wasn't easy, but you made it through this day."

"Barely."

"Want to talk about it?"

Jesse stood leaning against the window, his thumbs hooked on his jeans pockets, and told Elliot about the incident at lunch with Bull Hanson.

"What could I say? I brought it on myself," Jesse said. "I just sat there and took it with everyone watching. But I really wanted to punch Bull in the nose."

The corners of Elliot's mouth twitched. "I'm glad you didn't. Getting yourself suspended from school would've just made everything worse."

"Plus, Bull would've flattened me. One more thing to live down."

Elliot got up and put his arm around Jesse. "I know it probably seems like nothing will ever be the same. I suppose in one way it won't. You learned the importance of telling the truth and the consequences of lying. But that doesn't mean you won't ever have friends again. Or even that you and Dawson won't find a way to stay friends."

"I don't see how." Jesse stared at his shoes. "He can't be friends with me and still be friends with his teammates."

"That remains to be seen. But it's possible that God has *other* friends in mind for you. Friends that you might not have even considered if you and Dawson were still tight."

"I sure hope so. It's kind of depressing being the only seventh grader without a friend to hang out with."

"I know." Elliot tilted Jesse's chin. "But you trust God, don't you?"

"Sure. But He's probably mad at me for getting myself into this mess."

"Just talk to Him," Elliot said. "Tell Him the truth, ask His forgiveness, and then trust Him to make something good out of it. Remember what it says in Romans 8:28? 'And we know that in all things God works ...'"

"'... for the good of those who love him, who have been called according to his purpose,'" Jesse said, proud to finish reciting this verse he had memorized in Sunday school. Did "all things" include his lying to save his family? Because right now, he didn't see another way.

"I know it's been rough going"—Elliot patted Jesse's shoulder—"but you will get through this. And things will get better."

"I hope you're right."

"Jesse, when I was about your age, my dad stressed the importance of always trying to do the right thing. He said it might be costly in the beginning. But in the long run, it would pay off. It took me a few mistakes to understand what he meant and the wisdom of his words. But I've tried to live my life that way."

"What if I'm not sure what the right thing is?"

Elliot looked into his eyes. "Most of the time, the answer can be found in the Bible. But when in doubt, ask yourself two questions: By making this choice, am I showing that I love God with all my heart, mind, soul, and strength? And am I treating the other person the way I want to be treated?"

"I guess I flunked that test a lot lately," Jesse said.

"We all flunk. Adults too. More times than we would like to admit. Jesus told us that whatever we do to anyone else, we do to Him. Not just the kind things, but also the ugly things."

"So if I would've punched Bull in the nose, even though he deserved it, it would be like punching Jesus." Jesse sighed. "Doesn't seem fair."

"Sometimes it isn't. But you can never disappoint God by refusing to repay evil with evil. Jesus didn't even lash out at those who were going to kill Him. He took *all* the punches on the cross—every cruel or careless word or action of every person who would ever live. He died in our place. That sure wasn't fair."

"I guess when you compare it to that," Jesse said, "being humiliated in the cafeteria was no big deal."

"I wouldn't say it was no big deal. It was hurtful and you felt defenseless. But as a Christian, it's actually *you* who had the power."

"I did?"

"Absolutely," Elliot said. "Because Jesus lives in you, you have His power to choose to do the right thing, no matter what anyone says or does to you. But it requires putting your feelings away and deciding to act instead of react. Does that make sense?"

"I think so. Is it the same as dying to self? We talked about that in Sunday school."

Elliot nodded. "Our spirits come to life when we're born again. But it's a lifelong struggle to put to death our sinful desires and become more like Jesus, which is the process of sanctification. For example, all week long you've encountered difficult and sometimes painful situations. But in each instance, you had a choice of responding out of personal feelings or responding out of obedience to God's Word."

Jesse felt his cheeks burning. The only reason he didn't take a swing at Bull was because he was afraid. Obedience had nothing to do with it. Doing the right thing in obedience to God's Word, especially when he didn't want to, would be a huge sacrifice. He sure didn't feel like praying for his enemies or forgiving them.

"What I'm trying to say, Jesse, is that how we feel isn't as important as how we act. And as Christians, we no longer have to let feelings determine our behavior."

Jesse folded his arms across his chest. "Sounds pretty impossible."

"All by yourself it is. But nothing's impossible with God. He's always got your back. And the reward will be greater than the sacrifice."

Jesse let Elliot's words settle in his mind. "Thanks. I think I get it. I just need to keep asking myself those two questions."

"Still works for *me*." Elliot brushed his hand through Jesse's hair. "Come on, sport. How about we go see if dinner's ready? Your mama's frying up some of that crappie you and Hawk have been catching hand over fist. I saw her making hush puppies too."

Jesse was hungry. But not even his mother's cooking could distract him from the guarded secret that weighed heavily on his mind. For his family's sake, he would bear it alone. One slip of the tongue—and someone could die.

CHAPTER 22

Virgil sat at his desk, sipping his first cup of coffee.

It had been seven days since Billy Gene and Jason began the covert assignment to keep a close eye on Jesse Cummings. So far, they had not noticed anything out of the ordinary. Kate said there were no unidentified calls on Jesse's cell phone or emails on his computer. And that he seemed more relaxed. His schoolwork wasn't suffering.

Virgil questioned how long he could afford to invest valuable manpower this way when nothing supported his gut feeling that Jesse might have been coerced into recanting his story.

Kevin knocked on his open door. "You said you wanted to talk to me before the morning briefing."

"Come in and have a seat," Virgil said.

Kevin sat in the vinyl chair next to Virgil's desk, his navy uniform shirt clean and pressed, his wavy red hair neatly combed.

Virgil mused. "I've done some soul searching since you posed your poignant question asking whether I would have gone to this extreme had the situation not involved Kate's son."

"Listen, Sheriff, I'm really sorry about that. I was out of line."

Virgil held up his palm. "No, you weren't. You're the one person who has earned the right to ask it. The answer is yes. I honestly think I'm treating this case as I would any case, given these same circumstances. But I need your opinion about something. I'm aware that it's putting pressure on the whole department for me to keep Billy Gene and Jason out on covert assignment. The practical side of me says it's time to stop wasting manpower on a dead end. But my gut instinct tells me Jesse isn't telling us everything. What's your take on it?"

"Truthfully?" Kevin leaned forward, his hands folded between his knees. "I think we can make better use of Billy Gene and Jason right now. We've got a string of assaults, thefts, domestic violence cases, some gang-related vandalism, and a dog-fighting ring that aren't getting enough attention. We're doing the best we can to pick up the slack, but things are getting missed. I know the relationship you have with the Cummings family. And if we knew for certain that Jesse was a witness, I'd agree to do whatever it took to protect him. But at some point, without any evidence to the contrary, we have to accept his admission that he made the whole thing up."

"So you think we should shut it down and get Billy Gene and Jason back working other cases?"

"I would."

Virgil took a sip of coffee. "All right. Suspend the operation effective immediately."

"But you think it's a mistake?"

"I don't know, Kevin. My gut is right more times than it's wrong. But maybe I'm too close to it."

❧

That afternoon, Liam sat next to Colleen in the office of Randal Holmes, their mother's estate attorney. The big moment had finally come. He was about to be freed from the ball and chain of debt, freed to pursue a better future.

His mind wandered back to the river and those final moments with his mother. He wished he had thought to say thank you. The sound of Randal's voice caused him to come back to the present.

"It gives me enormous pleasure to present each of you with a distribution check for your half of the trust." Randal's thick white hair was a sharp contrast to his three-piece charcoal suit. He handed each of them a letter with a check paper-clipped to it. "One hundred and seventy-five thousand, two hundred and eighty-four dollars each. That's after my fee. The letter gives a full accounting. All I need is Colleen's signature on these papers, and your mother's trust will be officially closed." He smiled warmly and handed the papers and an expensive-looking fountain pen to Colleen. "It was an honor working with Dixie all these years. Your mom was one of the most determined ladies I've ever known. After your dad passed away, she was intentional about living modestly so she'd never have to touch the principal on her investments. And she succeeded because she never lost sight of her goal to leave her children a significant portion of what she and their father had saved and invested over the years. I have to believe they're both smiling down on us at this very moment."

Liam stared at the check, still trying to process what it would mean to his future. "We don't owe taxes on this money, right?"

"That's correct," Randal said. "But you do need to report it to the IRS when you do this year's taxes. I filed K-1 forms with the federal government and with the state of Arkansas so that these agencies know that neither of you has any outstanding fiduciary responsibilities as beneficiaries of the trust. You will be getting copies of those in the mail."

Colleen handed the signed papers back to Randal and dabbed her eyes. "I can't thank you enough for all you did to help Mom all those years and for advising me along the way. And for handling these final details."

"That goes for me too." Liam wiped his sweaty palm on his trousers and shook Randal's hand. "Seriously, man. Thanks. This is exactly what Mom wanted."

"It is, indeed," Randal said. "Give me a call if you have any questions. But this officially closes out your mom's trust."

Colleen rose to her feet, her pale face expressionless. "Thanks again, Mr. Holmes."

"You are very welcome."

Liam felt almost giddy as he slid his arm around Colleen and walked out of Randal Holmes's office, the fear he'd been carrying now turned to relief.

"I guess it's finally over," Liam said.

Colleen looked over at him, her eyes brimming with tears and determination. "Not for me it isn't."

Liam walked Colleen to her car and spent several minutes consoling her, trying not to show his impatience with her unwavering mission to prove their mother was murdered. When she finally seemed composed, he bid her good-bye and said he'd be home for dinner but had a few things he needed to do.

He walked to his car, surprised to see an envelope under his wiper blade. He picked up the envelope—plain white with his name typed in big letters across the front—then slid in behind the wheel. He opened the envelope and pulled out a single sheet of white paper with letters cut from a magazine. He held it out so he could read it.

"I SAW HOW YOUR MOTHER DIED. PAY ME $50,000 OR I'LL TELL THE SHERIFF. YOU'LL HEAR FROM ME AGAIN SOON." His heart banged so loudly he thought the glass might shatter in his old Caprice. So much for Jesse Cummings not knowing his identity. He should have gotten rid of the kid when he had had the chance.

Liam's thoughts screamed louder than two disgruntled grackles on the sidewalk fighting over a candy-bar wrapper. He took a deep breath and let it out slowly, then did it again. Jesse wasn't gutsy enough to pull this off by himself. The kid must have told someone. Someone who decided to use the information to extort money from Liam. He looked at the note again.

"I SAW HOW YOUR MOTHER DIED." Liam pounded his fists on the steering wheel. His alibi was solid. He was reasonably confident that no one could prove he was anywhere near the river when his mother drowned. What if he was wrong? All it would take to wreck everything was for someone to come out and back Jesse's claim. That would compel the sheriff to put Liam under close scrutiny. And though he had covered his tracks, he wasn't sure his alibi would hold up if the sheriff got suspicious and started checking street cams and store surveillance cameras.

Liam's hands shook. He looked around and then glanced in his rearview mirror. He didn't see anyone lurking. If he paid the fifty grand, he would still have more than enough to pay off his looming credit-card debt, pay cash for that new fully loaded Silverado he wanted, and cover the cost of tools and materials while he built clientele for his business. He could stay with Colleen as long as he needed to but would have to rent a storage facility and turn it into a workshop. Without that fifty thousand, he could forget buying a home of his own.

Liam spit out a swear word, then wadded up the note and stuffed it into his pocket. He needed time to think. He wasn't about to hand over that kind of money without knowing how much this extortionist wannabe really knew.

He started the motor and pulled out of the parking lot, furious that his long-awaited thrill had lasted less than ten minutes, and feeling as though he had walked into someone else's nightmare.

Jesse sat in the porch swing, eating a chocolate-chip cookie and holding half a dozen more in his other hand. He'd made it through another week at school without a major incident. The guys on the football team snickered anytime they saw him, but no one had bullied him. Or tried to befriend him. Dawson avoided him altogether.

Hawk came outside and sat next to him. "So, little brother, how's it going in Munchkin Land?"

"No one's pushing me around," Jesse said. "But no one will hang out with me either."

"That'll change. This whole thing will eventually blow over."

"Dawson and I are done," Jesse said. "That's not going to change."

"Maybe not. But you'll make new friends."

Jesse sighed. "I've already had this pep talk a hundred times. It doesn't make me feel better."

"Sorry." Hawk bumped shoulders with him. "How about you and me go fishing tomorrow?"

"On Saturday?" Jesse said. "Seriously?"

"I've decided to take the day off. Let's go back to our new favorite spot."

Jesse turned to Hawk and studied his expression. "Could we stop by the sporting goods store on the way? I'd like to get some new lures."

"Sure. Since the fish haven't been biting until late morning, why don't we swing by the sporting goods store about nine? You can take your time and look around."

Jesse grinned. "And you can hang out with Laura Lynn at the doughnut shop?"

"That, too, wiseacre."

"Okay, cool. I really didn't want to go by myself." Jesse shuddered, remembering his last encounter with the man who threatened him.

Hawk snitched a cookie out of Jesse's hand. "How can you chunk down all those cookies and still eat dinner?"

"I'm a bottomless pit, remember?" Jesse laughed and moved his hand full of cookies out of Hawk's reach. "After dinner, we'd better make some sandwiches to take with us."

"Sounds good." Hawk stood. "In the morning, let's plan to be in the Jeep, strapped in our seat belts, at twenty till nine. I want to sample the glazed doughnuts while they're still warm."

"More like Laura Lynn's warm lips."

Hawk grinned and pulled Jesse's cap down over his eyes, then went back inside.

Jesse turned his hat around and peered out into the distance, wondering if he would ever know who it was that had turned his life upside down. It had been eight days since the guy had last threatened him. Since then, Jesse had gotten off the school bus every afternoon and run all the way home, almost without stopping. He had skipped fishing last Saturday, choosing instead to stay in and watch college football. He was sure his mother thought it was because he was depressed about school. At least he could use that excuse to explain his dark mood.

Liam sat at the dinner table, moving his spoon slowly back and forth in a bowl of potato soup.

"Something wrong with the soup?" Colleen said.

Liam was startled by her voice and realized he'd been lost in thought. "No. It's great. I just don't have much appetite. Probably finality sinking in. I don't always show it, but today was pretty emotional for me too."

"Really? You seemed over-the-top excited to get your inheritance check."

"On one level, sure." Liam lifted his head. "I really want to quit my job and work for myself. But it's also bittersweet. It's sad that it took Mom's death to make it possible. Kind of bummed me out."

"You *have* been awfully quiet. I can't get over the difference in your demeanor between this afternoon and this evening." Colleen stood and picked up his bowl. "Don't worry about the soup. It'll keep. Are you sure that's all that's bothering you?"

Liam looked her in the eyes. "Yes, I'm sure."

"Did you deposit your check?" she said.

"I did. But it wasn't as satisfying as I thought it would be."

"In what way?"

Liam shrugged. "I don't know. It just wasn't."

"When are you going to give notice?"

"I suppose Monday morning. Look … I'm not really in the mood to talk right now. I'm going to hang out in my room for a while. I need to be alone with my thoughts."

Liam paced in his room, his mind reeling, his emotions torn between rage and helplessness. It seemed surreal that after he finally got the Cummings kid scared into silence, he might have to pay someone a big chunk of his inheritance to keep quiet. What guarantee did he have that the person wouldn't come back later and demand more?

He was tempted to leave town and just disappear. The only effective way to do that would be to cut off all ties with Colleen and leave no forwarding address. After which the failed extortionist would likely make good on his threat to tell the sheriff, and Liam would be looking over his shoulder for the rest of his life. It would be impossible to lie low and be inconspicuous while, at the same time, passing out business cards and trying to attract customers. And how long would his money last if he struck out on his own? Especially if had to pay rent and all his own living expenses while he was struggling to make a go of his handyman business?

Foggy Ridge was his home, and Colleen was all he had. He loved his sister and couldn't imagine just vanishing from her life. It made more sense to stay put and try to sort things out.

Liam kicked the trash can. He'd risked everything to get his inheritance. No way was he parting with fifty thousand dollars of it unless whoever wrote that note had proof that Liam had drowned his mother. Which was highly unlikely. But if Liam refused to pay and was wrong, things could go south rather quickly. Jesse Cummings, with someone else to back his story, might feel empowered to talk. And with two people pointing a finger at Liam, the sheriff would be compelled to put him under a microscope.

Liam felt as if his face were on fire. He pulled his handgun out of the bottom drawer of his dresser, then turned on the ceiling fan and flopped on the bed. He had to know if the kid had talked. And who it was he told. This time, things could get ugly.

CHAPTER 23

Jesse sat in the passenger seat of Hawk's Jeep and looked around as they drove into Foggy Ridge on Saturday morning. He could hardly wait to see the new shipment of fishing lures that Evans's Sporting Goods had received earlier in the week.

He loved to come to town, but it was sure different from Angel View. Up on the mountain, things were so quiet he could hear the wind in the pines. The air was fresh. And the only people he saw were guests and staff.

Foggy Ridge reminded him of an anthill that had been disturbed. Tourists moved in all directions. The air was heavy with car exhaust. But there was so much to see and do.

Jesse looked out at Main Street. Giant trees, starting to turn various shades of red, orange, and yellow, lined the sidewalk on either side, their branches growing together and forming a leafy roof overhead so that only glints of sunlight could get through. Quaint two-story buildings that were older than Grandpa Buck had been remodeled into every kind of souvenir shop, eatery, candy shop, and ice-cream parlor imaginable. After dark, Main Street was a kaleidoscope of neon lights. Foggy Ridge even had a classic video-game and pinball arcade as well as a city park with a public swimming pool. It was a fun place to spend time and money. At least it had been, when he was friends with Dawson.

Hawk turned right on Pine Street and drove through a residential area to the north end of town, and then pulled into the parking lot at Evans's Sporting Goods.

"All right, little brother," Hawk said, taking the keys out of the ignition. "Have at it. How about I meet you back here in exactly one hour? That should give you plenty of time to check out the new lures and me a chance to savor those warm doughnuts I've been dreaming about."

"Okay. Bring me two of the jelly filled." Jesse unfastened his seat belt and plugged his cell phone into the charger, and set it on the floor.

"You aren't taking your cell phone?" Hawk said.

"The battery's almost dead. I won't need it while I'm in Evans's. Tell Laura Lynn I said hey. Try to get all that kissy stuff out of the way so you can focus on fishing."

Hawk got out of the Jeep, a silly grin on his face, and tucked in his shirt. "See you at ten o'clock straight up."

"I'll be here, raring to go."

Jesse got out and walked to the front entrance of the sporting goods store and pulled open the glass door.

"Hey there, Jesse." Mr. Evans stood at the checkout and looked over the top of his glasses. "You're my first customer today. What can I do you for?"

"I'd like to take a look at the lures. I called and the guy said a new shipment came in."

"Yep. Right on time. Let me know if you need somethin'."

"I will."

Jesse turned down aisle two, which was stocked to the hilt with every imaginable fishing lure. He took his time and browsed every inch of both sides of the aisle, finding it hard to choose how to spend his ten dollars. He totally forgot about the time until he glanced at the clock on the rear wall. Hawk wouldn't be back for twenty minutes.

Jesse returned to the shelf where he had started and looked more closely at the variety of spinner baits, half listening to Mr. Evans talking with a customer.

"Just the ammo today?" Mr. Evans said.

"That'll do it," replied the male customer. "I'm going out of town and thought I'd get my Smith and Wesson out of moth balls and carry it for protection."

Jesse froze, his pulse racing. He knew that voice!

"I'm really sorry about your mama, Liam," Mr. Evans said. "Alzheimer's leaves you helpless as a kitten. If they find out Dixie was murdered, they oughta string up the lowlife who took advantage of her."

His mama? Jesse's mind raced to process what that meant. The killer was the victim's son, which meant he was also Miss Berne's brother!

Jesse stood behind the shelving and peeked out at the checkout, finally getting a good look at the man. Liam Berne wore jeans and a red-and-black plaid flannel shirt. And the same brown boots he wore the last time he threatened Jesse. He looked to be around fifty, average height and weight. Brown eyes. Dark hair with a little gray.

Five o'clock shadow. He studied him carefully, sure he would never forget that face.

"Is the sheriff making any headway?" Mr. Evans said.

"Nah, he's hit a wall. To tell you the truth, I don't think a murder investigation is even necessary. I've always believed that Mom just wandered off and the drowning was accidental. I just wish Colleen would accept that. But I guess it never hurts to be thorough."

What a liar! Jesse thought.

"Sheriff Granger'll get to the truth of it." Mr. Evans put Liam's purchase in a bag. "I hope it's soon so you can put it to bed. Take care now. Appreciate you coming in."

Jesse moved to the front of the aisle and watched Liam from behind as he headed toward the front entrance.

Mr. Evans remained at the register, his eyes looking down as he wrote something in a ledger. He said in a loud voice, "How're you coming, Jesse? Holler if you need help."

Liam stopped, then turned and stared at Jesse.

Jesse froze, his heart racing like a scared rabbit's. He saw panic in Liam Berne's eyes. The man knew Jesse recognized him.

Run!

Jesse ran down the aisle and into an alcove where the restrooms and drinking fountain were located. He turned into a hallway and slipped into what appeared to be Mr. Evans's office and hid behind a file cabinet. He waited for what seemed an eternity and didn't hear footsteps. He noticed a door that led outside. He pushed it open, closed it without making a sound, and raced across the back parking lot toward the undeveloped wooded area beyond it.

He leapt off the edge of the pavement onto a low-lying grassy strip and then crossed the tree line into the damp, dark woods, high-stepping over the thick ground cover and winding his way around the trees, low branches slapping his face. He reached in his jacket pocket for his cell phone and remembered he'd left it in the Jeep.

Jesse tripped over a tree root and fell forward on the ground. He picked himself up, then slipped in behind the trunk of a tall oak tree. He listened intently, the only sound the wild pounding of his heart, which felt as if it might explode at any moment.

He wiped the sweat off his forehead and tried to think about what he might use to defend himself if Liam followed him. He spotted a fallen tree branch about three inches in diameter and eighteen inches long. He picked it up. Not much of a defense against the gun for which Liam Berne had bought ammo. But he felt less afraid with something in his hand.

Jesse peeked out from behind the tree and didn't see anyone. Even if he hadn't been followed, he knew that just keeping his mouth shut wouldn't be enough to satisfy Liam now that Jesse knew his name.

Jesse crouched behind a tree. He would wait. If Liam didn't show, then he probably didn't know where Jesse was. As soon as it felt safe, Jesse would run over to the courthouse and tell Sheriff Granger everything. Once Liam was arrested and put in jail, this awful nightmare would be over.

Minutes ticked by and seemed like hours. Was it safe yet? Should he make a run for it?

"Jesse!"

The sound of Liam's voice shattered the quiet and sent chills crawling up Jesse's backbone. He didn't move. Or breathe.

"I know you're out here. I'm not going to hurt you. I just want to talk."

The all-too-familiar voice was somewhere behind him. It was impossible to tell how far.

"Don't be scared." Liam's tone was surprisingly friendly. "I know you told someone what you saw. And I'm not mad. But I need you to deliver a message to him."

What was he talking about? Jesse hadn't told anyone.

"Look, it's just you and me," Liam said. "Come out in the open. Let's negotiate, man to man."

His voice sounded closer. He must be moving this way. Jesse slowly stood, then gingerly stepped over a fallen limb and moved away from the voice.

"Come on, Jesse. Talk to me. I'm sorry I threatened you. Let's forget it okay? Everything's changed since I got the note."

What note? Could he trust Liam? Or was it a trick? *God, what should I do? I need Your help!*

"How can I make you believe I'm not going to hurt you?" Liam said. "Or your family? I just want you to deliver a message for me, that's all. Besides, you deserve a cut of the fifty grand your buddy's trying to extort from me. I'll make it worth your time to forget what you saw."

"I don't know what you're talking about," Jesse hollered, trudging farther into the dark woods. "I did exactly what you said. I didn't tell anyone."

"Stop with the games, kid. Let's deal. You need to trust me."

Could he trust a man who would kill his own mother and threaten to gut Jesse's family unless he kept quiet about it? Jesse peeked out from behind a tree and saw Liam walking ever so slowly in his direction. He was carrying a gun!

Jesse ducked behind the tree and turned around, feeling as if his back were cemented to the trunk. The deeper he went into the woods, the less chance he had of finding his way back. If Liam meant him no harm, then why was he carrying a gun? Jesse was curious about the note. And the fifty thousand dollars. But not enough to show his face.

"How about it?" Liam said. "Can we call a truce and talk business?"

"Put down that gun first," Jesse hollered. "If you're serious about not hurting me."

"Okay, I'm going to set it here in this hollow log." Jesse watched from behind the tree as Liam turned his back and pretended to do what he said, but instead tucked the gun in his waistband. He turned around and raised his hands. "Okay, no more gun. I'm unarmed."

Liar. Jesse didn't bother answering and moved away from Liam, quickly and quietly into the dark unknown.

God, You saved Abby and Jay from that crazy mountain man and brought Riley back home to us. I know You can keep me safe from Liam Berne. But I'm really scared.

⁂

Hawk sat in the Jeep, his fingers tapping the steering wheel. Why wasn't Jesse here at ten, as they had agreed? His brother was usually punctual to a fault, especially when fishing was involved. He wasn't in the sporting goods store. Hawk and Mr. Evans had checked thoroughly. No one saw him leave. Of all times for Jesse to have left his cell phone in the car.

"The kid couldn't have just vanished," Hawk mumbled to himself. He glanced at his watch. He would have been angry had he not been so concerned.

Mr. Evans walked outside the store and waved at Hawk, then hurried over to the driver's-side window of the Jeep.

"I thought of something," Mr. Evans said. "One other customer was in the store at the same time Jesse was. Maybe he saw something that'd help you find him. Might be worth a jingle. Here's his name and home phone number."

"Thanks." Hawk took a slip of paper from Mr. Evans. "I'll call him right now."

"Let me know when you find Jesse." Mr. Evans patted Hawk's shoulder. "I need to get back and mind the store."

"Sure. Thanks again."

As Mr. Evans walked back to the front door, Hawk read the name on the paper. *Liam Berne.* Wasn't that the guy whose mother had drowned? Talk about coincidence. Calling him would violate the agreement the Cummingses had with Sheriff Granger. But under the circumstances, what choice did he have? He keyed in the phone number and let it ring. And ring. And ring. He started to hang up when someone picked up the phone.

"Hello," said a woman, sounding out of breath.

"May I speak with Liam Berne?"

"Liam's not here. This is his sister, Colleen. Can I take a message?"

"Yes, ma'am. This is Hawk Cummings. You know my mother, Kate Cummings, from church. Is there any way I can reach Liam? Maybe a cell phone?"

"You sound upset. What's this about?"

"I'm trying to find my younger brother, Jesse. He was at Evans's Sporting Goods this morning and was supposed to meet me at the car at ten. He didn't show. Mr. Evans said Liam was in the store at the time and might've seen where Jesse went. I'd just like to ask him."

Hawk waited for several seconds, but she didn't answer. "Ma'am, you there?"

"Uh, yes. I–I'm here. Are you aware that I've been instructed not to have contact with Jesse—or anyone in your family?"

"I just want to ask your brother if he saw where Jesse went," Hawk said. "Please … this is important."

"All right, Hawk. Give me your number. I'll get Liam on the phone and have him call you right back."

Hawk gave Colleen his cell number, relieved when she ended the call without further conversation. He glanced again at his watch. If this call didn't yield anything useful, he would have no choice but to involve his mother.

Liam wandered through the woods, unable to evoke any further response from Jesse. He was tired of fooling around. He wanted answers. And he wanted them now. Maybe the kid didn't know about the note. But he'd told somebody that he'd seen Liam in the river, and Liam needed to know who.

His cell phone vibrated. The call was coming from home. "Hey, Colleen. What is it?"

"I just got a call from Hawk Cummings, of all people. He's looking for Jesse."

"Why would he call *you*?"

"He didn't," Colleen said. "He called for you. Apparently Jesse's missing. Mr. Evans told Hawk that you and Jesse were at the sporting goods store at the same time this morning and that you might have seen Jesse leave …" Colleen said something else, but her voice broke up. The cell signal was down to one bar.

"Colleen, listen," Liam said. "You keep breaking up. If you can understand me, call Hawk and tell him I didn't see Jesse. I didn't even know he was in the store … Colleen? Colleen, can you hear me?"

She said something indistinguishable, and then he heard a whooshing sound. And then nothing.

Liam crouched behind a tree, his heart racing almost as fast as his thoughts. He quickly removed the battery from his cell phone. He couldn't stay off the radar for long without raising suspicion. Nor could he escape the inevitable, ugly as it was. He was sure now that Jesse knew his identity. The kid had to be silenced. This time for good.

CHAPTER 24

Kate stood at the stove, stirring in the extra basil and oregano she had added to the pasta sauce she'd made for Saturday's spaghetti dinner. She put the tasting spoon to her mouth.

Mmm. Perfect.

She put the lid on the pan and sat at the table, savoring the wonderful aroma that had filled the house. The phone rang and no one else answered it, so she grabbed it on the fourth ring.

"Hello."

"Mom, it's Hawk. I didn't want to have to call you, but we've got a problem. I'm at the sporting goods store. I left Jesse here to look at lures while I walked down to Bella's to say hey to Laura Lynn. Jesse was supposed to meet me back at the Jeep at ten o'clock sharp. He didn't show. Mr. Evans and I searched every inch of the store. He's not here. I went in all the shops nearby and no one's seen him."

"Did you call Jesse's cell?" Kate heard the front door open and close and Elliot's cheerful voice calling her.

Hawk sighed. "He left his cell phone in the Jeep. His battery was low and he wanted to recharge it. I'm sorry. I never thought he'd leave Evans's. I checked, and he hadn't made any calls since he talked to Dawson on Wednesday night."

Kate's heart sank. "Are you sure he didn't walk over to the arcade? He might have lost track of time."

"I checked the arcade, but no way would Jesse lose track of time when we were going fishing. And get this: Mr. Evans gave me the phone number of a customer who was in the store at the same time. Turned out to be Liam Berne, Colleen Berne's brother. I called to see if he saw Jesse leave the store, and Colleen answered the phone. Talk about awkward. Liam wasn't home. She called him on his cell and then called me back. Liam told her he didn't even see Jesse at Evans's. I'm out of options."

"Well, let's not panic." Kate saw Elliot in the kitchen doorway and motioned for him to come in. "I'm putting you on speaker so Elliot can hear you. Any chance Jesse misunderstood where he was supposed to meet you?"

"What's to misunderstand? I parked the Jeep in Evans's parking lot, right next to the front entrance. All he had to do was walk outside and meet me there at ten o'clock."

"Maybe he's playing a trick on you." Kate stole a glance at Elliot, who seemed to have picked up on the seriousness of the conversation. "What if he walked to the river and knew you'd figure it out and meet him there?"

"That'd be pretty lame." Hawk sighed. "But that's one place I didn't think to check. I'll drive down there right now. It'll take me ten minutes to get there and another twenty to park the car and walk out to the flat rock. If he's not there, we need to call the sheriff."

Kate cleared her throat. "Hawk, there's something Elliot and I have been keeping to ourselves." Kate felt Elliot's hands on her shoulders. "Virgil isn't convinced that Jesse made up the story about seeing a man in the river with Dixie Berne. He has a real concern that Jesse may have been coerced into recanting his original statement."

"And you didn't *tell* me? Why?"

"Virgil asked us not to tell anyone, not even family. He had a deputy watching Jesse anytime he left the house. Even Jesse didn't know."

"Then the sheriff can tell us where he is."

"No, he can't!" Kate said, her voice shaking. "Virgil stopped the operation yesterday—after they'd watched Jesse for a week and didn't see anything unusual."

"Well, I'd say Jesse pulling a disappearing act more than qualifies as unusual."

"I know. I know. But we *have* to stay calm. We need to think," Kate said, more for her own comfort than Hawk's. "If you don't find him at the river, I'll call Virgil."

"All right, Mama. But I'm ninety-nine percent sure Jesse wouldn't pull a stunt like that. I'll call you as soon as I know. If he's not there, I'll keep asking around town. Someone must have seen him."

"I can't just sit here waiting for your call. I'm going to go out looking for him too."

"You'd be smart to let Elliot drive when you're this upset," Hawk said.

"He's right here." Kate reached up and took Elliot's hand and realized hers was trembling. "Call me on my cell. Elliot and I will check the places up here on the mountain where Jesse and Dawson liked to hang out. I'll have Abby and Jay stay here with Riley and Grandpa, in case Jesse comes home."

There was a long moment of dead air.

Finally, Hawk said, "I can't believe we're doing this again. Two years ago, we were out looking for Abby."

"And we found her," Kate said. "We'll find Jesse too."

But as Kate disconnected the call, fear gripped her heart like an iron fist. She wasn't sure of anything.

Virgil took the last delicious sip of coffee, and set his blue china cup and saucer with the empty dishes on his breakfast tray. He folded Saturday's issue of the *Northwest Arkansas Times* and turned to Jill Beth.

She sat snuggled next to him, her back against the headboard of their antique mahogany poster bed, the morning sun casting a warm glow on the soft yellow walls. She was perusing the engagement and wedding announcements in the *Foggy Ridge Forum*, the town's weekly newspaper.

"I love it when you spoil me," he said. "Your cranberry coffee cake was terrific. Hard to believe it was low fat."

"I knew you'd like it." She smiled, never taking her eyes off the paper. "Well, what do you know? Andrew Hardy's getting married. To some pretty young lady from Bentonville. One of these days, our sons will be featured here."

"I'm sure they will, darlin'. But they're only twenty-seven. Kids today don't get in a big hurry. Besides, can you really see just one of them getting married? The way they do everything together, we may be in for a triple wedding."

Jill Beth turned to him, her face aglow, her cheeks matching her pink cotton nightgown. "I've dreamed about it. And about having grandkids staying with us on weekends and holidays. I miss the pitter-patter of little feet around here."

Virgil laughed. "We haven't had *little* feet since our three musketeers were in sixth grade and measured an inch taller than you. But I do remember the sound."

His cell phone rang.

"This is such a relaxing morning," Jill Beth said. "Can't you let it go to voice mail?"

"Let me take a look." Virgil picked it up and glanced at the screen. "It's Kate Cummings. She wouldn't call my cell unless it was important." He put the phone to his ear. "Hello, Kate."

"Virgil, thank heavens you're there. Jesse's missing!"

"How do you know he's missing?" He looked at Jill Beth and mouthed *Jesse*.

He listened as Kate told him about Hawk and Jesse's plan to go fishing, where each was to be between nine and ten o'clock, and how Jesse never showed up at their rendezvous point.

"Jesse was beyond excited to go fishing with Hawk," Kate said, sounding out of breath. "Trust me, he wouldn't have lost track of time. Something's wrong. Hawk looked all over town for him and even called the other customer Mr. Evans said was in the store at the same time as Jesse: Liam Berne, of all people. I know you asked us not to have contact with the Bernes, but Hawk didn't see another option."

"I take it Liam wasn't helpful?"

"Actually, he was out running errands. Colleen answered the phone. She called Liam's cell and got back to Hawk. Liam told her he didn't see Jesse and didn't even know he was in the store."

Virgil combed his hand through his hair. "Can you think of any place Jesse might have gone?"

"Hawk has checked them all. Even their fishing spot on the river. No one's seen him except for Mr. Evans, who greeted Jesse when he came in the store to see all the new fishing lures. Mr. Evans let Jesse browse and was busy doing other things. Jesse could have left without being seen. But why would he? He had ten dollars he couldn't wait to spend on new fishing lures. He didn't buy a thing."

"That is odd," Virgil said. "Where are you now?"

"Elliot and I are checking Jesse's favorite hangouts on Sure Foot Mountain. Hawk's talking to people in town. Abby and Jay will stay with Dad at the house, in case Jesse comes home."

"Have you searched the house, Kate?"

"Why? We know Jesse's not there."

"Are you sure about that?" Virgil said. "I can't tell you how many times a big search operation was done in vain, because the child was hiding at home. Before I send my deputies out looking, I need you to search every conceivable place in the house where Jesse could be hiding. Check the attic. The basement. Closets. Under the beds. In trunks, boxes, large containers, storage units. I'll send some deputies to search the grounds and any buildings Jesse has access to. If he's hiding, we'll find him."

"Is that really necessary? Why would he be hiding?"

"Has he seemed okay to you? Have you noticed anything odd lately?"

"You mean, other than admitting he lied, losing his best friend, and feeling like an outcast at school?"

"I mean does he seem secretive? Is he staying indoors when he normally would be outside? Does he seem unusually jumpy? Or clingy?"

"All of the above," Kate said. "I thought it was because of the mess he's gotten himself into—and feeling a little lost without Dawson. They've been best friends since kindergarten."

"That might be all it is. But if someone is threatening Jesse, he would probably keep it from you, especially if he threatened the family."

"Now that I think about it," Kate said, "he recently started closing all the blinds as soon as it gets dark. I saw him peeking outside through the slats and asked what he was looking at. He stammered for a moment and said he had watched a spooky movie where aliens hid in the dark, watching their victims through the windows, and that he just feels better with the blinds closed. I thought he was embarrassed. I believed him." Kate began to cry. "Oh, Virgil … you tried to tell me. I should've listened. What if something terrible has happened to him?"

"Come on, Kate. Don't assume the worst. Let's not get ahead of ourselves. Can you tell me what he was wearing?"

"Yes. Blue jeans, a white T-shirt with the Razorbacks logo on the front, a hooded denim jacket, and red-and-white Nikes."

"All right. I'll put out an APB. Go home and search the house from top to bottom. If you don't find him, search it again. My deputies will be at your place shortly. I should be in my office within thirty minutes. If we determine Jesse is not at Angel View, Kevin and I will have a plan. Try not to worry. Most of the time these things turn out to be nothing."

"Thanks for being there," Kate said. "I'll get Abby and Jay, Dad, and Elliot to help me search the house."

Virgil ended the call and told Jill Beth everything Kate had said.

"She must be scared to death," Jill Beth said.

"Of course she is! Can you blame her?" Virgil said a swear word under his breath. "I should've listened to my gut and kept an eye on Jesse awhile longer."

"You think whoever killed Dixie Berne went after him?" Jill Beth's eyes were wide and questioning.

Virgil shrugged. "I don't know, but I can't afford not to take a hard look at the possibility. I mean, what are the odds that Jesse just happened to go missing the day after we stopped watching him?"

"Can you issue an Amber Alert?"

Virgil shook his head. "It's premature. We don't know that he was abducted. And we have no suspect or vehicle description. Amber Alerts can be very effective if used properly, but we're not there yet." Virgil kissed Jill Beth on the cheek. "I'm going to get dressed and go down to the office. I need to stay on top of this. Hopefully, it'll turn out to be a false alarm. Either way, I want Kate to know I'm doing everything I can to bring Jesse home safely."

"But what if you can't, Virgil? What if the killer got to him?"

"*What ifs* won't get it done, darlin'. I need to stay focused and get the facts."

Virgil rummaged through his dresser, snatched some clean clothes, and went into the bathroom, trying not to overreact to Jill Beth's comment and the doubt that still taunted him. He hadn't been able to bring Micah Cummings home alive. Even Abby and Riley's safe return couldn't change that fact.

He picked up his cell phone and keyed in the number for Kevin Mann, who picked it up on the first ring.

"Hello, Sheriff. Didn't expect to hear from you today."

"What's your twenty, Kevin?"

"I'm in my office, cleaning out my in-box."

"Jesse Cummings is missing. I need you to put out an APB right away. He was wearing blue jeans, a white T-shirt with a Razorbacks logo, a hooded denim jacket, and red-and-white Nikes. Last seen at nine o'clock this morning at Evans's Sporting Goods at Fourteenth and Pine in North Foggy Ridge. Call in Billy Gene and Jason, and meet me in my office in thirty minutes. Get Police Chief Mitchell to join us. This has got to be a joint effort."

"I'm on it."

Virgil put down his phone and looked at his reflection in the bathroom mirror. What if this situation had already escalated beyond his control? Could he ever forgive himself for not listening to his instincts and scrapping the covert operation that could have prevented this from happening?

CHAPTER 25

Jesse leaned his back against the trunk of a tall pine tree and caught his breath. He listened for the sounds of traffic, people talking, or children playing—anything that would indicate he was nearing the other side of the woods. All he heard was the unmistakable chatter of chickadees. He had no idea how much distance he had covered or even which direction he was going. He had expected to exit the woods on the other side. Instead, he was swallowed up in a dark forest that seemed to have shut the door on any chance for escape.

How long could he hide from Liam and refuse to talk? It was already twelve thirty. By four o'clock, the sun would be low enough in the western sky that it would be nearly impossible to see anything in these woods. Unless he could find a way out before then, neither of them was going anywhere. Even if he found a clearing and could remember how Hawk had taught him to start a campfire by rubbing two sticks together, he couldn't do it without Liam knowing where he was.

Jesse sighed. No one would think to look for him here. The denim jacket he was wearing wouldn't keep him warm once the temperature started to drop. If Liam didn't kill him, hypothermia might. Unless he starved first. What he wouldn't give for a plate of his mother's Saturday-night spaghetti.

A twig snapped. Jesse sucked in a breath and held it, listening intently, his heart racing. He ducked his head and continued weaving around the trees, hoping he wouldn't get shot in the back. The grim reality of his situation brought tears to his eyes.

Lord, I'm really scared. Show me the way out of here.

"Jesse!"

Hearing the killer's voice so close filled him with dread.

"Come on, kid. I know you hear me. The clock's ticking. Your mother's got to be worried sick. Just tell me who's trying to get fifty grand of my money, and I'll show you the way out of here."

Virgil pulled his squad car into his designated space in the courthouse parking lot, then turned off the motor. Why did he feel such a heaviness in his heart? He had dealt with missing kids before. But Jesse was Kate's boy. Kate, who had suffered unspeakable mental and emotional anguish every single day of those five years when Micah and Riley were missing. And during those torturous hours when Abby and Jay had disappeared on their foolhardy mission to snatch Riley from the clutches of Isaiah Tutt. And then again after the final, raw realization that Micah wasn't coming home …

Kate got a bottle of water out of the fridge and sat across from Virgil. "What was so important you couldn't tell me on the phone?"

"I waited to say anything until I was sure." Virgil held her gaze and spoke softly. "Kate … we found Micah's remains. Buried in a wooden box under the root cellar at the Tutts' where Abby and Jay were held hostage. The dental records match."

Kate stared at him, almost blurry eyed, seeming to let the gravity of his words sink in. "You're ***sure*** it's Micah?"

"Absolutely. We recovered his entire skeleton. And his gold wedding band—his initials and yours were engraved on the inside of the band, along with your wedding date, just the way you told us."

Kate put her fist to her mouth and pushed down the emotion that he wished she would just let go.

"We immediately confronted Isaiah," Virgil said. "He admitted to burying Micah under the root cellar but still claims that Jay shot and killed him. However, the medical examiner found a distinct scrape on Micah's breastbone, consistent with a deep stab wound. If it's the last thing I ever do, I'm going to get Isaiah to confess to Micah's murder. I'm going to nail him, Kate."

"I know you will." Kate lifted her gaze and exhaled. "At least now I finally know what happened, though it doesn't seem real yet."

"After what you've been through, it'll take time for this to sink in. But it's definitely Micah's remains we found. It's over, Kate. It really is."

But it wasn't over. Not for Virgil. He had gotten a confession out of Isaiah—the same one that Isaiah had indeed told Abby and Jay but later denied: that he had stabbed and killed Micah and kidnapped two-year-old Riley. But Virgil considered it a personal failure that he had been unable to solve the case. That it took two brave teenagers to unravel the layers by putting their lives on the line to do what law enforcement had failed to do. Abby and Jay accomplished in just a couple weeks what Virgil couldn't do in five years—five long years that had taken a huge toll on the Cummings family, especially Kate.

Virgil gripped the steering wheel. What if he couldn't find Jesse either? Maybe his decision to ignore his gut feeling and call off the covert operation would turn out to be a fiasco. Maybe they were too late. Maybe Jesse would never be found—at least, not alive.

Virgil took a slow, deep breath, then let it out. Poor Kate. After finally getting her life back, would she be shackled again with the cruel uncertainty of whether another of her children was dead or alive? He couldn't let that happen. Jesse's disappearance had to be related to the Dixie Berne drowning. Whoever was responsible either believed that Jesse saw something damaging or just wasn't taking any chances. Either way, Jesse was a target unless they found him first.

Virgil got out of the car and walked across Commerce Street toward the back door of the courthouse. He couldn't allow the regrets of his past to color his judgment now. There was no room for self-pity or doubt. He had a job to do. He needed to embrace the belief that they were going to find Jesse and bring him home, and then lead his deputies with confidence and resolve. He couldn't fail Kate again. He just couldn't.

Liam held tightly to his gun. He was done playing cat and mouse with Jesse. His anger and frustration should make it easier for him to do what was necessary. Jesse had to die—or Liam would be spending the rest of his life in prison, instead of spending his inheritance.

Listen to yourself. Mom would be horrified.

Liam blinked away the thought. He was in way too deep to wrestle with his conscience. He cupped his hands around his mouth. "Jesse … you're stuck here until you tell me who's after my money … Come out and let's get this done so we can both go home."

The silent forest seemed to taunt Liam. What if Jesse had eluded him? What if he'd found a way out of the woods? "Kid, you're really starting to tick me off! Stop acting like a baby. Man up and give me a name."

"I didn't tell *anyone*! Just leave me alone!"

Liam smiled. *There you are.* He began moving surreptitiously in the direction of Jesse's voice, low branches scratching his face. He needed to get this over with before he lost his nerve.

Kate had Elliot drive her home, where she then conveyed to Abby, Jay, and her father the conversation she'd had with Virgil. She assigned each a portion of the house to search. And when none of them found Jesse, they set out to search it again, agreeing to meet on the front porch when they were finished.

Kate, her heart heavy and her emotions fragile, pushed open the front door, went outside, and sat in the porch swing next to Riley.

"Guess you didn't find Jesse." Riley lowered the library book she was reading.

"No. But let's wait and see if the others do."

"Mama, don't be sad." Riley's bright blue eyes were wide and filled with hope. "I came home again. Jesse will too."

Kate put her arm around her youngest daughter and choked back the tears that were just under the surface. How could Riley understand the gut-wrenching anguish Kate had suffered in those years she was missing? Riley had only been two when she was taken. She had no memory of being stolen from her family. She knew nothing of their suffering, other than what she'd been told.

Kate blinked the stinging from her eyes, but not before a tear escaped down her cheek. She quickly whisked it away just as Abby came through the door.

"I told you Jesse wasn't here." Abby went over and stood at the railing, her auburn hair draping her shoulders and shining like copper in the sunlight. "We should be out looking for him instead of wasting all this time."

Kate sighed. "Virgil was insistent that often the missing child is hiding at home."

"Not this time."

Kate moved her gaze to the doorway as her father and Jay, wearing somber expressions, came out on the porch.

Dad put his hand on Kate's shoulder. "Sorry, honey. No soap."

"I'm sure I covered every inch of the attic, Mrs. Cummings." Jay pulled a strand of cobweb from his sandy-colored hair. "If Jesse was up there, I would've found him."

Elliot appeared in the doorway. "He's definitely not in the basement."

Kate heard car doors slamming and rose to her feet. Seconds later, four uniformed deputies walked up and stood at the bottom of the porch steps. Kate recognized Billy Gene Duncan and Jason Hobbs, who had helped in the search for Abby and Jay, and before that when Micah and Riley were missing.

Please, Lord. Let Jesse be all right. Help us find him. I can't go through this again.

Billy Gene came up the steps and extended his hand. "Afternoon, Mrs. Cummings. The sheriff sent us to search for your boy."

Kate nodded. "We've already searched the house twice. Jesse's not here."

"You may be right, ma'am," Billy Gene said, "but since we've done this a time or two, we might could think of places to search that wouldn't occur to you. Never hurts to do one last sweep before we rule it out and move on."

"All right, go ahead," Kate said. "We'll stay out of your way. When you're finished, I'll take you to the other buildings Jesse has access to and you can search there."

"Yes, ma'am."

Billy Gene motioned for the deputies to follow him inside.

As Elliot took a step back, holding the door for the deputies, Kate's mind flashed back to all the times he had been there for her. How he had been present through every family crisis since Micah went missing. Always a friend. Always putting her needs ahead of his own, even before his feelings for her had turned romantic.

"So what now?" Abby pulled back her hair and fastened it with a ponytail band.

"We wait." Kate walked over and linked arms with Elliot.

"Mama, we'll go nuts just standing around." Abby exhaled and looked at Jay. "There must be something we can do."

"How about you and me go up the mountain," Jay said, "and pick up where your mom and Elliot left off? They can always call us, if they find him. Or if Hawk does."

Kate nodded. "Good idea. Go."

Jay grabbed Abby's hand and the two of them hurried down the porch steps and out to his car.

Kate's dad turned to Riley. "Sugar, how about you walk with Grandpa Buck down to the pier so we're outta the way while the deputies do their searching?"

"Okay, we can feed the geese." Riley jumped up out of the swing, her blue quilted jacket matching the sky and the hair bands holding her dark braids. "We don't need to take any food. We left that big sack of corn in the boathouse."

"So we did." Buck glanced over at Kate and winked. "We might as well see if the fish are bitin'. I've got my cell phone."

Kate smiled appreciatively. How she loved her dad. He had worked hard at filling in for Micah during the years she'd been raising kids alone.

"Zip your jacket," Kate said to Riley. "The breeze is picking up, and it'll be chillier near the water."

Riley obeyed and flashed her a toothy grin. "Mama, I know how to stay warm. I'm nine. I'm not a baby."

"No, but you're *my* baby." Kate tugged one of Riley's braids, then bent down, hugged her tightly, and whispered in her ear, "I've never, ever stopped loving you—not for one minute."

"Not for a teeny-tiny second?" Riley whispered back.

"Not for a single heartbeat."

Kate smiled, vividly remembering the first time they spoke these words, when they were reunited after Riley had been missing five years. From that day on, this affectionate mantra was a reassuring expression of love that each enjoyed repeating from time to time. The words also reminded Kate that Riley had come home despite hopeless odds, and that nothing was impossible with God.

Riley rested in Kate's embrace as if she understood, and then she pushed back and looked over at her grandfather. "Don't forget your walking stick."

"It's right there under that bottom step," Grandpa Buck said. "We'll see y'all after a bit."

"'Bye, everyone," Riley said.

Kate linked arms with Elliot and watched her father and younger daughter talking and laughing as they headed down the hill toward the pier. Life had become normal again. Kate had finally let herself trust the God who had broken her heart, who had allowed unspeakable suffering to befall her. And yet here she was again in the throes of fear and anguish, the fate of still another of her children totally in His hands.

Lord, am I willing to give up my son, if that is what You require of me?

She wanted to believe yes, but her heart screamed no with every fiber of her being. God had given Jesse to her, and she wasn't finished raising him. She wanted to guide him through adolescence, reassure him before his first date, see him off to the prom, and watch him graduate from high school. She wanted to share his excitement as he went off to college, got his degree, found his true love, got married, held his firstborn in his arms.

Kate blinked away the slideshow of Jesse that flashed through her mind. She had to be strong and believe that things would work out as God had ordained. And that she would be able to handle whatever was to come. But deep down, under the cool facade, the demons of the past taunted her unmercifully. Anything was possible. Even the unthinkable.

CHAPTER 26

Jesse, the pounding of his heart almost audible, stood with his back pressed against the trunk of a huge old pine, listening to the sound of dried pine needles crunching underfoot. He held his breath and tightened his gut in an effort to muffle the gurgling sounds coming from his stomach.

If Liam found him, he was a dead man. Jesse felt hot all over. He had to find a way out of these woods. *Lord, what do I do? Help me!*

A proverb he had memorized in Sunday school popped into his head. *Trust in the Lord with all your heart and lean not on your own understanding; in all your ways submit to him, and he will make your paths straight.*

That's what he needed! A straight path out of there. A way of escape. *Lord, I do trust You. Please show me a way out. I just want to go home.*

"Jesse!"

Jesse leaned into the tree trunk as if it could hide him. That demanding tone sounded more like the Liam he knew. All the sweet talk had been a ploy to draw him out.

"I'm getting tired!" Liam shouted. "And I'm starved. Come out, son. Tell me who you told. Then we can both go home. Aren't you tired of playing games?"

Virgil disconnected a call and set his cell phone on the conference table in his office. He looked across the table at Kevin and Police Chief Reggie Mitchell, who had been anxiously awaiting a status report from the search team he'd sent to Angel View.

"That was Billy Gene," Virgil said. "The team's done searching. No sign of Jesse."

"Perfect timing. I've finished creating the search grid." Kevin slid his laptop into its carrying case. "The mobile command post is ready to roll. I'll have it in place and fully functional in thirty minutes."

"I'll meet you there," Virgil said. "I want to call Kate first."

Kevin put on his sunglasses, then hung the strap of the carrying case over his shoulder and left the office.

Reggie stood. "I've got a few loose ends to tie up, and then I'll head over there."

Virgil shook his hand. "Thanks for sharing your turf. We're going to need the combined manpower."

"Always glad to work with you, friend."

As Reggie walked out the door, Virgil took his cell phone and keyed in Kate's phone number.

"Hello."

"Kate, it's Virgil. Since we didn't find Jesse at Angel View, I'm setting up a command post and going forward with a full-scale search of the area. We'll be set up in the back parking lot of the new Walmart. That'll afford us a central location, the use of restroom facilities, and several fast-food places nearby. We'll be up and running in thirty minutes. We want to make use of every minute of sunlight."

"Where do you even begin?" Kate said.

"We already have by eliminating your house and the lodge facilities. We're in the process of pulling together teams made up of my detectives, police officers from Foggy Ridge, and core volunteers from the community. We've also contacted Dawson's mother and gotten the names of the other football players. The game just ended, so we'll talk to all those kids and their parents and see if that leads anywhere. I still don't have enough information to issue an Amber Alert. But we're making up fliers with Jesse's picture. I'll talk to the media and get Jesse's face on the news."

"I can't thank you enough," Kate said. "Deputy Duncan mentioned you were going to send someone to stay with us and keep us informed."

"Yes, that's the most efficient way to get information relayed to you quickly. Also, two of my deputies are going to come talk to your family members, one on one. The more we can learn about Jesse, his habits, his fears, his strengths, his impulses, the easier it will be for us to consider every angle of how he might respond if he's being threatened."

Kate sighed. "You've said all along that you thought he was being threatened. I should've listened."

"I hope I'm wrong. But I've never believed his recanting was sincere. If he's being threatened, he could feel very alone. Hiding would be a natural impulse."

"But he has to know I'd be worried sick," Kate said. "I just don't see Jesse doing that to me."

"Me either. Unless he's afraid."

Kate let out a whimper and sounded as if she'd started to cry. "Sorry ... I'm just so afraid something awful has happened to him."

"We don't know that. Jesse's smart. And he knows these hills like the back of his hand. There's a good chance he's hiding to stay safe. I'm going to do everything in my power to find him. I need you to get a piece of Jesse's clothing that hasn't been laundered and give it to the two detectives who come out to question the family. If we get a good lead, I'll call in the bloodhounds."

"Find him, Virgil."

"We're going to turn Foggy Ridge upside down. Sure Foot Mountain too. If he's out there, we'll find him."

Virgil put his phone on vibrate and put it back in his pocket, not nearly as confident as he'd sounded. What if his best effort still wasn't good enough?

As Kate hung up the phone, the gravity of the situation buckled her knees. She fell backward onto a kitchen chair.

Elliot hurried over to her, grabbed her hand, and steadied her. "You okay? You look pale."

"All of a sudden, I'm weak as a kitten," Kate said.

Elliot dabbed the perspiration off her forehead. "I'm not surprised. You need to eat something. Let me make you a sandwich."

"I would probably throw it up. Maybe a glass of milk."

Elliot opened the fridge, poured her a glass of milk, and set it on the table. He pulled out a chair and sat facing her. "Kate"—he seemed to look right past her defenses—"God knows where Jesse is. We need to stay positive and not give fear a foothold, or it will eat us up."

"I know," Kate said. "Easier said than done."

Elliot took his thumb and gently wiped a tear off her cheek. "I'll help you."

"You're *always* helping me. My life is just one crisis after another."

"Come on, Kate. Things have been great for two years." Elliot's eyes seemed to search her thoughts. "This is not your *fault*. And I'm right where I want to be."

Kate squeezed his hand. "Why didn't I see this coming? Virgil did."

"Virgil's a professional. It's his job to be suspicious."

"I believed Jesse," Kate said.

"So did I. He's never given us cause to doubt his word before. Poor kid. Had to be hard lying to us. He's got such a tender conscience."

Kate nodded. "Jesse's so sensitive that I'm not sure he would even fight back, if someone tried to hurt him."

"But he's also a smart boy. And his faith is strong. He has amazing spiritual insight for a kid his age." Elliot tilted her chin and held her gaze. "If he's in over his head, he knows who to turn to."

"That's what Hawk just said, right before I hung up the phone."

"Is Hawk coming back to the house?"

"No, he's going to hang around the command post. He said he would keep us updated."

"Do you want me to take you there?" Elliot said.

"Not yet. I think I'd rather wait here, in case Jesse comes home."

Kate folded her arms across her chest and rocked back and forth in the chair, then buried her head in Elliot's chest, not even trying to stop the tears.

Lord, are You going to take Jesse from me? Haven't I suffered enough? I want Your will to be done. You know that. And I've come a long way in trusting You again. But this is so hard. I'm just not ready to let him go.

Virgil sat between Chief Deputy Kevin Mann and Police Chief Reggie Mitchell at the computers in the mobile command post, a used motor home that had been remodeled for the specific needs of the sheriff's department. He had put his chief deputy in charge.

"All right, Kevin," Virgil said. "Tell us the plan."

Kevin took a pen and pointed to the left monitor. "This is a detailed map of Foggy Ridge, divided into four sectors. As we discussed earlier, Chief Mitchell's officers will cover all four, which are numbered and shaded in blue. Our deputies and the chief's core volunteers will join to do a foot search of these areas outside the city limits, which I've also divided into four numbered sectors and shaded in red."

"Looks good." Reggie rubbed his chin and studied the graphic. "And what about the specific people that need to be questioned?"

Kevin clicked the mouse, and a different graphic appeared. "Those folks are divided into four groups: Friends and family. Schoolmates and teachers. Youth group and youth pastor. And miscellaneous. Chief Mitchell, your field interview teams will handle the two groups shaded in green, and our deputies will handle the two shaded in orange. We'll be using handheld radios and operating on two separate frequencies, one for search and one for field interviews. They'll be monitored here at the command post and information compiled minute by minute, enabling us to pass pertinent information back and forth so all teams are on the same page.

"I've also got people assigned to handle media questions and disseminate information," Kevin said. "They'll make sure that fliers with Jesse's picture and our phone number are widely distributed, and will oversee any incoming leads.

"A search-and-rescue helicopter should be in operation shortly. And the sheriff's department in Fayetteville has been alerted that we may need the bloodhounds brought in. The dogs are in use at the moment, but the sheriff will let us know as soon as they're available. In addition, I've assigned Deputy Roberta Freed to stay with the Cummings family and relay any information they need to know."

Reggie nodded. "Good. Have we caught up with Liam Berne? I don't see his name on the list of folks to be interviewed."

"Not yet, Chief," Kevin replied. "We're trying to reach his cell number, but the calls aren't going through. His sister did talk to him on his cell, just after eleven. Liam told her that he didn't see Jesse in the store, but his voice cut out before they finished the conversation. She said his phone's been acting up off and on for weeks."

"So we don't have a twenty on Berne?"

"Not yet," Kevin said. "He told his sister he had a long list of errands to run, and not to expect him home until dinnertime. The sheriff offered to follow up with that."

Virgil nodded. "I put Deputies Duncan and Hobbs on it. They'll locate him and see if he remembers anything that can help us."

Reggie seemed lost in thought, his dark skin shiny like fine mahogany under the fluorescent overhead lights. Finally, he turned to Virgil. "Sheriff, should we have concerns about Berne, since he and the kid were in the sporting goods store at the same time and neither's been seen since?"

"What concerns? Liam Berne isn't a suspect."

"I know," Reggie said. "I just meant the possibility that Berne might be missing too."

"Since his sister talked to him after he left the store, I'd rather not spend our resources on him. Duncan and Hobbs will let me know when they catch up with him. Let's focus our efforts on finding Jesse while we still have daylight." Virgil stood and arched his back. "Anybody else want coffee?"

"No, thanks," Reggie said. "I already have a caffeine buzz."

Kevin shook his head. "I'm coffeed out."

Virgil went over to the counter and poured himself a cup. "Kevin, how close are we to getting under way?"

"Minutes. The core volunteers are all here, and the teams are being briefed. I'm waiting for confirmation from each team leader that they're ready to go." Kevin turned his chair around and seemed to study Virgil. "I know that look. This is not your fault, Sheriff."

Virgil pursed his lips.

"I've been in your shoes, Virgil," Reggie admitted. "I know it's easy to second-guess yourself, but don't go there. You made a good call."

"And you sure didn't tell Jesse to shoot off his mouth at the middle school," Kevin said.

"I should've never called off the covert operation. I should've listened to my instincts."

Kevin raised his eyebrows. "Instead of your chief deputy?"

"It was my call," Virgil said.

Kevin turned back around and looked at the map. "Finding that kid'll be like searching for a needle in a haystack. Should we at least *consider* calling in the feds? Jesse could be in any one of seven states by now."

"Or he could be right *here*," Virgil said, more adamantly than he intended. "There's no indication that Jesse was taken across the state line, and I don't need the feds breathing down my neck. Let's use our own resources and find Jesse and end his mother's agony over another missing child. No one in this town has suffered more than Kate Cummings."

Virgil hated that he sounded defensive. This was personal and everyone knew it. He would conduct this search the same as he would for any missing child and use every resource he had. But he couldn't fail. Not this time. Not with this kid.

❧

Jesse moved as quietly as he could, darting from tree to tree, and trying not to breathe too loudly. Though he hadn't actually seen Liam in a while, he could hear him, and the image of him closing in with a gun in his hand was still vivid in his mind. The sun was getting lower in the sky, and very little light was filtering through the canopy now. He wondered if it were even possible to find a way out of these woods before it got dark.

Jesse sat down on a hollow log and laid his head on his knees. It felt good to rest, though he didn't dare stop for long. He couldn't remember ever being this hungry. Or this thirsty.

God, please help me. Show me the way out. And don't let Mama get too worried.

"Jesse … I know you can hear me. I'm right on your heels."

The sound of Liam's voice made him shudder.

"We're losing our light, kid. In another couple hours, it's going to be hard to see in these woods. Just talk to me. I'm not going to hurt you."

Jesse sprang to his feet and leaned against the trunk of a hardwood tree. It sounded as if Liam was behind him. Or maybe to his left. He could hear the swishing of leaves and pine needles crackling beneath Liam's feet. The guy was on the move.

"The sooner we talk, the sooner we can both go home," Liam shouted. "I'm getting *really* tired of playing hide-and-seek."

Jesse clung to the tree, paralyzed with fear, and waited for what seemed an eternity. The forest was silent again. He took in a deep breath and let it out, then ever so slowly peeked out from behind the tree.

"Olly olly oxen free!" Liam let out a wicked laugh, grabbing Jesse by the collar of his denim jacket, the gun barrel pressed flush against his forehead. "I'm done with hide-and-seek. Start talking."

CHAPTER 27

Jesse glanced up at the barrel of Liam's gun, his surging heartbeat audible, his tongue feeling as if it were glued to the roof of his mouth.

"I'm out of patience. You do *not* want to mess with me." Liam's gruff tone was as intimidating as ever. "Who else knows that you saw me in the river with my mother on the morning she drowned?"

"I–I didn't tell anyone. Honest."

"You're lying."

"I'm not!"

"Spit it out, kid! Or I swear I'll pull the trigger."

Jesse considered making up a name. But if Liam could tell he was lying, he might kill him anyway. He decided to stick with the truth and hope Liam could read him.

"I'm t-telling you the truth." Jesse hated that his voice was shaking. "I can't give you something I d-don't know."

"If you didn't tell anyone, then who's trying to extort fifty grand out of me, huh?"

Jesse felt the hard steel barrel of Liam's gun pressing closer and closer to his brain. "I–I don't know. Maybe someone else saw you. If I knew, why wouldn't I tell you? I don't want to die."

Liam wore an ugly scowl and a stone-cold glare, as he tightened his grip on Jesse's collar. "You'd better not be lying to me." Liam let go of Jesse but kept the gun pointed on him. "If you kept your mouth shut, then whoever left me that note might be bluffing." Liam looked somewhere beyond Jesse and seemed to be talking to himself. "Probably one of the deputies trying to hit the jackpot. He's thinking if I'm guilty, I'll pay him. If I'm innocent, I won't. By staying anonymous, he has nothing to lose and might walk away with fifty g's. Clever. I almost fell for it."

"I kept my word," Jesse said. "Can I please go now?"

"You're a good kid, Jesse. But I know you overheard my conversation with Joe Evans. It was one thing when you only got a glimpse of my face at fifty yards. It's another now that you know exactly who I am. And be honest. If you get out of these woods, your conscience will compel you to go to the sheriff and spill your guts. I get it. That's what a good kid would do. But that would mean I'd go to jail for the rest of my life. I've invested too much to let that happen."

Jesse's eyes clouded with tears. It was pointless to try to talk his way out of this. Or even to plead. What Liam said was true, and Jesse couldn't deny it.

Help me, God, or I'm going to die.

"Look, I'll make this quick and painless," Liam said. "Kneel down on the ground and keep your hands clasped behind your head. If you don't try and fight me, you won't feel a thing."

Jesse stood frozen, his mind whirling with thoughts of his family and how hard this would be for them. Also the fact that a split second after Liam pulled the trigger, Jesse would be with Jesus. And would get to see his father again.

Lord, help Mama not to grieve so long this time. Convince her to marry Elliot. They're really good for each other. And Riley needs a dad.

Jesse tried to think of anything he needed to make right before he saw his Savior face to face.

"Stop stalling. Let's get this over with." A brisk breeze came up and blew the trees. A weird scraping noise caused Liam to look up, and he spit out a swear word. "This place gives me the creeps. Come on, kid. On your knees."

"*Wait* … I need to tell you something." Jesse swallowed hard, a tear escaping down his cheek. He looked up at Liam, his lips trembling, but unable to make a sound.

"You think I *want* to do this?" Liam said. "It's the only option that makes sense. I'm done talking about it. You're not going to change my mind."

"I know. I f-forgive you," Jesse said, relieved the words finally came out. "I just wanted you to know."

"Whatever makes you feel better. Now turn around and kneel, hands behind your head."

Liam spun him around. "For what it's worth, I never intended for this to happen. But I've got to play the hand I was dealt."

Jesse's heart pounded wildly as Liam cocked the gun, but he was strangely at peace. *God, I don't get why this is happening. But I trust You.*

A loud cracking sound split the silence, and something powerful forced Jesse forward, facedown on the ground. Had he been shot? Maybe he was dead.

He opened his eyes, lifted his head, and looked around, trying to get his eyes to focus. Liam lay motionless on his belly, his legs pinned by a huge tree limb. The gun was on the ground. Jesse got up on all fours and grabbed it, then sat on his heels, realizing how narrowly he had escaped being shot *and* being crushed.

Liam slowly opened his eyes and seemed disoriented, then cried out with moaning and swearing as he struggled to get his legs free.

"Not fun being helpless, is it?" Jesse said, his voice shakier than his hands holding the gun.

Liam sighed. "Go ahead and gloat. I suppose I have it coming. But either give me a hand or shoot me."

Jesse laid the gun down and pushed the fallen limb as hard as he could, grunting and straining, but to no avail. "I'm not—strong enough—to move it."

"My legs are probably busted," Liam said. "Just put me out of my misery. No one would blame you, after what I did."

"They'd probably thank me." Jesse rubbed a cramp out of his arm, sizing up the man who had scared him into silence and tried to put a bullet through his head. Liam was totally helpless pinned underneath that limb. Served him right.

You can never disappoint God by refusing to repay evil with evil. Jesus didn't even lash out at those who were going to kill Him.

Jesse considered Elliot's words. He'd been willing to forgive Liam when he thought he was going to die. Was he willing to stand by it, now that he was going to live?

"Did you hear me?" Liam said. "Get on with it."

"I'm not going to shoot you."

"Why not? That's what I'd do."

"Well, I'm not you."

"Then get out of here and save yourself." Liam winced. "Take the keys out of my right back pocket. There's an LED light on the key ring. It'll be dark soon. That should be enough light to help you see where you're going."

Jesse pushed the gun out of Liam's reach and stuck his hand in Liam's back pocket and found the key ring. "I'll send help as soon as I can." Jesse scrambled to his feet.

"Wait!" Liam said. "In case I don't make it, tell me the truth. You've got nothing to lose now. Who's trying to get money out of me?"

"I don't know. I never said a word to anyone. I didn't want you to hurt my family."

Jesse looked around in all directions, suddenly feeling sick to his stomach. How would he ever find his way home?

"What are you waiting for, kid?"

"I'm turned around. I'm not sure how to get back."

"You're facing the right way. Just start walking. Trust me. I'm good with directions. Go! You're running out of daylight. Take the gun. You might need to scare off a black bear or a wild hog."

Jesse reached down and grabbed Liam's gun, and took off running, his fear of the dark forest less ominous than his fear of never seeing his family again.

Thank You, Lord! I knew You would hear me!

Jesse zigzagged around the trees, wrestling with low-lying branches that scratched his face as he fought his way through the maze. He was cold. And hungry. But at least he was finally free.

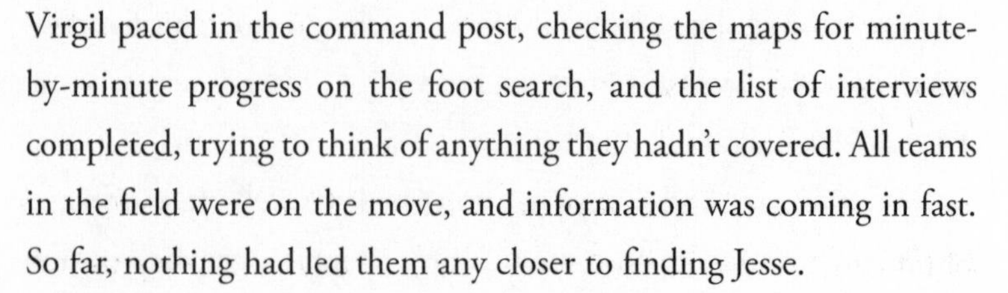

Virgil paced in the command post, checking the maps for minute-by-minute progress on the foot search, and the list of interviews completed, trying to think of anything they hadn't covered. All teams in the field were on the move, and information was coming in fast. So far, nothing had led them any closer to finding Jesse.

Reggie came and stood next to Virgil. "The one person we still haven't interviewed is Liam Berne. My mind's all over the map, wonderin' why he's so hard to reach."

"Mine too." Virgil threw his paper cup in the trash can. "Come on. Time to speed this up."

Virgil stepped over to Kevin's station, Reggie on his heels.

"Kevin, Liam should've surfaced by now. Think we should put out an APB on his Caprice?"

Kevin smiled. "You're reading my mind, Sheriff. Consider it done."

Virgil patted Kevin's shoulder, then turned to Reggie. "I'm going to step outside. I'll be right back."

Virgil went down the steps and out from under the awning that covered two tables, one arranged with an extra large coffeemaker, bottled water, and doughnuts. The other with battery chargers and recharged batteries.

He turned his back to the media, then took out his cell phone and keyed in the number for Billy Gene.

"Hello, Sheriff."

"What's the holdup on locating Liam Berne?"

"Sir, me and Jason have been runnin' our wheels off tryin' to track him down. One of us has called his cell phone every fifteen minutes. We've been to every establishment on the list his sister gave us. If he's out doin' errands, you'd think someone would remember seein' him. No one does."

"Change of plans," Virgil said. "I want you to do a couple things for me. First, on the bookshelf in my office, behind the framed photo of Jill Beth and me, is an empty Coke can. I want you to bag the can and take it to the lab. Give it to Ginger. Have her run a DNA test and compare it to the piece of bubblegum you recovered in the Dixie Berne investigation. Tell her to put a rush on it."

"Yes, sir. Copy that."

"Then I want you and Jason to go back to the Bernes' place and interview Colleen. Find out if Liam has acted out of character lately. You know, seemed anxious. Depressed. Angry. Aloof. Anything different. And pay close attention to *her*. I want to know if she acts nervous or like she's hiding something."

"We'll get right on it, Sheriff. So … does that Coke can belong to one of *them*?"

"I'll fill you in when I have time. Just take it to the lab and go question Colleen. If you think she knows something, don't be afraid to push her. Call me when you're done. I need to get back to the command post."

Virgil put his cell phone in his pocket, the eerie reverberation of the search-and-rescue helicopter starting to get on his nerves.

His instincts were on overload, but he knew better than to jump to conclusions. The DNA test wouldn't come back sooner than ten days, even on a rush. What he really needed was to find Liam Berne.

Jesse moved slowly through the dark forest, holding tightly to the loaded gun, the tiny light on Liam's key ring illuminating only a concentrated swatch of ground in front of him. Strange animal noises coming from the shadows made him edgy. Hawk told him that wild animals are more afraid of people than people are of them. Jesse was counting on it.

He found a tree stump and sat, the mingled scents of pine and wet earth turning his thoughts to Angel View. He wanted to go home, so why couldn't he stop thinking about Liam? It was hard to tell how injured the guy was. Or whether he was in shock. And even a healthy person could die of hypothermia in these nighttime temperatures.

Jesse looked down at the gun. He could never have shot Liam, no matter how much the man deserved it. But leaving him out there, wounded and vulnerable, with no protection from the cold, seemed just as wrong. Yet who would blame Jesse for fleeing from the monster who almost killed him—and would probably try again, if he had the chance?

Jesse sighed. Why did he feel so pulled to go back? He planned to send help once he got out. It was crazy to go back and help a guy who wanted him dead. It made sense to get home to the family who wanted him alive. So why the tug-of-war in his gut? Which decision was right—should he keep going or turn around?

Then Jesse remembered the advice Elliot got from his dad. Which decision best showed that Jesse loved God with all his heart, mind, soul, and strength? And which decision treated Liam the way Jesse wanted to be treated?

Jesse immediately thought of the parable of the Good Samaritan and mulled it over in his mind. If he left Liam behind, how was he any better than the priest and the Levite who walked past the wounded man and left him to die? If Jesse were the one trapped under a limb, he wouldn't want to be left alone at night in that cold, creepy forest.

He wrestled with that thought for a few minutes. Going back would be hard. Way out of his comfort zone. But wasn't putting someone else's needs ahead of his own what the Bible meant by loving his neighbor—even Liam Berne?

Lord, I really want to go home. But this seems more important than doing what I want.

Jesse pulled his hood over his head and stood, holding tightly to the gun in his right hand. He shone the blue light on the ground in front of him, then made an about-face and began walking the other way.

CHAPTER 28

Kate sat on the porch swing, zipped up in her red anorak jacket, her mind jumping from one thought to another before she had time to really process any of it. The one thought that *had* sunk in was tonight's forecast calling for the temperature to dip below freezing. Jesse wasn't dressed for a cold snap. How she hated the feeling that she couldn't protect him.

Kate's mind flashed back to the hospital on the night Jesse was born. The nurse brought her newborn son and placed him in her arms …

"He's a little punkin," the nurse said. "Didn't even squawk with all the poking and prodding. Have you named him?"

"We're thinking about Jesse Buckley Cummings," Kate said. "The middle name is after my dad."

The nurse studied the baby and smiled. "I like the sound of it. Suits him just fine."

"It really does." Kate looked over at her husband, Micah, who crouched next to her recliner, studying the baby's tiny foot.

"When you and the kids came up with the name, I thought I would need a while to see if it fit, but he *looks* like a Jesse."

"Great. Then it's unanimous." Micah kissed his son's tiny foot. "Okay, buddy, it's official. Your first name's Jesse. Your middle name is after your grandpa Buck, who's about the kindest man you'll ever know."

"I'll leave you two to get acquainted with this little doll," the nurse said. "Use the call button when you're ready for me to put him back in the nursery."

"We will. Thanks," Micah said.

"I can hardly wait for Dad to see his namesake." Kate smiled, gently brushing her fingertips through her newborn's fine dark hair. "This little man has no idea how loved he's going to be. Abby and Hawk are already fighting over who gets to rock him first in the pine rocker you made when I was pregnant with Hawk."

Micah smiled. "I wouldn't trade those late-night feedings alone with Hawk and Abby for anything."

"So does that mean you're taking the night shift with Jesse too?"

"Absolutely. And if by some miracle, he wants to sleep through the night, I'll get up and rock him anyway."

Kate chuckled. "Oh really?"

"Yep. I want the whole experience. Hear that, Jesse? Your ol' man is all in."

"Mama is too." Kate looked into her baby's round dark eyes. "We just want you to be happy and carefree and not grow up too fast."

Kate blinked the stinging from her eyes. Micah didn't live to keep that promise, and she was failing miserably. Why hadn't she been able to read the signs that Jesse was keeping something from her, or at least that he was troubled? Was it because he had never given her cause to doubt his word before? Or was it because she'd been too self-centered and preoccupied?

The door opened, and Elliot came out on the porch, carrying her pink and ivory afghan, and sat next to her in the swing.

"You've been out here a long time." He opened the afghan and draped it over her legs. "How are you holding up?"

Kate shook her head and swallowed the emotion that threatened to steal her composure. "Why can't Virgil find Jesse? They've turned Foggy Ridge and the outlying areas upside down. Search and Rescue has flown over every inch of Sure Foot Mountain."

"They're not finished yet. But don't forget, the Lord knows where Jesse is. If he's in trouble, there's no doubt in my mind that Jesse will rely on God to help him."

"I know," Kate said. "It's how God will respond that makes me nervous. There, I finally said it."

Elliot didn't flinch at her admission and just looked into her eyes as if he understood.

"Don't forget," Kate said, "I lived through five years of God's silence while my husband and two-year-old daughter disappeared from my life. I want more than anything to trust God to bring Jesse home. But I'm struggling with doubt, no matter how much I don't want to." Kate buried her face in her hands and stifled a sob. "I'm so sorry. My faith isn't as strong as yours. Or Jesse's."

Elliot put his arm around her. "It's not a contest, honey. You've been through more than most people will face in a lifetime. Just don't lose sight of the fact that God also brought Abby and Riley home unharmed. Let's take it one step at a time."

Kate heard a knock, and then the door opened.

"Excuse me," Deputy Roberta Freed said. "Just checking to see if I can get anything for you."

"We're okay." Kate dabbed her eyes. "No news from the command post?"

"Not yet. But don't be discouraged. Sheriff Granger and Chief Mitchell are using every available resource. I've seen situations like this turn on a dime."

Virgil sat at his station in the command post, tapping his fingers on his desk. What was taking Billy Gene and Jason so long to report back on their interview with Colleen Berne?

Reggie came over and stood next to Virgil's chair. "No success yet with the APB on Berne's car. How're we comin' with leads?"

Virgil smiled. "Oh, since Elliot Stafford offered a five-thousand-dollar reward and Jesse's picture was shown on the five o'clock news, leads're pouring in faster than we can sift through them. Nothing useful. Just the usual deluge of flaky people making up information in hopes of cashing in."

"That kid didn't just disappear from the face of the earth," Reggie said. "Somebody knows somethin'. And I keep thinkin' that somebody might be Liam Berne. The longer Berne's incommunicado, the more suspicious he looks."

Virgil's cell phone vibrated, and he glanced at the screen. "Excuse me, Reg. I need to take this." Virgil turned around and faced the computer, the phone to his ear. "Were you able to find out anything useful from Colleen Berne?"

"Sheriff, this *is* Colleen Berne. Deputy Duncan insisted I call you on his cell phone so I could get through faster. I haven't heard back from my brother. But I have something important you need to see. Deputy Duncan said you're not in the office. Is there someplace we can meet?"

"I'm currently at the command post we set up to manage our search for Jesse Cummings. I can't leave right now. Could you show it to my deputies or have them bring it to me?"

"No. I need to show you myself. Believe me, it'll be worth your time."

"I suppose Duncan and Hobbs could bring you here," Virgil said. "It's kind of crazy, but I'll find us a place where we can talk privately."

"All right. Hold on a minute."

Virgil heard Colleen talking to someone, and then Billy Gene took the phone. "Sheriff, we can have her there in ten minutes."

"Any idea what this is about?"

"No, sir," Billy Gene said. "She's being real closed with us. Whatever she's got, she's only willing to share with you."

"Did you bag the Coke can and take it to the lab?"

"Sure did. Right before we came over here. Said they'd move it to the front of the line but would need ten days, at the very least."

"Okay, Billy Gene, thanks. See you soon."

Virgil put his cell phone in his pocket and sensed someone standing next to him. He looked up into Reggie's inquiring eyes.

"I supposed you overheard me talking to Colleen Berne," Virgil said.

Reggie folded his arms across his chest. "Did she tell your deputy where her brother is?"

"Come with me." Virgil rose to his feet. "I need to tell you and Kevin about a new development."

Jesse inched his way through the thick, inky blackness of the forest, feeling disoriented, much like he did in a blinding snowstorm. As far as he could tell, he was moving in the right direction. But how could he really know for certain?

He stopped and set the key-ring flashlight between his feet, then blew on his hands and rubbed them together. The night air felt even colder than he had anticipated. What if he wasn't able to start a fire by rubbing two sticks together? He'd only done it one other time, and Hawk had helped him.

Jesse's thoughts turned to his brother. Hawk probably felt responsible for losing track of Jesse.

Lord, don't let Hawk get in trouble or blame himself. He's the best big brother I could ever have.

Jesse's mind drifted back to the first time he could remember feeling a closeness with his brother …

Jesse lay on his back in his sleeping bag, his hands behind his head, staring up at the moonlit sky.

"I'm sorry Dawson got the stomach flu," Hawk said. "I know how long you waited for Mama to let you camp in the backyard by yourselves."

"Only my whole life."

Hawk smiled. "If it's any consolation, I had to wait until I was eight too. And even then, Mama and Daddy made me pitch my tent so they could see me through the kitchen window."

"Did you stay out alone?" Jesse said.

"Are you kidding? I was too chicken. Of course, I wouldn't admit it. I asked this kid, Joey Ray Miller, to camp out with me. You should've seen us. We shrieked every time the breeze moved a leaf." Hawk laughed. "I think we scared ourselves."

"So you had fun?"

"Oh, yeah. We lasted until midnight. I was just starting to nod off when Daddy stuck his head inside the tent and nearly scared Joey Ray to death. That kid let out a scream I'm sure every guest at Angel View could hear. He was so shaken and embarrassed that he started to cry."

"I'll bet Daddy felt bad."

"For sure. He was just checking on us."

"So did y'all go back to sleep?" Jesse said.

"Nope. Joey Ray wanted to go home. So Mama called his parents and they came and got him."

"Then you stayed outside by yourself?"

A grin spread across Hawk's face. "Absolutely not. I was as freaked out as Joey Ray, just quieter about it. Daddy said I could stay out if I let him sleep in the tent with me. I was glad. There were a lot more sounds in the dark than I remembered hearing when I'd gone camping with the family."

"Did you still have fun?" Jesse said.

"There's no way you could spend time with Daddy and not have fun. He stayed out with me all the next day, and we hiked, collected interesting rocks, and caught some fish for dinner. He started a small campfire and fried the fish and some potatoes in an iron skillet. Later, we got real comfy in our sleeping bags and he told me stories about when he was a kid. I was fixin' to listen all night, but he finally fell asleep in the middle of a sentence."

Jesse sighed. "I wish I could remember him better. I have a few memories that are clear in my mind. But I don't remember his voice. Or what he was really like. Most of what I know about him, I learned from Mama and Grandpa, you and Abby."

Hawk turned on his side and draped his arm over Jesse. "I'm sorry he's not here while you're growing up. Just remember that *I'm* here for you. I can't take the place of a father. But if anybody bullies you, he'll answer to me."

Jesse looked up at the round, full moon that seemed to have chased the stars away.

"I do remember something Daddy whispered in my ear when he kissed me good night."

"Cool. What was it?"

"He said, 'I love you to the moon and back.' It's from a storybook he used to read to me. I was too young then to totally get it. But now that I do, it's even harder to think I might never see him again."

Neither of them said anything for half a minute. And then Hawk said, "Maybe now it's up to us to love each other like that. I don't know whether we'll see Daddy or Riley Jo again. But if I can love you and Abby, Mama and Grandpa with all my heart, I know it would make him happy—and proud."

The deep reverberation of a helicopter brought Jesse back to the present. He wondered if Search and Rescue was looking for him. He bent down, picked up the key ring, and held up the beam of light, waving it back and forth until his arm got tired. It was no use. The canopy was so thick he couldn't even see the stars.

He set the key ring on his knee, then blew on his hands and rubbed them together. He thought of his family and how worried each of them must be.

Tears stung his eyes. "I love you to the moon and back," he whispered, regretting that he'd never told them so.

As desperate as he was to get home, the pull to go back and help his enemy was stronger. Surely the God who talked to Moses from a burning bush could help him get a fire going and keep Mr. Berne alive until they were found.

Jesse started walking, mumbling under his breath. "Lord, I hope this is the right decision. Because unless You help us, we're both going to die."

CHAPTER 29

Virgil sat in a folding chair at Kevin's station in the command post, and finished giving Reggie and Kevin the details of his conversation with Billy Gene.

Virgil turned his gaze to Kevin. "We're not exactly set up for an interview like this. Where do you want me to meet with Colleen Berne?"

"Why don't you take the back room," Kevin said. "We can clear everyone out of there until you're done. How long do you think you'll need?"

"Thirty minutes, maybe less," Virgil said. "Whatever it is she has to show me, we need to cut to the chase. If she knows where Liam is, or has any information that can help us find Jesse, that's our first priority."

Kevin nodded. "Agreed. I'm eager to get your assessment. Maybe we were too quick to eliminate Liam Berne as a suspect in their mother's drowning."

"Guess we're about to find out." Virgil looked at Reggie. "Let's do this."

"Won't have to ask me twice," Reggie said. "I've been itchin' to question her all day."

"Okay, then." Virgil rose to his feet. "Reggie and I will go clear the room and get it ready. Billy Gene and Jason should be here with Colleen by the time we're finished."

Virgil walked down the hall and knocked on the door to the back room and asked the deputies working there if they would move their work to his and Reggie's stations until they finished conducting their private interview.

Virgil and Reggie moved the table to the center of the room and set folding chairs on both sides.

"Well, it's not exactly state of the art," Virgil said. "But it'll do."

A loud knock at the door caused both men to turn, just as Billy Gene came through the doorway with Colleen Berne.

"Sheriff, me and Jason will be waitin' outside to take Miss Berne back, whenever you're done."

"Thanks," Virgil said. "Why don't you two take a break, have some coffee and doughnuts?"

A wide grin spread across Billy Gene's face. "Don't mind if I do. The wife's been pressurin' me to go easy on the sugar. Tried to make her understand that, when it comes to working cases, doughnuts are brain food and practically a food group all by themselves."

Billy Gene turned and went back down the hallway.

Virgil extended his hand to Colleen. "Thanks for coming here. I'm not comfortable leaving the command post while information is pouring in. You remember Police Chief Mitchell. He's assisting in our search for Jesse."

"Yes, hello again." Colleen shook hands with Reggie.

"Can I get you a bottle of water?" Virgil said. "Or coffee, juice, or a soft drink?"

"Thanks, but I'm good," Colleen said. "Where would you like me to sit?"

"Right here at the table." Virgil pulled out a folding chair and seated Colleen, then took the seat across from her and next to Reggie.

"We don't have much daylight left," Virgil said, "so let's cut to the chase. Colleen, as you know, Jesse Cummings went into Evans's Sporting Goods this morning at nine and hasn't been seen since. Our two departments have joined resources and are currently immersed in a massive search for this boy. Your brother was at that store this morning at the same time as Jesse. He hasn't been seen since either. Our persistent efforts to contact Liam have failed. And no one at any of the establishments you listed remembers seeing him today. It's rather perplexing."

"Why is it so important for you to question Liam?" Colleen said. "He already told me he didn't see Jesse in the store and never knew he was there."

"I know that's what he told you. My question is"—Virgil held her gaze—"do you believe him?"

Colleen's pale face was suddenly bright pink, and she looked down at her hands. "What are you implying, Sheriff?"

"Is it possible your brother deliberately misled you?"

Colleen paused for several seconds and coughed to clear her throat. "Of course, it's possible. If you'll hear me out, what I have to say might help you fill in a few blanks."

"Please go on. We're listening."

Colleen bit her lip. "You have to understand how hard this is for me. I love Liam. He's the only family I have now. I've always trusted him. Leaned on him. But some things have happened that didn't seem like a big deal at the time. But now, in combination, are impossible to ignore."

Virgil grabbed the pencil and ruled pad. "Tell us in order, if you can remember the sequence."

"The first thing was that the dark green shirt Liam wore the day Mother drowned—when he went out to run errands—is not the green shirt he put in the laundry. It was the same color, brand, and size as the one I got him for Christmas, but this one had a button-down collar and no pocket. The one I got him had a pointed collar and a pocket."

"Are you sayin' he came home wearin' a different shirt than the one he left in?" Reggie said.

"Honestly, I didn't pay attention to the shirt he came home in." Colleen looked from Reggie to Virgil. "But he was wearing the shirt I got him when he left the house. I'm sure of it. And I searched his closet and dresser drawers. The shirt I gave him isn't there, and I haven't seen it since he left that morning."

"Did you ask Liam about it?" Virgil said.

"Yes, but he blew it off and insisted it was the same shirt. So I let it go until some other things started to bother me."

Virgil arched his eyebrows. "What other things?"

"Liam has come home late from work a few times, which is something new. I left messages on his cell phone, but he never returned them. Each time I asked where he was, he said he was driving around and had his cell phone turned off. He always gave a reason: grief over Mother's death. Trying to get up the courage to quit his job. Just trying to clear his head. It's obvious to me that he's established a pattern of turning off his cell phone when he doesn't want to account for his whereabouts."

"Like he did the day your mother drowned," Virgil said.

Colleen hung her head. "Yes. And again today. He should've been home before now, or at least called. There's something else—and this was the last straw for me." Colleen reached into her jacket pocket and pulled out a piece of crumpled white paper and handed it to Virgil. "This is what I wanted you to see. Just before your deputies arrived to question me, I found this wadded up in the trash can in Liam's room."

Virgil put on his reading glasses, then opened the paper and smoothed it out so he and Reggie could read it. The letters had been torn from a magazine and pasted on:

"I SAW HOW YOUR MOTHER DIED. PAY ME $50,000 OR I'LL TELL THE SHERIFF. YOU'LL HEAR FROM ME AGAIN SOON."

Virgil laid his glasses next to the note on the table. "What do you think this means?"

Colleen's eyes brimmed with tears. "The same thing *Liam* thought it meant: that someone saw him drown Mother and wants hush money."

"The note's not specific." Virgil rubbed the stubble on his chin. "It could mean a number of things."

"It doesn't."

"What makes you so sure?"

Colleen's face suddenly looked like cold gray stone. "Because … *I* made the note and put it on Liam's car windshield in order to test him. I knew if he had nothing to hide, he would come to me with it. I wanted him to be innocent. I gave him plenty of chances to talk about the note. But he chose to hide it from me."

"When did you leave the note?"

"Yesterday afternoon," Colleen said, "right before I walked into the Gordon Building to meet Liam at the attorney's office to receive our inheritance checks. I wanted to be sure Liam had the means to pay an extortionist before I put him to the test."

Virgil sat back in his chair and exhaled, his mind spinning. "So did you assume by his silence that he was planning to pay it?"

"I don't know what he was planning. But if he believes Jesse was involved in an extortion attempt, he might have gone after him."

"Why would you think Jesse might be involved?" Virgil said.

"Oh please." Colleen rolled her eyes. "Just because Jesse publicly recanted his story doesn't mean I believed he lied about what he saw. There was a reason you didn't want me talking to Jesse and had him moved out of my English class. Liam and I both believed Jesse witnessed something. I just never dreamed that *something* was Liam."

Reggie leaned forward on his elbows. "Did your brother tell you why he was going to Evans's Sporting Goods?"

"No. But he liked the store. He went in there all the time."

"According to Mr. Evans, he bought ammunition for a handgun."

Colleen's eyes grew wide. "Liam has a permit to carry one, but he never does. He keeps it in the bottom drawer of his dresser in case we have an intruder."

"Do you know if it was there this morning?" Reggie said.

"No, but I'll check when I get home."

"Do you think he's capable of hurtin' the boy?" Reggie said.

"I would never have thought so. But I do believe he drowned our mother. So why not?" Colleen wiped a tear off her cheek. "I've said everything I came to say, Sheriff. I don't know what more I could tell you. Do you have more questions for me?"

Virgil glanced at his watch. "Not right now. We need to get back to the search. We appreciate your candor. I know it wasn't easy." Virgil stood. "I'll have the deputies take you home and wait with you in case Liam calls. You can check to see if the gun is missing. We'll probably have more questions later as we investigate your mother's death. But knowing these facts might help us to find Jesse."

"I hope so, Sheriff. He's such a sweet boy. If anything happens to him …" Colleen's voice trailed off, her lower lip quivering.

"Come on, I'll walk you out." Virgil led her into the hallway and to the side exit. "Thanks again for your willingness to come forward. I know what it cost you."

"I keep hoping I'm wrong. But what are the odds?"

Not in Liam's favor, Virgil thought, as he pushed open the metal door and followed Colleen down the steps.

When they reached the bottom, she looked at him, her eyes filled with angst. "Sheriff, please promise me you won't hurt my brother."

"We'll do everything in our power not to," Virgil said. "But I'm sure you understand that if he's holding Jesse against his will, we have to consider Jesse's safety first."

"I understand. Just know that Liam's not a bad person. He really isn't. He loved our mother. If he drowned her, he saw it as a mercy killing. That's the only way he could've justified such a horrific act."

Virgil motioned for Billy Gene to come. "You did the right thing, Colleen. Let us find Liam and sort out the facts. If you'll excuse me a moment, I need to speak with Deputy Duncan before he takes you home."

Virgil took Billy Gene aside and gave him a quick rundown of his interview with Colleen.

"I want you and Jason to stay with her at the house," Virgil said. "Check to see if the gun's there. And see if we can get the GPS coordinates on his cell phone; though if he doesn't want to be found, he's probably removed the battery. Get set up, so if he calls her, you can trace it. I've got enough now to issue an Amber Alert. Let's hope it's not too late."

CHAPTER 30

Jesse shivered in the frigid night air, tediously trying to retrace every step back to Liam, and feeling as if he'd been trudging through the forest all night. He held the flashlight to his watch. It was only eight forty. After he left Liam, he had gone an hour and a half before changing his mind and turning around. He had to be getting close. Unless he was lost.

Jesse heard gurgling sounds coming from his hollow stomach, and images of starving children popped into his mind. He wondered if his family had enjoyed his mother's Saturday-night spaghetti—or if they had been too upset, worrying about him.

He still wasn't sure how he was going to start a campfire when he caught up with Liam. But the feeling of being half frozen was a powerful incentive to figure it out.

Jesse came to a pine tree and spotted the initials LRV carved into the trunk. He *had* come this way! He was right on track. It wouldn't be long now.

Thank You, Lord. Now if You'll just help me know what to say when I find him.

Him. It occurred to Jesse that he had never called the man by name. Should he address him as Liam or Mr. Berne? Jesse had been taught that, as a sign of respect, he should not call adults by their first name. Calling the man Liam would feel weird and awkward. Addressing him as Mr. Berne would seem more natural, even if he didn't deserve the respect.

Jesse walked around the pine tree and spotted a fallen log that he remembered seeing earlier. This was definitely the way he had come. He thought of something else that hadn't occurred to him until now: What would he do if Mr. Berne was dead? He'd never even seen a dead person for real. The thought of being out there with a corpse through a cold, dark night was creepier than he wanted to think about.

The deep reverberation of a helicopter shook the ground again.

Jesse held up the tiny flashlight and waved it wildly, back and forth under the canopy, even though he held little hope that Search and Rescue would see it. Maybe if he could find a small clearing and build a big enough fire, the rescuers would be able to spot the flames, or at least the smoke.

He picked up his pace. As soon as he found Mr. Berne, that's exactly what he planned to do. Maybe they would be found yet tonight!

❧

Kate sat on the floor in the living room of her big log house, hugging her knees in front of a crackling fire. Thoughts of Jesse consumed her. After Roberta told them that Virgil had issued an Amber Alert and that Jesse was believed to be with Liam Berne, she had more questions than answers. Had Liam refused to believe Jesse's retraction that he was an eyewitness to Dixie Berne's drowning? Was he going to try to make Jesse talk?

"Honey, can I get something for you?" Elliot's voice startled her.

"No. I'm fine. Well, not fine. But I don't need anything—other than Jesse home safe and sound."

Elliot sat beside her, pulled her into his arms, and held her. How she needed his strong presence and seemingly unshakable faith.

Minutes passed in silence, Kate feeling no need to spoil it with words that would expose her fear and doubt. Why couldn't she have the faith that Elliot did? Or like that of her dad and her children? Every time she thought she had grown past her anger at God for the five agonizing years she had spent grieving her missing husband and daughter, her old demons slithered out of a dark place buried deep in her subconscious. They tormented her, relentlessly at times, with flashbacks so real that she feared all over again that God could not be trusted.

Kate sighed. Anytime she started to question God, it served only to provoke her anger and perpetuate her agony for however long it took for her to come to her senses. Why was her faith so fragile?

Kate sensed someone else had come into the living room.

"How's she doin'?" Buck said to Elliot, barely above a whisper.

"She's hardly said a word since the Amber Alert was issued."

"You don't have to talk as though I'm not here," Kate said, looking up at her dad, his shiny head and round glasses reflecting the glow of the fire. She reached up and took his hand. "I'm as all right as any of us can be, under the circumstances. Why don't you sit in your easy chair and get warm by the fire?"

"Aw, I don't wanna disturb you two."

"You're not," Kate said, "as long as I don't have to move."

Buck eased into his rocking chair. "I talked to Pastor Windsor. He called in the elders and the prayer team to pray for Jesse's safe return. He offered to come wait with us."

"Please tell me you told him *no*," Kate said, louder than she meant to. "I can't handle—"

"I know. I know. Don't worry," Buck said. "I told him you cope better with a little solitude. And that all of us are mighty grateful for the prayers."

"Thanks, Dad. You're a dear." Kate's cell phone rang, and her heart nearly stopped. She sat up straight, grabbed her phone, and read the caller ID. "It's Hawk." She took a deep breath and put the phone on speaker. "Did they find Jesse?"

"No," Hawk said. "But something's going on. Colleen Berne was here earlier with two deputies and went inside the command post. She was in there almost thirty minutes and then came out a side door with the sheriff and left with the same two deputies. Right after that, Sheriff Granger issued the Amber Alert."

"Did you ask him what she said?"

"No, the area is roped off and I can't get to him. But there's a lot of law enforcement coming and going—deputies *and* police officers. Mostly drinking coffee and grabbing doughnuts and fresh batteries. I suppose if they had found Jesse or had a hot lead, they would all jump in their squad cars, turn on the sirens, and rush out of here.

They're not. I think you should call the sheriff's cell and ask him what Colleen Berne said."

"Oh, I hesitate to do that." Kate looked over at Elliot. "After Virgil told us about the Amber Alert, he promised he'd call if something happened that we need to know. He's always been good about doing that."

"Who determines what we need to know?" Hawk replied. "I want answers. I'm not getting them here. There's nothing to stop me from talking to Colleen myself."

"Hawk, you know Virgil asked us not to do that."

"We're talking about my little brother's life. I can't just sit around and do nothing!"

Kate didn't bother arguing with him. She knew her eldest son's determination would trump any effort on her part to stop him.

"Unless you're going to call Sheriff Granger," Hawk said, "I'm going over to the Bernes' house and talk to Colleen."

Kate looked at Elliot and then at her dad. Both shrugged as if to say it was her call.

"Hawk, I'm honestly not comfortable calling Virgil at this point. At least not until you find out what Colleen has to say."

"All right, Mama. Sit tight."

❧

Virgil moved around the command post, studying maps and charts and every bit of new information as it came in. *Jesse, where are you?*

Reggie came over and stood next to him. "I need to run something by you."

"Shoot."

"My officers have finished covering all four sectors in town, including businesses along Pine Street, door to door in the neighborhoods, and every business downtown. We're close to wrappin' up the interviews on our list." Reggie folded his arms. "The only areas left to search are the acres of undeveloped land within the city limits. We only searched about a hundred yards in because they're so densely wooded. And without the bloodhounds, it would take my officers and the core volunteers an inordinate amount of time to search them. I'm wonderin' if our resources might be better spent by joining forces with your deputies and the core volunteers and finish searching the outlying areas first. And then, if Jesse isn't found, bring everyone to town and search deeper into those undeveloped areas. All that manpower combined will get it done faster. Just a thought."

"Sounds like a good move." Virgil mused. "I'm really disappointed the Amber Alert hasn't produced some leads."

"Yeah, me too," Reggie said. "What are we missing?"

"Darned if I know." Virgil put his hand on Reggie's shoulder. "Come on. Let's go run your idea by Kevin."

Virgil walked over to Kevin's station with Reggie, a hundred thoughts bouncing off his brain. But the one thought he continually dismissed was his fear that Jesse had been missing too long and was already dead.

God, I don't deserve any special consideration. I know I haven't been to church in a while. But I'm not asking for me. Help us bring Jesse home to Kate.

Jesse stopped walking and looked around, his frustration coming out in an audible groan. Suddenly the trees all looked alike. Why couldn't he figure out how to get back where he had started? He was cold. Hungry. Tired. And not in the mood to deal with another crisis.

Jesse cupped his hands around his mouth. "Mr. Berne," he shouted into the dense darkness. "Can you hear me? Mr. Berne!"

It was no use. He was never going to find the man. Coming back here was a lame idea.

He sat down on a hollow log, then blew on his hands and rubbed them together. Whether he found Mr. Berne or not, he needed to start a fire and thaw out—or risk frostbite or hypothermia. What if he couldn't get a fire started? What then?

Jesse felt trapped. His heart pounded and he broke out in a cold sweat, light-headed and sick to his stomach. He breathed in slowly and let it out. Then did it again, aware that he had sweat all over his face and was shivering. He wondered if he was having a panic attack like the ones his mother used to get.

God, don't let me do this. I need to get a fire started before I'm too cold to move.

He heard a noise and turned his ear toward the sound and listened.

"Help! I'm over here."

"Mr. Berne?" Jesse called. "Is that you?"

Jesse sprang to his feet and moved toward the voice, winding through a maze of tree trunks. He came to a small clearing and stopped. It looked familiar. This had to be the same open space he had crossed when he left.

"I'm almost there," Jesse hollered. "Call me again. I need to follow your voice!"

"Over here …"

Jesse crossed the clearing, shivering but excited that he had finally made it and thinking how good it would feel to sit by a roaring fire. He stopped and looked around. "I just crossed the clearing. I'm really close. Call me again so I can get my bearings."

He listened intently for a voice. Instead, everything was quiet. Too quiet. "Hello? Mr. Berne?"

A twig snapped in the stark stillness, sending a chill crawling up Jesse's spine. He stood still and tightened his grip on the gun, his hands shaking, not knowing what he was going to encounter. The woods were quiet except for the hooting of an owl and Jesse's breathing.

Jesse moved forward, taking slow, silent steps. He heard a dull thud, and the back of his head felt as if someone had blown it up with a stick of dynamite. The gun fell out of his hands as his knees gave way. He knew he was falling, but it seemed as if it were happening to someone else. His shoulder hit the forest floor with a powerful jolt, the side of his face pressed into a prickly mound of pine needles. He lay dazed, unsure of what had happened.

When he finally opened his eyes, he could barely make out a shadowy form crouched next to him. In the eerie stillness, he could hear it breathe in, breathe out. Breathe in, breathe out. Terror seized him.

God, I need Your help!

Jesse clamped his eyes shut and lay still as stone, the rhythm of his heartbeat wild and erratic, sounding like a war drum pounding in his head. He felt something warm and wet under his cheek. Blood! Had he been attacked by a black bear? Had the bear come back to finish him off?

And then he heard it—a still-fresh-in-his-mind sound that filled him with dread—the unmistakable click of a gun being cocked. Jesse took a shallow breath and didn't exhale. The shadowy form was human. And he was going to die.

CHAPTER 31

Kate sat on the couch with Elliot, comforted by the sound of her dad's light snoring as he napped in his rocker. She took a sip of warm tea and heard the door handle turn. The front door flew open and Hawk stumbled in, followed by a swirling blast of cold air and dried leaves.

"Stupid wind." Hawk leaned on the door with his back and closed it.

"Please tell me you don't have bad news." Kate put her hand over her heart.

"No, I came to get my down jacket and a stocking cap. It's freezing out there."

Hawk picked up the dried leaves and tossed them in the fire, then patted his grandfather on the head and sat on the piano bench that had hardly been used since Micah died.

"Did you go see Colleen Berne?" Kate set her cup and saucer on the side table.

"I did. Big waste of time," Hawk said. "Deputies Duncan and Hobbs were there with her and I didn't get past the front door. I did ask her why she went to see the sheriff and whether she knew something that would help us find Jesse."

"And what did she say?"

"Just that she was sorry about Jesse and knew about the Amber Alert. But that she'd been instructed not to talk about the case. Duh. I should've known. How many times have we heard *that*?"

"Does she understand that her brother is suspected of taking Jesse?" Elliot said.

"I'm sure she does." Hawk leaned forward, his hands clasped between his knees. "But Deputy Duncan never left us alone. She couldn't say anything even if she'd wanted to."

"Colleen was just doing what she was told to do," Kate said. "We know how that works."

Hawk's eyes turned to slits. "Yeah, but I'd sure like to know what she said to the sheriff. Mama, I really think you should call Virgil. There's more going on than he's telling us."

"Anything we *need* to know," Kate said, "will be forthcoming through Roberta. I trust Virgil. I'm surprised you don't."

Hawk sighed. "It's not that. I just don't like being left out of the loop. I'm about to climb the walls. I feel responsible for what happened to Jesse."

"Don't," Kate said. "He should've been perfectly safe at Evans's. We all know that."

Hawk rubbed the dark stubble that had almost become a mustache. "You should've seen Colleen's face. She knows something."

Kate squeezed Elliot's hand. "Do you think I should talk to Virgil?"

"Sometimes it's good to be proactive. Probably should run it by Roberta first."

"Run what by me?" Deputy Roberta Freed stood in the doorway between the kitchen and the living room, her dark skin blending into the evening shadows.

Kate told Roberta about Hawk's brief conversation with Colleen Berne and his concerns.

"I was just coming to tell you that Sheriff Granger called," Roberta said. "He wanted me to let you know that after he and Chief Mitchell met with Colleen Berne at the command post, they're convinced that Liam has Jesse or knows where he is."

"Let me guess," Hawk said sarcastically, "the sheriff didn't say what it was that Colleen told him?"

"No, he didn't."

Hawk rolled his eyes. "Of course not. He acts like it's none of our business. Only it *is* our business. We have a right to know."

"Hawk, I can imagine how frustrating this is," Roberta said, her voice calm and reassuring. "The sheriff is taking every measure we have available to find your brother."

"I just wish you'd keep us informed," Hawk said.

Roberta smiled. "I just did."

Hawk held Roberta's gaze, his jaw set. "But what I *want* to know is what Colleen told the sheriff. We know she heard the rumor at the middle school that Jesse was an eyewitness to her mother's murder. She must've told Liam. The fact that Liam is suspected of taking Jesse makes me think one of two things: Either he didn't buy Jesse's retraction and decided to make him talk. Or *he's* the one who killed his mother, and wants to shut Jesse up."

"It's dangerous to make assumptions." Roberta folded her arms across her chest. "Believe me, I understand that you want answers. But I don't have them."

"Or aren't authorized to tell us."

"Hawk, that's enough," Kate said, trying to process the implications of Liam Berne having killed his own mother.

Roberta went over and sat on the piano bench next to Hawk. "Hey, we're all on the same team here," she said softly. "The sheriff will tell me what you need to know. I trust him. You should too."

"Listen to Roberta," Kate said. "Virgil has always been straight with us. Let him do his job."

Hawk's eyes were suddenly dark pools, his chin quivering. "Jesse's been missing for *ten* hours. With that monster. We have to find …"

Elliot stood and held out his hand to Kate. "How about we get the rest of the family in here and pray again. The sheriff may not know where Jesse is, but God certainly does. We need to be strong and trust Him to help us."

Everyone nodded in agreement, and while Hawk went to round up the others, Kate's mind flashed back two years, to the command post where her family nervously waited for news about Abby, never dreaming that God planned not only to bring her home safely but also to bring Riley back after five long years.

The Lord had proven Himself faithful. Kate chose to believe He would do it again. But if He didn't, if His will was to take Jesse from her the way He had taken Micah, could she handle it?

Jesse trembled, waiting for the gun to fire, hoping his death would be instant. Instead, he felt the tip of a boot prod him in the ribs.

"Get up!"

Jesse knew Liam's voice. That wasn't him.

"You deaf, boy? Up on your feet!"

Jesse's eyes flew open. He scrambled to his feet, face to face with what appeared to be a tall, thin, bearded man holding two guns, one of which was likely the one Jesse had dropped.

"Who're you?" the man demanded to know. "And what're you doing in these woods?"

"My n-name is Jesse. Cummings."

"Stop your stuttering and finish answering my question," the man said. "Why're you here?"

"I–I came back to help Mr. Berne." Jesse's head hurt so bad he wanted to cry. "His legs are pinned under a tree limb, and I—"

"Where're the others?"

"There's no one else. I'm by myself," Jesse said, immediately regretting having admitted that to a man holding two guns on him.

"How come? I thought you were going to fetch the sheriff and those medical folk."

How did he know that? "I–I was. But I changed my mind. I thought if it took too long, Mr. Berne might not make it. It's really cold. So I came back to get a fire going."

"No need to worry about ol' Liam. He's just fine."

Liam? "You know Mr. Berne?" Jesse said.

"Let's just say we've been getting acquainted. He's a tad cranky. But we had us a little chat about attitude. He's thinking on it. My name's Slick. You two are staying the night at my shelter. It's just over yonder."

Jesse glanced at the two guns pointed at him. "Mister, you don't need those. I'm not a threat."

"Now *that's* the right attitude, boy." He handed Jesse a flashlight. "Turn around, why don't you, and start walking. Keep your hands so I can see them, and that light so we can see where we're going."

Jesse did what he was told, wishing he could take one of the painkillers that had helped Hawk when he sprained his ankle. "Did Mr. Berne tell you why he's here?"

"Yep."

"So you know he drowned his mother?"

Slick laughed. "To hear him tell it, he did her a favor."

"The sheriff doesn't see it that way," Jesse said. "I'm sure he's looking for us. I heard the Search and Rescue helicopter fly over a couple times."

"Cops are crawling all over Foggy Ridge too, going door to door, asking about the both of you. They came to my place and showed me photos. Asked if I'd ever seen you or Liam. I told them no, but I didn't like the way they were eyeing me. So, soon as they left, I stuffed some essentials into my backpack and took off running in the woods. Thought I'd just camp out here till the ruckus dies down."

"Why, are you in trouble with the law?" Jesse said.

"Let's just say I'm pretty sure the cops that came to my door looking for you recognized me. I'm *not* going to jail, I promise you that. And you, young fella, are my insurance policy." Slick gave him a shove. "Keep walking. It's not far now."

"Your insurance policy?" Jesse asked.

"Yep. If the cops find us, I'll have leverage. I can offer you and Liam in exchange for them letting me walk. And seeing as how the whole town wants you home, and Liam's already killed once—and will surely kill you if he isn't locked up—they're going to want you both back a whole lot more than they want to lock me up."

"But they may not even come here," Jesse said. "They can't search everywhere."

"Then I won't be needing you."

"So you'll let us go, right?"

"You ask too many questions. Walk." Slick shoved him again. "If the sheriff does show, you better hope he's agreeable to doing things my way. Because I'm telling you straight out: I won't hesitate to blow your head off—and Liam's—if the law tries to pull a fast one with some smooth negotiator and fancy SWAT team. If they try and take me down, you're going with me."

"Don't worry," Jesse said. "The sheriff is a friend of my family. He'll listen to me. I'll make sure they don't try anything."

"I like your attitude, young fella. You might oughta convince your buddy Liam that it isn't going to do him any good to fight me again. Keep moving. The shelter's just up yonder."

Jesse pushed himself, step after step, even though the back of his head throbbed, his legs were shaky, and he felt as if he could throw up. His face stung where he'd been scratched by low tree branches. He couldn't imagine being any more hungry, thirsty, or cold. The only upside to his precarious predicament was that Slick's shelter would be warmer than the outdoors. He crossed a small clearing, stars twinkling overhead, and approached the embers of a campfire just inside the tree line.

"That's far enough," Slick said.

Jesse stopped and looked around. "Where's the shelter?"

"There, to the right of the fire."

Jesse turned and moved the beam of light to the right. "All I see is a huge pile of tree limbs."

"Yep, that's the shelter. Mighty fine handiwork, if I do say so myself."

Jesse felt as if his heart had sunk down to his toes. "How are we supposed to stay warm in that?"

"Look closer, knucklehead. The shelter's open on this side so the fire can take the chill off. Stop complaining and get over there."

Jesse walked past the slowly dying fire and held the flashlight so he could see whatever it was Slick had constructed.

"Go on, boy. Take a gander inside."

Jesse sat on his heels and shone the beam of light into the shelter, startled to see a man sitting upright, his ankles and wrists bound with rope, his face bruised and bleeding. One of his eyes was black. The right leg of his jeans was torn and bloody. Jesse recognized the brown boots.

"Say hey to your ol' buddy, Liam." Slick laughed. "Don't look so shocked. I told you me and him had a little talk about attitude. Since he isn't hollering anymore, I guess he got my point."

Liam looked at Jesse and shook his head slightly, as if he was trying to send a warning.

Slick grabbed Jesse by the collar. "I've got enough rope left to tie your wrists. Kneel here with your hands behind your head and don't try anything stupid. If I have to talk to *you* about attitude, you'll end up looking like your buddy there. There's sure no need for it. Just mind your p's and q's. Now don't move and keep your mouths shut, both of you."

Jesse did what he was told and couldn't stop staring at Liam. That must have been some beating. If Liam had kept the gun instead of giving it to Jesse, could he have protected himself? Jesse had a lot of questions but didn't want to risk looking like Liam. He sized up the shelter, which resembled a small cave crafted of tree limbs and branches. It would take more than a smoldering campfire to stay warm in that.

Slick came up behind Jesse. "Put your arms behind you. Nice and slow." Jesse lowered his arms, and Slick grabbed both his arms and pulled them behind him, tied his wrists, then gave him a shove. "Get in there. Sit or lay, doesn't matter to me, long as you behave. Just because I ran out of rope doesn't mean I haven't got my eye on you, boy. You try to run and I'll shoot your kneecaps. No need for you to suffer like that, so don't be stupid."

Jesse, his heart nearly pounding out of his chest, his wrists secured behind him, walked on his knees into the enclosure, then sat cross-legged next to Liam.

"All right then," Slick said. "I need to feed that fire before it goes out. You two have a nice time, catching up. If either of you tries to get away, I'll have to hurt you real bad."

CHAPTER 32

Kate stood in the family prayer circle between Elliot and Hawk, a warm fire crackling at her back, her eyelids heavy and her burden even heavier, as she listened to Elliot close out their second family prayer session since Jesse disappeared.

"And so, Father," Elliot said, "in faith we come to You once again as a family, knowing that You love Jesse even more than we do, and far more than we can imagine. Nothing can cross his path that You don't allow. Your Word tells us in Romans 8:28 that in all things You work for the good of those who love You, who have been called according to Your purpose. Jesse loves You. He gave You his heart and put his life into Your hands. Lord, we know it's You, and not Liam Berne, who is in control. And that, ultimately, You will use this circumstance for Your glory. Protect Jesse, Lord. Help him not to be afraid. Speak to Liam's heart. Make his conscience tender and give him the grace to do the right thing. Wrap us in Your peace and answer our prayer as is fitting in Your sight, for it's in the Name of our Lord and Savior, Jesus Christ, that we ask these things. Amen."

Kate didn't move, but let the family amen settle over her. Finally, she opened her eyes and turned to Elliot. How could he look so at ease? He was as concerned as she was for Jesse's safety.

Elliot stroked her cheek. "It's going to be all right, honey. Trust Him."

Kate nodded on the outside, but inside she wrestled with fear and doubt. It was only going to be all right if Jesse came home alive. God could do anything. She believed that. So why did He sometimes allow something dreadful to happen in order to make something good come of it? Sometimes Scripture made no sense. At least, not to her. The only thing that made sense right now was getting her son home safely.

Her dad rubbed his eyes and put his glasses back on. He came over and put his arms around her. "Jesse's strong, Kate. More than you know. He and I talk about spiritual things quite a bit. That youngster takes his faith seriously. Way beyond his years. Wherever he is right now, he and God are talkin'."

"Buck's right," Elliot said. "Jesse knows he's not alone out there."

Kate didn't say anything but squeezed Elliot's hand in agreement. Jesse's faith was stronger than hers. But he was only twelve. How much could a boy his age trust God if his life was being threatened? Especially when God hadn't chosen to spare Jesse's father.

Abby tugged one of Riley's braids and winked at Jay. "Let's go cut into that chocolate cake the women from church brought over. I told Pipsqueak she could make us chocolate shakes to go with it—as long as she's willing to help clean up afterwards."

Riley clapped her hands. "Yay!"

"Count me in," Jay said.

"Me too." Buck smiled. "Roberta, you need to get in on this. Riley's been practicing on her ol' grandpa, and I promise you're in for a treat."

"Come on, Riley," Abby said. "We need to get started if we're going to get you in bed by nine."

Kate looked at Abby and mouthed the words *thank you*.

As Abby, Jay, Riley, and Dad escorted Roberta into the kitchen, Hawk came over to Kate and kissed her cheek, then shook Elliot's hand. "I'm going back to the command post. I'll see what I can find out and call you if I hear anything new."

"Promise me you won't get in Virgil's way," Kate said.

"I promise not to impede the investigation." Hawk slipped on his down jacket and zipped it, then put on his stocking cap and pulled it down over his ears. "But I can't promise I won't push the sheriff for information."

"Then use a little restraint," Kate said. "Remember, Virgil's on our side."

Hawk nodded, then went out the front door and pulled it shut.

Kate blinked to clear her eyes. Hawk's take-charge attitude and unwavering tenacity reminded her so much of Micah.

Micah. Her mind raced back in time, through all the drama and pain of those five years he was missing. And of that moment when Virgil told her they had found his remains. She wondered if she could ever handle that kind of pain again.

Lord, please don't take my son from me. But if You do, hold him close. Take the fear out of his heart. And give me the courage to work through the grief without falling into anger, despair, and unbelief. I'm trying so hard to trust You.

Jesse sat on the cold, hard ground in Slick's shelter made of tree limbs, his hands bound, the man who'd tried to kill him now as helpless as he.

"You stupid kid," Liam whispered. "Why'd you come back here? Why didn't you run while you had the chance?"

"I did," Jesse said. "But I changed my mind."

"Why would you do that?"

Jesse shrugged. "It wasn't right to leave you."

"Says who? You had a chance to save yourself. You should've taken it."

"Not if it meant leaving you out here to die."

"That's crazy," Liam said. "If the tables were turned, I'd have left you in a heartbeat. Seriously, kid. What were you thinking?"

Jesse glanced over at Liam's badly beaten face. "I was thinking about the Good Samaritan in the Bible. You probably don't know who that is."

"Of course I do," Liam said. "Despite what you think, I'm not a heathen. I used to go to church every Sunday. I know that story."

"Then you know why I couldn't leave you out here."

Liam was quiet for about half a minute. Then he said, "Yeah, but the man the Good Samaritan decided to help hadn't tried to kill him."

"That's not the point," Jesse said. "The Good Samaritan didn't know anything about the man he helped. He just knew it was wrong to pass by and leave a wounded man out there where he could die."

"You didn't leave me out there, kid. I *told* you to go."

"But I think God wanted me to come back. It wasn't a good idea to leave you out here in the cold where you might freeze to death. Or get hypothermia or something."

"I can assure you, Almighty God couldn't care less about me right now."

"You're wrong."

"And you're a fool," Liam said. "Coming back here was stupid. Now both of our lives are in jeopardy. Are you going to tell me *that's* what God wants?"

"No." Jesse sighed. "I don't know. Maybe. There could be a reason we don't understand."

"How about we stick with what I *do* understand. We can't trust that creep."

"That's why we have to trust God."

Liam lowered his voice. "I don't need to be preached to by a seventh grader. I don't know what misguided baloney they feed you at that church of yours, but don't try and feed it to me. We're in over our heads, kid. *Way* over. We'll be lucky to get out of here alive."

Jesse looked out the open side of the shelter and saw Slick piling wood on the fire and whistling as if nothing were wrong. Jesse considered the seriousness of the situation. He'd had a gun pointed at his head twice today, and both times he thought he was going to die. He didn't want to die at twelve. He thought again about his family and how hard it would be on them if he were murdered. He so wanted to say good-bye and tell them how much he loved them. He blinked away the tears that stung his eyes.

"You scared?" Liam said.

Jesse shrugged. "Sort of. I mean, I'm scared of getting shot. But heaven's going to be awesome. I'll see Jesus face to face. And my dad and grandma are there, so I'll get to see them again. But I'm worried about my family. I know how scared *they* are. They were miserable all those years when Daddy and Riley were missing. It's not fair they have to go through it again."

"I'll never understand how you Christians can love and worship a cruel and sadistic god who puts you through stuff like that."

"You still don't get it, do you?" Jesse felt bold and didn't care if Liam got mad about what he was going to say. "It's guys like you and Slick and that crazy mountain man who took my sister and killed my dad that cause suffering, not God. He sure didn't kill your mother."

"You don't know the first thing about why I took my mom's life," Liam said. "What are you, twelve? What do you know about having to make tough choices?"

"You think it was easy forgiving *you*?" Jesse said. "Or coming back here? Because it wasn't."

"It wasn't smart either. I hope it was worth dying for."

"How was I supposed to know that guy was out here?" Jesse felt the heat from the fire, which was now burning brightly. "I thought you were pinned under a tree limb and helpless. I just wanted to be like the Good Samaritan. That's why I came back to help you. So when I think of it that way, it was worth it."

"Whatever." Liam rolled his eyes and then seemed to stare at nothing. Finally, he turned again to Jesse. "So tell me something—the gut-honest truth—why did you say you forgave me when I was about to shoot you?"

"We're supposed to love our enemies, not hate them," Jesse said. "And I pretty much hated you. I didn't want to die feeling that way. But just because I forgave you didn't mean that what you did wasn't wrong. God would've held you responsible."

"Then why bother saying it?"

"I guess because Jesus forgave the soldiers who crucified Him and He said it out loud. Maybe they needed to hear it. I thought maybe you did too."

"Jesus also said they didn't know what they were doing," Liam said. "I *did* know. And if that tree limb hadn't fallen on me, I'd have pulled the trigger."

"I couldn't stop you. But forgiving you made me feel stronger and not so afraid." Jesse thought for a moment. "And I knew if I died, I'd be in heaven, happier than I could ever imagine. What about you? Where will you be when *you* die?"

Liam spit out a swear word. "How about you spare me the repent-or-burn spiel? Colleen's been on my case for years. I'll tell you what I told her: thanks, but no thanks. I do not need *or* want a personal Savior or a stupid set of rules controlling my life. I sure don't think that's grounds for eternity in hell."

"Sorry," Jesse said. "I wasn't trying to upset you."

"That's not what I'm upset about. You have *no idea* what we're facing here."

"Then tell me," Jesse said. "I'm not a little kid."

Liam paused for what seemed an eternity, then glanced over at him. "After you left, I had time to think about everything. I was actually relieved the limb fell on me and knocked the gun out of my hands so I couldn't shoot you. I knew if I survived, I was going to prison for the rest of my life, and I accepted that. I really did. But then Slick came along and *rescued* me," Liam said sarcastically. "Now I'm more trapped than before."

"How'd he get you out?"

"With a lot of grit. Took him forty minutes to pry that limb up enough for me to pull my legs out. I have a nasty gash on this one, but it's not broken."

"That's good," Jesse said. "Bet it felt great to be standing."

"Yeah, for about thirty seconds before Slick stuck a gun in my back. Said he'd seen my face all over the news and knew I was wanted by the police as a suspect in your disappearance. He told me that a couple months ago he robbed a bank in Higgins Springs and shot and killed a cop. He came to Foggy Ridge, grew a beard, and kept a low profile—until the cops went door to door looking for you. He's afraid they may have recognized him, so he decided to hide in the woods until the dust settles and he can move on. He figured if the sheriff found him out here, he could use me as a bargaining chip and trade me in exchange for his freedom. And if the sheriff didn't show, he'd set me free and we'd go our separate ways."

"Can't you still do that?" Jesse said.

"Just hear me out. When we heard you calling in the forest, I told Slick who you were. Only took him a few seconds to figure out that holding you hostage would give him twice the leverage if the sheriff showed up. So he captured you, and here we are. Thing is, it's doubtful the sheriff will even search these woods, since the Amber Alert indicated that the authorities suspect I drove you somewhere and are looking for my car. Once Slick feels it's safe for him to return to Foggy Ridge, he won't need to hold us hostage anymore."

"Then he'll let us go, right?"

"Not exactly." Liam sighed. "Look, kid, the only way Slick will cut me loose is if I …"

"If you what?"

Liam's lips trembled. "If I … kill you first."

Jesse studied Liam's profile, his heart about to pound out of his chest. "That's crazy. Just tell him you won't do it. Once he's left, we'll figure out how to get untied. We don't need him to get out of here."

Liam didn't comment and just stared at the ground.

"You're not telling me everything," Jesse said. "I need to know."

"Killing you isn't exactly an *option*, okay?"

"What does that mean?" Jesse said.

The muscles in Liam's neck tightened. "Look, kid. Unless I kill you, Slick's going to kill us both."

CHAPTER 33

"What?" Jesse stared at Liam, trying to process the gravity of his words. "Slick wants you to *kill* me?"

"That's right, or we're both dead," Liam said. "It's so weird. A few hours ago I had my finger on the trigger, ready to take you out, then that tree limb saved me from doing something I would've regretted the rest of my life. But now I *have* to kill you. It's not like I have a choice."

"That's insane," Jesse said, hardly able to catch his breath. "Why does he want me dead?"

"Because if Slick lets you go, he knows you'll tell the sheriff everything and the authorities will pick up his trail again. On the other hand, if he gets me to kill you, I can't go to the sheriff because no one would ever believe I did it only because he forced me. He's got me over a barrel."

Jesse blinked the stinging from his eyes. "I'm sorry, Mr. Berne. I came back to help you, not to make things worse."

"*Mister* Berne?" Liam exhaled and his whole being seemed to deflate. "Why do you have to be such a nice kid? This wouldn't be so hard if you were a smart-mouth. Or had some attitude."

The fire outside the shelter was putting off a lot of light, and Jesse looked—really looked—into Liam's eyes for the first time. "How do you know Slick will let you go, after you kill me? How do you know he isn't planning to shoot you dead and then disappear?"

"I don't," Liam said. "But the whole purpose of making *me* do it is so that I can't go to the sheriff. The only chance I have of getting out of this alive is to kill you and hope that Slick keeps his word."

"Maybe he's bluffing."

Liam shook his head. "He isn't."

"I don't think God would send me back here just to die this way," Jesse said. "Sheriff Granger will find us before that happens. But then you'll have to go to jail."

"Jesse, be realistic." Liam's voice was suddenly softer, almost tender. "Even if the sheriff shows up, which is doubtful, he's not going to give Slick what he wants. He's a cop killer. And the minute Slick realizes he's not in control, he'll kill us both."

Jesse didn't say anything but couldn't take his eyes off Liam. Finally, he said, "You don't look like a murderer to me."

"What do you think a murderer should look like?"

Jesse shrugged. "Not like you."

Slick came over and crouched at the open end of the shelter. "You fellas making yourselves at home?"

Neither Jesse nor Liam said anything.

"Aren't real chatty, are you?" Slick crawled inside and checked Liam's wrists and ankles to make sure the knots were secure and then checked Jesse's wrists. "Well, talk or don't talk. It's up to you. That fire should be thawing you out. I didn't bring enough food and water to share, but I'll keep the fire going to keep you comfortable."

"If the search teams don't find us," Liam said, "when are you planning to go back to Foggy Ridge?"

"I figure things should calm down by tomorrow night. Can't go back to my place, so I'll move on." Slick flashed an annoying grin, moving his gaze from Liam to Jesse and back to Liam. "Is the boy up to speed on the plan?"

"I told him what I'd have to do and why," Liam said.

"Well then. That's that. You have anything to say, boy?" Slick waited for Jesse to respond, and when he didn't, Slick backed out of the shelter and started to get up on his feet.

"Wait!" Jesse blurted out. "Do you have a mother who loves you?"

Slick crouched down, the expression on his face somewhere between puzzled and amused. "I do, as a matter of fact. What's it to you?"

"Well, so do I," Jesse said. "My dad was murdered, and both my sisters almost were. My mother's suffered enough. You don't have to do this. I won't tell the sheriff I even saw you. I promise."

"A promise you can't keep," Slick said. "Don't worry, boy. You won't feel a bullet in your head at close range. It'll be quick and painless."

"Not for my mother, it won't."

Slick chuckled. "Liam, doesn't it just warm your heart to know young Jesse here's worried about his mama? Seeing as how she's going to fret forever and a day, wondering what happened to her boy, maybe I'll go put her out of her misery—just to show I really do have a heart." A grin spread across Slick's face. "I might could make it look like an accident."

Jesse's eyes burned with tears. He pressed his lips tightly together, knowing that, if he verbalized what he was thinking, he would probably get a beating too.

Lord, this jerk makes me so mad. Don't let him hurt my mother.

"You can turn on those crybaby tears all you want," Slick said, "but my mind's made up."

Slick got up and left.

Jesse couldn't stop shivering, though he wasn't cold anymore. He watched Slick disappear in the shadows, whistling. Jesse thought it odd, coming from a man with murder in his heart.

A few minutes went by. Finally, Liam said, "Don't let him get to you, Jesse. He's not going after your mom."

"That was a horrible thing to say."

"It was. I said worse, but I would never have hurt your family. He just wants to scare you so he can feel in control."

Jesse sat for a few moments, at the same time angry and terrified. Finally, he turned to Liam. "Remember you asked me what I thought a murderer should look like, and I said, 'Not you'? Well, Slick's got evil in his eyes. He *looks* like a murderer. The guy scares me."

"Yeah, well, try not to think about him. You getting warm yet?"

Jesse nodded.

"Why don't you try and sleep some while you can?" Liam said.

"If I'm going to die, I don't want to sleep away the only time I have left."

"Look, Jesse, I doubt my apology means anything to you, but I'm sorry you got pulled into this. I'd give anything to change that."

Jesse studied Liam's profile. "Can I ask you something? You don't have to answer, but I'd really like to know. Why did you kill your mother? You don't seem like a bad guy."

Liam glanced over at him and then looked at the ground. "My mom had Alzheimer's. For all practical purposes, the woman I knew and loved was already dead even before I put her out of her misery. I know the law calls it murder, but I couldn't sit back and let that disease steal my mom's mind and allow the medical expenses to eat up the inheritance she wanted me to have."

"So that's it … You killed her to get what *you* wanted, just like you're going to do with me."

"That was a cheap shot. I loved my mom! I really did. I was gentle with her, and it was over before she realized what was happening."

"You can't know that." Jesse, his heart heavy, wondered how any man who loved his mother could drown her.

"The situation Slick put me in is entirely different," Liam said. "I would only kill you to keep from being killed. You'd do the same thing to me, if you had to."

Jesse shook his head. "I wouldn't *have* to. Because it's a choice, and I would never choose to kill you or anyone."

"You might, if it was the only way to save your own neck."

"No, I wouldn't."

"It's self-defense," Liam insisted.

"Maybe so, but I couldn't do it because my life would be ruined after that."

"So you'd rather die?"

"If I killed someone in cold blood," Jesse said, "even to save myself, I'm pretty sure I'd feel dead on the inside for the rest of my life. I'd rather just die for real and go to heaven."

"How can a kid who's not old enough to shave already know what you would or wouldn't do in this situation?"

Jesse shrugged. "Because I believe we're supposed to love our neighbor as ourselves. And sometimes that means forgetting about what we want, and doing what's right for another person, even if it's hard."

"Even if it kills you?"

"I wouldn't *want* to die. And I'd be scared. I just know I couldn't kill an innocent person."

"I believe you. You're a remarkable kid and a better man than I am. But my philosophy is we have to play the hand we're dealt. And there's nothing to be gained by both of us dying." Liam was quiet for a few moments. "My mom believed all that Bible stuff, and Colleen does too. I can't say any of it has stuck with me, but I do wonder about heaven. I kind of hope my mom *is* there. She really wanted to be."

Jesse just listened.

"Well, if heaven does exist," Liam said, "I won't be going there. Not after what I've done and what I'm about to do. If anything, I deserve hell."

"So do I."

Liam looked as if he were going to smile. "Yeah, right."

"I do. Everyone does."

"Oh, that's right," Liam said. "This is the part where you tell me that we're all sinners. And the only way to be forgiven and go to heaven is to repent and accept Jesus's sacrifice for my sins. I told you, I've already heard it all. It's not for me."

"Why not? All you have to do is ask."

"Well, I don't need to be forgiven. I'm the only one who had the guts to do the right thing for my mother, and I'm not sorry for that. I'm not."

"Aren't you sorry for other things?" Jesse said. "Like threatening to kill my family, and then trying to shoot me?"

"I don't know. Aren't you tired of talking so much?"

Jesse sighed. "I just want to be sure you know God can forgive you, that's all."

"Why do you care anyway? It's my problem."

"Because you're going to feel really guilty if you kill me now, and I don't think it's fair that Slick's making you choose between your life and mine."

Liam rolled his eyes. "Then stop making it harder by being so nice."

"I might not have the courage to say this stuff later. I want you to know that I don't blame you—"

"Enough already!" Liam said. "Not another word or I'll ask Slick to put a gag on you."

Jesse stopped talking and looked down at the ground. He was scared. Far more than he was letting on. Death didn't scare him, but being shot sure did.

He stole a few well-spaced glances at Liam and decided the man's silent language didn't match the gruffness of his words. He was struggling with the choice he would have to make. And he looked scared too.

CHAPTER 34

Virgil dabbed the perspiration off his forehead. "You hot?" he said to Reggie.

"Not really. The command post actually feels cool to me." Reggie flashed a crooked smile and patted Virgil on the shoulder. "My guess is you're workin' up a sweat because your mind's in fast motion."

"That's the only speed it knows." Virgil glanced at his watch. "I had hoped to see some sign of Jesse, Liam Berne, or Liam's car. Our teams are almost finished searching the hills around Foggy Ridge. Where *are* they?"

"We may have to accept that Berne took the boy out of the area," Reggie said. "He could've been long gone before we were even on to him."

Virgil ran his hands through his hair. "I'm a long way from accepting that. Even if Liam left, which my gut tells me he didn't, I don't think he would have risked taking Jesse with him, dead or alive. We need to complete our search-and-rescue operation."

"We still have a number of densely wooded, undeveloped areas in the city limits to cover," Reggie said, "if we could just get those hounds over here."

Virgil nodded. "I know. The dogs are still in use to track a registered sex offender who snatched two girls from a retreat center near Fayetteville. If the dogs aren't here by the time our teams are ready to search the remaining areas, I'm not sure Kevin will give the green light and chance upsetting the handlers by letting us go in ahead of them. It's his call."

"I understand his reluctance," Reggie said. "You know how touchy the handlers are about us trampin' on their turf before the dogs've been over it."

"Yeah, well, they're the least of my worries." Virgil hated the tension in his voice. "I've got a potential young victim and a distraught family to think about. Time is everything."

"Relax, Sheriff. Kevin's on top of it."

Virgil sighed. "You're right. He hasn't missed a trick. I'm just restless. I hate the waiting."

"Of course you do. But let him have the reins. That's why you put him in charge."

Virgil looked out the window at what appeared to be a team of police officers just returning from their search. "You know Kate Cummings is a friend. The last thing I want to do is hand her another devastating heartache."

"Good grief, man. It's not like you're *responsible* for any of it."

Virgil turned around, his arms folded across his chest. "I know, Reg. It's just personal, that's all."

Reggie raised an eyebrow. "You have … feelings for this woman?"

"No, no. It's nothing like that. Actually, Kate's more like a sister, and her kids like nieces and nephews. I just care a whole lot about them, and I can't imagine Kate's life without Jesse. He's one fine kid. More tenderhearted than the average twelve-year-old. Maybe because of all his family's been through."

Reggie's eyes seemed to probe Virgil's thoughts. Finally, he said, "You don't think we're gonna find Jesse alive, do you?"

"I refuse to go there," Virgil replied. "I need to stay focused on what we're doing. We don't have time to waste."

"You think we shouldn't wait for the hounds, if we're ready to roll and the handlers aren't?"

"I'm leaning that way." Virgil's cell phone rang. "Sheriff Granger."

"Sir, this is Deputy Northridge. I'm outside with a young man named Dawson Foster. Says he and the Cummings kid were like brothers. I've told him the status, but he insists on talking to you. I already told him you can't see him. I just wanted him to see me make the call."

"Actually," Virgil said, "I wouldn't mind talking to him. But I need you to bring him to the south side of the command center, away from the media. I'll be right out."

"Yes, sir."

Virgil put his cell phone in his pocket. "I'll be back in a few minutes, Reg. There's someone I need to speak with."

Virgil motioned to Kevin that he would be outside, then slipped out the side door and walked around to the south side of the command center, careful not to make eye contact with anyone from the media.

The night air was downright cold, and the scent of pine wafted under his nose as he rounded the corner and saw Dawson standing with Deputy Northridge.

Virgil extended his hand to Dawson. "Good to see you again."

"Yes, sir," Dawson said. "Same here."

Northridge excused himself, and Virgil looked at Dawson. "What can I do for you, son?"

"I want you to tell me straight, Sheriff. Do you think Jesse's still alive?" Dawson stood tall and brave, his eyes brimming with tears.

Virgil put his hand on the boy's shoulder. "I have no information that leads me to believe otherwise. We're searching the town and the hills around it, looking for Jesse, the suspect, and the suspect's car."

"Is the guy you suspect of takin' Jesse really Miss Berne's brother?"

"Yes," Virgil said.

"Isn't it true most kids don't survive more than a few hours, once they're kidnapped?"

"If we were dealing with a sex offender, I'd say yes. But we're not. This situation is entirely different."

"You think the guy's tryin' to make Jesse talk? You can tell me, Sheriff. Jesse and I are like brothers."

Virgil was filled with compassion and glad Dawson couldn't see the images that kept popping into his mind. "I know this is hard for you. But I really can't discuss the particulars of an ongoing investigation."

Dawson sighed. "That's what everyone says."

"There's good reason for it. It helps to protect Jesse. I know you want that."

"Well, what *can* you tell me?"

"I can tell you we're on top of things. We know what we need to do, and we're out there doing it. I want Jesse found unharmed as much as you do. The Cummingses are like my own family. This is personal."

Dawson nodded. "Yes, sir. It is for me too."

"Have you had contact with Jesse lately?" Virgil said.

"Not since Thursday night when he called and asked me to tell the guys on my team that he lied about bein' a witness. At first, I was really mad because it made me look bad with them, and I knew they'd make life miserable for Jesse. But then after I thought about it, I was sure he told the truth in the first place."

"You sound pretty positive about that."

Dawson shrugged. "'Cause I know Jesse. He's not a liar. Sure, he exaggerated a little to impress me, when he told me he witnessed the drowning *and* got a good look at the killer's face. But he trusted me not to tell anyone. If I'd kept his confidence instead of blabbin' it to Bull Hanson, none of this would be happenin'. It was only after the whole school found out that Jesse called me and said he'd made the whole thing up. But I don't believe he did. He's a straight arrow. He never lies about anything, even if he gets in trouble."

"I don't believe Jesse's a liar either."

Dawson smiled. "Good."

"Let me ask you this," Virgil said. "If you thought Jesse was hiding, where would you look for him?"

"I already told the officers who interviewed me that I'd search the mountain. I even took them to four different spots where Jesse likes to hang out. We didn't find him, but he must be somewhere up there. Are they done searchin' the mountain?"

"I can't get into where we've searched, but rest assured we're leaving no stone unturned. If Jesse's up there, we'll find him." Virgil put his hand on Dawson's shoulder. "I need to get back inside. I've got to stay focused."

"Is there anything I can do, Sheriff?"

"Hang on to hope … and pray. I think that's what Jesse would want."

CHAPTER 35

Kate's eyes flew open. She was curled up on one side of the couch, nestled comfortably under an afghan. She spotted Elliot sitting on the floor in front of the fire.

"What time is it?" Kate said.

"A little after ten." Elliot got up and sat on the side of the couch. "You dozed off and I was hoping you could sleep."

"Has Virgil called?"

"He called Roberta and reported that they've finished searching the mountain. The teams are on their way back in."

Kate wanted to scream. What if they never found him? What if she had to live with the debilitating pain and grief all over again? *Lord, I can't bear it. I just can't. Please don't let that happen.*

Elliot pulled her into his arms, and Kate quietly sobbed, trying not to give in to the despair she felt. God was faithful. That she knew. But His timing often left room for suffering in the midst of the unknown. What if His plan was to call Jesse to his ultimate home? Could she accept it?

"Mama, don't cry."

Kate lifted her head and saw Riley standing next to the couch, barefoot and dressed in her blue-and-white flannel nightgown. Kate sat up straight and patted the couch. "Come here and sit with us. You're supposed to be sleeping."

"I wasn't tired, so Abby was reading me her journal she wrote on our camping trip to Colorado. But she fell asleep." Riley sat on the couch, nestled between Kate and Elliot. "Are you sad?"

"I'm tired, sweetie," Kate said. "I just want your brother home."

"Don't worry. God brought *me* home." Riley looked up at Kate, unquestioning faith twinkling in her eyes. "I prayed that God would send Custos, or one of His other angels, to keep Jesse safe and bring him back to us."

Kate glanced over at Elliot. Riley hadn't mentioned Custos in a long time. But the angel, real or imagined, that she claimed saved her from drowning during the time she lived incognito with the Tutts had made a seemingly indelible impression on her.

"God can do anything," Kate said. "I suppose He can use angels to do whatever He wants."

Riley nodded, the wispy dark curls around her face adding to her look of pure innocence. "Remember when Hawk aimed and shot the rifle out of Isaiah's hand so Jay didn't get killed and me and Abby could come home? And he said he felt a humongous wing and something holding him steady?"

"I remember." Not that Kate could ever forget the incident that had caused her eldest son to turn loose of his cynicism and embrace his Christian roots.

"Well, *I* think God uses angels a lot," Riley said. "And since I prayed He would now, I believe He will."

Kate smiled and cupped Riley's cheek in her hand. "I know He listens to you." If only her own faith could be that simple.

"What's going on?" Abby's sleepy voice came from behind Kate. "Did they find Jesse?"

"Not yet," Kate said.

Abby came into view, dressed in a green-and-pink plaid nightshirt, her thick hair draped over her shoulders. She stood next to her younger sister.

"I was reading to Riley and must've fallen asleep. I guess I'm drained from worrying about Jesse. Have you been able to sleep?"

"She dozed off for about a half hour," Elliot said. "I wish you would all try and get some rest. I'll be glad to stay and wait for Virgil to call Roberta with an update. I'll wake you if anything changes."

"Will you tuck me in?" Riley linked arms with Elliot and looked up at him, their momentary pose fit for a Norman Rockwell painting. "I always sleep better when you do it. You say good prayers."

"Sure I will." Elliot winked at Kate, then stood and put his arm around Riley. "Come on, doll. Let's send you off to dreamland."

Kate relished the warm smile on Abby's face as Elliot escorted Riley to her room.

"She adores him," Abby said. "For a guy who's never had kids, Elliot's got fatherhood down pat. Are you ever going to marry him?" Abby arched her eyebrows. "I'm serious, Mama. What are you waiting for? This man is perfect for you and we all love him."

"You don't think you're going to resent him when he starts giving you advice and getting involved in your life, day to day?"

Abby shook her head. "He's already doing that. I don't resent it. I look up to him. Hawk does too. The little kids think the sun rises and sets on him. What about you? Do you know how many women would give anything to have a man care about them the way Elliot does you? Do you even notice the way he looks at you?"

Kate's cheeks warmed. "Of course I do. I love that about him."

"Was Daddy like that?"

"Very much so. I told you when we went back to the high school for homecoming, five years after we graduated, that he proposed to me in front of the entire student body during halftime. Did I ever tell you he added to our wedding vows during the ceremony, totally off the cuff?"

"Nooo." Abby came over and sat next to Kate, a silly smile on her face. "I want details."

"We had exchanged traditional vows and I was relieved to have recited my part without getting too emotional. Suddenly, it was as if he and I were the only two people on earth. Micah looked at me, a little choked up, and said, 'Kate, you are my dream come true. The other half of my soul. The song in my heart. The answer to prayer. This union was meant to be—and it's forever. I don't know what the future holds for us, or whether the road will be bumpy or smooth, but I promise I'll be there, right beside you …'" Kate reached for Abby's hand and held it, fighting back the emotion. "I've often wondered if, while your dad lay bleeding to death, he thought of me and hoped I would know how sorry he was that he couldn't keep this promise—"

"We'll never know," Abby said, dabbing her eyes. "But you don't have to wonder how he *felt* about you. How did you remember word for word what he said at your wedding?"

"A friend recorded our vows and typed them out for us. I must have read your father's words a hundred times after he disappeared."

"And Daddy ad-libbed the whole thing. That's so cool. Thanks for telling me. It's one more special thing about him I didn't know before."

"Elliot is just as romantic," Kate added. "He's very different from Micah, and yet he has most of the same wonderful qualities. Plus a few besides."

"What a blessing, Mama, that you've been loved that way by *two* men. Most widows never find another man who can measure up to the husband they lost. So why aren't you setting a date?"

"Why is everyone in this family pushing me on that?"

"Because"—Abby tilted Kate's chin and looked into her eyes—"he makes you happy. You hardly ever smiled before, and now you smile all the time. Sometimes you giggle like a schoolgirl."

"No, I don't."

Abby nodded. "You do. And we kids love it. Our house is happy again because of Elliot. He's here half the time anyway. You should just marry him."

"It's not that simple."

"It shouldn't be complicated either. If you love each other, don't you want to be together? Sometimes Jay and I can hardly bear to say good night."

Elliot came out of the hallway into the living room. "Mission accomplished. That sweet angel is somewhere in dreamland."

Abby rose to her feet. "Here, I'll give you your seat back. I think I'll go try again before I'm too wide awake to go back to sleep. Good night." Abby winked at her mother as she walked off.

Kate was glad for the pleasant-but-momentary distraction and hated to come back to the reality that Jesse was still missing.

"Excuse me." Roberta stood in the doorway to the kitchen. "I'm going to brew a pot of coffee. Any takers?"

"Yes, ma'am." Elliot raised his hand. "Count me in."

"Me too," Kate said. "I want to be awake when Virgil calls."

Kate tried not to look afraid, but on the inside, she had completely lost the battle.

Liam, stiff and aching, lay on his side, facing Jesse, grateful that the crackling fire outside the shelter had taken the chill off. He heard the deep rumbling of the Search and Rescue helicopter in the distance and wondered how long Slick would wait before he decided to split and force Liam to do the unthinkable.

"Mr. Berne," Jesse whispered. "Mr. Berne, are you awake?"

"Wide awake. Every inch of me's throbbing."

"I hope I'm not bothering you. I just feel better hearing your voice."

"I don't know why," Liam said. "You know what I have to do."

"What you *think* you have to do."

"Whatever."

"I'm not going to try talking you out of it," Jesse said. "I'm just lonesome."

"And scared? I sure am."

"I'm trying hard not to think about that. I've been thinking about how awesome it'll be seeing Jesus, and I'm kind of excited to see my dad. I was only five when he disappeared. I didn't get to know him very well."

"I went to high school with Micah," Liam said. "I was a couple years older, but I knew who he was. Now that I think about it, you look a lot like him."

"Everyone says that."

"He was a real nice kid. I'd say you're a chip off the ol' block."

"Thanks. I'd like to be." Jesse sighed. "I wish the sheriff *would* show up. At least we'd stand half a chance of getting out of here alive."

"What are the odds?" Liam said. "That helicopter's been zigzagging all across the area for hours. I expect they'll give up looking before long. With this thick canopy, I doubt they can see the campfire. Or would even suspect anything if they did. My guess is they're concentrating on Sure Foot Mountain."

"You're probably right," Jesse said. "Who would think to look in the woods, right here in the middle of town? Especially since they already went door to door."

"What're you two night owls whispering about?" Slick crouched in front of the open side of the shelter, his grin as annoying as ever.

Liam didn't answer, and neither did Jesse.

Slick crawled inside and made sure they were still bound. "You better not be planning something. Doesn't matter if you give me the silent treatment, just so you toe the line."

Good, Liam thought. *Now leave!*

Slick got up in Liam's face. "Are you starting to feel the thrill of the kill? I know I am. You might could say I'm feeling trigger happy." Slick pushed Liam's arm with the palm of his hand, then backed out of the shelter, howling as if he'd cracked the pun of the century.

"I really hate that guy," Liam said. "I suppose this is how you felt when I intimidated you. If I could go back and undo it, I would."

"I already forgave you, remember?"

"I do. I just don't understand how you can keep from hating me."

"I never said it was easy. But I'm supposed to forgive my enemies and not try to get even with them."

"I'm *not* the enemy, Jesse. None of this was my idea. I fully admit that I'm a coward. You're the only real man here."

"I sure don't feel like a man," Jesse said. "But two times today I thought I was going to die, so at least I know what to expect."

"So you're going to take it on the chin, just like that? You're not even going to fight for your life?"

"Why, so Slick can feel even more powerful? He's not going to change his mind." Jesse's big round eyes were fixed on Liam. "I don't want to die, but I'm ready. You're not."

"Ready? Really, at twelve?" Liam hated the sarcasm in his voice.

"I'm guessing heaven is awesome at any age. The Bible says this isn't our home anyway."

"Good grief, kid. Can't you forget the fairy tale for one minute? *This* is real. This is now. You're going to die. Do you get that?"

Jesse's eyes pooled, a tear trickling down the side of his face. "I get it, Mr. Berne. Do you? You're the one who has to live with it. Only you'll be dead on the inside."

CHAPTER 36

Sheriff Virgil Granger paced in the command post, waiting for Chief Deputy Kevin Mann to get off the phone. Police Chief Reggie Mitchell stood, his hands clasped behind him, surveying the map of Foggy Ridge and the outlying areas.

Kevin put his cell phone in his pocket, got up, and walked over to Virgil. "Two things," he said. "One, the bloodhounds are finished tracking the rapist in Washington County, but they'd been on the guy's tail for nearly twenty hours, and the hounds are spent. The trainers don't want them going back out until they're rested. And two, the National Weather Service has issued a heavy fog advisory for northwest Arkansas from eleven p.m. until after sunup. Visibility in many places could be zero. Sir, with all due respect, there's no way we should send the teams out tonight. The fog will make our job impossible. We need to wait until morning, and that'll give us time to get the dogs here too."

Virgil glanced over at Reggie and then back at Kevin. "What about Search and Rescue's thermal imagining?"

"Unreliable in thick fog, and add the density of the trees, nearly impossible. Look, gentlemen, I know this is disappointing," Kevin said, rubbing the stubble on his chin. "But we've already searched about a hundred yards into each of these undeveloped areas. If we send those teams deeper into the woods, and that fog rolls in, they'll be stuck wandering in circles, blinded by their own flashlights. We're all tired. In my mind, the risk of continuing in the fog outweighs any chance we have of finding them tonight."

Virgil glanced at the clock on the wall and mumbled a swear word under his breath. "My gut tells me they're still here. Our Amber Alert didn't reap one valid sighting. Not one."

Reggie folded his arms across his chest. "Virgil, let's assume they *are* here. It's still a waste of manpower and resources to proceed in the fog. Kevin's right. It makes sense to wait till after sunup when the fog starts to clear and we've got use of the bloodhounds. We've been thorough with every step. Would be foolish to risk missin' somethin' critical just to try to get it done quickly tonight."

Virgil pulled up a chair and sat. Was he even capable of being objective where Kate's son was concerned? He leaned forward in the chair, his elbows planted on his knees, his hands clasped together. He took a slow, deep breath and let it out.

"Humor me a minute," Virgil said, "and rewind back to the initial planning point. Maybe we're missing something. If the IPP is wrong, we may be chasing our own tails."

"Sir, it's not wrong," Kevin said. "It's indisputable that Jesse was last seen at Evans's Sporting Goods."

"But," Virgil said, "it's also true that Mr. Evans never physically saw Jesse again after he greeted him at the front door around nine a.m. So what isn't clear is when and how Jesse left, and why."

Kevin nodded. "Right. Evans is sure that Jesse entered the store at nine. And that Berne came in just after nine thirty and checked out at nine forty-five. We can't be certain where Jesse was during that time. We assume he was in the store. We just don't know."

"What we do know," Virgil said, "is that after Jesse failed to rendezvous with Hawk at ten o'clock, Hawk and Mr. Evans searched the store and Jesse wasn't there."

Kevin nodded. "A short time later, police officers and deputies searched Evans's store and found no indication which of the three exits Jesse had used—the front door, a west side door, or the private exit door in Evans's office. Each opens into a different area of the customer parking area. After your meeting with Colleen Berne, we've since hypothesized that Jesse spotted Liam Berne in the store, recognized him as Colleen's brother, and assumed he'd heard the rumor that Jesse was a witness. Jesse then sought to avoid Berne by slipping out one of the exits. Of course, it's also possible that Berne had been threatening Jesse, and when Jesse saw him, he ran."

Virgil sighed. "And it's certainly in the realm of possibility that it was Berne who saw Jesse in the store, recognized him as the kid who claimed to be the only eyewitness to his mother's drowning, and went after him."

"*I'm* leanin' that way," Reggie said. "Berne's vehicle hasn't been spotted. And my officers went door to door in Foggy Ridge, and not one person reported seeing Jesse. We've searched the first hundred yards of the undeveloped areas in town, including the woods behind Evans's, and that effort didn't yield any clues. We've searched nearly every inch of those hills with no sign of either of them. I have to wonder if Berne took off with the kid long before we issued the Amber Alert. Maybe he's holed up somewhere, waitin' for the dust to settle."

Virgil stood and stretched his lower back. "Maybe. But my gut instincts tell me Jesse's here somewhere. It helped to revisit what we know from earlier in the day. Thanks. Colleen Berne's statement blew this case wide open, and I wanted to be sure we're not missing something."

"Why don't we call it a night?" Kevin said. "Let's all go home and get some rest and meet here at daybreak. I'll go tell the teams to come back then. We'll go deeper into the wooded areas and use the bloodhounds, but I've got to tell you, Sheriff, I'm not that hopeful we're going to find them."

Virgil stood. "Sounds like a plan. I need to tell Deputy Freed what we're doing so she can inform Kate. Better yet, I'll head up the mountain and tell Kate myself."

Virgil called Deputy Freed and told her the plan, and asked her to let him tell Kate. He asked her to tell the family he wanted to talk to them, and for her to reassure them that he wasn't bringing grim news.

He encountered thick patches of fog on Angel View Road as he drove up the mountain. By the time he pulled into the driveway of the Cummingses' log house, the fog was severely impairing visibility. Kate was at the door waiting. He got out of his squad car and walked toward the house.

Kate opened the door, took Virgil's hand, and pulled him inside. "Roberta told us you wanted to update us on the search."

Virgil took off his hat and followed Kate into the living room, where Buck, Abby, Hawk, and Elliot were waiting. Kate sat on the couch next to Elliot, and Virgil sat in an upright chair facing them.

"I wanted to come in person to explain where we are in our search to find Jesse. As you know, we went door to door in Foggy Ridge and didn't find Jesse or Liam Berne and got no actionable leads. We've now finished searching the hills, and we didn't find either of them or obtain any clues leading to their whereabouts. Berne's car hasn't surfaced, despite the Amber Alert. We wanted to search even deeper into the few wooded areas in town yet tonight, but the National Weather Service has issued a heavy fog advisory from eleven p.m. until after sunrise. Search and Rescue's thermal imaging won't work in thick fog, and I can't get the bloodhounds from Washington County until morning. So we made the decision to suspend the search until tomorrow morning after the fog lifts. We'll be able to make good time if the bloodhounds pick up their scents."

A tear trickled down Kate's face. "Poor Jesse. It's freezing out there, and all he has on is a denim jacket."

"Don't worry, Mama," Hawk said. "He's a resourceful kid. If he's outside, he knows how to start a fire. I showed him myself."

"Where could he be?" Kate said. "Why can't anyone find him?"

A heavy sense of failure came over Virgil. His heart ached for Kate, but he couldn't find any words to say that would give her hope.

"The Lord knows exactly where Jesse is," Elliot said. "We've been praying all day, and we need to keep on. We certainly appreciate all that Virgil's deputies and volunteers are doing to find Jesse."

Kate nodded. "We *are* grateful. I'm just scared."

"We're all scared, Mama." Abby got up and stood by the fire. "But we can't let that cripple us right now. We need to hang on to hope and trust the Lord to bring Jesse home to us."

"How many times do we have to go through this?" Kate said. "Every one of my children has been in grave danger. You'd think we'd get a break."

Elliot put his arm around Kate. "Just remember that each of those children has come home alive and well."

"Am I just supposed to forget that their father *didn't*?"

The silence in the room was more profound than anything anyone could have said.

Virgil cleared his throat, determined not to dwell on what he considered his deepest failure. "No one is sorrier that Micah never came home than I am. But Jesse's situation is entirely different. Let's stay focused."

"The sheriff's right," Hawk said. "We have to stay focused. Jesse knows we won't give up until we find him. He's counting on us."

"Just like Jay and I and Riley counted on you," Abby said. "I never gave up hope of being found because I knew y'all wouldn't stop looking."

Virgil rose to his feet, his six-foot-four frame shaky in the knees. "You hang on to hope. I *am* going to find Jesse. I can promise you that." Virgil turned his gaze to Kate and placed his Stetson firmly on his head. "You have my word."

CHAPTER 37

Jesse was tired of lying on his side with his hands bound but didn't want to risk a beating by complaining. He opened his eyes and glanced outside at the fire, surprised to see a rolling carpet of white had reduced visibility considerably.

"Mr. Berne, look."

Liam sighed. "I already saw it. Might as well kiss good-bye any chance of the sheriff searching for us tonight."

"You don't know that," Jesse said. "He's a friend of my family. He's not going to stop looking."

"Wise up, kid. He's not going to have a choice. No search-and-rescue operation is going to tackle these woods at night in the fog. Truth be told, I doubt they're going to search them at all."

"Don't say that." Jesse's pulse began to race. *Lord, please show us a way out of here alive.*

He heard footsteps and then saw Slick's face peering in at them.

"I'm glad to see you fellas are still awake." Slick's toothy grin nearly glowed in the dark. "I've got something to tell you, so listen up. I caught the radio station in Foggy Ridge on my shortwave, and dense fog is moving into the area. There's not going to be any search party tonight. I've decided to wait till midnight, then head on back to my place, get my stuff, and be ready to roll out of town as soon as the fog starts to lift."

"What makes you think you can see to get out of these woods?" Liam said.

"Because I marked the trees when I came in. And I've got a fantastical sense of direction; that's how." Slick looked at Jesse and pointed to his watch. "It's six past eleven. In fifty-four minutes, Liam here's going to decide whether he's got the guts to finish what he started earlier tonight before he got waylaid by that falling tree branch. Or whether he's going to chicken out and die a coward alongside the eyewitness whose execution he botched, namely you—the same eyewitness, I might add, who'd sell us both down the river, if you could get to the sheriff."

"I wouldn't do that," Jesse said. "I just want to go home."

"Save it, kid." Slick crawled over to Liam, took a gun out of his waistband, and held it to Liam's head. "Personally, I don't see a conflict. It's simple. Either you take out young Jesse—or I take out both of you." Slick laughed. "Either way, I'm leavin' at midnight."

Slick backed out of the shelter on his knees. "Talk it over, don't talk it over—it's up to you."

"Wait," Jesse said. "Can't you just leave us out here tied up? What are the odds the sheriff will ever find us? Even if we somehow manage to get free, you'll be long gone. You don't have to make him kill me."

"Oh, but I do," Slick said. "And Liam told you why—because you can identify me, and I don't want the law to know I was in Foggy Ridge and start looking for me again."

"But you said the officers recognized you already," Jesse said. "Isn't that why you came out in the woods?"

"Maybe they did. Maybe they didn't. I wasn't taking any chances. But the law sure won't give *me* another thought when they find you shot dead with a bullet from Liam's gun. They'll start tracking him down instead of me. Poor Liam won't have any defense, if they catch him. No lawman is going to believe I made him shoot you when the whole county knows that was his intention all along. Isn't that right, Liam?"

"Does it matter what I think?"

Slick let out a wicked laugh. "Nope. You know my offer. I'll be back at the stroke of midnight carrying two firearms. You off the kid, and you're free to go."

"How do I know you won't kill me anyway?" Liam said.

"I guess you don't." Slick wore a smug grin that reminded Jesse of Bull Hanson. "But it's a perfect plan. Why would I mess it up? I want the kid dead without me adding another murder to my record. That's where you come in, Liam. But if I have to kill the kid myself, I'm going for a twofer—and put you both six feet under."

"Yeah, we get it," Liam said.

"Then I'll leave you to your thoughts. I'll be back at the stroke of midnight."

Slick got up and disappeared in the fog. Jesse wished he would disappear forever.

"I really loathe that creep," Liam said.

"He reminds me of the quarterback on our football team. He loved humiliating me and making me feel really small. I guess it made him feel really big."

"I'm sure Slick feels powerful, since he's a control freak who's calling *all* the shots."

"So I guess that means you're going to shoot me," Jesse said.

Liam sighed. "Sorry, Jesse. I don't want to, you know that. But there's no point in both of us dying."

❧

Virgil looked through the lace curtain on the beveled glass of his front door and turned the key just as Drake rounded the corner, skidded on the wood floor, and then sat at the door, whining and yelping, his tail swishing back and forth.

Virgil pushed open the door, then closed it, pleased that Drake continued to sit. "Good boy. I guess all that obedience training stuck." Virgil bent down and rubbed Drake's chin, then ran his hands along his sleek coat. "I know. I'm glad to see you too, fella." Virgil patted him and then stood up straight.

Jill Beth came out the kitchen doorway, pulling her robe tighter around her in the nighttime chill. She walked over to Virgil and put her arms around him. "What a dreadful day. It's a real kick in the teeth that Mother Nature sabotaged your search."

Virgil kissed her warm lips and found solace in her embrace. Finally, he took off his jacket and hung it on the coat tree. "It's been intense. I didn't want to quit for the night, but Kevin and Reggie talked some sense into me. Driving home just now, it was really hard to see the road. Thank God we didn't do something foolish like searching blind. We'll try it again after sunup, but we've searched almost everywhere. Only thing left is to go deeper in the undeveloped, wooded areas in the city limits."

"How's Kate?" Jill Beth said.

"Holding her own. She's plenty scared."

"Who wouldn't be? At this point, do you even think you're going to find Jesse?"

"Absolutely. We have to." Virgil walked into the kitchen and opened the fridge.

"But what if you can't?"

"Can't is not an option. Period!" Virgil grabbed a bottle of water, shut the fridge door, and turned around. He slowly exhaled and studied Jill Beth's startled expression. "I'm sorry I snapped at you, darlin'. I refuse to give doubt an inch, that's all."

"But isn't it better to be realistic?"

"I *am* being realistic." Virgil unscrewed the cap and chugged down several swallows of water. "Nothing's happened to make me think that finding Jesse isn't possible."

"Has anything happened that makes you think it is?"

"We didn't get a single hit on our Amber Alert." Virgil went over to the table and sat. "That makes me think Liam Berne didn't leave town."

Virgil told Jill Beth all the details of his conversation with Colleen Berne, including the fact that Liam had wadded up and trashed the anonymous note demanding hush money that Colleen had secretly left on his windshield.

"How awful it must be for Colleen to suspect her brother of killing their mother. I got the impression that Liam was devoted to her."

"Ironically, on one level, I think he was. According to Colleen, Liam had been helping to care for Dixie at home and was distressed at the thought of her living out her days in the Alzheimer's center. Colleen thinks if he did drown her, he saw it as an act of mercy."

"Do you buy that?" Jill Beth said.

"Maybe. I don't know. What I *do* know is after Dixie Berne's trust was distributed, Liam and Colleen each got one hundred and seventy-five grand. And when Colleen planted the anonymous note, and Liam thought someone was trying to blackmail him, he never went to Colleen."

"Is it possible he didn't want to worry her?" Jill Beth said.

"She doesn't think so. They talked about everything. She planted that note because she suspected him. She knew he wouldn't keep something like that from her unless he was actually considering paying off whoever left the note."

"So where does Jesse come into all this? Surely Liam doesn't think Jesse planted the note?"

"I'm not sure what Liam's thinking." Virgil blew out a breath and folded his hands on the table.

"Poor Jesse," Jill Beth said. "He can't tell what he doesn't know. Do y'all think Liam would hurt him to make him talk?"

Virgil felt his gut tighten. "We have to assume he would. Liam has no history of violence. But if he did kill his mother, it's hard to say what he might do to silence anyone who knows it. Or to what extent he might brutalize Jesse in an effort to get him to tell who it is that's blackmailing him." Virgil blinked away an image of Jesse's badly beaten face.

Jill Beth reached across the table and put her hand on Virgil's. "I doubt you're going to sleep tonight, but let's get you to bed. At least your body can rest before you go out again in the morning."

"Sounds good to me."

Virgil stood, put his arm around Jill Beth, and walked down the hall and into their bedroom. He saw no need to tell her he would lay in the dark with his eyes wide open, hoping to avoid seeing images of the outcome he feared the most.

CHAPTER 38

Jesse lay on his side, his wrists bound, every muscle in his body aching. He accepted that he was going to die this time. He'd finally reached the point where he didn't even blame Liam for being willing to kill him in order to survive.

Lord, I guess I'm going to see You sooner than I thought. I really wish You'd get us out of here, but if You don't, it's okay. Just help me to be brave. I'm scared, but I know You'll be with me when Mr. Berne pulls the trigger. Would You help him find a relationship with You so he won't have to deal with guilt the rest of his life? He's really not so bad.

Be with Mama and Elliot so this won't ruin their chance to be happy. Please help Hawk not to blame himself, and help Abby, Riley, and Grandpa Buck not to take it too hard. Don't let Dawson blame himself either. He's been my best friend all my life.

Jesse opened his eyes. Slick must have added wood to the fire because he could see flames instead of just embers. He caught a glint of light on something just inches from his face. He focused on it for a moment and realized it was a buck knife! It must have fallen out of Slick's pocket.

"Mr. Berne, wake up!" Jesse whispered.

"There's nothing more to talk about. Don't make this harder, okay?"

"You need to open your eyes and look between us on the ground. I think it's Slick's buck knife."

"What?" Liam's eyes flew open and he raised his head up off the ground. "Hot dog! That's what it is, all right. Can you turn over and grab it with your hands?"

"Okay." Jesse glanced outside and didn't see Slick's silhouette. He turned over on his other side and backed up, groping the ground with his fingers. "Can you see it? Am I close?"

"Come back a few more inches."

Jesse backed up a little more and still didn't feel the knife.

"You're right where you need to be," Liam said. "You're practically touching it."

"Found it!" Jesse held tightly to the knife and rolled over, facedown. He drew up his knees under him, and rolled backward and then forward into a sitting position, facing Liam.

"You must be made of rubber," Liam said. "Can you open the knife?"

"I think so." Jesse's hands were cold and he dropped the knife. He felt along the ground until he found it, then dropped it again. Finally, he had a good hold on it and managed to get the blade out partway. "I wish … I could see … what … I'm … doing. The angle's wrong."

"Let me help," Liam said. "Turn around and back up an inch at a time until I say stop. Whatever you do, don't drop the knife."

"I won't."

Jesse used his legs and feet to turn himself around. He backed up, an inch at a time, clutching tightly to the knife, and noted that Liam's breathing sounded labored. Or was it his own?

"Stop there," Liam said. "Make sure you've got a strong grip on the handle. I'm going to grasp the blade with my teeth and try to pull it all the way up, preferably without slicing off my tongue. What I need you to do is hold the knife blade still as a rock when I start pulling. If you let go suddenly, you're liable to cut my throat. Understand?"

Jesse nodded. "Hurry." He heard the sound of Liam's teeth clamp down on the metal blade and then felt tugging. He held a firm grip on the knife.

"Ouch! That blade is sharp," Liam said. "All right, it's open about halfway. See if you can take it from here. Try not to cut your fingers."

Jesse felt for the sharp side of the blade. He placed his thumb and forefinger on the dull side and pulled it all the way up. "Done."

"Can you control the knife to cut the rope on your wrists?"

"I'm used to cleaning fish. I'm sure I can." Jesse tried to slide the knife blade under the rope. But the rope was tight, the angle of his hand too awkward for precision, and the clock was ticking toward midnight. Instead, he placed the knife blade on top of the rope and ever so carefully slid it back and forth. "It's a little risky, but I know what I'm doing."

"I hope so, kid. We won't get another chance."

Jesse kept sawing until he felt a sharp sting and realized one wrist was free. "I did it!" he said. Jesse pulled his aching arm out from behind him and peeled off the rope that was stained with drops of blood where he'd nicked himself. "Let me cut you loose, Mr. Berne."

"You go," Liam said. "I've got a bum leg, and have lost a lot of blood. My body's been bent for hours. I'm not even sure I can stand up straight. I'll just slow you down."

"I'm not going without you." Jesse cut the rope on Liam's wrists, and then his ankles. "There you go. You're free. Stretch for a minute, and then we need to get out of here." Jesse crawled over to the open side of the shelter and peeked out. "The fog is so thick, I can't see more than three or four feet in front of me."

"Which means Slick will have a hard time finding us, if we can just get into those woods. Big *if.* I'm totally turned around since Slick moved me in the dark. I don't have a clue where we are."

"I do," Jesse said. "I found my way back here, and I paid attention when Slick forced me to walk from there to here. I'm pretty sure I can get us out. We might have to hide in the woods until we can see better."

Liam pushed the button on his watch and the face lit up blue. "Good grief, it's five minutes to twelve! We've got to go *now*, before he comes back toting both guns."

"Okay, Lord," Jesse said aloud. "We're trusting You to guide and protect us."

Jesse looked in every direction, but all he could see through the sea of white was the flickering campfire. "Come on, Mr. Berne. We can do this."

Liam, grunting and groaning under his breath and dragging his injured right leg, made it to the open side of the shelter. He held up his hand, and Jesse pulled him to his feet.

Liam stood for a moment, bent at the waist, and slowly straightened his back. "There's nothing on me that doesn't hurt. What I wouldn't give for a shot of morphine about now."

"I'm sorry it hurts so much," Jesse whispered. "But we need to go. Follow me." Jesse took deliberate steps, able to see only four feet in front of him, and moved toward what he hoped was the clearing he'd crossed earlier, just before he had reached the campfire. "Once we lose sight of the fire, we might as well be blind." Jesse heard something and stopped. "Shhh. Listen. Do you hear whistling?"

"I hear it, all right. It's midnight straight up. We need to find a place to hunker down. When Slick realizes we're on the run, he's going to go ballistic and is liable to start shooting in all directions."

CHAPTER 39

Jesse kept moving forward in pitch blackness, his heart pounding so hard he thought he might die of fright.

"Try to keep up, Mr. Berne," he whispered. "There's no place to hide until we cross this clearing."

Gunshots pierced the darkness, followed by a string of obscenities and then the long, anguished roar of a man outsmarted.

Jesse kept walking, his knees shaking, and hoped he knew where he was going.

"The deal's off, Liam!" Slick bellowed. "Prepare to meet your maker, because neither of you's going to get out of these woods alive."

Shots reverberated, and Jesse felt a bullet whiz by his ear.

Liam gave Jesse a shove. "He's shooting both guns. We've gotta find a place to get down low or we're liable to take a random bullet."

"I'm pretty sure we should be coming to the end of the clearing soon," Jesse said. "We should be able to see some trees once we're close enough."

"Jesse!"

Slick's voice filled him with dread.

"Either you get back here right now, or I'm going for your mom. Even if you make it back home, she'll be dead. And it'll be on you."

More shots rang out, and a bullet ricocheted off something nearby.

Jesse squinted and could just make out what appeared to be a dark wall. "Look, Mr. Berne. Trees! We made it across the clearing. We're going the right way."

"Now you're talking," Liam said. "Keep moving."

Jesse stepped up his pace, then gingerly entered the woods, groping the tree trunks as he felt his way. "Are you okay?"

"Okay enough," Liam said. "Come on, let's get out of the line of fire."

"Can you tell if Slick's following us?" Jesse said.

"Not really. But if you're right about where we are, he has to assume we would head back the way we came."

Jesse was able to make out the trunks of trees and maneuver around them, but it seemed as though he and Liam were moving at a snail's pace.

"I'm not sure where we should hide," Jesse said. "We need to find something quick or Slick's going to hear dried leaves and twigs snapping under our feet. Why is he so quiet all of a sudden?"

"I don't know. Maybe he's trying to spook us," Liam said. "Let's cut to the left. If we can find a spot that has enough limbs and dried leaves, we can cover ourselves up and lay low."

"Good idea." Jesse turned left and felt his way through a maze of trees, wishing he could see better and move faster. The silence from Slick was almost worse than the fury and gunfire. "Do you really think he could be following us?"

"It stands to reason he'd expect us to flee this way. The only good news for us is that he can't use a flashlight in this fog or he'll just blind himself. And don't worry, he's not going after your mom. He's just trying to rattle you."

"Well, it worked."

"Shhh." Liam put his hand on Jesse's shoulder and kept him from moving forward. "Did you hear that?"

"No, what?"

"I'm not sure. Something."

Jesse held his breath and listened intently. He realized he was shaking. *Lord, please don't let Slick find us.*

"Whoo. Whoo."

Jesse put his hand over his heart. "It's just an owl."

"Good. Keep moving," Liam said. "We're a couple minutes ahead of him. We need to dig in somewhere and wait until morning. Maybe he'll give up and go back to his place, pack up, and leave town, like he planned."

Kate sat with Elliot in the porch swing, the patchwork quilt her mother made her wrapped snugly around them.

"I'm so tired of feeling helpless," she said.

Elliot pulled her closer. "None of us likes to feel out of control. But the truth is, God's in control all the time, even when we think *we* are."

"Your faith never falters," Kate said. "Why can't I be like that?"

"Don't be so hard on yourself. I remember a time when you didn't trust God at all. Look how far you've come."

Kate looked up at Elliot and wondered how he was going to handle it if Jesse wasn't found alive. "Elliot, when Pam died, how did you handle the grief?"

"By the seat of my pants. I really didn't have a formula. I was so glad that I had a chance to say good-bye to Pam and tell her how much she'd meant to me. I took comfort in the fact that she was a believer and I'd see her again. But the only way I found to cope with her absence was to seek the Lord's presence and live each day for Him. He used me in all sorts of ways I never would have anticipated. The most satisfying was being a support to you and the kids."

"So you only helped us because God nudged you?" Kate poked him in the ribs with her elbow.

"At first. But it wasn't long before I was crazy about the whole lot of you. I trained myself not to think of you in a romantic way since you were still married to Micah. I really wanted him to be found alive because, more than anything, I wanted you to be happy."

"Even if it meant *you* weren't?" Kate said.

"I was happy just supporting you and praying that God would bring Micah and Riley home. I had no expectation that anything personal would ever come of my feelings for you. That was a gift."

Kate nodded. "For both of us." Elliot had brought laughter and joy back into their home. But all that would change if Jesse died.

Jesse lay on his back on the cold, damp forest floor, Liam lying next to him, tree limbs clumsily spread over them.

"I wonder where Slick is," Jesse whispered.

"Odds are he won't come *exactly* the way we did," Liam said. "But he could be out there just waiting for us to make a sound. You cold?"

"Kind of," Jesse said, his teeth chattering. "Actually, I'm freezing."

"Put your hood on," Liam said. "Maybe our shared body heat will keep us from getting hypothermia."

Jesse tied his hood snugly around his head and stuffed his hands into his jacket pockets. He started to say something, but didn't, then decided it had to be said. "Mr. Berne … you know there's a good chance … we won't make it out alive, right?"

"You kidding? You'll be home by lunchtime. Right now, that's all I'm thinking about. You're a great kid, Jesse. You deserve to go home to your family. We both know I'm going to prison. So let's focus on getting *you* home."

"I'll bet your sister's missing you and scared that something's happened to you."

"I doubt it," Liam said. "Colleen and I have always been close. But she'll never forgive me for what I've done."

"It might take awhile," Jesse said. "But I think she will. She's a Christian."

"Yeah, well, not all Christians take their faith as seriously as you do, especially when it comes to forgiving someone who's betrayed their trust. I wouldn't blame her if she couldn't forgive me."

"You might be surprised. You never thought I would either."

"I still don't get it, after the way I treated you."

"What you *did* was wrong," Jesse said. "But there's more to you than that. You're not a bad person."

"Give me a break. I tried to kill you once, and then was willing to shoot you to save my own neck. You had it right before. I'm a coward."

"You're not perfect," Jesse said. "You made some bad choices, but I'll bet you made a lot of good choices before that, right?"

"I suppose I did. But if there is a God, He's going to judge me and punish me for what I've done."

"If you died today, He would for sure. You'd be judged guilty and sentenced to hell, and there'd be no going back—ever. But you're still living, so it's not too late. You can totally choose where you're going to spend eternity."

"Yeah, I know," Liam said sarcastically, "by putting my faith in Jesus, confessing my sins, and receiving God's forgiveness. I've heard it all my life. I happen to think the whole God thing is a crutch."

"Okay. But what if you're wrong? Are you willing to gamble your eternal future on it? Maybe the real reason God wanted me to come back here is because He loves you and doesn't want you to die unsaved."

Liam offered no rebuttal. He turned on his side with his back to Jesse.

Jesse lay shivering in the steely silence, sobered by the gravity of the words he'd just said.

We really are *going to die. And I've completely blown it. Mr. Berne's never going to listen.*

Kate sat on the floor, her back leaned against the love seat, aware that her dad and Elliot were dozing, and that the fire needed another log.

She'd been sitting in the same spot for hours, thinking back over the past seven years and the horrible events that had tested both her sanity and her faith. God had never abandoned her, even when she had left Him and all but cursed His sovereignty. And He had used each devastating blow to strengthen her family and cause them to grow closer to one another—and to Him. Despite the trials—or perhaps because of them—Hawk's scathing cynicism gave way to a newfound faith that was compassionate, strong, and solid. Abby and Riley had learned to trust the Lord almost without question. And Jesse's relationship with Jesus was so simple and pure and uncomplicated that he was often an example to the rest of the family. Micah would have been so proud of his children.

And Kate could see that she had grown too. Her first tendency had typically been to fall victim to fear and begin to question God's goodness. But it was in that process that she had learned what it meant to die to self, even though her natural inclination to be in control never surrendered easily and she suffered many self-inflicted wounds because of her headstrong nature. But there had invariably come a point at which she died to her own desires and accepted whatever the Lord had ordained. There had been great freedom in letting go. Would she be able to do that again if the Lord took Jesse from her?

It was nearly daybreak, and she didn't have any fight left. *Lord, why do I always struggle so, as if I had any control over the outcome? You're either Lord of my life or You aren't. I either trust You or I don't. And I want to, more than anything.*

She felt strangely peaceful, despite the ache in her gut and the ominous feeling that Jesse wasn't coming home. When she'd lost her beloved Micah, God had shown her compassion and given her the grace to survive. And had gifted her with another soul mate to walk with her through the remainder of her life's journey. Whatever the outcome of Jesse's situation, God would give her grace sufficient to cope. If she'd learned nothing else, she'd learned that.

Virgil hit the snooze button on the alarm, the aroma of fresh-brewed coffee permeating the room. He put his arm around Jill Beth and held her close. Soon the teams would be searching again for Jesse and Liam Berne. What were the odds they'd find Jesse alive at this point?

"I hear the wheels in your head turning," Jill Beth said. "You didn't sleep, did you?"

"Not a wink. But my body's rested. I need to get back to the command center. The teams will be gathered by sunup, and as soon as we get the green light, we'll head out again. I've got to say, this is one time I'm grateful Kevin is at the helm. I realized last night when I wanted to keep searching in the fog that I'm too emotionally immersed in this."

"Of course you are." Jill Beth turned over and looked into his eyes. "How could you not be after all you've been through with Kate's family? On some level, I think you've felt responsible to watch out for Jesse since Micah disappeared. But this is not your fault."

"I know that with my head. But my heart is so heavy. I don't think I can bear to give Kate any more bad news."

"Are you afraid that's what's going to happen?"

Virgil pulled her head to his chest and swallowed the emotion that was just under the surface. "I don't know. I hope not. Liam has already killed once. He hasn't got anything to lose. And it's been twenty hours since anyone's seen Jesse. I can only imagine how Kate's feeling."

"You need to stay focused, Sheriff," Jill Beth said. "You're always telling me it ain't over till it's over. The coffee's ready. Go grab a cup and add a dash of that Granger optimism you're known for, then go do your job. Kevin may be at the helm, but it's you those deputies are taking their cues from. Caring deeply makes it tougher on you. But you're the strongest man I've ever known."

Virgil kissed her forehead. "Thanks for the pep talk. That's exactly what I needed to hear. I'd better get going."

"Call me when you know something."

"I will."

CHAPTER 40

Jesse opened his eyes and moved a small tree branch ever so slowly from his face, surprised to see pink sky through the canopy. The fog had thinned considerably, and he could see trees all around him.

He reached over and tapped Liam on the back. “Mr. Berne,” he whispered. “Wake up. It’s morning.”

Liam groaned as he turned over on his back. “I must’ve fallen asleep.” He rubbed his eyes, then pushed the button on his watch. “Good grief, it’s seven forty-five.”

“The fog has thinned out a lot,” Jesse said. “I think we can see to keep going. I wonder if Slick went back to town.”

“I wouldn’t count on it. As mad as he was, I doubt he’s going to give up finding us that easily.”

Jesse moved the branches off him and sat up, his muscles sore and the back of his neck throbbing where Slick had hit him with the gun barrel.

Liam worked his way up into a sitting position. Jesse was startled at first to see his battered face, which looked considerably worse in the light and even more troublesome than the gash in his leg.

"We're too exposed here," Liam said, looking around. "Let's move to where there are more trees." He tried to get up but fell back on his behind, spitting out a swear word that would have gotten Jesse grounded had *he* said it. "I feel like I've been flattened by a semi. And this bum leg hurts like the devil."

"Take my hand, Mr. Berne. I've got this." Jesse offered Liam a hand and pulled him to his feet, concerned about the moaning sounds he made.

"I think this leg's infected."

"Don't worry. You can make it. I'll help you. I'll reverse our steps from last night. And if I can get us back to the edge of the clearing, I think I know the way to Foggy Ridge." Jesse gently patted him on the back. "We'd better get moving, if you're going to get me home by lunchtime."

"I did tell you that, didn't I? Okay then, a promise is a promise."

The two walked over to where the canopy was denser.

"We angled left after we crossed the clearing," Jesse said. "As slowly as we were going, we couldn't have gone much distance."

"Probably not," Liam said, "but do you even know what you're looking for?"

"Not exactly. But I think I'll know it when I see it."

"I hate the idea of backtracking," Liam said, "but I have no idea how to get us out of here, so you're the boss."

"Okay, let's angle back the way we came."

Jesse led the way, weaving around one tree after another, hoping to come to the clearing. Instead, the woods just got denser and darker.

"We've been moving at a pretty good clip for twenty minutes," Liam said. "Last night, we moved at a snail's pace and stopped after twenty minutes. This can't be right."

"I know." Jesse paused and let out a big sigh. "I'm so turned around. I didn't think it would be this hard. I guess we're lost. What should we do?"

Liam sat down on the trunk of a fallen pine tree. "Take a break. We're both too hungry, weak, and tired to push ourselves."

"Not to mention thirsty," Jesse said, imagining himself downing a bottle of ice-cold water. He sat down next to Liam.

Neither said anything for several minutes.

"Hey, about last night," Liam said. "I'm sorry I shut down on you. I know you meant well."

"It's okay. You made it pretty clear how you felt. I should've left it alone."

"For what it's worth, Jesse—and I sincerely mean this—you're the finest kid and the most authentic Christian I've ever known. Bar none. Regardless of how this ends, it's been an honor getting to know you. You're the real deal."

Jesse swallowed hard and blinked to clear his eyes. *Lord, You gave me a job to do and I failed. Mr. Berne needs more time. I just can't reach him.*

Liam grabbed Jesse's arm. "Do you hear that?"

"What?"

"That."

Jesse stood slowly, listening intently. "I can barely hear *something*. What is it?"

"I'm not sure. Help me up."

Jesse reached for Liam's hand and pulled him to his feet.

"It's getting louder," Liam said.

Jesse nodded. "It's a weird sound. Maybe logging equipment?"

"Wait—" Liam held Jesse's arm, his swollen lips seeming to smile. "Those are bloodhounds!" he whispered. "They're either tracking Slick or tracking us. Either way, they're our ticket out of here."

"We should yell so they can hear us," Jesse said.

"No. Let's wait and see where they go. If they're tracking us, they'll find us."

"But what if they're tracking Slick? He said he thought those officers recognized him. Shouldn't we let whoever it is know we're here?"

A twig snapped. Before Jesse could react, he heard the dreaded sound of a gun being cocked.

"Then again ol' Slick might could blow your head clean off before those dogs get here." Slick laughed. "Well, gents. Let's see those hands in the air."

Jesse felt his hands go up, but the rest of him was paralyzed.

"Well, isn't it rich I caught up to y'all? I don't appreciate being played for a fool. Not one bit. And you're going to pay big time."

"Slick, come on. Let the kid go," Liam said. "It's over. Your beef's with me anyway."

"You got that right," Slick said. "If only you'd done what I told you. It was a beautiful plan, and the both of us could've walked away."

"So use us for a bargaining chip when the sheriff shows up with those hounds," Liam said. "That was the other part of the plan."

"*Was.* The plan's changed. I'm going to gamble it's you they're looking for. I'm going to kill you both, just like I said I would, and then hightail it out of here—"

Jesse saw Liam lunge backward and heard the thud of flesh hitting flesh.

"Jesse, *run*!" Liam shouted. "Run! Don't look back! I'm right behind you!"

Jesse ran as fast as he could, aware that the bloodhounds were getting closer.

Two shots rang out in succession.

Lord, help Mr. Berne. Don't let him die.

Jesse felt as if his legs had turned to rubber. His foot hit a rock, sending him sailing through the air until he crashed into something, the earth seeming to spin faster and faster until he fell off into a black vacuum.

Virgil ran up to the two adult males lying on the ground, both of whom had been shot by Deputy Billy Gene Duncan.

"Berne's still alive, Sheriff." Billy Gene looked up at Virgil. "Bullet went clean through his shoulder."

"What about the other man?" Virgil said.

Jason Hobbs shook his head. "Not good. He's got a weak pulse. Suffered a gunshot wound to the chest and is bleeding pretty badly."

"I aimed for his shoulder," Billy Gene said. "He was fighting Berne and turned just as I fired."

"The medic is here," Kevin said. "Step aside."

Kevin put his hand on Virgil's shoulder. "The hounds found Jesse. He's alive." Kevin spoke into his walkie-talkie. "Search and

Rescue, bring the bird in. We've got two adult males with gunshot wounds—one critical. And a twelve-year-old male suffering from exposure and a compound fracture to his right arm. Over."

"Copy that. Out."

"Where's Jesse?" Virgil said, aware that someone had grabbed his arm.

"Come on." Reggie held his walkie-talkie in one hand and pulled Virgil by the other. "Over this way. They think he tripped and hit a tree as he was running away."

Virgil and Reggie jogged through the woods about thirty or forty yards until they saw the handlers with the bloodhounds and several members of law enforcement standing around. The officers moved aside and let the sheriff through.

Virgil bent down next to Jesse, who was dazed but conscious. *Thank You, God. I owe You one. A big one.* Virgil brushed Jesse's hair off his forehead. At that moment, he was flooded with the emotion of a father with three boys of his own. "I'm sorry it took us so long to find you, buddy. But you're going to be all right. It's over. Your mother and your family will be waiting for you at the hospital."

Virgil stood. He turned and walked briskly past Reggie and away from the group of officers. When he was sure no one had followed him, he knelt on one knee, put his head on his arm, and wept.

CHAPTER 41

Kate sat with Elliot, Grandpa Buck, Hawk, Abby, and Riley in Jesse's room at Foggy Ridge Medical Center, waiting for Jesse to come down from recovery after he'd had surgery to set his fractured right arm.

She listened as Virgil briefed them on what had happened to Jesse over the past twenty-six hours. She hung on every word Virgil said and tried to imagine all that her son had gone through.

"I'll tell you what," Virgil said. "Jesse is one tough kid with enough faith to make an apostle jealous. I'm amazed at the character that boy shows at such a young age. I can't say I agree with his choice to go back and help Liam after Liam tried to kill him, but I am impressed with his Good Samaritan attitude." Virgil turned to Elliot. "Whatever the recent advice you gave Jesse, he said to tell you it worked."

Elliot smiled and squeezed Kate's hand.

"What about Liam Berne?" Hawk said. "I guess he's going to pull through?"

Virgil nodded. "The doctors say he should fully recover from the gunshot wound. It's unfortunate that he was shot, but when Deputy Duncan saw Liam fighting with Slocum, each with a gun in his hand, and Jesse running away, he thought Jesse was in danger of imminent harm and acted accordingly. However, Liam's also suffering from dehydration, loss of blood as well as cuts and bruises from the beating he took, and an infection in the leg that was gashed when the limb fell on it. He'll need to be in the hospital for a while. Of course, he's in sheriff's department custody and will be under armed guard twenty-four-seven while he's here."

"What happens when he gets out of the hospital?" Kate asked.

"When he's well enough to be released, he's going to the county jail until his court date. He's already waived his right to an attorney and pleaded guilty to capital murder, kidnapping, and attempted murder. There might be more charges filed later, but a judge will decide his sentence. On the charge of kidnapping and attempted murder, it should work in Liam's favor that, in the end, he risked his life to save Jesse."

"Will Jesse have to testify?" Elliot said.

"No, because there's not going to be a trial. The judge will want to hear Jesse's side of what happened, but that can be done privately."

"Sheriff, who was this Slick fella?" Buck said.

"His real name was Painter Reed Slocum, Caucasian male, age forty-five, of Little Rock. He was wanted for bank robbery and killing a police officer in Higgins Springs. He has a record a mile long for breaking and entering, assault and battery, aggravated assault, illegal possession of a firearm, grand larceny, cruelty to animals, dog fighting, and the list goes on. And that doesn't count the charges of kidnapping, aggravated assault, conspiracy to commit murder, or attempted murder of Liam and Jesse that would have been filed. I'm never happy when a man dies on my watch, but in this case, I'd say justice has been served."

"The dude was sadistic and evil," Hawk said. "I can't believe what he put my brother through."

Virgil raised his eyebrows. "Pretty sick. But I also can't wrap my brain around the fact that Liam put his life on the line to save Jesse after he'd already tried to kill him once, and then was ready to do it again to save his own neck."

"My poor Jesse," Kate said. "I hope he's still the same sweet boy after all this."

Virgil moved his gaze from Kate to Elliot, then back to Kate. "Oddly enough, it wouldn't surprise me if he is. I mean, listening to Jesse's reasoning about why he went back to help Liam and what he hoped to achieve is amazing enough. But when things didn't go as planned, Jesse told me he was prepared to die, if that's what God had required of him. I don't understand that. How does a twelve-year-old—or anyone, for that matter—have that kind of resolve and peace in those circumstances?"

"Only by death," Elliot said. "Not physical death, but the spiritual process of dying to self. It's really the story of the Christian life—or should be. Jesse and I talked about it when he was struggling at school. Of course, I had no idea that it would ever be tested like this, or that he would respond with such spiritual insight. I'm so proud of him."

"We all are." Kate dabbed her eyes. "I'm just grateful he escaped with nothing worse than he did. And that the blow he took to the back of his neck didn't cause permanent damage."

"After a few days here of eating like a prince and getting those fluids replenished, he'll be ready to go home." Virgil rose to his feet. "I imagine that arm is going to be sore for a while, but I think we all agree, it's a miracle we found him alive."

Kate got up and put her arms around Virgil. "Thank you so much for not giving up when it looked hopeless. You have been such a blessing to this family and I can never thank you enough."

"It's thanks enough that Jesse's going to be okay," Virgil said. "But I'm not going to tell you I was just doing my job. I think you know this was personal. Y'all are like family."

"Which is why you and Jill Beth must come for dinner after Jesse comes home. You should share the joy."

"We'd be honored." Virgil blinked to clear his eyes. He reached over and shook hands with Elliot, Hawk, and Buck, then kissed Abby and Riley on the cheek. "I'm going to get out of your hair and go speak to the media. Jesse should be coming down from recovery anytime now."

Jesse felt the softness of cotton sheets against his skin and realized he was toasty warm and not shivering. He smelled rubbing alcohol—and coffee. And heard the *beep ... beep ... beep* of a machine that sounded like the one in Grandpa Buck's hospital room after he had his hip replaced. He slowly opened his eyes at the sound of his mother's voice. For a few seconds he was confused and couldn't figure out where he was. And then … he remembered. He was at Foggy Ridge Medical Center. He was safe.

"Jesse's waking up," Kate said. She smiled and gently brushed her fingers through his hair. "Jesse, you're in the hospital. Virgil rescued you. You've had surgery to repair a compound fracture of your right arm. Do you remember?"

Jesse nodded. He counted six smiling faces looking down at him. "I … love … you to … the moon … and back," he whispered.

"We love you too," Kate said.

"I've been wanting … to tell you … but I never thought … I ever would."

Elliot squeezed Jesse's hand. "I can't know what you've been through, but Virgil said you had enough faith to make an apostle jealous."

Jesse felt a grin stretch his cheeks. "The sheriff … really said that?"

"He sure did." Grandpa Buck's lips quivered. "We were prayin', but I knew you were talkin' to God out there. Never a doubt in my mind."

"You know you're going to be a hero at school," Hawk said. "You have every right to be proud of that cast. Now everyone's going to know the truth about my little brother. Even Bull Hanson."

Jesse touched the cast on his right arm and the sling holding it in place. "Cool. Y'all have to sign it."

"We will. Later," his mother said. "The nurse ordered you a cheeseburger for lunch. I don't know if you're up to eating, but—"

"Are you kidding me?" Jesse said. "I'm starved. All I thought about all Saturday night was your spaghetti."

"*Of course* you did." Abby laughed.

Riley touched his cast with her index finger. "I'm glad you're coming home. I've only had you for my brother for two years. I told God that wasn't long enough."

"I couldn't stop thinking about all of you," Jesse said. "I was sorry I never told you how much I love you."

"I guess we all learned that lesson." Grandpa Buck winked. "Best we tell the people we love how we feel while we still can. Never know what's down the road."

"What happened to Mr. Berne?" Jesse said.

"Liam and Slick were both shot by Deputy Duncan," Elliot replied. "He had every reason to think you were in grave danger."

"Are they … dead?"

"Slick died before they got him to the hospital. But Liam should recover fully from the gunshot wound. It's going to take awhile. He also has a badly infected leg, and is suffering from dehydration. Plus, he had cuts and bruises and had lost a lot of blood from the beating he took."

"He's not really a bad man," Jesse said. "I know he did some bad things. But he was sorry. All he wanted was to get me home safe."

Hawk rolled his eyes. "I'm not sure I'm ready to hear about what a good man Liam Berne is."

"I know he's going to prison," Jesse said. "I want to talk to him before he goes. Do you think Sheriff Granger would let me?"

"I'm not even sure *I'll* let you," Kate said. "Why would you want to do that?"

Jesse shrugged. "I care about him."

"There'll be plenty of time to talk about this later," Elliot said. "For now, let's just enjoy having Jesse back."

"Elliot, would you check on Mr. Berne? Please?" Jesse's eyes were pleading. "It would mean a lot to me if you could just let him know I'm thinking of him. And that I'm grateful he risked his life so I could get away."

Elliot looked over at Kate and then at Jesse. "If Virgil gives the green light, and it's okay with your mother, I don't suppose it could hurt."

Kate nodded. "*If* Virgil says it's all right."

Elliot glanced at his watch. "I'll head down to Liam's room and see if the guard can page Virgil before he leaves the building."

Elliot walked to the end of the shiny marble corridor and saw Virgil talking to the armed guard outside Liam Berne's hospital room.

"Just the man I want to see," Elliot said.

"What's up? Jesse okay?" Virgil said.

"Yes, he's fine. We're all thrilled to have him back." Elliot glanced over at the armed guard and then at Virgil. "Jesse's concerned about Liam's condition and pleaded with me to go check on him. He wants Liam to know he's grateful Liam risked his life so he could escape."

"He also tracked him down and nearly killed him." Virgil's eyebrows came together. "You really want to eyeball Liam Berne after all he put Jesse through?"

"Not really. I want to relay Jesse's sentiments to Liam because it's important to Jesse."

Virgil sighed. "You do know it's not uncommon for a victim to get attached to his captor, right?"

"Jesse went back to help Liam before he had time to get attached. I think this is more akin to the Good Samaritan feeling the need to check on the man he went back to rescue, who ended up rescuing him. Only Jesse can't do it so he asked me. I don't need to stay long."

Virgil seemed to be thinking. Finally, he said, "All right. But I want to be present. Let me caution you not to get into the specifics of what happened. This is still an open investigation."

"Fair enough."

Virgil said something to the armed guard, and then Elliot followed Virgil inside.

Liam lay in the hospital bed, one eye swollen shut, his face badly cut and bruised. He was hooked up to several IV drips, one containing blood. His right leg was bandaged and elevated, and his upper right arm and shoulder were layered with bandages. Elliot was surprisingly moved with compassion.

Virgil walked over to his bedside. "Liam, there's someone here to see you. Elliot Stafford. He's a close friend of Jesse's family."

"If you came here to chew me out, there's nothing you could say to me that I haven't already said to myself a hundred times."

"That's not why I'm here," Elliot said. "Jesse insisted I come check on you. He wants you to know that he's thinking about you. And that he's grateful you risked your life so he could get away."

Liam's eyes glistened. He swallowed hard. "That Jesse's something else. Never met anyone like him."

"A lot of us agree with that, especially his mother."

"For what it's worth, I thanked God he's going to be okay," Liam said, his voice softer. "The world needs more people like him."

"Amen to that." Elliot ran his finger along the bed rail. Should he stop there or say what was on his mind? "I want you to know that the family is sorry you got shot. The authorities had no way of knowing that you were trying to protect Jesse."

"Of course they didn't. I don't blame them." Liam looked away and seemed to be thinking. "Can I ask you a question?"

"Go ahead."

"How does a twelve-year-old kid get sold out to God?"

Elliot smiled. "One day at a time. Jesse's got a tender conscience and a sincere desire to please God. He takes his walk with God seriously."

"I suppose you know the only reason Jesse ended up in Slick's clutches is because he was afraid I wouldn't survive the night out in the cold and came back to help me," Liam said. "Despite the fact that I nearly killed him."

"Yes, the sheriff told us that Jesse wouldn't leave you out there."

"I got all over him for it, and he said he wanted to be like the Good Samaritan. Said he couldn't leave me in the woods injured and unable to function."

"Sounds like Jesse."

"Says a lot about what he's made of." Liam lifted his head and looked Elliot in the eyes. "I need to say something. I–I can't tell you how sorry I am for all the pain I caused Jesse, and his family. I'm not making excuses and I don't expect them to forgive me for it. But I really am sorry. I'd give anything to go back and undo it."

"Jesse forgave you. I assure you he's not holding any hostility. He just wants to be sure you know how grateful he is that you put your life on the line *for him*."

"He's a bigger man than I am," Liam said. "Would you tell Jesse something for me? Tell him I'll see him again."

"Gentlemen, this visit is over." Virgil stepped over to the bed, his arms folded across his chest. "You need to get something through your head, Liam. You're going away for life. And there's zero chance you're going to see Jesse—ever."

"Ever's awfully final, Sheriff."

"That's my point."

Elliot took a step back. "It's okay, Virgil. I said what I came to say. I should get back to Kate and the kids. Thanks for letting me be the messenger. It was important to Jesse."

"Please tell Jesse what I said." Liam's voice sounded weak. "That's all I ask."

Elliot was uncomfortable with the idea of any back-and-forth conversations between Liam and Jesse and didn't know how to respond, so he said nothing and stepped out into the hall with Virgil.

"Sorry for being so abrupt," Virgil said. "I think we should put an end to whatever relationship these two think they have. It's a no-win, and I don't want Jesse being manipulated by this guy."

"Fine with me. I'm sure Kate would agree. Thanks for letting me do this one thing for Jesse. Hopefully, it will give him some closure."

CHAPTER 42

Kate sat with Elliot on the couch in her living room, a crackling fire warming her to the bone, the glow in the room matching the way she was feeling.

"I'm so glad Hawk insisted on staying with Jesse at the hospital tonight," Kate said. "It feels good just to sit here and enjoy the peace. Yesterday, my heart was breaking. And today, I'm overjoyed that my son was found alive and will be home soon. I still can hardly believe it."

"I know what you mean." Elliot pulled her a little closer. "It's a bit surreal."

Kate stared at the flames flickering in the fireplace. "This is the first chance I've had to talk to you about this, but something happened to me in those final, difficult hours of waiting for Virgil to find Jesse. I stopped fighting. I mean, really stopped. I accepted on a new and deeper level that God was in control of my son's life, but I was strangely at peace with it. I felt as if He'd lifted a thousand-pound weight off my chest, and I could breathe. Does that make sense?"

"Perfect sense."

Kate looked up at Elliot. "It's odd, but I realized for the very first time that Jesse really is just on loan to me, that God is his Father and has a plan for his life that is much bigger than my selfish desire to nurture him."

"I think the desire to nurture is one of the most beautiful aspects of motherhood, but I know what you're saying. It's small in comparison to God's desire for Jesse."

"Why couldn't I see that until now?" Kate said.

"You've come to this point, little by little, trial after trial. Even the apostle Paul said he died daily. I think that's what he meant. Dying to our own desires is a lifelong struggle. I know it has been for me."

"Does it get easier?" Kate said.

"I suppose that depends on how long it takes us to surrender. Jesse is certainly an inspiration, and he's only been a believer for two years. I want to be just like him when *I* grow up—" Elliot's voice cracked and he paused for several seconds. "You know I seriously love that boy. It's been a joy watching him grow. I'm so proud of him."

"You've been a wonderful influence on Jesse—well, on all of us. Your fingerprints have been on everything we do for so long that I can't imagine life without you."

"I'll always be there for you—as long as you'll let me."

Kate nestled closer to Elliot. She took a moment to process what she was feeling, then looked up into Elliot's eyes. "I know that, I mean *really* know that, to the depth of my being. You've stuck by me through the darkest of times, when seeing me so devastated had to have hurt you too, especially since you had romantic feelings for me and no freedom to act on them. You're the most selfless man I know. I am head over heels in love with you. Heaven knows, you're already a part of the family. So what am I waiting for? It's time we started planning our future together."

"You mean it?"

"I do."

In the next instant, Elliot's warm lips melted into hers, and Kate became wholly immersed in a longing, lingering kiss that took her breath away. "Yes, we most definitely need … to be together."

Elliot smiled. "Most definitely."

Elliot bent down to kiss her again—but the sound of the phone ringing spoiled the moment. She reached over and groped the end table until she found the phone. "Hello, Virgil."

"I'm sorry to bother you so late."

"You're not. I was just sitting here, talking with Elliot. I hope nothing's wrong."

"Well, I guess that's a matter of perspective. Liam Berne is dead."

CHAPTER 43

Early the following morning, Kate and Elliot went to Foggy Ridge Medical Center to tell Jesse that Liam Berne had died unexpectedly.

"It's too soon. I don't think he's going to take this well." Kate walked briskly down the long, shiny corridor, her heels clicking, Elliot keeping in stride.

"I don't know, Kate. After all Jesse's been through, I don't think this will throw him over the edge. He seemed remarkably calm yesterday. You want me to do the talking?"

"Would you? I don't know what to say."

"Sure." Elliot slid his arm around her as they walked. "It's going to be fine."

Kate slowed as they approached Jesse's room, and then they walked inside.

"Hey there. I'm surprised to see you two so early." Hawk walked over and hugged Kate and shook Elliot's hand. "Jesse had a great night. Slept straight through."

Kate went over and kissed Jesse on his forehead. "Hi, sweetie. How're you feeling?"

"Sore all over. And my arm kinda hurts. But it's not so bad. I had eggs, bacon, hash browns, toast, and oatmeal for breakfast. Man, did it ever taste good." Jesse patted his middle.

"Has the doctor been by yet?" Kate said.

Hawk shook his head.

Elliot pulled up a chair for Kate and one for himself, and sat next to Jesse's bed.

"We have some news," Elliot said. "It might be hard for you to hear."

"What?" Jesse's face went blank. "Tell me."

Elliot leaned over closer to Jesse, his arms folded on the bed rail. "Liam died last night. It was very sudden. The way Virgil explained it, his heart gave out."

Jesse's eyes welled with tears. "What time?"

"Around nine forty-five."

Jesse wiped a tear off his cheek. "I didn't even get to say thank you."

"I told him for you," Elliot said. "He knew how grateful you were that he risked his life so you could get away from Slick."

Jesse was quiet and seemed to be thinking. "I don't get it. Why would God want me to go back and help Mr. Berne if he was going to die anyway before I could make him understand?"

"Understand what?" Kate said.

"That God loved him and would forgive him if he just asked. That last time, I told Mr. Berne maybe the real reason God wanted me to go back there was because God loves him and didn't want him to die unsaved. Mr. Berne closed down and wouldn't listen at all after that. I know he said he didn't need a Savior, but I could tell he didn't really believe that. I asked God not to let him die, that he needed more time." A tear trickled down the side of Jesse's face. "I failed. I tried so hard, but I couldn't reach him."

Elliot put his hand on Jesse's arm. "Not necessarily. Liam asked me to tell you something. He was adamant. He said, 'Tell Jesse I'll see him again.'"

Jesse's eyes grew wide. "Were those his exact words?"

"Yes. And when I started to leave, he pleaded with me again to tell you."

"Why didn't you?"

"Jesse, Virgil put an end to our visit the minute Liam said to tell you he would see you again. Virgil told him in no uncertain terms that there was zero chance he would see you again. And yet … Liam pleaded with me to tell you anyway."

"Because his heart changed!" Jesse wore a grin from ear to ear. "Mr. Berne wanted me to know that he was a believer—that he'd put his faith in Jesus!"

Elliot looked over at Kate and then at Jesse. "Thinking back, I believe that's exactly what he was trying to say."

Hawk came over and stood at the bed rail. "Man, we couldn't make this stuff up. The dude killed his mother, tried to kill Jesse once, then agreed to kill Jesse to save his own neck, then put his neck on the line to save Jesse. And then he got saved because of Jesse. And died. Is that about right?"

Elliot stood and put his arm around Hawk. "Sounds like it."

Kate stood and took Jesse's hand. "What happened in Liam's heart is something only God knows. But you didn't fail, Jesse. You were obedient to what you felt God was calling you to do. I know God protected you because it's nothing short of a miracle that you survived."

"I couldn't shake the feeling I needed to go back," Jesse said. "I just wanted to go home. But I couldn't leave Mr. Berne out there to die. I remembered what Elliot told me about the importance of always trying to do the right thing. He said it might be costly in the beginning. But in the long run, it would pay off. Plus, I kept thinking about the parable of the Good Samaritan. God told us to go and do likewise, right? I'm really glad I went back. I can't know for sure what happened between Mr. Berne and God, but he knew how to be saved, and I choose to believe he had a change of heart."

"Me too," Elliot said.

Kate nodded.

Hawk smiled. "Hey, you're talking to a guy who felt an angel's wing and had a permanent change of heart. It doesn't take a lot to convince me of what God can do. But you're one brave dude, little brother."

CHAPTER 44

Four days later, on Thursday morning, Jesse waited and waited at the hospital until the doctor finally released him. His mother and Elliot were eager to get him home, but there was one stop they had planned to make first.

"There it is." Jesse pointed to a green canopy, beneath it a bronze casket covered in gold and orange flowers.

"Everyone's driving away." Kate sighed. "Jesse, I'm so sorry. Looks like we're too late for the graveside service. We tried."

"But it's not too late to at least say something to Miss Berne," Jesse said. "Isn't that her, standing by the casket with Pastor Windsor?"

Kate nodded.

"I hate to interrupt them," Elliot said. "Let's park here and wait a few minutes. They might need some privacy, now that the others have left."

Elliot turned off the motor, the sun flooding in the car windows, taking the chill off the frosty October morning.

Jesse looked out across the rolling slopes of Blessed Redeemer Cemetery, high atop Sure Foot Mountain, remembering a difficult day just over two years ago when they stood not far from this very spot and said good-bye to his father, a man he'd never had time to really know. He felt a tinge of guilt that the feelings he had today for a man who'd tried to kill him were stronger and easier to understand than his feelings on the day of his father's funeral. Back then, his sorrow was mostly for his mother, who had suffered deeply for five long years, not knowing whether his father and younger sister were dead or alive. Today his feelings were raw, personal. Joy and sorrow mixed. *What ifs* and *if onlys* tugging at his heart.

It was impossible to feel sorry for Mr. Berne now. He was with God. But how hard it must be for his sister who'd lost her mother by her brother's hand. Jesse wasn't sure what to say to Colleen Berne—but he knew he had to say something.

"It looks like Pastor Windsor is ready to leave," Elliot said. "Let's go pay our respects to Colleen, and not stay too long so she can be alone with her thoughts."

Jesse opened the door and slid out of the back seat and onto his feet. Elliot linked arms with Jesse and with Kate, and the trio walked across the frosty brown grass and arrived at the green awning just as Pastor Windsor was getting in his car.

Kate walked over and put her arms around Colleen. "I'm so sorry."

Colleen nodded. "Me too."

Elliot hugged Colleen and offered his condolences.

"We wanted to be here for the graveside service," Kate said, "but were delayed getting Jesse released from the hospital."

"I–I can't believe you came at all. I never expected it." Colleen turned and opened her arms to Jesse.

He walked over and unabashedly yielded himself to her embrace. "I'm so sorry, Miss Berne. I can't imagine how awful you must feel."

"I do feel awful." She pushed back and looked into Jesse's eyes and then gently touched the sling on his arm. "No kid should ever have to endure what my brother put you through. Saying I'm sorry seems inadequate. I'm just grateful you're going to be all right."

"I am," Jesse said. "Really. I have so much I want to tell you sometime when you feel like it."

"I would love to hear it now. Why don't we all sit down? Tell me what's on your heart."

Jesse sat next to his mother and told Miss Berne about how he'd felt compelled to go back and help Liam, even after Liam's failed attempt to kill him. He told her about the spiritual conversations he'd had with Liam after Slick accosted him and prodded him to the shelter at gunpoint, including that final conversation in the foggy woods as they lay covered in tree limbs, hiding from Slick and thinking they might not make it out alive. He shared how excited he was to hear the last words Liam had said to Elliot—and why.

"I have to believe Mr. Berne was trying to tell me he'd opened his heart to Jesus," Jesse said, sounding out of breath. "It's so cool. The Lord knew it was Mr. Berne's time to die, and He never gave up on him."

"And neither did *you*." Colleen dabbed her eyes. "There's something I've been waiting to tell you. I was with Liam about an hour before he died. He told me all about the conversations you'd had with him. I don't know when it happened, but you got through to him. He told me that everything Mom and I had been telling him all these years finally made sense to him … all because he'd *seen* the gospel at work in a twelve-year-old kid, so sold out to God that he was less concerned for his own life than saving a killer from dying in the cold. Jesse, Liam asked me to pray with him to receive Jesus. I'd never seen him so radiant. Afterwards, we both cried. That had to be why he asked Elliot to tell you he'd see you again. He knew you'd understand what that meant. And, of course, he hoped the sheriff would let him tell you the whole story before he went to prison—" Colleen's voice cracked. "Only he's not going to prison. He's been pardoned forever by the same Jesus he thought was nothing more than a cliché, until he experienced the love of God working through you."

Jesse's eyes pooled and he blinked to clear them, but not before a tear escaped down his cheek. "It's awesome Mr. Berne chose to follow Jesus. It's just so sad you've lost your mom *and* your brother."

Colleen lifted his chin. "But ultimately, I haven't lost them. Yes, it's tragic that Liam killed our mother, and I'll grieve them both for a long, long time. But if he hadn't done such a terrible thing, he would never have encountered you and probably never seen the profound effect eternal hope can have on a believer. And because he chose to trust Jesus as his Lord and Savior, I'll see him again. It was worth the price, Jesse. I can never thank you enough for listening to God and being obedient. Already at twelve years old, you've done more to further the kingdom than most Christians do in a lifetime."

Jesse couldn't make any words come out of his mouth. He imagined Mr. Berne standing in heaven, with no black eye, cuts, or bruises. No gash or infection in his leg. No gunshot wound in his shoulder. Just pure joy on his face, and his mother beside him.

"It *was* worth it," Jesse finally said. "There was so much going on in my head when I left Mr. Berne to go get help. Even though I'd chosen to forgive him, I was mad and scared. I really wanted to go home. But then I worried he might die out there in the cold before I could get help to him. I had to go back. I'm so glad I did."

"Liam said you were trying to be a good Samaritan, and he was angry you came back because he knew what Slick wanted him to do. It was a terrible choice for anyone to have to make."

Jesse felt his cheeks get hot. "I knew that. I was mad and scared, but so was Mr. Berne. That's when I started to see him differently. I didn't understand how he could kill your mother. But he wasn't a bad man."

"Thank you, Jesse. Liam had a lot of good in him. That's how I want to remember him."

"I think if I'd known him longer, we might've become friends. And he risked his life so I could get away from Slick. I wish I'd had the chance to thank him in person."

"Elliot spoke for you. And you can thank Liam face to face someday, though he will probably beat you to it." Colleen smiled, her eyes brimming with tears. "You'll always be my hero, Jesse Cummings. I loved my brother, and as awful as his actions were, it gives me great comfort that God trusted you to offer him kindness in his darkest hour and show him the way home. You are truly a man after God's own heart."

CHAPTER 45

Kate had spent two days preparing her usual traditional Thanksgiving meal, much to the delight of her family. Grandpa Buck ate a second piece of pumpkin pie and finally pushed back from the table, not to be outdone by Jesse, who had eaten a slice each of Dutch apple, black bottom, *and* pumpkin pie.

"Aren't you miserable yet?" Hawk said to Jesse, a grin twitching his cheeks.

"No, I'm just right." Jesse patted his middle and then started laughing. "Just don't stick me with a pin or I'll explode."

Abby stood and tapped her water glass several times with a spoon. "Attention, everyone. It's time to give Mama our surprise."

Riley reached down and picked up something and then handed it to Abby under the table.

"What's going on?" Kate said.

"As you know," Abby continued, "we unanimously decided that your pasta sauce was the best and should be sold in the gift shop here at Angel View, paired with a cookbook of your pasta recipes. Our goal was to have it in our gift shop and the shops around Foggy

Ridge in time for Christmas. You agreed to let us have the fifty jars of pasta sauce you canned last summer if we designed the cover and handled all the details. I'm happy to announce that the first fifty books arrived yesterday. Mama, we present to you *Secrets from Kate's Kitchen*."

Kate took the thin hardback book, about the size of a novel, from Abby and couldn't stop looking at the full-color glossy cover, which featured a flattering image of Kate standing at her stove, wearing her red bib apron and tasting her pasta sauce with a spoon. "This is really nice! Who took this picture—and when? I have no recollection of it."

Elliot raised his hand. "Guilty. I used my telephoto and shot it from the living room. You didn't even know what I was up to. But look closer. Jay painted that cover image from the photo and then painted the red-and-white checked border."

Kate smiled. "Goodness. It's so perfect I almost can't tell. Jay, this is beautiful. Your talent never ceases to amaze me. This is absolutely going to pop on the shelf."

"We all thought it turned out very cool," Jay Rogers said. "I'm glad you like it."

"Like it? I *love* it." Kate thumbed through the pages of her fifteen best pasta recipes. "I never envisioned anything quite this beautiful. So well done. Thank you all. And thank you for believing my pasta sauce was worthy of such recognition."

Abby held out her palm. "Wait, there's more. We ordered self-adhesive labels that match the cover design to stick on the front of the pasta jars, and those have come in. Jay and I also found a source for really cute white cotton mesh bags to hold each cookbook and jar of pasta sauce. Just close the drawstring at the top, staple the product ingredients tag we also had printed, and we've got attractive, see-through, reusable, and inexpensive packaging. And since we already have fifty jars of pasta sauce, all we have to do is get a family assembly line going and we can have the gift sets packaged and ready to go in a day."

Grandpa raised his hand. "I volunteered for that."

"However, there is a hitch in the plan we didn't anticipate," Abby said. "According to the Arkansas Cottage Food Law, we're allowed to home-can the pasta sauce and sell it here at Angel View, at farmer's markets, and at special events. But in order to sell it to retailers, we would have to be licensed by the health department and go through a lot of hoopla, which we might want to revisit later. But to start, we can sell the gift sets here at Angel View."

Kate laughed. "Honestly, I'm *fine* with just selling it here. Oh dear! My business head is spinning. So is someone making sure everything's compliant with state law? And tracking expenses? And figuring out how we're going to handle our cash flow?"

Elliot tapped his water glass. "As a matter of fact, *I* am. Kids, your mother and I have been waiting to tell you something. But first I have a surprise for her." Elliot got up and knelt next to Kate's chair.

Kate sucked in a breath, her hands to her cheeks. Was he really going to do this now? In front of the entire family?

"Darling," Elliot said, "there is nothing on earth I would rather do than spend every moment with you and this beautiful family. But honestly, I've been a freeloader long enough." He took a small black box out of his pocket and opened it, displaying the most beautiful halo diamond ring Kate had ever seen. "Marry me, Kate, and let me start giving back. I love you more than words can express. And I love each person in this family as if they were my own flesh and blood. I don't want to change anything. I just want to be a part of everything for the rest of my life. So, my darling Kate … will you be my wife, my life partner, the other half of my heart—and let me start pulling my weight around here?"

Kate laughed. "Well, when you put it that way, yes!"

Elliot slipped the ring on her finger, a perfect fit, and kissed her tenderly.

"Way to go, Elliot," Jesse said, his face beaming. "Took you long enough."

"Yay!" Riley clapped her hands. "I'm going to have a daddy."

All the kids sprang to their feet and rushed over to Kate and Elliot.

Abby held Kate's cheeks and looked into her eyes. "Mama, I'm so happy for you—for all of us!"

"Me too." Kate reached for Jay's hand, streams of joy trickling down her face. "When we say family, that includes you. You know that."

Jay nodded, his cheeks suddenly pink. "When the time is right for me and Abby to get engaged, I hope she looks as happy as you do."

Hawk shook hands with Elliot and then pulled him into a hug. "I couldn't be happier, man. You two were obviously meant to be together."

From across the table, Grandpa Buck caught Kate's gaze and nodded, his eyes glistening.

"Mama, I'm *so* jazzed you said yes!" Jesse picked up her hand and looked closely at her engagement ring. "It's humongous because that's the way Elliot loves you … Do you think it would be okay if I call him Dad after you get married? I mean, would that be too weird?"

Kate smiled, her heart pounding and thoughts racing with images of past, present, and future. "Not at all. I'm sure your father would be happy that a fine man like Elliot wants that responsibility. And I promise you, Elliot will be thrilled."

"Hey, everybody," Riley hollered, "look outside. It's snowing!"

Kate grabbed Elliot's hand and hurried over to the giant living-room window that looked down over Beaver Lake. Snow had nearly covered the ground. And as far as they could see, huge white flakes were falling from the sky.

Elliot flashed a toothy grin. "Okay, coats and boots, everyone. The way this is coming down, I see a snowball fight just waiting to happen."

The kids raced for the coat closet, Riley's unmistakable squealing a happy contrast to the silence of those empty years when laughter had lost its voice.

On his way to the back door, Jesse tossed two ski jackets to Elliot, then held up his left arm. "Expect no mercy. When it comes to snowball fights, I'm ambidextrous."

Elliot chuckled as the herd of Cummings kids, big and small, stampeded out the door, Grandpa Buck on their heels. He helped Kate put on her jacket and then slipped into his own, zipped it, and put his arms around her.

She looked up into his twinkling eyes, her heart overflowing, and just relished the moment.

"I love you," Elliot said, pulling her closer. "You're not disappointed that I proposed in front of the kids, are you?"

"Nothing you do disappoints me," Kate said. "Did you see their faces? I can't remember the last time I saw them this happy."

He smiled. "You look pretty radiant yourself."

"I *feel* radiant. And the ring … my goodness"—Kate held out her hand and admired how the diamonds sparkled in the light—"it's magnificent. I never expected anything like this."

"I intend to surprise you for the rest of your life."

Elliot gently pressed his lips to hers, just as the first snowball hit the window, turning their kiss into a mutual smile.

"We can't let that go unanswered," he said.

"Definitely not." Kate put on her gloves and stocking cap, then turned and walked out onto the deck, where the snow was rapidly accumulating.

She stood at the railing and breathed in the crisp mountain air, aware that Elliot had ducked and a snowball had hit the house, evoking a round of laughter from the kids.

Elliot fired back, then put his arm around Kate, a boyish grin overtaking his face. "I hope they never outgrow this kind of fun."

"Well, even if *they* do"—Kate heard herself squeal as a snowball hit Elliot's sleeve—"we're bound to have grandkids."

Kate picked up a handful of wet snow, formed it into a ball, and threw it randomly over the railing. She was delighted by the sound of her children's playful voices and imagined it echoing all the way to heaven. Micah would always be her first love and her children's father. But God, in His faithfulness, had filled the aching void of Micah's absence with an exciting new love, who was everything her heart desired and the most fitting father figure her children could have hoped for.

A familiar honking sound caused Kate to look up. Her eyes found a flock of Canada geese gliding southward across the snowy Arkansas sky, powered by nothing more than what God had programmed into their DNA. She had no more idea of what the future held than they, but she no longer felt the need to control it. No matter what direction her future took, or what obstacles she might face on the journey, she trusted the Lord to get her to the final destination—right on time.

... a little more ...

When a delightful concert comes to an end,

the orchestra might offer an encore.

When a fine meal comes to an end,

it's always nice to savor a bit of dessert.

When a great story comes to an end,

we think you may want to linger.

And so, we offer ...

AfterWords—just a little something more after you

have finished a David C Cook novel.

We invite you to stay awhile in the story.

Thanks for reading!

Turn the page for ...

- **A Note from the Author**
- **Discussion Guide**

A NOTE FROM THE AUTHOR

"The mind governed by the flesh is death, but the mind governed by the Spirit is life and peace." Romans 8:6

Dear friends,

I think the process of crucifying the flesh is one of the most difficult, ongoing challenges of the Christian life. Many believers sincerely want to be conformed to the image of Jesus, but once the battle rages between flesh and spirit, they are unwilling to make the personal sacrifice necessary for transformation to take place.

Kate's faith took a terrible beating in those agonizing hours while she waited for Virgil to find Jesse. She bemoaned having the same faltering faith that had crippled her efforts to trust God in tumultuous times past. But this time, Kate's fear and crushing pain were more than she could bear, and she surrendered Jesse's fate into God's hands … and was both surprised and relieved to feel her burden lift.

Ultimately, she was able to look back on those miserable years she had spent in a crucible of uncertainty, fear, and despair and see that nothing had been wasted. The very trials she thought would destroy her had been used by God to reshape her thinking, strengthen her faith, and restore her trust. Little by little, Kate had died to that part of herself that needed to be in control, and she found the freedom to face the future with Elliot.

In contrast, Jesse, with childlike faith, took God at His word and was willing to be obedient, even if it meant he could lose his life. Jesse modeled what it is to be dead to self, alive in Christ, evidenced by his need to tell Liam he had forgiven him, even as Liam was ready to pull the trigger. It was also evidenced by his unselfish choice to go back, despite the risk to his personal safety. And by his unrelenting passion to make Liam understand the need for a Savior.

Not that Jesse gave up his own desires without a struggle. He was desperate to go home. To get warm. To satisfy his hunger and thirst. To be safe. But when he weighed what he wanted versus what he believed God was asking, there was no contest or delay. Jesse was simply and solidly sold out to God. And because it was no longer Jesse, but Christ living in him, Liam was able to see the living God and believe.

Let us embrace for ourselves this mystery of the faith proclaimed by the apostle Paul in Galatians 2:20: "I have been crucified with Christ and I no longer live, but Christ lives in me. The life I now live in the body, I live by faith in the Son of God, who loved me and gave himself for me."

When the world looks at us, who they see will depend on the choices we make. Let us choose well.

Join me for the finale, *A Treacherous Mix*, where Hawk finds himself caught in a web of deceit and learns a valuable lesson about the consequences of moral compromise.

I would love to hear from you. Join me on Facebook, where you can find me at www.facebook.com/kathyherman, or drop by my website at www.kathyherman.com and leave your comments in my guest book. I read and respond to every email and greatly value your input.

In Him,

Kathy Herman

DISCUSSION GUIDE

1. Can you put into your own words what Romans 8:12–13 is saying to us? "Therefore, brothers and sisters, we have an obligation—but it is not to the flesh, to live according to it. For if you live according to the flesh, you will die; but if by the Spirit you put to death the misdeeds of the body, you will live."
2. Have you experienced what it is to die to the flesh? If so, was it difficult? Was the outcome worth it? Do you think dying to the flesh is a onetime experience? Or do you think it happens little by little? Explain your answer.
3. Which character's struggle could you most relate to: Liam's, Jesse's, or Kate's? Which character's struggle do you think would be the hardest for you to deal with? Why?
4. In Galatians 2:20, the apostle Paul said, "I have been crucified with Christ and I no longer live, but Christ lives in me." Now let's make this personal: *I* have been crucified. *I* no longer live. After Christ lives in me, how am *I* different?
5. Do you think having Christ living in us should change the way other people see us? Do you think the change should be seen as physical? Or can it be seen in our attitudes and actions?
6. Are you able to see Christ in other believers? If so, how does that look? Do you see it all the time, or just sometimes? Do you think members of the body of Christ *should* look different from everyone else? If so, how?

7. Can we grow as Christians without dying to our sin nature? Why, or why not?
8. Do you think Liam would have drowned his mother if there had been no inheritance? Do you agree with Colleen that, had it not been for that horrible choice, Liam might never have given his heart to God?
9. When Kate's fear of losing Jesse became second to the pain and anguish she was feeling, she finally gave up fighting God—and, to her surprise, found peace. Why do you think that was? Is there comfort in accepting that the circumstances we're in are bigger than we are—and that God is bigger than both?
10. Jesse struggled with life issues as any twelve-year-old boy does, and sometimes made immature and hurtful decisions. But when he was confronted with the hardest of all decisions—whether he was willing to risk death rather than abandon what he believed God wanted of him—he showed amazing spiritual conviction and resolve. Why do you think that was? Which do you think helped him more—his childlike faith, or spiritual wisdom?
11. Is it possible that the easiest way to handle dying to our sin nature is to approach it with childlike faith and trust instead of analyzing how hard it's going to be and fighting it every step of the way? Have you experienced both? Which was easier for you?
12. What was your takeaway from this story?